OUR POLLY

OUR
POLLY

Anna Jacobs

Hodder & Stoughton

Copyright © 2001 by Anna Jacobs

First Published in Great Britain in 2001
by Hodder and Stoughton
A division of Hodder Headline

10 9 8 7 6 5 4 3 2 1

A CIP catalogue record for this title is available
from the British Library

ISBN 0 340 75060 X

Typeset by
Phoenix Typesetting, Ilkley, West Yorkshire
Printed and bound in Great Britain by
Mackays of Chatham plc, Chatham, Kent

Hodder and Stoughton
A division of Hodder Headline
338 Euston Road
London NW1 3BH

This book is dedicated with great love to my husband, David Jacobs, who has been loving and supportive about my writing from long before I got published, and is still my final wise reader for each new book. As this goes to press we've been married for 38 years. Living that long with a writer deserves a medal – a big, gold medal!

Anna Jacobs is always delighted to hear from readers and can be contacted:

BY MAIL:

PO Box 628
Mandurah
Western Australia 6210

If you'd like a reply, please enclose a self-addressed envelope, stamped (from inside Australia) or with an international reply coupon (from outside Australia).

VIA THE INTERNET:

Anna now has her own web domain, with details of her books and excerpts, and invites you to visit it at http://www.annajacobs.com

Anna can also be contacted by email at jacobses@iinet.net.au

If you'd like to receive email news about Anna and her books every month or two, you are cordially invited to join her announcements list. Go to http://www.egroups.com/group/AnnaJacobs

CHAPTER ONE

November 1919

Polly stumbled along the track to the farm, her feet slipping in the mud. She should have changed into stouter shoes. She still forgot sometimes how muddy the countryside could get because she'd been brought up in the terraced streets of Overdale, not here on the slopes of the Pennines. She hoped she could find her son before she had to ask for help; she was still regarded as an outsider in the village of Outshaw, and her husband, Eddie, was pitied for having married a townie.

He was a little devil, her Billy was, always into things, often going missing, but you couldn't help loving him. When a child smiled like that and gave you smacking great kisses, you knew you were lucky. Polly jumped up and down to look over the drystone wall. He was nowhere in the village, but surely he couldn't have come so far? What if he'd gone the other way and wandered on to the moors?

This would give Hilda Scordale yet another reason to criticise her. Polly had tried hard to get on good terms with Eddie's mother, but had slowly come to realise that the older woman was jealous of his love for his wife. Whoever he'd married, it would have been the same. And Eddie worshipped his mother, so could see no wrong in her. She was the only reason they ever quarrelled because his mother was always telling them what to do – well, telling Eddie and expecting him to convince his wife.

Things had improved a little after Billy's birth, but had started going downhill again once he began toddling and getting into mischief. Mrs Scordale said it was up to a mother to keep an eye on her children, but Polly defied anyone to keep Billy in check all the time. He was not only adventurous but clever enough to figure out how latches worked. They'd thought they'd got him safely penned in the garden with the new latch Eddie had fitted to the gate, but obviously he'd figured that one out now and you couldn't keep your gate padlocked when so many things had to be delivered to this isolated hamlet.

. Just before she got to the farm she saw her husband walking towards her with Billy in his arms, and stopped to clutch her side and sigh in relief.

Eddie grinned at her as he held their son up in the air and gave him a mock shake. 'I think we need a cage for this one!'

Billy crowed with laughter.

Polly tried to look severe, but could not help smiling at Billy's rosy little face with its mop of soft brown hair, like her own in colour but with a rebellious curl to it when you tried to comb it neatly for church. 'Have you time to come back for a cuppa, love?'

'Nay, lass. Farmer Snape wasn't best pleased with our Billy turning up like this. I'd best get straight back to work.'

She nodded and took Billy from him. The child flung his arms round her neck, planting a wet kiss on her cheek with wind-chilled lips. 'You're a naughty boy, Billy Scordale!' Polly scolded.

'Naughty boy,' he echoed solemnly, peeping sideways at her. 'See the horsies.'

Eddie kissed her other cheek. 'You don't even sound angry with him, Pol.'

She smiled ruefully. It was true. She did find it hard to stay angry with her son – with anyone, in fact. She knew she was too soft, but there was enough unhappiness in the world without creating more. Setting the child down, she took his hand firmly in hers and led him home.

Her mother-in-law was standing at the door of their house

opposite and greeted her with, 'Have you given him a good smacking?'

Polly suppressed a sigh. 'You know I don't believe in hitting children.'

'He'll never learn to behave if you don't chastise him.'

'I'll find other ways.' She waited till Hilda had gone inside, then let out her breath in a long sigh that turned into a near sob. Once inside her own home, she changed Billy's muddy clothes and set his little boots to dry in front of the fire, tears filling her eyes. If only there was someone her own age here, someone to talk to. Eddie worked such long hours at the farm, and the other women in the hamlet were all Hilda Scordale's age, and cronies of her mother-in-law.

When Billy fell asleep on the rug in front of the fire, Polly tiptoed out into the kitchen to stare blindly out of the window. There wasn't enough to keep her occupied in one small house. She'd been a maid at Mrs Pilby's before her marriage, working in a large house with several other staff members to chat to, lots to keep them busy and all the gossip from the town filtering through the kitchen. Here in Outshaw nothing much happened from one day to the next and she couldn't think what her mother-in-law did with herself once Mr Scordale had gone to work in the quarry.

Polly went to glance into the front room. How could she get angry at Billy who was the only small child in Outshaw and had no one to play with, poor little soul? Clicking her tongue in annoyance, she told herself not to brood on things, just get on with her life. And she'd certainly be busy for the next few days because as soon as she got word that her sister Lizzie's baby had been born, Polly was going to stay with her for a week. She brightened at the thought. There'd be plenty going on at Lizzie's. The Deardens lived in busy York Road over the large grocer's shop they owned, one of the posh shops which served the gentry.

✻

Dearden's delivery van turned up the very next morning with old John the driver calling out before he even got out, 'The babby's arrived!'

'What is it?' Polly asked eagerly.

'A little girl. Hadn't been born when I left work last neet, an' your Lizzie sitting packing sugar in t'back room. But when I got in this morning I heard a babby skriking upstairs. Eh, it's got a right pair of lungs on it, yon has.'

It only took Polly a few minutes to get ready. As she had arranged, she took Billy across to her mother-in-law's and for once was not greeted by a sour face. Hilda Scordale would enjoy having her son and grandson to herself for a few days. She'd soon find out what a handful Billy was, thought Polly, smiling as she got into the van. Maybe then she'd be more understanding. And maybe not.

In the living quarters above the shop, Lizzie greeted her youngest sister with, 'Come and meet your new niece.'

Polly hung over the cradle. 'Isn't she pretty? And you look well, too.'

'This one was much easier than the first.' She stretched. 'In fact, I'm already fed up of lying in bed.'

'You enjoy your rest.'

Lizzie pulled a face. 'Who wants to rest?'

With her husband Peter and his mother busy in the shop below, the two sisters were looking forward to a few days together. Beth was a placid baby and her brother Matt was an easy child to look after compared to his cousin Billy, playing quietly with his toys while the two sisters talked for hours.

'What's up?' Lizzie asked after a while.

'What do you mean?'

'I mean what's making you look so unhappy underneath?'

Polly sighed. 'It's just – well, it's a bit lonely at Outshaw and try as I will, I don't really get on with the Scordales – especially *her*.'

'There's something wrong with anyone who can't get on with

you, my girl. You'd be better moving away from there and so would Eddie. In fact, it'd do you both a world of good.'

'Eddie wouldn't go. His mother was so upset when his sister went to Australia, he promised her he'd never leave Outshaw. Besides, the house goes with the job and there aren't many farms which would take on a lame man.' Polly shrugged. 'Any road, I manage. I have Billy, which makes up for a lot. Eh, I'm missing him already.'

The next day a letter arrived from the middle Kershaw sister, Eva, who was a schoolmistress over near Rochdale where she lived with her friend and former teacher, Alice Blake.

'Eva says Alice hasn't been well, so she can't come over this weekend to see her new niece.' Lizzie pulled a face. 'Oh, dear, they've had to have the doctor in again.'

'Poor Alice. She's having a bad year of it, isn't she?'

'Yes, poor thing! But me, I'm having a good year. Never been so happy in my life.'

'So you should be with Peter doting on you like he does.' Polly felt her sister deserved her happiness because she had had a bad time with her first husband, Sam Thoxby, who had been a wife-beater and a thief. Even when Lizzie had run away from him during the war, he'd found her and dragged her back. It had been a relief for them all when he'd been killed in an accident towards the end of the war, though you ought not to be glad of such a thing. Then Lizzie had been able to marry Peter Dearden, whom she'd known for a long time and they were so happy together it did Polly's heart good to see them. And though Polly's Eddie was not the most lively person to live with, he was a kind husband, a good father and a loving son. She had nothing to complain of, really, and didn't know why she was letting things get her down.

'Are you two going to have any more children?' Lizzie asked idly one day. 'You're leaving it a bit late if you want them to be friends.'

Polly could feel herself blushing. 'We've been trying, but no luck so far.'

'Well, you've proved once that you can do it, so there's no need to worry.' Lizzie grinned. 'You just have to keep practising till you get it right.'

Polly could feel her face heating up still further. She didn't tell her sister that Eddie was often too tired to love her. That sort of thing was private as far as she was concerned and she'd never been able to discuss intimate things in the casual way Lizzie did.

Polly was sorry when the week came to an end, despite all the interrupted nights, and was thoughtful as she packed to go home. She had enjoyed the bustle of living above the busy shop and got on well with Peter Dearden and his mother. And, eh, the new baby was a pretty little thing, with a look of her Auntie Eva.

Polly would have loved a daughter. But if she had one the baby would no doubt have its mother's mid-brown hair and plump, placid face. Polly knew her own shortcomings only too well. She had never been able to sparkle with life like Lizzie, or talk intelligently about the world as Eva did – nor was she as pretty as her clever sister. She was just ordinary. And so was her husband. She should be ashamed of herself for finding him rather dull, but she did – and was dreading going back to Outshaw.

Two months after the birth of Lizzie's child, the Mercer family gathered in a small village on the north Fylde coast to mourn the death of old James Mercer with due pomp and circumstance, though with little real grief. Indeed, there were expectations in more than one breast that there might be something to celebrate after the will had been read, so the gathering had a cheerful undertone to it.

Richard Mercer, who attended the funeral at the tiny church of St Paul's with his wife, Florence, was one of the few to feel genuinely sad because he had liked his Uncle James for all the old fellow's fussiness. After the service they walked from the church back to the house along the sea front, pausing for a moment to look back towards the eastern end of the village, where the only hotel stood. It had changed its name since his last visit and was now Hotel Bella Vista, a stupid name for a hotel in Lancashire. They passed the long row of boarding houses or large private homes that graced the foreshore. Poorer people lived at the rear of the village in rows of cottages. The older ones were white-washed and had thatched roofs; the newer ones were built of brick and tile but were still small.

As they turned from the shore down Seaview Close, with its select group of seven houses, Florence grumbled about the loose gravel path and the lack of amenities in Stenton-on-Sea, but Richard let her complaints wash over his head. Instead he breathed deeply, enjoying the bracing sea air and wishing they lived in a place like this instead of a grubby little town like Overdale.

Seaview House was at the end of the short close, looking down to the sea from a slight rise. It was one of the largest houses in Stenton and had a new wing at the rear where the servants were housed because old James had valued his privacy.

Richard gave his coat and hat to Doris who had been his uncle's maid for as long as he could remember and whose eyes were reddened from weeping. He joined the other mourners in the sitting room, but went to stand on his own in the big square bay window with a glass of his uncle's fine dry sherry in his hand, staring out towards the water. He did not feel like chatting to his relatives. His parents had died while he was fighting in France and he had lost touch with most of the rest of his family.

His cousin George was fussing over the ladies as usual. It always upset Richard to see the old aunties simpering at the handsome young man and watching him fondly as he moved on because he knew what his cousin said about them afterwards and it was never flattering. He touched his cheek, feeling the scar, knowing it gave him a sneering expression these days which made people wary of approaching him. There were other scars on his body, because he'd copped a few minor wounds over the long years of combat, and sometimes he felt that there were scars on his mind, too. But George seemed untouched in any way by the fighting and muck and deaths, even boasting of having had a 'good war'. Trust *him* to come through unscathed!

'Well, at least old Georgie livens things up,' Florence muttered, waving and smiling brightly across the room. 'I hate funerals. Still, this one might be worth coming to. I expect your uncle's left you something – you and Georgie are his only nephews. He was a funny one, though, old James, and you could never count on him doing the right thing. I'm not surprised he never married.'

A minute later she was off again. 'You know, he refused to let me live with him while you were away and yet there was only him in this big house. It'd have been so convenient to have servants to help me look after Connie. It's not even as if I'd have been here all the time.'

Richard replied when he had to and felt only relief when she left his side, though he was not pleased to see her gravitate towards George. Those two were birds of a feather, he thought glumly. He should never have married her, but she'd been expecting his child so what else could he have done? Back in 1910 you did not even try to get out of doing your duty. He'd often wondered since what had attracted him to Florence – or her to him – for they were an ill-matched couple.

He now realised that their brief affair had been the result of sheer lust on Florence's part. She was the first for him, though he was clearly not so for her. He had believed her to be a friend in need after she had listened so patiently to his ramblings about the boredom of figures and office work when his father had forced him to become an accountant. He had been too naïve in those days even to know that women like her existed: decent to all appearances, but with the hearts and bodies of whores. He was quite sure Constance, whom they always called Connie, was his child, however, because his daughter had the fair Mercer hair that was neither brown nor blond, and she looked very like photos of his mother as a child.

He sighed and took another sip of sherry as he sifted through memories of coming here to Stenton-on-Sea as a child: paddling happily in the tranquil water, cycling along the rutted country lanes in a world without the hills of his home town. The Fylde coast could be bleak in winter, though, with the wind tossing white foam off the waves and howling across the flat land. But the air was always clean and tangy and he couldn't seem to get enough of it after the stink of the trenches.

A burst of laughter made him twist round and scowl at these vultures who had descended on Seaview House and who cared nothing for James Mercer. He'd be relieved when today's fuss was over. There had been too many deaths and funerals in the past few years – and he had had to stand there in his Captain's uniform without betraying his emotions at the loss of another young life. Since the fallen comrades were men from his company, the least he could do was offer them the outward trappings of military respect, but sometimes, when it was a particularly young lad in the simple coffin, some of whom he guessed to be well under the age of enlistment, it had been hard to suppress his own grief and bitterness at the waste. Many a time he had gone back to his bunker and sat there with tears in his eyes as he wrote to tell the usual lies to their families about a quick and painless death.

There were only a few men left now from the original 'Hellhounds', as the men of his company had called themselves in those early, enthusiastic days when he became first their Lieutenant, then their Captain. He might have left the Army now, but he hoped the few remaining Hellhounds wouldn't lose touch – hoped they knew they could always turn to him if they were in trouble. And if that was blindly idealistic, as Florence had told him scornfully, he didn't care. She simply could not understand how little class and money had mattered out there, or how important such camaraderie had been in seeing you through. Still was. Peace wasn't proving easy after so many years of war, and Richard had been in the Army from the very beginning.

Someone cleared their throat and he jerked back into

awareness of where he was to find his Uncle James's lawyer standing next to him. They shook hands and exchanged a few platitudes then Richard fell silent, waiting to see what Quentin Havershall wanted.

'Your uncle asked me to read the will in his study. Just you and your cousin George involved. Would now be convenient?'

Richard could see Florence watching eagerly from a few feet away, her lips avidly parted, showing the line of pink gum behind the bright red lipstick he hated so much. 'Yes, of course.'

'I'll find your cousin, then.'

When the old lawyer had moved away, she darted across and hissed, 'What's he want?'

Suppressing a sigh he told her. She beamed up at him, her dark bobbed hair swinging forward over her cheeks, the glossy strands touching a corner of the garish mouth beneath a small feathered hat that was pulled right down to her eyes when all the other women were wearing broad-brimmed hats. Even her skirts were shorter than theirs, coming only to mid-calf, and the material of her dress was too shiny. 'Art silk, my dear,' she had said when he'd mentioned that. 'It washes much better than the real thing. I'm going to trim this one up afterwards and use it for an evening gown.' She looked like a painted doll, he thought in disgust. Not even a soft, cuddly doll nowadays for she had lost a lot of weight since they first married – no, a wooden, peg-top doll come to life, with that cropped hair and over-thin body.

His wife made a little noise of satisfaction in her throat. 'That must mean your uncle's left you something. How much do you think he was worth? He certainly lived comfortably here.' She stared round covetously. 'It'd be wonderful if he'd left you this house, wouldn't it? Not that I'd want to live here but we could sell it and get out of Overdale, buy one of those smart new villas in London, perhaps.'

He stared at her bleakly. She had not uttered a single word of regret since they'd heard the news of his uncle's death, just gone on and on about money. He was relieved when Havershall beckoned from across the room. 'Excuse me.' He joined the lawyer, walking in silence across the big rectangular hall behind the fussy little man who barely reached his shoulder. As they passed a mirror, Richard grimaced at the sight of himself. He looked gaunt still after the years of privation and was beginning to wonder if he'd ever flesh out again. Beside him walked George, six foot three to his own six foot and a bit beefy now, though he had been a scrawny child. They had always hated one another, right from the first time they'd met. George, the younger by a year, had been spoiled rotten by his elderly parents while Richard had been very strictly brought up – which he now considered preferable.

In the study Havershall took the big leather chair behind the desk, then reached into his briefcase and brought out some papers which he set out in precise piles. George plumped himself down in one of the two other chairs which had been arranged in front of the desk, sprawling like a schoolboy.

He grinned sideways at his cousin. 'The moment of truth, eh?'

Richard could not return his smile. Uncle James had hinted that he would be left something, but not what.

'My client asked me to give you these letters to read before I go through the will.'

George snatched his envelope and tore it open, dropping the pieces on the carpet.

Richard stared at the one in front of him, reluctant even to pick it up. The spidery handwriting had always been difficult to read and yet Uncle James had been a faithful correspondent throughout the war. His letters had brought a welcome breath of sanity into the filth and mayhem. Florence had written very infrequently, mostly just postcards sent from so many different places that he'd wondered what she was doing travelling round – and what she'd done with their daughter.

And after a while, he'd started to wonder who she was with as well.

He reached out to pluck the letter opener from the stand, but even before he'd inserted it into the corner of the envelope, George was cursing beside him.

'Mr Mercer, please! This is hardly the occasion for—'

Ignoring the lawyer, George turned to glare at his cousin, flicking one finger at the piece of paper in Richard's hand, still folded and unread. 'You needn't bother with that. Our dear departed uncle says in mine that he's left you everything so your years of toadying have been richly rewarded!'

They stared at one another, Richard with a vivid memory of how things had been when they were children. George had always mocked him for his bookishness and quiet ways. They'd fought several times, once because George had taken all the eggs from a bird's nest, leaving the poor mother fluttering around in blind panic. And although Richard had won that fight, George had stamped on the eggs – and then laughed uproariously until his cousin's fist smacked into his mouth again. That blow had given Richard immense, savage satisfaction, and he didn't care that his parents had punished him afterwards for fighting. They hadn't been able to make him apologise.

Nowadays George contented himself with patronising Richard and flirting with Florence, who had once been his girl and who still called him 'Georgie-boy' in caressing tones. Neither of them seemed to realise that this flirting meant less than nothing to Richard; that the only thing which did matter nowadays was his daughter – and to a lesser extent his men.

With a sigh, he unfolded the single piece of paper, sure that this was going to cause trouble.

My dear boy

I've not been noted for my bluntness in the past, but this time there is no other way than to say it straight out. I'm leaving everything to you because George has turned into a gambler and would only waste it, as he must have wasted his inheritance from his father. All he gets is my gold watch. The rest is for you.

I've been careful over the years, invested my money prudently – and I hope you'll continue to do the same. It's not a huge fortune, but there will be enough to allow you to live comfortably if you are not extravagant — and maybe even write that novel you were always talking about.

Do not, if you care at all about my wishes, let George get his hands on the money. Do not even lend him any, whatever tale he spins you. He will not repay it, for he has not proved trustworthy in his dealings with me.

I have not been feeling well for a while and shall not be sorry to go, my dear nephew. I've enjoyed life in my own way, but I don't fit in with this scrambling modern world. I'm pleased that we've beaten the Hun at last — though I never doubted we would — and am greatly relieved that you've survived that dreadful carnage.

Havershall will advise you about the money. I'd be happy to think of you living in Seaview House, but that's your choice. If you sell it, please make sure that the servants are looked after. I've left Mrs Shavely and Doris small bequests and they have agreed to stay on with you. Indeed, this is as much their home as mine now.

Yours affectionately,

James Mercer

Richard stared at the heavy silver desk furnishings and the inkstand blurred into a gleam of light against a dark background. He blinked furiously to clear his eyes, for he did not wish to weep in front of George, and made a mental resolution to do exactly as his uncle had wished, even to living in this house for this quiet, windswept village would suit him very well. It would be good for his daughter, too. Connie needed somewhere settled to live. Florence had dragged her hither and thither while he was away, often dumping her with relatives or neighbours for days on end, and the child seemed very fretful and anxious. And, of course, the accident had left her lame and even more reluctant to face the world.

Richard was grimly determined on the need for these changes, no longer the malleable young man who had married sophisticated Florence Hawley, as she would find out during the next few weeks. He had been forged in the flames of war and as an officer had been responsible for other men's lives – and deaths. Did his wife really think she was going to lead him around by the nose? Villa in London, indeed!

As soon as the lawyer had handed over James's gold watch, George left the library without another word, slamming the door behind him.

Havershall and Richard exchanged glances, then the lawyer began to explain the practicalities of obtaining probate and taking up the inheritance.

When Richard returned to the drawing room half an hour later, conversation faltered and he found himself the focus of a battery of disapproving gazes. Clearly George had wasted no time in spreading the word that Richard had wormed his way into James's good graces and stolen his cousin's inheritance. However, his wife positively beamed at him from across the room and hurried to join him, threading her arm through his and giving it a quick tug as he lingered to speak to his second cousin Jane.

'You don't mind if I steal my husband away, do you?'

'Oh, no, no! Of course not.' Jane moved back to her mother's side.

'There was no need for that,' Richard protested.

'There was every need! I can't wait a minute longer to find out exactly what happened.'

'Uncle James has left everything to me – except his gold watch, which George gets.'

Florence threw back her head and laughed, laughing again even more loudly as a shocked murmur arose from those standing nearby.

Her jubilation was as hard to bear as George's jealousy and Richard took her away soon afterwards, first promising Mr Havershall he would return the following week to take formal possession of the house.

The village's one cab, an elderly horse-drawn vehicle, was

waiting outside to take them to the station in Knott End.

'We could almost have walked,' he said. 'Knott End is only a mile or so down the road.'

His wife looked at him incredulously. '*You* might have walked, but I am not dressed for the country. This skirt is too tight for walking and these,' she waggled her feet in their high-heeled shoes, 'are too high.'

'Then why do you wear them? Why not choose something more sensible?'

Florence gave a trill of laughter. 'Because I believe it's a woman's duty to look smart.' She looked back at the house as the cab turned on to the sea front. 'How much do you think the place will be worth? Oh, Richard, isn't it wonderful?' When he didn't answer, she nudged him. 'What's the matter, you old sobersides? The funeral is over and we've left all the fuddy-duddy relatives behind so we don't have to pretend to be sad any longer.'

He could only stare at her in disgust at this crass speech.

'Aren't you even glad you've inherited?' she demanded.

He would have preferred to wait until they got on the train to say it, but she was tapping her foot impatiently. 'Let's get two things straight, Florence: I am genuinely sad that my uncle has died and I'm *not* going to sell the house. I love the place and always have done. I shall be happy to bring up our daughter here.'

For a moment her smile faded and her hand tightened like a claw on his arm, then she took a deep breath and said in a toneless voice, 'No need to make a decision yet. We'll have lots to discuss.'

'I shan't change my mind.' But as he listened to her humming a few minutes later, he realised she was still confident of being able to get her way. Well, once she might have done, but not now. Unfortunately for him and Connie, until Florence resigned herself to the situation, life was going to be uncomfortable for everybody. She had a gift for creating a bad atmosphere in a house and it made him sad that even at the age of nine, Connie tried so hard not to upset her mother.

CHAPTER TWO

November 1919

It was after dark when the Mercers reached Overdale, after a train journey spent alternately bickering and sitting in a heavy antagonistic silence. When they got home, however, Richard immediately forgot about the inheritance, forgot everything, because his little daughter, whom they had left in a kindly neighbour's care for the two days they had been away, was ill.

'It looks like that Spanish influenza, I'm afraid,' Mrs Broughton said, her eyes pitying. 'The doctor's rushed off his feet with it so I put her down on the sofa and –'

But Richard wasn't listening. He rushed into the front room to find his daughter flushed and feverish, with the oldest Broughton girl trying vainly to cool her by sponging her face. Connie didn't even recognise him. As Florence hovered in the doorway, making no effort to come near her child, he cast her one scornful glance and gathered his daughter gently in his arms. 'I dare say you'll manage to open our front door for me, Florence, if you try really hard.'

She flounced off, muttering to herself.

He sent the Broughtons' eldest son for the doctor, but the lad brought back a message that the doctor himself had come down with the influenza.

'We'll have to take her to the hospital, then,' Florence declared. 'I haven't the foggiest idea how to nurse a child.'

'We're not taking her anywhere in this condition. Surely there's another doctor round here?'

'I think there might be a woman doctor – Marriott's her name – but I haven't a clue where her surgery is. You're the one who insisted on staying in this dreary little house after your parents died. I hate it here. You might have grown up in Overdale but I didn't, and since you've seen a bit of the world now, I've never understood why you came back.'

'I came because our home and my job were here.'

'Well, there are other jobs, aren't there? Plenty of them.'

'My father's business may be small, but at least it's mine now.'

Florence made a vulgar sound with her lips and he turned away, biting back an angry retort. Because she seemed to dislike looking after their child, he sent her to fetch some boiled water and began to undress his daughter himself. Connie was alternately shivering and burning with fever.

After getting her to bed, he sat beside her, pulling off the covers or piling them back on as needed, and coaxing her to take sips of water at regular intervals. As the night passed Connie's temperature rose until she was hallucinating and screaming at them to stop hitting her. He'd seen high fevers before – he some-times thought he'd seen too many of mankind's woes in the trenches – so stripped all the bedding off yet again and began sponging her down with lukewarm water.

When he passed the other bedroom on his way for more water, he saw that Florence was sound asleep. It was then that the thought first came to him: perhaps he'd have enough money now to divorce her. If he offered to make her a generous settlement, surely she'd agree to it? He didn't want a messy, contested divorce, but a quiet one that wouldn't upset Connie. He'd have to think about it, find out what he'd have to do – then persuade Florence.

The following morning Richard hired a woman who was not a nurse, but who often 'helped out' in times of illness. Mrs Chittock soon showed why she had such a good reputation and together they watched over the child, taking turns to sleep and leaving Florence to deal with the housework with the assistance of their daily help. Mostly she just lounged around giving contradictory orders and leaving a trail of untidiness behind her.

It was touch and go for a few days before Connie was out of danger – days during which Florence continued to do no more than appear in the doorway of her daughter's room occasionally to ask how she was; days during which she and Richard quarrelled several times over her failure to supply decent cooked meals in the evenings, days during which fear lay on his heart like a heavy stone.

Florence grew sulky when he ordered her not to leave the house except to do urgent shopping. In fact, they quarrelled so often that Richard moved into the big attic bedroom, desperately needing to get away from her.

He had wanted to move up there when he first came home because he had longed for some peace and privacy after the trenches, and had tried to explain that to Florence. But she in turn had protested strenuously that he was her husband and what *she* needed was a man in her bed. Although she had encouraged him to make love to her, he had been unable to for he no longer found her in the slightest bit attractive. He had found out about her infidelities during one of his short stays back in Blighty and simply couldn't take other men's leavings. Now he didn't want to touch that boyish body or have those bony, restless hands touch him.

That had caused their fiercest quarrels.

When Connie was out of danger and beginning to recover, Richard thanked Mrs Chittock and paid her a generous bonus. 'You've been wonderful,' he told her.

'I wish you luck, Captain,' she said ambiguously, her eyes flicking towards Mrs Mercer.

He did not move back into what he now thought of as his wife's bedroom. The attic suited him fine with its views of Overdale's grey slate roofs and distant glimpses of the Pennines. As far as he was concerned, Florence's refusal to care for her sick child had set the final seal on their estrangement.

He would make sure their daughter was never left in her sole care again. Connie still believed that her mother loved her, but he knew better. Florence had never satisfactorily explained the accident that had left their child with a permanent limp, but he suspected it had happened through her neglect.

It was strange, too, how Connie always insisted she didn't remember what had happened. The doctor said she had probably bumped her head when she fell down the stairs.

In Overdale Dr Toby Herbert, former Medical Officer in the North Fylde Rifles, stared down at his patient, who was tucked firmly into the bed. Eric was clean and freshly shaved, but apart from that no other treatment had been offered to him. All the progress they had seen in the past few months before the man was brought here seemed to have vanished. Eric's eyes were now dull and unfocussed. Even his skin seemed paler.

Fury coursed through Toby. Dr Browning-Baker at work again, no doubt. But he had better make sure what was going on here before he created a fuss. He turned to the nurse. 'Why is this patient lying down?'

She stared down her nose at him and did not at first reply, her huge starched head-dress flapping gently to and fro at the slightest movement of her head.

It was a ridiculous piece of headgear, Toby thought. The brave nurses who'd looked after the lads at the front would not have been able to wear such monstrosities; wouldn't have wanted to, either. They were more concerned with their patients' welfare than their own appearance; with keeping the injured lads cheerful, not pinning them neatly to beds so that the ward 'looked tidy'.

'Well?' he demanded.

'Dr Browning-Baker is in charge here and I'm afraid his orders must take precedence over yours, Dr Herbert.'

'But this man is *my* patient,' he protested, keeping his voice steady only with an effort. 'And his current treatment is not helping him to get better.'

Her expression showed nothing but scorn. 'I'm afraid you'll find that we follow tried and tested methods here. And, I repeat, I cannot go against Dr Browning-Baker's orders.'

'Then I shall go and see him myself.'

'As you wish.' She bent forward to smooth an invisible wrinkle from the bedspread and continued her round without another glance at poor Eric who might have been a doll for all the stimulation he received now.

The secretary said Toby could make an appointment to see Dr Browning-Baker the following week, but he was very busy now.

Toby could hear voices coming from the doctor's comfortable office. Just as he was debating whether to agree to the appointment or not, the door opened and Dr Browning-Baker showed out a man as formally dressed as he was – and as full of self-importance.

Toby stepped forward. 'I need to see you, sir, on a matter of urgency.'

'Do you have an appointment?' Dr Browning-Baker looked down his nose at him, as he had been doing ever since some of Toby's patients had been sent here to recover because the well-endowed hospital had spare capacity.

'No. But, as I said, it's urgent.'

The look Dr Browning-Baker threw at his secretary boded ill for her. The look he gave Toby was even more disapproving. 'I'm afraid I cannot rearrange my schedule at such short notice.' He turned and went back into his office.

Toby followed him inside, closed the door and stood against it, arms folded. 'Why have my instructions for Eric Nesby been countermanded? He's losing what little progress we had made.'

'I am in charge of the medical side of this hospital and I do not approve of these radical new treatments. They give false hope to the families and promise cures which they cannot deliver. Head injuries are difficult enough to assess and while Mr Nesby is in *my* hospital he will receive only treatment of which I approve.'

'Mr Nesby is not here as one of your patients. He is merely occupying a bed which was empty until *I* can find him a permanent home.'

'I do not intend to argue.' Dr Browning-Baker moved some papers across the desk and began to read them.

Toby breathed in deeply then turned on his heel. It would be no use arguing with this old sod. He'd seen them before: tinpot dictators who hated to be crossed. The only way to get anywhere was to go through army channels and clarify the situation officially. He sighed as he drove back to his rooms in Manchester, which were not nearly as luxurious as those he had just left. It would all take time, and although he was pretty sure he would win the army's support, he would have made an enemy of a powerful doctor.

Well, he didn't care about that. The Government was paying him to look after these badly injured soldiers and he intended to give them the best care he could. And he knew a hell of a lot more about treating severe head injuries than a doctor who had never been to the front, never had to deal with the carnage there.

He did win, but it took several weeks and by that time Eric had reverted to a near-comatose state and Dr Browning-Baker had written to the army to protest that his case was hopeless and the fellow should be sent to St Jude's.

Not if Toby Herbert could help it! The nuns of St Jude's were devoted women, but they also placed too high a value on tidy bodies in tidy beds. The only patients he had allowed to go into permanent care there were those whom his methods had not helped at all, those who truly were the living dead – or, worse, incurably deranged by their horrifying experiences at the front. The sort who were never mentioned in newspaper articles eulogising 'our brave lads'.

✿

Little Connie Mercer was slow to recover from the influenza. It left her very lethargic, with a tendency to sleep a lot. She wept if asked to stand up or walk for long, complaining that it made her bad leg ache and that she hurt all over. She spent a lot of time lying on a sofa near the window in her bedroom, attended by a young girl whom Richard had hired to look after her and keep her company, even though Florence had protested about the expense.

With his uncle's money behind him, he put the family accountancy firm up for sale and when a buyer appeared within three weeks, left the place as soon as he had handed his clients over and made sure things would run smoothly. Apart from that he spent most of his time with Connie. Although Dr Marriott said reassuringly that she would probably recover completely from the 'flu within a month or two, there was still the question of his daughter's leg.

When Dr Marriott suggested she should see someone about the limp and referred them to Dr Browning-Baker, the senior doctor at the hospital, Richard agreed. If he could help his daughter in any way, he would. His wife certainly hadn't made any attempt to get the leg examined.

The consultation was a nightmare from start to finish. Florence had to be coerced into accompanying them because she hated hospitals. Connie wept and begged them not to make her go, saying doctors always hurt you. And when they got there Richard himself took an instant dislike to the arrogant doctor with his pair of attendant nurses, both of whom were as uncommunicative as he was and snapped at the already distressed child instead of treating her kindly.

Distress turned into screams and Richard ignored the nurses' orders to wait outside and burst into the examination room, to find one woman holding Connie down while the doctor brusquely manipulated her bad leg.

'Please leave the room at once, Father! It's better for the child if she is not distracted by the presence of her parents,' he declared.

'I have a name, Doctor, and so does my daughter! And how can it be good for her to be hurt so badly?' Richard went to stand by his daughter, clasping her hand and speaking to her soothingly. This was no way to treat a sick child. Why the hell couldn't the man have been gentler and taken the time to reassure Connie, instead of reducing her to this pitiful state?

The doctor frowned at him.

One of the nurses whispered, 'It really is better if you leave the child with us, Mr Mercer.'

'I'm not leaving.'

Browning-Baker sighed, then shrugged and began to manipulate the leg again.

Connie screamed.

Richard could not understand why the fellow had to be so rough. 'I think that's more than enough,' he said, using a crisp officer's tone.

The doctor eyed him narrowly and moved away.

Richard went to the door and called his wife in. 'Help Connie to dress while I have a word with the doctor.'

In Browning-Baker's well-appointed office Richard sat down without waiting to be asked and glared across the wide polished desk. 'Well? What has all that unpleasantness proved?'

'Let me tell you, sir, that I do not appreciate your tone . . .'

'And I don't appreciate your rough treatment of my child!'

For a moment there was silence then the doctor made a little snorting sound. 'I fear your daughter has been encouraged in her weakness and consequently has a hysterical condition.'

'What does that mean?'

'There's little or nothing wrong with her leg. She may have broken it once, but children's bones heal quickly. She is now playing upon your sympathies, probably to avoid going to school. A sound spanking might have cured it in the beginning, but as the condition has been going on for a long time you may never rid her of the neurosis now.'

'It's real enough to give her pain if she walks much,' Richard protested.

'Phantom pain only, I'm convinced. She may improve somewhat once she recovers completely from the influenza. Or as she grows up. But there is nothing physically wrong with her leg.'

The doctor's expression was so smug and superior that Richard felt a sudden urge to smash his fist into that plump face. While he had been fighting for his country, while other doctors had been serving at the front, this fellow had been lording it here. Well, Richard wasn't submitting Connie to any more rough treatment from him. 'Thank you for your trouble.' He stood up and walked out.

After that he did not take his daughter to see any more doctors. When Connie recovered completely from the 'flu he would arrange for a tutor to come and supervise her lessons. In the meantime, he spent time with her and ensured that she had plenty to occupy herself with, buying her books and toys, whatever caught her fancy, glad that she seemed at least to enjoy reading.

Florence made little effort to help in any way. 'Never been good in sickrooms,' she said airily when he asked her to go and entertain the child occasionally. 'You do that sort of thing far better than I ever could. I dare say it's your wartime experience. It's hardened you to distress.'

'On the contrary.'

But she had already turned away and was lighting another cigarette – a habit he despised – inserting it into a long holder and exhaling clouds of smoke, watching the curls and twists of vapour writhe upwards as if they were the only thing on her mind.

CHAPTER THREE

April 1920

The following April, on a showery Saturday afternoon, Polly leaned back in her seat, enjoying the ride from Outshaw into Overdale. These new motor omnibuses had made a big difference to people in outlying districts, allowing them to come shopping whenever they wanted. Even her mother-in-law used them. Polly particularly appreciated being able to visit her sister without relying either on the carter or waiting for Sunday so that her husband could borrow a trap from his employer.

Beside her Eddie was holding their son on his lap. Well, Polly was now five months pregnant as a result of their loving reunion following her stay with Lizzie and her lap was not as large as it had been. Certainly it did not provide much room for a lively lad of almost three. She was pleased about her condition. In fact, everything had seemed better during the past few months, even her mother-in-law behaving in a more friendly way once she found out that Polly was expecting another child.

As the bus topped the rise just outside Outshaw, the sun broke through the clouds and she smiled at her husband, gesturing towards the view spread out below them. 'From here I always think Overdale looks like a giant cat curled up against the foot of the Pennines. Don't you, love?'

He looked out of the window then shook his head. 'I can't see it myself. Just another of your fancies, Pol. Hey, you sit still, my lad.' For Billy was in a fractious mood that day, refusing to settle on his father's knee, stretching his arms out to his mother and grizzling to go to her.

By the time the bus stopped in Market Square, it was raining again and the sky was leaden. Eddie got off first with Billy, setting the child down for a moment as he turned to help Polly off. When he looked round, there was no sign of the boy. 'Drat him! Always running away. Wait here and I'll find him, love.' He limped off round the back of the bus.

Polly watched him in some concern. It seemed to her that Eddie's bad leg, legacy of a childhood injury, was giving him more trouble lately, but he would never discuss it with her and usually tried to ignore it completely. Working on a farm couldn't be good for it, but what else did he know?

There was a shout from the other side of the bus and the sound of squealing brakes, followed by thump and a grating sound, then a whole chorus of screams and shouts. The traffic blocking her way stopped. Passers-by moved instinctively towards whatever lay beyond the bus. The babble of noise abated only slightly.

As Eddie still hadn't returned Polly went after him. She didn't want Billy gaping at an accident. But the spectators were blocking her way and it took her some time to push her way through them. By this time she was starting to feel really anxious. Why hadn't her husband come back to reassure her?

Between the bobbing heads and bodies that had spilled over on to the road, she saw a figure lying half underneath a bus with blood pooling beside it. She didn't recognise it at first because she was looking for Billy, then something drew her back to stare at the still figure and she saw that it was wearing Eddie's clothes! Only – it didn't look like her husband any more.

She could not move, could not even breathe properly for the terror that clamped hard around her chest. Then, as the terrible details sank in, nausea made her stomach lurch and her skin feel suddenly clammy. People were whispering around her, but they seemed a long way away.

'Eh, what a brave fellow!'

'Is he dead?'

'Did he save the child? Where is it?'

Polly tried to move forward again. She could not afford to give way to shock, not yet. She had to find Billy. 'Excuse me. Could you let me pass, please?'

An older man with a kindly face put out his arm to stop her. 'Better stay back, love. It's not a pretty sight for a woman in your condition.'

'He's – I think it's my husband who's hurt.' The words seemed to be spoken by someone else and to echo faintly in her head.

'Stay there a minute, lass, till we find out . . .' Letting the words trail away, he shuffled sideways to block her view, saying, 'You're better not looking, love.'

So she stood next to him, feeling frozen, terrified, bewildered. All she could think of was Billy. Where was he?

Another man came back, shaking his head and looking at her pityingly. She stared at him in horror. 'He's not – Eddie can't be –'

The kindly man put his arm round her shoulders. 'I'm that sorry, love.'

'Is she all right?' a woman's voice asked from Polly's other side.

'It's his wife,' the man explained.

'Eh, the poor thing's expecting an' all.'

The woman had whispered the words, but they were still loud enough to be heard and everyone in the vicinity now turned round to stare at Polly.

She felt tears fill her eyes. When she blinked them away more followed and spilled down her cheeks. *All right!* How could she possibly be all right with her Eddie dead? Suddenly her legs turned boneless and she would have fallen but for the man's arm round her waist. 'My son?' she managed. 'A little boy. Where's my son?'

'I can't see him, love.'

'There was a little lad ran out into the road. Your husband was chasing after him then he slipped and fell in front of the bus, poor soul.' the shrill-voiced woman informed her.

'I must find Billy.' Polly moved forward again. The stranger went with her and she was glad of his strong arm supporting her.

'She's his wife,' he kept saying and the words opened a path for them through the onlookers who had flocked on to the road to gape. She didn't dare glance in Eddie's direction, keeping going only because she had to find Billy.

Beyond the bus they found her child lying on the ground, as still as his father, his head covered in blood. Polly stopped in terror. 'No! *No!*' For a moment she could not move then she jerked forward, shoving a woman out of the way and throwing herself to the ground beside her son.

'Don't touch him!' an onlooker said sharply. 'We've sent for the ambulance.'

'He's my son. I –' Polly saw one of Billy's arms twitch and forgot about the other people. 'He's alive! Oh, thank God, he's alive!' Tears of relief began to trickle down her face and she leaned over him, saying gently, 'Billy, love! Your mammy's here.'

He didn't answer, but she could see his chest rising and falling and she focused on that. As long as he was breathing, she could breathe too.

She didn't know how much time had passed, but when someone took hold of her arm and said, 'Let the doctor see to him, lass!' she sat back on her heels.

Dr Marriott knelt beside Billy, her fingers light against his pulse. 'Has someone sent for the ambulance?'

'They phoned from the butcher's. It's on its way.'

Polly looked at Dr Marriott, the woman who had been her doctor when she'd worked for the Pilbys. 'Is he – will he live?'

'We can't tell anything yet.' The doctor's eyes went to Polly's stomach and she called over her shoulder, 'Someone get the mother a chair.'

But before anyone could obey, a bell clanged in the distance and as the sound drew nearer the crowd shuffled backwards to make way for the ambulance, leaving only the small group around the bus and the two still figures. Some of the passengers from the bus were also standing nearby, one holding a bloody handkerchief to his forehead and an old woman weeping hysterically, supported by a younger woman whose face was chalky white.

When Billy had been lifted on to the stretcher, Dr Marriott had a quick look at the other people's injuries, but there was nothing seriously wrong so she returned to the child, her face showing her anxiety.

They let Polly go in the ambulance with Billy and the doctor sat beside her, keeping an unobtrusive eye on the mother as well as the still figure on the stretcher.

'Is he – very badly hurt?' Polly asked, surprised at how hoarse her voice sounded.

'It's a head injury.' Dr Marriott hesitated then added quietly, 'They're the hardest to judge, I'm afraid. We must wait for your son to recover consciousness, then we'll know.'

'Know what?'

'Whether he's been injured in other ways.' She reached out to clasp Polly's hand. 'But you need to –'

'*What ways?*'

'Well, head injuries can affect the brain or the body's movements.'

Polly stared at her in sick horror, remembering a boy from school who had hurt his head falling off the roof and had never been the same since. 'Turn people into idiots, you mean? No, not my Billy! *No!*'

Shh, now. Keep calm. There's nothing you can do but pray, my dear.' As the doctor studied Polly's stomach, she added, 'And I think we'll admit you to hospital as well. In your condition, we can't afford to take chances. And anyway, if we do that you'll be nearby in case – well, in case they need you quickly.'

Polly shivered and asked no more questions, concentrating

on watching Billy's chest moving up and down with his slow breaths. If it weren't for the bandage round his head, you'd think he was just asleep. He fell asleep sometimes when he got overtired. She'd found him in the scullery once, curled up on the stone floor as if it were a soft feather bed. She and Eddie had chuckled over that. She bit her lip. Eddie . . . She mustn't think about her husband yet. There was nothing she could do for him now. It was their son who mattered. For him she had to be strong.

When the ambulance arrived at the hospital, they took Billy away on a trolley and wouldn't let her go with him.

'We'll need your name and particulars,' a nurse said.

'Scordale – and my son is Billy. *Please* let me go with him!'

'I'm afraid that isn't allowed.'

Polly could not hold back a sob and tried to push past the nurse who prevented her gently, eyes pitying.

Dr Marriott stepped forward. 'Please calm down, Mrs Scordale. You have the baby to think of as well as Billy.'

Polly stared down at her stomach. It didn't seem real. Nothing seemed real. But she didn't have the strength to argue so she let them do with her what they wanted. After they had examined her – she kept telling them she hadn't been hurt! – they wanted to know who to contact so she gave them Lizzie's name. Then at last they left her alone, lying on a narrow bed in a small cubicle surrounded by green curtains on metal frames.

She should be crying, she thought, as she lay there staring at the folds in the curtains. When you lost a loved one, you were supposed to weep. But her tears had dried up and everything seemed unreal, as if she were watching a film at the cinema. She couldn't believe Eddie was dead, couldn't believe this was anything but a nightmare. Surely, surely it was?

When a woman came in and sat beside the bed, it took her a moment to recognise her own sister.

'Polly, I came as soon as I heard. Someone recognised you and ran into the shop to tell me. Oh, love, I'm so sorry.' Lizzie waited a minute and added gently, 'You – you do know that Eddie is . . .'

'Dead? Yes, I saw him.' Polly could not stop her voice from wobbling. 'There was blood all over the road – and him such a little man, too. You wouldn't think he'd have so much blood in him. But Billy was still alive when they took him away. I could see him breathing. Only they wouldn't let me go with him. Have they said anything to you about him?'

'No.'

'If they'll just let me know he's all right, I can cope, but till I know – well, I can't seem to think of anything else. Can you find out, *make* them tell us how he is? I wanted to stay with him but they wouldn't let me.' She began to weep softly. 'I feel too dizzy to stand up. I don't know why I feel so dizzy. I wasn't the one who was hurt.'

Lizzie leaned forward to kiss her cheek then got up, nodding in the determined fashion in which she did most things nowadays. 'If you'll promise to stay here, I'll go and ask about Billy.'

'I promise.'

Lizzie pushed the green curtain aside and walked out.

Noises floated round Polly, people walked past the cubicle and once a nurse came to ask her something, but she couldn't think properly, let alone give a sensible answer. Lizzie would find out what was happening. Lizzie would tell these people what they needed to know. She closed her eyes for a minute, waiting for her sister to return.

She did not open them again until a hand took hers, then she looked up and sighed in relief. 'I didn't see you come back.'

Lizzie squeezed her hand. 'You were dozing, love. It seemed a shame to wake you.'

'Billy?'

'He's still alive, but the doctors are going to keep a careful watch on him.'

'I should be with him.' Polly tried to sit up.

Lizzie pushed her back. 'He hasn't regained consciousness. He won't know what's happening. If they'd needed you, I'd have woken you, but they want you to stay quiet, and I think you should, too. For the baby's sake.'

'Yes.' Polly laid one hand on her stomach and its gentle curve was a comfort. Only – Eddie would never see the child now. She pushed the thought of him away again, unable to face it yet, just lay there in silence, holding tightly to her elder sister's hand, as she had done so many times when they were children.

Later a nurse came into the cubicle. 'We need to get you up to the ward now, Mrs Scordale. And I'm sorry, Mrs Dearden, but visiting hours are over.'

'Can't I stay with her? Surely she shouldn't be left alone?'

The nurse pursed her lips and gave Lizzie a severe look, her starched head-dress standing out around her plump face. 'I'm sorry, but there are several other patients in the ward who need their afternoon rest. The best thing you can do is go and bring some nightclothes for your sister. You can leave them with the porter then visit her again this evening.'

What worried Lizzie most as she walked away was that Polly didn't protest about this, just closed her eyes again, still with that frozen expression on her face. She dreaded to think what her sister would be like once it really sank in that Eddie was dead. When Lizzie's first husband had died, she had felt only relief because she'd hated Sam by then, but Polly and Eddie had been happy together in their own quiet way.

Lizzie hurried back along York Road to the shop, rushing in like a whirlwind to toss information at her husband then pound up the stairs to their living quarters with him following. There she continued to talk and speculate as she packed up some of her own maternity clothes and nightgowns for Polly. When she had finished, she glanced at the clock. The young lass who looked after her two children so that she could work in the family shop would be back from the park soon with the pram and Lizzie usually took a few minutes off to have tea with them before the evening rush.

'Tell Jen I won't be in for tea – and give Matt and Beth a kiss from me!' she called over her shoulder to Peter as she clattered down the stairs.

A brisk fifteen-minute walk took Lizzie back to the hospital. After leaving the bag of clothes with the porter, she hesitated then made for the town centre. Before she got there, she turned off down a side street. Someone would have to let Percy know what had happened. Their brother would probably be at the yard now so she might as well go and tell him. She'd rather be doing something than sitting around worrying about Polly or facing customers in the shop who would tell her over and over about the accident.

However would Polly manage now? It was a good thing the Deardens weren't short of a penny or two. If her sister needed help, Lizzie would not hesitate to offer it — she had no need to ask her husband or his mother to know that it would be forthcoming. She considered Sally Dearden the best mother-in-law in the whole world and her Peter the kindest man on earth.

Lizzie brushed away a tear impatiently. Polly was kind, too, and her sister didn't deserve this.

At Cardwell's Quality Builders Percy Kershaw came out of the back room when he heard the doorbell. 'Lizzie, how nice to —' he broke off at the sight of his sister's expression. 'What's wrong?'

'Eddie's been killed in an accident.'

He gaped at her for a moment then yelled over his shoulder, 'Emma! Come quickly!'

When Lizzie had finished her tale, he asked simply, 'What can I do to help?' Beside him, his wife nodded.

'Drive over to Outshaw and make sure the Scordales know what's happened. They'll want to come into town to see the body, I suppose, and they'll need to see Polly and Billy, too. You could drive them in, perhaps. I don't think Polly is in a state to do much and — and there'll be things that need sorting out, as well as a funeral to arrange.' She looked at him, tears welling again in her eyes. 'Oh, Percy, our Polly looked *dreadful* when I saw her. She was so shocked she couldn't think straight and she was as white as the sheets on the bed.'

Emma gave him a push. 'You go and fetch the Scordales, Percy. I can manage here. And I'll tell Johnny what happened when he gets home. Your little brother is taking longer and longer to run errands.'

Percy hesitated. 'I hardly know the Scordales and they're a funny lot. They usually like to keep themselves to themselves, so maybe they won't want my help.' But both women insisted he should at least offer, so he shrugged and left.

At Outshaw a neighbour opened the door of the Scordales' house for Percy. Eddie's parents had not long since been told the news and were in the kitchen. His mother was sitting at the table, her head on her arms, weeping hoarsely, the sound shockingly loud in the quietness of the afternoon. His father, still wearing dusty work clothes, was standing beside her, patting her on the shoulder and mopping tears from his own cheeks with a grubby handkerchief.

Percy offered them his condolences, which they didn't even seem to hear, then said, 'I wondered if you'd like me to drive you into town? Someone has to — well, see to things.'

Hilda's tears stopped for a minute and as she looked up her voice grew sharp. 'Isn't your Polly doing that?'

'She's in hospital. They're worried about her losing the baby.'

'Some folk give way easily to shock.' Mrs Scordale sniffed and her voice took on an irritated tone. 'They think only of themselves, some people do.'

Percy was too surprised by this spiteful remark to do more than stare at her.

Mr Scordale intervened hurriedly. 'It's kind of you to offer, lad. Very kind. How's our Billy? No one seems to know.'

'It's a head injury, so they won't know for a while whether the accident has done more damage.'

The door burst open then and Eddie's brother Rodney rushed in, still in his muddy farm clothes. 'I just heard about our Eddie. Is it true?'

His mother started sobbing again, and his father muttered, 'I can't take it in, I just can't. I keep thinking there must be some mistake.'

Rodney turned to Percy. 'Is our Eddie really dead?'

'I'm afraid so. I came to see if I could help – maybe drive you all into Overdale. You being family and all.'

'Thanks, but I've borrowed Farmer Snape's car so I can take Mum and Dad into town.'

They all stared at Percy as if he were guilty of intruding and he decided, not for the first time, that they were a funny lot, always seeming suspicious of strangers. Eddie had been the best of them, but the mother was a sour creature. Fancy saying something like that about poor Polly. 'I'll leave you to it, then. But if there's anything we can do to help . . .'

Rodney escorted him to the door. 'Thanks, but I'll look after my parents. If you see to your sister, that'll help us most.'

And that was the way it went from then on – as if Polly was no longer a Scordale.

One day Richard Mercer received a letter from a firm in Fleetwood which dealt in property sales. As he read it he realised with growing indignation that Florence must have contacted them about selling Seaview House, and that a representative had actually been to look over it. She had clearly not given up her plan for them all to move to London when they left Overdale. Well, she could move there on her own – he was surprised at how strongly he wished she would – but *he* wasn't going anywhere but Stenton-on-Sea and nor was Connie.

He waited to confront her about this until after the evening meal, when their daughter was in bed, but as soon as she had cleared the table, Florence declared her intention of going to the cinema with her friend Susan.

'Go another night instead,' Richard ordered. 'You and I have something rather important to discuss.'

'I can't think what that is. Will it take long? Susan and I might still catch the second house if you hurry.' Florence glanced down at the little jewelled wrist watch that he suspected had been bought for her by one of her admirers because it was an expensive piece and he had not been able to supply her lavishly with money during the war years.

'No, it won't take long.'

'Hoe in, then.' She leaned forward, expression a parody of an eager child's, eyes already glazed with patent lack of interest.

'It seems you contacted Mindley & Sons in Fleetwood about selling my uncle's house.'

'Ah. Was there a letter from them in the second post?' She took a new cigarette out of the holder and pushed it back in again, fiddling around with it and avoiding his eyes. 'They seemed to think the place would sell quite easily when I spoke to them.'

'I have no intention of selling Seaview House, as I've already told you. I intend to move to Stenton almost immediately. I'm sure the sea air will do Connie good.'

Florence's face turned a dusky red and she said very loudly, 'Well, it won't do me any good, but you didn't think about my needs, did you? You never do. Well, let me tell you, I have *no* intention of spending the rest of my life in such a god-forsaken hole.'

'Uncle James didn't leave me a fortune, you know, Florence, and most of the money is tied up in investments. We couldn't afford to live half as well in London, and now that Connie is feeling a little better she needs –'

'Don't I have a say in where we live? I'll go mad in a small village. Stenton hasn't even got a cinema!'

'You'll have a larger house to run. I'm sure that'll keep you pretty busy, and I intend to write.'

She clapped one hand to her brow. 'Oh, my God! The great English war novel, I suppose? As if a cold fish like you could write with passion, when you can't even satisfy a woman! Shall we all have to tiptoe around you, then, while you apply your genius? It's really going to be *such* fun living there.'

He could feel himself flushing. 'Since you're not at home very often, I'm sure you won't be much affected by what I do.'

They went on to have an even more heated row than usual about the move, but Richard stuck to his decision that they should leave Overdale within the month. In the end Florence slammed out, saying she might be too late for the cinema, but she wasn't too late to see Susan and she'd best enjoy her friend's company while she could, because there was no one below the age of sixty in bloody Stenton.

The following day he telephoned the firm she had contacted, withdrew the house from the market and also informed them unequivocally that his wife had had no authority to act as she had done.

'But, sir — *you* signed the letter of authorisation.'

'No, I didn't.'

'But it's there, very clearly. Richard Mercer. Perhaps you were — um — busy and forgot?'

'Could you send me the letter in question, please? It sounds to me as if someone's been forging my signature.'

There was a gasp at the other end of the line, then, 'Certainly, sir. And I hope you'll accept our assurance that we acted in good faith?'

'Of course.'

When the letter arrived the following day by first post Richard stared at it in dismay. Even he would have thought it his own signature — only he knew he had not signed any authorisation to sell. It could only be Florence's doing. As he studied it, it suddenly occurred to him that she might have been signing his name to other documents, so he went to the bank and asked to see the manager. Together they checked his account carefully, and he realised in dismay that she had been withdrawing considerable sums of money during the past few weeks while he'd been busy selling the family business.

Richard didn't intend to cover up what had been going on. 'I'm afraid my wife has been forging my signature,' he told the manager.

The man goggled at him. 'Oh, my goodness! I hope you will absolve us from any complicity in this?'

'Yes, of course, but I wish to make sure it can't happen again.'

He changed his form of signature, setting up some safeguards to make sure any letters or cheques the bank received really were from him but saying nothing of this to Florence, merely telling her that he wished them to economise for a while so she was not to incur any extra expenses.

The following week the bank manager telephoned him to say in hushed tones that they'd received another cheque with the old signature forged on it and asking, with much clearing of the throat, if Richard wanted to call in the police.

'No. I'll deal with the matter myself.' He strode up the stairs two at a time, bursting into Florence's bedroom to find her standing with her breasts bared in front of the dressing table, studying herself in the mirror.

She made no attempt to cover herself. 'Goodness, have you had a sudden surge of passion? Are you going to throw me on the bed and have your wicked way with me?'

His expression must have shown how unattracted he was to her because she tossed her head and went to put on her kimono. 'Well? What's so urgent that you have to rush up here and burst into my room?'

'I came to tell you that if you try to forge another cheque on my account, I'll call in the police and have you arrested.'

She glared at him. 'You shouldn't be so mean with your money, then.'

'Careful is not the same as "mean". What's more, if you try to run up any debts in my name, I'll put an announcement in the newspaper to make sure the local tradesmen understand the situation. It'll be even easier to do that in Stenton, I should imagine.'

Her face suddenly set in harsh lines, making her look far older than her years. 'How do you expect me to manage, then?'

'The way other women do: by working out a budget and sticking to it.' He hesitated, then added, 'Perhaps we should seriously consider getting a divorce? I am prepared to make a modest settlement on you, which will give you some independence.' His family would be horrified at the mere hint of a divorce, but he was finding it increasingly difficult to live with Florence. He'd been trying to find a tactful way to broach the idea for a while and had found it harder than he'd expected.

She stared at him, an ugly expression on her face. 'Oh, you'd like that, wouldn't you? To get rid of me now that you've come into money. Find yourself a new wife, one who wants a litter of children, then give *me* a pittance to manage on. Well, I'm not doing it. I'm your wife and I'm staying your wife.'

'Why? You don't care two hoots for me – or for our child. It's just the money you want. Well, I'll make sure you don't get your hands on it, believe me – if I have to put you in prison for forging cheques to do so.'

She snatched up a perfume bottle and he moved forward quickly to take it out of her hand as she raised it in the air. 'I don't like having things thrown at me. It doesn't solve anything. Whereas a quiet divorce –'

'No!'

'But surely –'

Suddenly she shrieked, 'Get out . . . *get out*! I can't stand the sight of you for a minute longer. And if you try to divorce me, I'll make such a fuss the whole world will hear of it!'

Without another word he set about making arrangements for their move. Perhaps spending time in Stenton-on-Sea would make her change her mind about a divorce though he could not even imagine her coping on any allowance, however generous. Florence had been deeply in debt when he got back from the war, but he wasn't going to give her his Uncle James's money to waste. For Connie's sake, as well as his own.

CHAPTER FOUR

April 1920

It was two days before a doctor came to see Polly about her son, two long days during which she fretted so much that they took her in a wheelchair to sit by the boy's bed. He wasn't conscious and his face didn't look like her Billy's any more. Not only was it badly bruised, it also had a stillness and emptiness to it, as if there were no one present inside the poor, battered skull. She wanted to weep, was aching with the weight of her grief, but the tears seemed dammed up inside and her thoughts were just tangled in formless misery.

When the doctor eventually came to see Polly, he was accompanied by the Ward Sister who pushed a chair forward for him then pulled the curtains closed around the bed and stood behind him.

As if that would stop the eight women in the other beds from listening! Polly thought. 'What's wrong with my Billy?' she asked, not waiting for them to speak.

'I'm afraid there has definitely been some brain damage, Mrs Scordale. He's not regained consciousness and his body isn't responding properly to stimuli.'

Her heart seemed to speed up and start thumping. When she tried to speak all that came out was a whining sound. She dug her fingernails into the palm of her hand and the pain helped her focus. 'Will he have to – have an operation, then?'

'I'm afraid that would be no use. These head injury cases are rather difficult. There is very little we can actually do about brain damage. We shall run more tests on your son, of course, but I'm afraid you must prepare yourself for the worst, Mrs Scordale.'

The room wavered around her. *'Billy's going to die?'*

'No, no. Not physically, at any rate. But we think his brain is so badly damaged that he will never be able to live a normal life.'

Polly clapped her hand to her mouth to hold back the agony that seemed to be filling her chest so that it was full of sharp, biting pain. Then she suddenly remembered what her old employer Mrs Pilby had done when her son was injured at his fancy school. 'I want to see a specialist.'

The doctor stared at her in astonishment. 'There really is no point. And besides, that can be very expensive. Can you afford it?'

She hung on to the thought. 'I want to see a specialist – even if it takes all my savings. I can earn more money, but I can't replace my Billy.'

'Well – our own Dr Browning-Baker does see some of these cases. I'll ask him if he has time to see you about Billy next week.'

'Not till next week?'

'Dr Browning-Baker is a very busy man. And anyway, it'll be better if he sees the child a little later – just in case there's any progress.'

The doctor pushed his chair back. 'In the meantime, you have another baby on the way, Mrs Scordale. You must draw your comfort from that.' He stood up and the Sister whisked aside the chair then followed him out, her starched head-dress crackling and rubber-soled shoes squeaking slightly on the linoleum-covered floor.

Polly was glad they didn't draw back the curtains. She did not want to face the other women's pitying gazes.

One of the nurses came to stand beside her bed. 'You all right, love? No, of course you're not.' She took Polly's hand and held it, patting it gently. 'You let it all out. It's best to cry.'

But the tears wouldn't come. They seemed frozen inside her.

Later the Ward Sister came back and said Polly could leave
hospital that afternoon and Dr Browning-Baker would see her
about Billy next Tuesday. 'Do you want me to telephone Mrs
Dearden to come and fetch you?'

Polly shook her head. 'No. I'll catch the bus home. It passes
the hospital and – and I think I'll be best on my own till I – get
used to things.'

The kind nurse came back later and scolded her for that,
saying she needed her family around her at a time like this, but
Polly didn't want anyone, not even Lizzie. She had never been
quick at working things out and she needed time now to sort it
all out in her mind. Eddie. Billy. Herself. What she was going to
do with her life.

No one was around to see Polly get off the bus at the end of the
lane that led to Outshaw, for which she was glad. A light rain was
falling as she hurried down the muddy track and the house
seemed cold and damp. She stood inside the door for some time,
pressed against it, breathing hard as if she had been running. Her
home. Two rooms upstairs, two down, plus a rear scullery – not
a big house but she kept it shining clean. Eddie had appreciated
that, had said so often.

A knock on the door brought her out of her reverie and she
sighed as she opened it. She knew that knock. 'Hello, Mrs
Scordale.' She waited, expecting some expression of sympathy,
some offer of help.

'*You* don't look too bad, any road.'

Polly was hurt by the unsympathetic tone but not really
surprised. It was only three days since she'd last been home, but
it seemed like an eternity. She felt like a completely different
person now, one who was no longer afraid of her mother-in-law.
Losing your husband did that to you.

What had Hilda Scordale come for? Polly wondered as she
watched the other woman staring round as if she had never seen

the front room before when not a day had gone past that her mother-in-law hadn't popped in for a few minutes, especially in the evenings after Eddie came home from work.

'You'll have to take good care of yourself from now on,' her unwelcome visitor said at last. 'The new baby will be all we have left of our Eddie.'

'What do you mean – all you have left? There's still Billy.'

Mrs Scordale gave her a scornful look as if she was half-witted. 'Our Rodney phoned the hospital this morning. They said Billy hasn't recovered his wits, so it stands to reason he'll have to be put in an institution. That's what they do with cases like that. I've seen it before.'

Polly gasped and took a step backwards. 'They haven't told *me* he'll have to go into an institution and I'm his mother. He just – hasn't recovered properly yet. They said no one can tell with head injuries. It takes time.'

'They're just saying that. People don't recover from such injuries and you'd better face it. Your Billy might as well be dead. In fact, it'd be easier if he were. You'll allus have the worry of him now.'

Polly felt anger start to rise in her. Until now her child had been 'our Billy' to his grandmother. Suddenly he was 'your Billy', rejected as if he no longer belonged to the Scordale family. Well, *she* wasn't going to reject him or give up hope, either. She'd decided that on the bus. It was the only thing she'd decided so far. The fact that her boy was badly hurt didn't stop her loving him and it never would. 'As long as he's alive, there's hope,' she said firmly.

'Don't be a fool to yourself, girl. They don't recover from injuries like that.' Hilda Scordale's voice became suddenly hoarse, her pain showing through. 'That's two children I've lost now. *Two*, think on! You're not the only one as is suffering.'

Polly didn't waste time pointing out that Mary was alive and well in Australia. Mrs Scordale always acted as if her daughter was dead. 'Look, I need to be on my own for a bit, if you don't mind, to think things through.'

'I'll bring you across some fresh milk. I'm making stew for tea so I'll bring you a bowl of that, too. You'd better get yourself to bed. Happen you'll be able *to think things through* there.'

Her tone was so scornful that Polly stared at her reproachfully.

'Eh, you're a moony one and no mistake! I don't know what my Eddie ever saw in you. I'll leave the milk on the doorstep. I can't stand around gossiping all day.' She walked out, slamming the door shut behind her as usual and crossing the lane to her own house.

Polly shot the bolt. She didn't want any more of the Scordales coming in to disturb her or give her bad news with as little tenderness as Eddie's mother had just done. And her Billy definitely wasn't going into an institution, not if she had anything to do with it.

She walked slowly up the stairs then stood in the bedroom for a moment, trying to remember what she had come up for and failing. Shaking her head, she walked downstairs again, feeling disoriented and woozy.

The door knocker rattled and a voice called 'I've left some milk on t'step!'

Not until the door across the road had slammed did Polly bring in the jug. As she put the kettle on the gas burner, she saw Eddie's big cup sitting on a saucer nearby, ready for its next fill, and tears welled in her eyes. He loved his cups of tea, Eddie did. *Had* loved them. Wouldn't drink any more out of this cup.

As she went to sit down at the table with her own cup, her hands began to tremble and she had to put it down hastily. Tears ran down her cheeks and she put her head on her hands, sobbing loudly, mouthing incoherent protests against the fate which had robbed her of her husband – and now seemed likely to rob her of her son, too.

As the fit of weeping eased Polly mopped her face with the tea towel and let out a long, shuddering groan. The tea was cold, but her throat ached from weeping so she drank it anyway. Then she went wearily up the stairs, feeling very alone and hating the silence of the house. As she lay down on the bed she saw Eddie's pyjamas and picked them up, clutching them against her breast as she huddled beneath the covers.

She was woken an hour or two later by a cramping pain in her stomach. When she looked down there was blood on the sheet between her legs. She screamed then, a thin, shrill wail of protest. 'No! No-o-o!'

Desperate for help, any help that would save her baby, she threw open the window and screamed at the top of her voice, 'Help! Someone help me!'

When the door of her mother-in-law's house was flung open, Polly shrieked at her to fetch the doctor, then collapsed on the bed.

By the time the ambulance came, she had lost the baby, a little girl so pale and tiny she seemed like a wax doll.

Lizzie got back from visiting her sister, who was in hospital for the second time, and walked through Dearden's, nodding automatically at the two women customers who said in lowered voices how sorry they were about everything. When Peter followed her up to the living room she threw herself into his arms and buried her face in his shoulder. 'I can't bear it!' she wept. 'Our Polly doesn't deserve this on top of everything else.'

'I know, love. Come and sit down.' He jerked his head in dismissal and Jen, their young nursemaid, picked up the baby and took little Matt's hand, leading him upstairs into what they called the nursery but was really only an attic that had been made into a bedroom and playroom for the two children so that they could all continue living over the shop.

Peter cradled Lizzie against him, rocking her a little and making soothing noises until she stopped sobbing, then fumbled in his pocket for a handkerchief and wiped her eyes very gently. 'Now, sit down and tell me what you've arranged with Polly.'

'Nothing, really. She doesn't want to come here when she gets out of hospital, she just wants to go home – so I had to tell her that Mr Snape wants the house back as soon as possible for his next farm-hand. She stared at me as if she'd lost her wits, Peter. When I said she was to come here so that I could look after her, she turned away and lay staring at the wall. She wouldn't even talk about it. They're going to keep her in for another day, but she definitely has to leave hospital tomorrow.'

'I'll come with you to pick her up. We'll take the van.'

'But what's Polly going to *do* with herself? Where's she going to live?'

'I don't know.' He hesitated. 'That's up to her now. You can't live her life for her.'

'I'm her sister. I want to help!'

'I know. I want to help, too, but sometimes there's not much you can do.'

That evening Lizzie's family held what they always called a 'Kershaw family powwow', even though she and Polly were no longer Kershaws. They all met at Percy and Emma's house – even Johnny, who at sixteen was not expected to have much to contribute, and Emma's elder sister Blanche, who owned half the house and lived on the third floor. She was, Lizzie thought, looking thinner than ever and was very quiet, as always. Blanche Harper was the only one who could make Lizzie feel plump and the other woman never looked really well. Johnny said nothing whatsoever, alternately scowling down at the carpet or staring from one face to another and jiggling little Matt on his lap as he listened to the discussion.

Although they talked for more than an hour, no one had any real idea of how they could help Polly apart from looking after her till she recovered.

'She'll have to find a way to earn a living,' Lizzie said. 'I suppose she could work in the shop, only she's not so quick at sums and she'd get flustered when there was a rush on. Perhaps – I don't know – perhaps she'll go back into service.'

'She won't like that after having her own home,' Emma said quietly. 'And there's still Billy to consider.'

'Mrs Scordale told me they'd have to put him into an institution,' Percy put in.

'I wouldn't do that,' Lizzie declared at once.

'She may have to, love,' Peter said quietly.

Silence fell for a few moments, then Emma stood up and asked who wanted a cup of tea. Lizzie bounced up and offered to help, glad of something to do.

Just as the Deardens got home the middle Kershaw sister, Eva, rang up from Rochdale to ask how things were going.

'Not well,' Lizzie said gloomily.

'I could have Polly here for a while if it'd help,' Eva offered. 'Alice wouldn't mind.'

'I don't know what she'll want. She just lay staring at the wall today and hardly said a word. I'll tell her you offered, though, and call you back tomorrow night. Eh, I don't know what we used to do without the telephone. It's a real blessing at times like this.' It was Peter who had insisted they get one, and now the big houses were able to phone in their orders instead of him having to go out to take down their lists of requirements once a week. And a good thing too. Since the war, rich folk didn't get fussed over quite as much.

When they had finished chatting, Lizzie hooked the earpiece on to the holder and tucked the wire carefully down the back of the table so that Matt would not be able to catch hold of it. He was into everything lately, that child was. She sighed as she watched the earpiece swing to and fro then gradually grow still. Poor little Billy was lying there in his hospital bed, motionless and without any expression on his face. *He* wouldn't be able to get into mischief.

Before she went to bed, Lizzie crept up to her children's bedroom and stared at her little son and daughter, sleeping so peacefully in their cots, baby Beth with one thumb in her mouth as usual and Matt with his arms flung wide. What would she do if her husband and children were killed? It'd tear you apart, that would. She could imagine nothing worse.

No, she decided as she tiptoed down again, there was no real comfort they could offer to Polly, none at all. Which wouldn't stop them trying, of course.

As for Eddie's family, they were worse than useless and old Mrs Scordale was a nasty piece of work. They'd held the funeral without waiting for Polly to come out of hospital for the second time and had even chosen a headstone without consulting her.

In bed Lizzie cuddled up to Peter. 'I'm dreading tomorrow, absolutely dreading it.'

'I'll come with you to fetch her, love.'

'They won't let Billy out of hospital yet. Polly has to go and see Dr Browning-Baker about him when she's better. Do you think he'll be able to do anything?'

There was silence beside her in the bed, then Peter sighed. 'I doubt it. And he'll not be gentle with her, that chap won't. He treated one of my mates once and Phil said he was an arrogant devil. Old-fashioned, too. Wants everyone to bow down before him.'

'It's a good job he isn't dealing with me, then. I don't bow down to anyone. But our Polly's so quiet he'll never know what she's thinking.'

'Mmm.'

Peter had had a busy day and was exhausted so Lizzie tried to hide the fact that she was crying – only he guessed and pulled her close again, which made her cry all the harder, thinking of the sister who had no one to hold her now and whose son didn't even recognise her.

The following morning, the Ward Sister bustled across to where Polly was sitting quietly beside the bed, dressed and ready to leave. 'Your sister is on her way up, Mrs Scordale. Do you have everything ready?'

Polly nodded listlessly. What did it matter if she left something behind? What did anything matter now? When Lizzie and Peter appeared at the door, she stood, picking up her bag of clothes but not moving.

Lizzie rushed across to hug her. 'Are you all right, Polly love?' She could only shrug.

'Well, come on. This place gives me the miseries and that Ward Sister has a face like a camel.'

Polly found it vaguely soothing that her sister filled the silence with cheerful chatter, so that she didn't need to speak.

When they got to the van, Lizzie asked gently, 'Are you sure you want to go home? You could still come to us.'

'I *need* to go home.' The thought of being surrounded by her own possessions was a great comfort to Polly.

At Outshaw Peter brought in the box of groceries they'd put together for her, then went to sit in the van, leaving the two sisters together.

When Polly didn't speak, Lizzie glanced sideways. Her sister's face might have been carved from ice. 'Do you want to talk, love?'

'What is there to say? And – and I don't want to see the Scordales.' Her eyes filled with tears at the thought of them holding the funeral without her, not even telling her. She'd never forgive them for that.

'But what are you going to *do*? You know you have to get out of this house.'

'I *want* to get out of here! I can't get away from Outshaw fast enough.'

'Won't you change your mind and come to us, just for a week or two?'

'No. Anyway, I've already arranged to rent a house in Bobbin Lane.'

Lizzie gaped at her. 'You never said. And how did you do that? You never left the hospital.'

'One of the nurses knew about it. She brought Mr Cuttler

in to see me and I gave him two weeks' rent in advance.'

'But you haven't seen the house!'

'I know it, though. You do, too. It's the one the Holdens used to live in. It'll do me till I can sort myself out a bit. It's close to everything. Not like Outshaw.'

'Oh. Well. Right, then. We'll come over and help you to move your things when you're ready.'

'How about Saturday afternoon?'

'So quickly?'

'The sooner the better. But if you've got any tea chests or boxes you could lend me, I'd be grateful.' Polly knew food was often delivered to the grocery store in packing cases, then the staff at Dearden's packaged it to suit their clients: sugar in blue paper bags for some reason, flour and currants in white — she'd often bought those items because Eddie had loved her currant soda-cakes for tea.

'I'll send Ted out in the van with them.'

Polly tried to smile, but failed. 'I am grateful, love, but I – I have to do this myself. I'm not just your little sister any more, I'm Billy's mother. I have to have somewhere ready for him when he comes out.'

'If they'll let you take him out of hospital.'

'Just let them try to stop me!' Polly's voice was low and fierce. She had had enough of people telling her what to do, treating her as if she hadn't got a mind of her own. Some of the doctors even spoke loudly and slowly to you, as if you were too stupid to understand them. She had never been one to stand up for herself – 'Too soft for your own good,' Eddie used to say – but she was learning how to do it now.

'Hey!' Lizzie tapped her sister's arm. 'Come back, wherever you are.'

The new tight-lipped Polly gave her a travesty of a smile. 'Sorry. What did you say?'

'Are you all right for money?'

'Oh, yes. I have plenty. Or I will have. Eddie had some life insurance. The nurse rang them up for me. I have to take the death certificate in and sign some forms then they'll pay me. Two hundred pounds it was. But don't tell the Scordales or they'll be trying to get some.'

'Polly, two hundred pounds! That's wonderful!'

'Is it? It doesn't feel wonderful.' She hesitated, then gave Lizzie a quick hug. 'Look, thanks for everything, but you get off now. You've got a shop to run – and don't think I don't know you had to get extra help in today so you could bring me home. I'm grateful, really I am, but I need to think and – and plan. I'll have plenty to keep me busy with the packing. If you just send those boxes and some old newspapers if you have any, I'll get everything ready for Saturday. I'll go into Overdale to see the insurance people and check the new house tomorrow.'

As Lizzie got into the van she said in a choked voice to Peter, 'Polly's so different.'

'She's bound to be. Death of someone close does change you.'

She knew from his voice that he was thinking of his own experiences during the war. Suddenly, not caring whether the Scordales were watching or not, she pulled his head towards her and kissed him hard, afterwards pressing her cheek against his and feeling the convulsive way his hands clutched her shoulders. The war had scarred him badly and his mother always said it was Lizzie who had brought him out of his deep sadness.

'I don't know what I'd do if anything happened to you, Peter love,' Lizzie murmured.

'You'd cope. Most people do.'

But even though he gave her another quick hug before starting the car, he was staring into the distance as if she wasn't there. She left him to his thoughts as they drove back into town. She knew from the bits and pieces he'd shared with her that he'd lost a lot of his comrades from Company A of the North Fylde Rifles during the war. They'd called themselves the Hellhounds and had been a close-knit group. He still saw Captain Mercer sometimes, because he lived in Overdale, only he was moving to the coast, it seemed. Peter also occasionally visited one or two of his old comrades who were still in hospital, poor souls, and always would be, because their injuries were so bad.

Captain Mercer was trying to raise money for a special rest home for them, which Lizzie thought a kind thing to do. Anything would be better than one of those big, echoing hospital wards. Polly had looked so small and pale in that immaculately made bed.

Oh, dear, she had to think of something else or she'd never stop crying!

The Mercers' move to Stenton went smoothly. Richard hired a removal company to do most of the packing and, anyway, they weren't taking all their furniture because the things at Seaview House were much better quality, even if they were horrendously old-fashioned according to Florence. She had refused point blank to lift a finger except to pack her own clothes, saying she didn't want to go so why should she help? Even Overdale was better than that stupid village.

Richard had already let Doris and Mrs Shavely know that he did not intend to sell the house and that the visit from Mindley & Sons, Estate Agents, had been due to a misunderstanding. He had also apologised for upsetting them.

When the Mercers arrived at the house, the two ageing women came out to greet them, smiling and saying how glad they were to have a family here again. Richard shook hands solemnly with the cook, Mrs Shavely, who was enveloped in a huge apron as usual, and then with Doris, who had a plump face and frizzy grey hair sticking out from under her cap.

Florence merely nodded to them, not even saying a proper hello, so he drew Connie forward, worrying about how badly she was limping today, and introduced her. Doris soon had the child smiling and Mrs Shavely asked what her favourite cake was. Richard could feel Connie's thin shoulders relax beneath his hands. Then he introduced Nan who looked after Connie.

He could not help looking round with a proprietorial air and saying to his daughter, 'I love it here in Stenton and I'm sure you're going to love it, too, darling. I'll take you down to the promenade later.' It was a grand title for the paved footpath and low wall that ran along the sea front, with shelters to sit in at either end, he thought in amusement.

'Don't be silly. It'll be too far for her to walk,' Florence said tartly. 'And are we going to stand outside all day? The removal men will be here soon with our things and I'm dying for a cup of tea.'

'I'll fetch a tray for you, madam,' Doris said, unable to hide her hurt at this rudeness.

Richard sighed and led the way inside.

After one day in Stenton, Connie's attendant handed in her notice, coming to see him, not Florence. 'I'm sorry, sir, but I'm not one for the country and I hadn't realised that this village was so small and so far away from everywhere. If I could just nip along the road to Fleetwood on my day off, it might not be so bad, but you have to go across on a ferry from Knott End and I'm not one for boats – let alone what would it be like in the winter? I'll stay on here till you find someone else, of course, I'm really fond of Connie, but I couldn't be happy living here, I just couldn't.'

Florence crowed in triumph at this and prophesied that he'd have trouble keeping any servants.

Within days Richard realised that she was deliberately trying to antagonise Mrs Shavely and Doris, presumably to get rid of them, too, so he had a quiet word with them, explaining frankly that his wife did not wish to live at Stenton-on-Sea and that this was making her bad-tempered. 'If she gives you any unreasonable orders or you have any other difficulties with her, you should come to me. I really want you to both stay on here.'

Mrs Shavely let out a gusty sigh of relief and beamed at him. 'Well, that's all right then, sir. As long as we know where we stand.'

He turned to leave and Doris cleared her throat. 'About Mrs Mercer's bedroom, sir?'

'Yes? What about it?'

'It's a bit hard for me to know where things go and, well, it's always very untidy. It's as if she pulls stuff out of the drawers on purpose.' Which Doris was pretty sure was what happened.

'I'll speak to her. Perhaps it's best if you leave her to tidy her own room. She can let you know when she wants it cleaning.'

Richard went upstairs and knocked on his wife's bedroom door. When he went inside he was shocked. Such chaos had never happened in Overdale, even with her. 'Are you clearing out your drawers?'

'No. Just looking through my clothes.'

'Doris won't be able to clean the room till you've put the things away again.'

Florence came to stand in front of him, hands on hips, chin jutting aggressively. 'Has she been complaining to you?'

'Yes. And rightly so.'

'How dare you take her part against me! She's a bloody maid and it's her job to clear up.'

'Not this sort of thing it isn't. I know what you're doing, Florence. I'm sure you helped Nan decide to leave, too.'

'She didn't need helping. She was as horrified as I am by this place. And as for that Doris, she's –'

'I'm not going to argue with you. Doris and Mrs Shavely report to me from now on and if you want something unreasonable doing, you can do it yourself.'

He left his wife screaming insults at him and took refuge in the library, where he sat for a while with his head in his hands.

After four weeks of discord and upsets, during which the house rang with quarrels and the servants sided with their master, Florence announced her intention of going to visit friends in London for a few days before she went totally mad from boredom. She had her story all worked out, but to her chagrin Richard did not even ask who she was going to stay with.

'You must do as you wish,' he said calmly, as if she was just popping out to the shops. 'I'm going into Manchester tomorrow. One of my men is in trouble. We can share a cab to the station and I'll help you with your luggage. I'm going to buy a new car as well. A bigger one.'

She glared at him. 'You'll go running off anywhere after those old soldiers of yours, but you don't care if I go away — or even ask where I'm going.'

'No, I don't, actually, though you'd better leave your address. If it were up to me, we'd apply for a divorce tomorrow. I'm quite prepared to provide you with the necessary evidence, if you'll change your mind about that.'

'No, thank you very much. If I'm going to be miserable, I might as well be miserable in comfort.' Sometimes Florence wished desperately that she had some money of her own, but her father's annuity had died with him and her parents' house had not been very big, so it hadn't brought much when she'd sold it. Like all her other friends, she had spent money like water during the war because you never knew what was just around the corner. She was regretting that now. If she'd been just a bit more careful she might have something of her own left instead of being dependent on *him* for every farthing.

Well, there must be some way of getting her hands on Richard's money, and she intended to find it. Pity he was so careful with his bank account now. She had enjoyed stealing from him. If she'd inherited so much money, she'd have gone abroad. She sighed at the thought of leaving him permanently to live in a warmer climate, a daydream she had long cherished. Maybe all was not lost and she'd find another way to get hold of the money, but before she could do anything she had to lull Richard's suspicions. 'Couldn't we try again with our marriage?' she asked, keeping her voice soft. 'If we went to live somewhere else and —'

'But I want to live here. I love this house.' He decided that he might as well set the ground rules. 'And while we're having this little talk, let me make it quite plain that I don't intend to share a bedroom with you again, Florence. *Ever.* You rouse nothing in me but disgust.'

She breathed in deeply, anger simmering, then something snapped inside her. 'Well, if that's the case, I shan't even pretend to be faithful. I'm young enough to need a man regularly.'

'You never have been faithful to me – not since Connie was born, and probably not before that, either. I certainly wasn't the first. Who was?'

'None of your business.' She wondered how much he knew, but you could never see behind that damned mask of a face, and although she knew his scornful expression was mainly caused by the scar, she often felt he really *was* sneering at her. Yet who was he to look down on anyone? A man who couldn't even make love to a woman. Only, since poor Georgie-boy was not exactly flush, she would be foolish to leave the goose that was sitting on some shiny golden eggs. She realised that Richard was speaking again, in that damned pedantic way he had, and banished the image of Georgie with a quiet sigh. He was so lusty and demanding, her very first lover and still the one she cared about most. There was no one quite like him.

'I should think rather carefully about being unfaithful again, Florence,' said her husband with icy civility. 'If I find you've taken a lover, I'll throw you out at once and use the evidence to start divorce proceedings. I'm not fathering someone else's child.'

She could not help laughing. 'Oh, you don't need to worry about *that*. I've learned my lesson in that department, believe me. One child was more than enough for me. Especially one who's lame and ugly.' There had been another man's baby started during the war while Richard was away, but she'd got rid of it. Messy process, but it had worked and she'd not allowed any carelessness from her lovers since, not even Georgie. 'How much of an allowance do you intend to give me?'

He named a figure. 'Paid quarterly.'

'You stingy bugger! How long do you think that will last?'

'That's up to you. You can always come and live here when it runs out. It'll be better for Connie anyway if you're at home part of the time. For some strange reason, she seems fond of you.' Or perhaps fond of the idea of a mother. Not quite the same thing.

When he started to turn away, Florence picked up the nearest ornament and threw it at him, relishing the expression of shock on his face as it whizzed past his ear and smashed against the wall. Then she pushed past him, slamming the door hard behind her and making the trinkets on the mantelpiece rattle.

Damn him to hell! she thought as she ran up the stairs. What was she going to do now? She'd never be able to manage on so little money. But if he tried to divorce her and fob her off with a pittance, she'd make a big fuss. He'd hate that.

CHAPTER FIVE

May 1920

One evening of sitting alone in her old house seared Polly with such painful memories that she could not wait to leave it. There was a half-finished sweater she'd been knitting for Eddie lying on a chair, with some of the stitches pulled off the needle. She stuffed it out of sight in a drawer. She'd pull it back when she was more settled and knit something for her son from the wool.

She kept finding herself turning round, half-expecting to see Billy playing in a corner or thinking she heard Eddie whistling while he worked in his little shed at the back. He had whistled so tunefully. They'd both loved music and the house had rarely been silent. She remembered how she had practised the songs Blanche Harper had taught her, doing the best she could without a piano. Percy's sister-in-law always said Polly had a lovely voice and Eddie had thought so, too. Time and time again, he'd asked for his favourites as they sat in front of the fire in the evening.

Polly doubted she would ever be able to sing any of those songs again without weeping.

She had expected the Scordales to pop across and see her, but they didn't. And though that hurt, she was glad not to have to confront them. Anyway, after the way they had behaved about the funeral, denying her the chance to say a proper farewell to her husband, she did not want to speak to them ever again. What mattered most to her now was not the grave or the headstone the

Scordales had chosen, but her memories of Eddie and their happy years together. Well, mostly happy.

She immediately felt guilty about qualifying this, but there was no getting round the fact that she had been very lonely out here. She had never complained, just got on with things, and that was what she intended to do now. Keep busy. Look after her son. Go and see her own family sometimes. Just – get on with things.

The following morning, the delivery man from Dearden's turned up quite early with some packing cases and old newspapers. When she found Ted had only one delivery before he went back to the shop, Polly asked if he could take her with him into Overdale. 'I could be ready in five minutes.'

'You take your time, Mrs Scordale. I'm sure Mr Dearden would want me to wait. And I'm right sorry about your husband. The little lad, too. Is he any better, like?'

She managed to say, 'It's early days yet.' Then had to stand quite still for a moment to keep from bursting into tears. She'd find it easier if people said nothing, but they always felt they had to offer their condolences. And what was worst of all, some of them talked as if Billy was dead – and he wasn't!

She asked to be dropped off in the town centre and went first to see the lawyer who had drawn up their wills. She'd thought Eddie mad to insist on their doing that, because it hadn't come cheap, but he'd said it was the proper thing to do for a family man. Mr Finch's secretary scolded her for not making an appointment, but fitted her in for a few minutes between clients. The lawyer promised to see to all the formalities for her, seemed uncertain whether to shake her hand or not, and showed her out again in less than five minutes.

Next she went to the insurance company, armed with Eddie's death certificate and the life insurance policy. They showed her into the manager's office and he spoke to her in a hushed voice, promising to have the money ready for her within three days.

Her final stop was the bank, to explain matters yet again and open a new savings account in her own name. They explained that she could not close the joint savings account until the will was sorted out. The new savings book they gave her was just like one she'd had as a girl – eh, she'd been a one for saving money, even in those days, always something squirrelled away. And she'd been the same since her marriage. She had a pot full of loose change in her pantry now because you never knew when you'd need a bit extra. It looked like she was going to need it till the insurance and will were sorted out.

Relieved to have got that over with, Polly walked briskly up the hill to the streets where she had grown up, trying to look as if she was in too much of a hurry to stop and chat to anyone. Number 27 Bobbin Lane, where she and Billy were going to live, looked run-down and in need of a coat of paint. Polly felt disappointed as she studied it from the street, because Mr Cuttler, the rent man, had said it was in 'pretty good condition, considering'. What did he consider bad condition, then?

As she was fumbling in her shopping bag for the key, a voice behind her said, 'Polly Kershaw! What are you doing back here?' and she turned to find Mary Holden staring at her. Lizzie's old enemy from their school days looked years older than her real age, with two grubby children clinging to her skirt and a baby in her arms.

'I've just rented this house.'

Mary blew out her cheeks in surprise. 'Eh, never thought a Kershaw would come back to Bobbin Lane. Thought you'd all gone up in the world. Sorry about your troubles, though. I heard about the accident. I live just round the corner.' She hesitated then said, 'Look, I know I didn't get on with you lot when I were younger, but I've growed up a bit since then so I hope you won't hold a grudge.' She glanced down at the children – not a fond glance, either. 'You have to grow up, don't you, when they're depending on you?'

Polly nodded and pushed the door open.

'Mind if I come in and have a look round, for old times' sake?'

'Not just now. I – I'm not good company at the moment.'

And before the other woman could speak, Polly whisked inside and shut the door.

For a while, she just stayed where she was, her eyes closed, reliving old memories conjured up by the sight of Bobbin Lane. Her father, who had been killed so tragically, and her mother, embittered by his death, growing increasingly strange and picking on Lizzie, who had been his favourite. Poor Lizzie might not have married Sam Thoxby if she hadn't needed to get away from their mother. Eva had left home as soon as she finished school to live with Alice Blake and become a student teacher, though Percy and their mother had had a blazing row before she would allow this. And Polly had been glad to leave, too, going into service as soon as she was fourteen. Only poor old Percy had been trapped there, for his wages had been needed to support his mother and younger brother, Johnny, who still lived with him and Emma.

Polly sighed and opened her eyes again, dismissing the memories. It did no good to dwell on the past. She had to concentrate on the future, on making this place into a home for her son. But as she looked round, the condition of the house shocked her. It was the usual two up, two down, with a dark scullery at the back leading out into the yard, which had a smelly earth closet at the far end. 'This'll never do for my Billy!' she said aloud. 'If the owner doesn't do something about it, I'll have to find somewhere else to live.'

It being half-past twelve by now, she locked up the house and marched off down the street to Mr Cuttler's much larger house on the corner opposite Minter's little shop, which never seemed to change. Knowing the rent man always went home for dinner in the middle of the day, she rapped smartly on the door. When he opened it, still chewing something, Polly did not wait for him to speak but said her piece quickly before she lost her courage. 'I've just been to look at number 27 Bobbin Lane, Mr Cuttler. It's a proper disgrace and I'm not taking a sick child to live there till it's been sorted out.'

He swallowed the food. 'Hold on – you've paid the first two

weeks' rent and signed the rent book so it's up to you now to –'

'I can afford to lose the money and if I give notice straight away, those two weeks are all you'll get paid for.' Staring him firmly in the eye, she demanded, 'Now, do you want a good tenant in that house or not?'

He frowned at her, head on one side. 'Got a job, have you?'

'No.'

'How are you going to pay the rent, then, now you've no husband to provide for you?'

'Eddie had life insurance. I've enough money to last me a year or two – though I'd be obliged if you didn't spread that information around.'

'Ah. That's all right, then.' He grinned unexpectedly. 'Didn't know you had it in you to stand up to me, Polly Kershaw. You never used to say boo to a goose.'

She found herself echoing Mary's words. 'Well, I've a sick child depending on me now. That makes a difference.'

In the tone of one offering her a great favour, Cuttler said, 'I'll go and see the owner about the house this afternoon. What needs doing?'

'Privy cleaning out, walls distempering, floors scrubbing properly – they've left it in a right old mess. And it needs doing quickly, too, because I want to move in on Saturday afternoon.'

She knew there were plenty of houses standing empty, because although there had been a lot of jobs going just after the war, for some reason things were slowing down now and men were being thrown out of work so families were doubling up to save on rent money. She should have waited to look round, really, but when the nurse told her there was a house going in Bobbin Lane, where she'd grown up, it had seemed meant to be.

He gave her a wry smile. 'All right, Mrs Fusspot. There's enough men seeking work to fettle up ten houses by Saturday.'

'Thank you, Mr Cuttler.' She began to turn away.

'And Polly lass – I'm right sorry about your husband.'

She froze, then stammered, 'Thank you.'

Funny, she thought as she walked away, she had always been afraid of Mr Cuttler, but today he seemed just a man like any other – and she'd got her own way, too. That knowledge and the bitter satisfaction of coping with problems herself took her all the way to the hospital to see Billy and Dr Browning-Baker. As she passed a pie shop, she wondered vaguely if she ought to get something to eat, but she couldn't be bothered. She hadn't really been hungry since Eddie died.

When it was her turn, a nurse showed her into a consulting room and followed, standing behind her near the door. Dr Browning-Baker peered at her across the desk, looking at her as if she was a worm, Polly felt indignantly. He tapped one index finger on his blotting pad as he spoke, seemingly in a hurry to get this over with. 'I've examined your son, Mrs Scordale, and I'm afraid there is no hope whatsoever of his making a full recovery. Little hope of even a partial one.'

Polly gasped and closed her eyes for a moment.

Someone leaned over her and the nurse asked, 'Are you all right, Mrs Scordale?'

She opened her eyes and saw the other woman's face close to hers. The doctor was reading some papers on his desk, not even glancing in her direction. Anger at his callous attitude stiffened Polly's spine. 'I was just shocked at the blunt way Dr Browning-Baker told me the news.'

He looked up with an expression of irritation on his face now. 'I'm a very busy man, Mrs Scordale, and I cannot afford to waste my time or anyone else's. I'm sorry for your loss, but I have other patients whom I *can* help, so I must think of them.'

'What shall I do then?' she asked helplessly. 'You haven't said what I should do.'

'I'm arranging to have your son put in an institution. You'd best forget about him and make a new life for yourself.' As she opened her mouth to protest, he held up one hand to stop her. 'It sounds harsh, but you are a young woman with a whole life ahead of you and you can do nothing for the boy now. Nothing whatsoever.'

'And if I don't want to put him away like that?'

'Then you will be devoting your life to the care of someone who will never be able to thank you for it, who will never even recognise you. And a very hard life it will be, too. Anyway, I've set matters in hand.' He nodded a dismissal and looked expectantly at the nurse who opened the door.

Outside, Polly sank into the nearest chair and burst into tears, not caring who saw her. She had told herself she would be brave, but suddenly it all overwhelmed her. The nurse, seeming irritated, put her in a cubicle to 'calm down', and after a time, she managed to stop weeping.

Someone came in and when she looked up, Polly saw the friendly nurse from the ward she'd been in, the one who had helped her to find a house.

'You all right, love?'

Polly could only shake her head.

'No, of course you're not.' The nurse glanced round and whispered. 'That man doesn't know how to break bad news gently. We're always having to deal with people he's upset.' She patted Polly's shoulder then glanced down at her fob watch. 'I can't stay too long, I'm afraid. They want you to fill in the papers now.'

'What papers?'

'The ones to send your Billy to St Jude's over in Manchester. It's run by nuns but you don't have to be a Catholic to go there. They look after – well, people like your Billy. And they're kind so you won't have to worry about him.'

'I want to look after him myself. I just can't believe there's no hope at all. He was always such a lively little lad.' More tears ran down Polly's cheeks, try as she would to hold them back.

The nurse st down beside her and put an arm round her shoulders, making soothing noises.

Polly gulped and tried to stop weeping. 'I'm sorry to be such a nuisance.'

'You have a right to cry.' The other woman hesitated and

lowered her voice again. 'Have you thought of seeing someone else about your son?'

'Someone else?'

'Mmm. You'll have to pay for another opinion, but you said your husband had life insurance and there are other doctors besides *him* – doctors who don't think kids like your Billy should be treated like vegetables and left to rot – only don't tell anyone I said this, or they'll haul me over the carpet good and proper.'

'Who should I see?'

'Well, there's Dr Herbert. He comes here, too, sometimes. He's quite young, but I've seen him help cases that were considered hopeless by *you know who*. Dr Herbert says he learned a lot during the war dealing with soldiers who had head injuries. He doesn't get on with *you know who*. In fact, they've had one or two big upsets and now we have to keep their patients in separate wards. Mind you, Dr Herbert's methods don't always work – there are some people who are beyond help – but he doesn't pretend to know everything, which is what I like about him.'

She let Polly think it over for a minute or two then added softly, 'Maybe it's worth a try, eh? After all, you can still put Billy in St Jude's later on, if you need to. Half a mo'.' She hurried out and came back with a scrap of paper and a pencil, scribbling something on it. 'Here are the address and phone number of Dr Herbert. You'll have to telephone for an appointment. He has rooms in Manchester.'

Polly felt the first tiny stirring of hope since the accident. 'Thank you, nurse.'

'Oh, heavens, call me Jane. I'm not nursing you now, am I? And if you don't mind, I'd be really interested to know what happens with Billy. I'm thinking of specialising in looking after children like him if I can get accepted at the children's hospital for further training.'

Polly folded up the piece of paper. 'I'm moving back into town on Saturday: 27 Bobbin Lane. You'd be very welcome any time. Drop in for a cup of tea.'

'You sure?'

'Yes. And — and thank you, Jane. I don't know what I'd have done without you today. I was feeling that down.'

Taking a deep breath, Polly left the cubicle and went to do battle with a very fierce Sister who tried to get her to sign a piece of paper and when she wouldn't, got angry with her, assuring her that she was making a serious mistake in even trying to look after her son herself and she'd soon be sorry she didn't take the advice of those who knew better.

But Polly knew she wasn't making a mistake. She had to try everything she could to help her Billy, she just had to. If nothing came of it, then at least she'd be able to live with her own conscience. If she put him away now without trying, she'd regret it all her life.

On the Saturday afternoon, once the main rush at the shop was over, Peter drove to Outshaw with his young brother-in-law Johnny, and although it took them three journeys, they carted all Polly's possessions back to Overdale — and with the final load, Polly herself.

'Do you want to say goodbye to the Scordales?' Peter asked when the last packing case had been wedged into the van, leaving a space for Johnny to perch on the end of the sofa.

Polly hesitated, then decided it was the proper thing to do. No need for her to forget her manners even if they were more or less ignoring her. She walked across the lane to knock on the front door of their house. She was doing this for Eddie, she told herself. He'd have wanted it. When Hilda Scordale opened the door, Polly said calmly, 'I've come to say goodbye.'

Her mother-in-law stared at her, not seeming to know what to say or do for once.

Jim Scordale came to join his wife. 'I'm right glad you did, lass. I wish you well, I do that. Where are you going to live?'

She told them her address and hesitated before adding, 'I'm

going to have Billy at home with me. I'll be fetching him from the hospital on Monday.'

'You'll regret that,' Hilda Scordale said at once. 'It's a thankless task.'

'You have to think of yourself, lass,' Jim Scordale said more gently. 'You'll need to build a new life now.'

'That's what I intend to to, build a new life for me *and* my son.'

'You allus were stubborn underneath that soft expression!' Hilda snapped.

Jim turned to his wife. 'Eh, Hilda, what's got into you lately to speak so sharply to our Polly?'

With a sob his wife went back into the house. He watched her go, his expression anxious, then sighed and turned back to Polly. 'Let us know how you get on, won't you, love?'

She felt glad she'd done the right thing. Nothing on her conscience now.

At number 27 Polly's brother Percy was waiting to see if he could help, too. The place smelled of fresh distemper and scrubbing soap, and furniture and boxes from the first two journeys were lying around in piles. For a moment they stood together inside the front room, which opened directly on to the street. He said quietly, 'Couldn't you have found somewhere better than this to live?'

'It'll do for the time being. The rent's cheap and it's nice and close to the shops. I'm going to get a wheelchair for Billy and take him out for walks. It can't do him any good to lie and stare at the wall all day.' It hadn't done her any good, either, in the hospital. She felt better now she had something to occupy herself with.

'If we can help in any way –'

'I'll come to you.' But she knew she wouldn't. A determination was growing in her to do things herself.

There was a shout behind them and they moved hurriedly out

of the way as Peter and Johnny came in with the sofa. Percy had a heart problem that had kept him out of the war, so he carried only the smaller stuff, while Polly told everyone where to put things and began unpacking boxes in the kitchen. She lined her shelves carefully with the kitchen paper she'd bought, getting the scalloped border hanging evenly over the edge of each shelf, then put her crockery away.

By the time they'd finished arranging the furniture it was getting dark.

'Good thing Lizzie packed you some food, eh?' Peter said.

'Yes. Tell her thanks.'

'She had to look after the shop while I was away, but she'll be over tomorrow to help you settle in. You can thank her yourself then.'

When they'd gone, Polly went to stand in the kitchen and look out at the back yard. It was a right old mess of bare earth and broken paving slabs. 'Flowers,' she said firmly. Eddie had loved them and had passed his gardening knowledge on to her. 'I'll plant some next week.'

But first she had to see the new doctor. When she'd explained her situation on the telephone, Dr Herbert's secretary had said to come on her own the first time. The doctor liked to talk to parents about his methods before he met the injured children. Oh, and she wasn't to think he could work miracles, either. He was only a man like anyone else. But he'd be happy to try.

Which is more than that Browning-Baker fellow would do, thought Polly. He thinks he's God's uncle, that one does.

Forgetting the food Lizzie had prepared, she went to sit in the front room, not bothering to light the gas, just sitting in the darkness listening to the noises of the street. They made her feel a bit better. There had been few sounds at Outshaw, and hardly anyone ever walked past.

Yes, it felt good to be close to other people again.

As Richard passed the door to his daughter's room, he saw her crying and the new maid patting her shoulder and looking helpless, so he went in. 'What's the matter, darling?'

Connie smeared away the tears, then accepted his handkerchief and wiped her eyes properly. 'I was missing Mummy!'

'Won't I do instead?' He stoked the hair back from her flushed forehead and murmured, 'Get a damp cloth to wipe her face.'

The maid rushed out.

As Connie's sobs subsided, he asked, 'Shall we go out together this afternoon? We could walk along the sea front. We'll take your chair for when you get tired.' He'd intended to work on his novel, but his daughter's welfare came first. When she shook her head and said she didn't want to go out, he set himself to persuade her, teasing her and making her laugh – but still she wouldn't go.

By that time he'd lost track of where he was in his story so instead sat in his study and stared out of the window. There were white caps on the sea but the wind was falling and the fisherman who had a tiny house down by the breakwater at the west end of the village had told him it was going to 'fine up'. Mrs Shavely said Owd Saul, who supplied them with fresh fish, was never wrong about such things.

'I ought to be happy here,' Richard said aloud. But he was worrying too much about his marriage to be happy. He hadn't heard from Florence for three weeks. Heaven alone knew where she was. If only she would agree to a divorce. He was dreading her coming home. He, Mrs Shavely and Doris got on really well without her, though he wasn't so sure about the new maid who couldn't persuade Connie to go for a walk, let alone supervise her lessons. Though she was a good reader, Connie was not very good at arithmetic and Richard was working through a book of sums with her that had been recommended by the headmistress of the school in Knott End.

Connie was now officially an 'invalid' and although Florence seemed happy enough with that, he wasn't. He wanted his daughter to make friends as other children did, and to go to school one day.

Richard's thoughts wandered back to his wife. He had been considering getting a detective to follow her and see if he could find the evidence needed for a divorce. He had even gone so far as to ask his uncle's lawyer to recommend one. But he shrank from actually taking such a step. It would all be so sordid. The family would be shocked and Connie would be dreadfully upset.

'Damned if I do, damned if I don't,' he muttered, then picked up his pencil and forced himself to start writing again. The words did not flow. He'd had this story in his mind for years, but life was too unsettled for him to concentrate on this new task.

'Oh, hell!' he exclaimed half an hour later, throwing his pencil down. He got up and put on a raincoat to keep the wind out because it was chilly for May then went for a brisk walk along the front, going as far as Knott End where he bought a cup of tea and a sticky bun.

He felt better as he walked slowly home. Walking always helped him sort out his thoughts and face unpleasant tasks.

CHAPTER SIX

May 1920

When his secretary had explained about Mrs Scordale's tragic loss, Toby Herbert had vaguely imagined her to be in her late twenties, perhaps older, with a worn face and scrawny body. But she wasn't at all like that. She looked very young and yet held herself with a simply dignity that touched his heart.

'You seem too young to have a son of three,' he said gently.

'I married young and we wanted children immediately. My husband was a few years older than me.' Polly stared down at her lap, then raised her eyes and said with a catch in her voice, 'I've lost my husband – I don't want to lose my son as well. One of the nurses thought you might be able to help me.'

Her eyes were clear and direct, of a grey-blue colour like a moorland stream reflecting the sky – but there were shadows under them. Her clothes hung on her as if she'd lost weight recently, and yet, if she were not so unhappy, she might have been described as pretty. He found himself staring at her, wondering if her nature was as sweet as her face suggested, then he realised how unprofessional this was and tried to pull himself together.

'Do you know how I work?' he asked, the same question he put to all new patients.

She shook her head.

'Then I'd better explain my general approach to anyone with

a head injury, whether it's a child or an adult, before we go any further.'

'Please.'

'I believe that if we treat these people as normally as possible, if we *expect* them to do things, scold them when they don't even try, show them again and again what to do – above all, give them time and attention – well, sometimes we can lighten their darkness.' She was looking thoughtful, so he waited until she nodded slowly before he continued.

'I also think we should move their limbs. Not exactly force them into exercise, but do it for them.' His voice rang with scorn as he added, 'Not leave them lying flat in a neatly made bed so that their muscles atrophy. We need to stimulate them in many ways, as we did when they were babies: sing to them, play games with their toes, encourage them to crawl – anything and everything. It doesn't really matter what. Sometimes, if we're lucky, they regain their senses – or partly regain them.' More often the latter, but he never told anyone that until it was necessary.

A further silence was followed by another slow, thoughtful nod. 'Yes, that makes sense.'

'I can show you how to do things – such as the best way to move the child's limbs – and I can keep an eye on your son's progress, but it'll be for you to do everything, day in, day out, whether you feel like it or not, whether your son weeps and frets or not. It definitely won't be easy.'

'I don't mind that. And anyway, I have nothing else to do.'

'You don't have to earn a living?'

'Not yet. My husband had some insurance. The money should last me a year or two.'

'Good. You also ought to know that some doctors don't agree with my methods and believe it's a waste of time. And very sadly sometimes we make no progress whatsoever with our patients, so I'm making no guarantees about helping your son, only about trying my best.'

Polly looked him squarely in the eye again. 'I don't expect

empty promises, but if I've done everything humanly possible, then *I* shall feel better, whatever happens. I can't just lock Billy away for the rest of his life, however kind the nuns are at St Jude's.'

Dr Herbert grimaced. 'They're too kind, actually. They do everything for the poor helpless creatures in their care, won't listen to me or try my ideas because I'm not a specialist. I'm just a plain doctor who had some experience with head injuries during the war. They did tell you that, didn't they?'

Only when she looked up and nodded again did he add, 'I'll have to see the child first, of course. And you'll have to inform the doctor presently looking after him that you're taking the boy out of his care. Who is it? Ah, yes, Browning-Baker. He definitely doesn't agree with my methods. You should write him a letter saying you're taking the child out of his care before we go any further.'

'Very well.'

'Take the letter to his rooms yourself and get a signed receipt for it.'

Polly looked at him in surprise.

'I can't explain but it's the best way, believe me. Dr Browning-Baker can be – difficult. Where is your son? Overdale Hospital? Oh, that's easy. I already have a few patients there and I'm going over to see them at the end of the week. I can examine your son at the same time – as long as you get that letter to Browning-Baker before then. If you'll telephone my secretary when you've done that, she'll make the necessary arrangements with the hospital. Any questions?'

'No, I don't think so.'

'Then I'll see you on Friday morning at nine.'

'Thank you. You've been very kind.' What a difference there was between him and the other doctor!

'You may not think I'm kind when we start forcing Billy to do things.'

He watched her walk out, her back straight in her brown

woollen suit with its ankle-length skirt and three-quarter-length jacket, a simple hat with a small brim and a beige ribbon trim set neatly on her head. From what his sister wore, he knew the clothes were old-fashioned, but they were probably Mrs Scordale's Sunday best. He hoped desperately that he'd be able to help her child. Some patients and their families became more special than others, however much you tried to treat them all alike. And this young woman was going to be one of them, he could tell that already.

'You're too soft, Toby my lad,' he muttered, then began to gather his things for his visit to the nearby home for disabled ex-soldiers where he gave his services free because they were so short of money. A former colleague of his from the Regiment was trying to raise the money to set up a similar place, a permanent residence for men who could make no more progress. He'd made a good start and if the Captain set his mind to it, the rest of the money would be found, however long it took. He was like that, Richard Mercer was, stubborn. He was searching for a suitable house for the rest home on the Fylde Coast, Toby knew.

The people running the Manchester home were so grateful for Toby's services that they were willing to try anything to help their charges. They let him try out his new methods there on those with head injuries – and he'd had a few minor successes, too. But although it was a slow business, he was fascinated by the work of rehabilitating such patients. He had fallen into it by sheer chance as an Army doctor during the war. In such an area no one knew very much – whether they admitted it or not – so you just tried anything and everything to help your patients. He was collating his results carefully, hoped to publish a paper on it one day. And in the meantime was in correspondence with a few like-minded souls.

It was quite a long way from the doctor's rooms to the railway station, but Polly walked because she needed to think through what Dr Herbert had said. She had liked him on sight, and he had not rushed her or treated her like a fool or as that Dr Browning-Baker had. *He'd* seemed to think her Billy was a charity case and that Polly ought to be grateful for ten minutes of his grudging attention.

What Dr Herbert had said made sense. His secretary had given Polly a little booklet which explained the methods he used. She was going to read it till she knew it by heart because if there was any way to help Billy, she intended to find it.

She stopped walking and for a moment terror squeezed her heart. There *must* be a way. She wasn't going to lose her son without a fight. Eddie was gone for ever, but she had to save Billy. She just had to.

Richard Mercer arrived at the soldiers' home in Manchester in time to share a cup of tea and a chat with those whose minds were not damaged, only their bodies. He had never quite come to terms with how mangled bodies could be and still continue living, and was certain that he would rather be dead than in need of permanent care like some of these fellows. How they stayed so cheerful he didn't know.

He made an effort to visit the home regularly, taking small presents to those who had once been under his command. But what mattered most of all to them, he knew, was the fact that someone from the Regiment still cared enough about them to visit. For some, he was the only visitor they had.

He had already raised enough money for the new rest home, but they also had to purchase equipment and pay the wages of those who would care for the maimed men, so he needed more. And although the Government would help, that would not be enough, either.

Florence mocked his efforts but the project meant a great deal to him. He had come to the conclusion that he couldn't really devote himself to writing his novel until his men were properly looked after. Well, they weren't exactly his men any more, but they still felt like his responsibility.

When a nurse signalled to him, he excused himself to his companion and went through into the south wing with her. He always dreaded this part of the visit because these men were mentally ill or brain damaged, and he found that a lot harder to deal with than physical disability.

'The doctor came early today,' the nurse said as she locked the door behind her. 'He's with Fred Bibby just now.'

'Right.'

She glanced sideways at him. 'There's been some improvement, Captain Mercer. Not a lot, but it gives you hope at least.'

Richard braced himself for that slack face which always looked empty, as if there were nothing left behind the one remaining eye and the badly scarred forehead, but this time Fred's eye focused on him for a minute. Richard stood still, reminded suddenly of the lively lad who had joined his regiment, probably under the minimum age of eighteen.

'Was that my imagination?' he asked Toby Herbert who was standing beside the bed. 'Or did his eye really focus?'

'Yes, it did. Watch.' Toby clapped his hands suddenly and Fred turned towards the sound, staring for a moment then relapsing again. 'I'm going to ask for more work to be done with him, but we need volunteers. Will you lend your name to an appeal for that sort of help?'

'Of course – for what good it'll do.' They both knew that money was far easier to find than people's time, though neither came all that easily.

They went on to visit the other man from the regiment who was also in this wing, but with him there was no sign of progress. He still cowered away if anyone came near him, still crooned tunelessly to himself when left alone.

'No sign of any changes here,' Richard said sadly.

Toby's voice was firm. 'No. But if we give up, there never will be any progress, will there?'

'However do you keep going?'

'Because I've seen these methods work sometimes and I'm trying to find out how.'

The two men parted at the door to the south wing, Toby to visit other patients, Richard to make his way to a teashop and sit for a while lost in thought. Pity Toby Herbert couldn't do something for people like Connie, but the man specialised in head injuries, not leg injuries that no doctor could explain to his satisfaction.

And only this morning the new maid had given notice.

Florence had been right, damn her! It was going to be hard to keep staff in Stenton. Perhaps he should get a proper nanny this time? Yes, he'd try that. It couldn't be worse than changing maids every few weeks.

In London Florence woke in George's arms and sighed happily at the memory of their love-making. Why hadn't she married him instead? She smiled wryly as she slid from the bed. Because he hadn't asked her, that was why. And because she'd been stupid enough to get pregnant by Richard.

As he turned over and muttered to himself, she smiled across the room. Not an early riser, her Georgie.

When she returned with two cups of tea, he opened one eye and muttered, 'I'd kill for that, you know.'

'You don't have to.' She waited till he'd heaved himself upright, then passed him the cup.

He drank half the tea in one loud slurp, sighed in pleasure and winked at her. 'You're damned good in bed, Flo my pet! Wasted on that stick of a cousin of mine.'

'Don't I know it! And Richard won't come near me these days. I don't know if he can't – or just won't.' She closed her eyes as bitterness surged through her. 'Why did I ever go near him in the first place?'

'Because you're not made to be faithful, any more than I am.'

Later, as they sauntered out together to buy lunch, George folded her arm in his and decided that, apart from enjoying her company, it added a further layer to his satisfaction to know that he had not only taken Richard's wife but could do with her as he pleased. And that wasn't all he intended to take. Somehow he and Flo were going to find a way to get hold of Richard's money as well. Damned if he was going to leave things as they stood! He was just as much a nephew of old James's and had been morally entitled to half the Mercer money, damn it.

It was at that moment the idea came to him. Widows inherited their husband's money, didn't they? He glanced sideways at Florence. She'd not weep for Richard, and it wouldn't be too bad marrying her because they were two of a kind. Not mealy-mouthed do-gooders like her bloody husband!

George began to whistle softly as they walked along, turning the idea over in his mind. The more he thought about it, the more he liked it, but being in the army had taught him to plan a campaign properly. If he was caught in this, they'd hang him. Was it worth the risk? He didn't know. But it was worth looking into, that was sure.

'You're very cheerful today,' Florence said.

'Yes, aren't I?' He slapped her rump playfully, but didn't share his thoughts with her. Not yet.

When Polly got home from Manchester, she took out her writing things, refilled her fountain pen and set to work on the letter to Dr Browning-Baker. She would be glad to get her son back, not just for his sake but for her own. Living alone was dreadful, something she'd never done in her whole life before this. At fourteen she'd gone from being one of five children to being a maid in a large house with ten indoor and outdoor staff, then on from there at seventeen to marriage.

By the time she'd finished the letter she was tired but determined to take it to the hospital that very day. Then perhaps she'd be able to sleep more soundly and not lie awake worrying, wondering whether Billy was awake too, and if so, whether he was aware of anything. Surely, surely, it must be good for children to be loved and cherished, even when they were so badly injured?

At the hospital, she handed the note to Dr Browning-Baker's secretary, insisted on a receipt for it as Dr Herbert had instructed, much to the woman's annoyance, then went up to see her son.

The bed was empty!

Terrified, Polly rushed along to the Ward Sister's cubicle. 'My son isn't there! Has he been moved to another ward?'

'He's been moved to St Jude's.'

'What?' Polly couldn't take that in for a moment, then she gasped, 'But how . . . why? I never gave permission for that! In fact, I said I definitely didn't want him to go there.'

The Sister looked down her nose at Polly. 'Dr Browning-Baker thought it would be better, you being so young, to take such a difficult decision out of your hands.'

'He had no *right* to do that.'

'He was thinking of the child. You should be grateful that an important man like him is taking an interest in your problems.'

Polly returned to the doctor's office, but even the secretary had gone for the day now. With tears streaming down her face, Polly started to walk home. How could they do this to her? Just take her son away, without even a farewell.

She didn't notice when the Dearden's delivery van drew up beside her. Peter had to get out and take hold of her arm to stop her walking on. 'Polly! What's wrong?'

She tried to find the words, tried to find the air to breathe, and failed in both, sliding to the ground in a faint before he'd realised what was happening.

A passer-by stopped to help and they got her into the front seat of the van, then Peter abandoned what he was doing to drive home and carry her upstairs.

When she opened her eyes, Polly stared round blankly, saw Lizzie and burst into tears. As she explained what had happened, her sister grew more and more indignant and Peter grew thoughtful.

'I didn't know you'd gone to see old Toby,' he said.

'Dr Herbert? Do you know him?'

'He was Medical Officer in our regiment at one stage. I also heard that he had a big quarrel with Browning-Baker a few weeks ago.'

'Will he help me get my son back, do you think?'

'We can ask him. I'll phone him for you tomorrow.'

Lizzie insisted she spend the night with them on their sofa, and bullied her into eating a proper meal, but Polly didn't get much sleep. She kept thinking about Billy and wondering where he was.

The following day Peter phoned Toby Herbert and told him what had happened.

'Heaven preserve us all from arrogant fools like that one!' he exclaimed.

'What should we do to get Billy back?'

'Do you have transport for him? Right, then. I'll rearrange my schedule and meet you at St Jude's tomorrow.'

The following day they found Dr Herbert waiting for them in the street outside, as arranged. He got out of his car and came straight across to Polly, keeping her hand clasped between his as he said, 'I'm sorry this has happened and even more sorry to tell you that the nuns won't want to give him back to you. Browning-Baker has done this before, you see, claiming the mother was incompetent. The courts upheld his decision, too.'

Polly gazed at him in white-faced shock. 'But how can they do that?'

'Because the man looks so impressive and is a well-known figure in the medical world.'

'Well, I won't let them take Billy from me.'

Toby Herbert glanced towards the home, which was in a large

old house set in its own grounds. 'I'll help you all I can, but I have to be careful or Browning-Baker will accuse me of unprofessional conduct. This is what we need to do . . .'

Together, the three of them asked to see the nun in charge and explained the situation to her. However, as Toby had predicted, she insisted she could not possibly let the boy go without Dr Browning-Baker's express permission.

Polly drew herself up. 'But I'm Billy's mother and I didn't agree to him coming here in the first place.'

'Then Doctor must have had some reason for what he did, and until we find that out. . .'

At this something snapped inside Polly. 'At least let me see my son. If necessary, I'll search every room in the hospital.' She could feel colour rising in her face and anger such as she'd only ever felt before when Sam Thoxby was beating her sister during the unhappy years of their marriage.

'There is no need to take such an attitude, Mrs Scordale. Of course you can see your son. We *encourage* the families to visit patients. It's not visiting hour yet, but I'll find the porter to take you up to his room anyway.' She looked at the two men. 'We don't allow three visitors at a time.'

'Dr Herbert is here at my invitation to examine Billy,' Polly said.

'Does Dr Browning-Baker know that?'

'I took a letter into his office two days ago saying I was withdrawing Billy from his care and wanted a second opinion.'

'I see. Please excuse me for a moment.'

When the nun had left, Toby whispered urgently, 'If you want to avoid a lot of red tape, I'd suggest you simply pick up your son and carry him out.'

'But what if we harm him?'

'I'll come up with you to see him and scratch my chin if I think it's safe to move him. Then I'll say I have another appointment and leave. I'd be grateful if you'd wait till you hear my car drive away before you do anything.' He grinned suddenly. 'But I'll come and visit your son tomorrow in Overdale so that if necessary I can swear you're looking after him competently. That man's so used to getting his own way, he's beginning to think he's God Almighty!'

Polly turned to Peter. 'Will you help me carry Billy out?'

He didn't hesitate. 'Yes, of course.'

The nun came back followed by a porter and took them up to the ward. There were ten children and each bed was tidy, each child immaculately clean – but also totally motionless. Every face was horrifyingly blank.

Polly gave her son a quick hug, then stood back to let Dr Herbert examine him. She saw the nun exchange meaningful glances with the porter, a burly man who had followed them up and was now standing behind them. He nodded, folded his arms and remained near the door.

The doctor spent a long time examining Billy who looked so small and helpless Polly could have wept. Just once the child's face screwed up as if he was about to cry. Otherwise he lay passive as the gentle hands moved him about, though he also twitched a little when the hands tickled.

'He still has some physical responses,' Toby said thoughtfully. He turned to the nun. 'Have you tried making him move about?'

'We move them every hour to avoid bed sores.' She looked at Polly. 'They could not possibly receive better care than we give them.'

Toby intervened. 'I know you do your very best, but there are other approaches being tried which sometimes help.' He scratched his chin as he took out his watch, then clicked his tongue as if surprised at the time. 'I'll have to leave now, I'm afraid, Mrs Scordale. I'll write out my report as soon as I get back to my rooms and put it in the post to you.'

She could take Billy home!

Relief and joy made Polly go weak for a moment, then she moved forward to take her son's hand, trying to speak calmly.

'Thank you, Dr Herbert. I'll look forward to hearing what you have to say.'

When Toby turned to leave, the porter hesitated then followed him out, leaving the nun to keep watch.

Peter moved forward to stand beside his nephew. 'The bruises have nearly faded now. He's looking more like our little lad, isn't he?'

From outside came the sound of a car engine starting. As it faded away Polly looked at her brother-in-law. 'Now, I think.' She drew back the covers and Peter scooped up the child.

'What are you doing?' the nun exclaimed.

'Taking my son home, where he belongs,' said Polly, moving to stand between the other woman and Peter.

'But you can't! It isn't allowed!'

'I can and will do it. He's *my* son, not yours, and I didn't give permission for him to be brought here.' She followed Peter out of the ward and down the stairs, with the nun twittering behind them.

In the hall, the porter stood up and came out of his cubicle. 'Hey! What do you think you're doing?'

Polly stepped forward. 'I'm taking my son home.'

'Not without the doctor's permission, you aren't.' As he started towards them, she moved even more quickly, taking him by surprise by pushing him out of the way.

Peter slipped outside with the child. Polly stood for a moment in the doorway facing the other two. 'You'll have to fight me every inch of the way to take my son from me!' she said, her voice very quiet and steady though her heart was pounding inside her chest.

It hung in the balance for a moment, then the nun shook her head. 'Leave them, John. I'll go and phone Dr Browning-Baker. He'll know what to do. We had this problem once before.'

Billy was already lying in the back of the van on the quilt from Polly's bed. As she clambered in beside him reaction set in and her voice wobbled as she said, 'Drive off as quickly as you can,

Peter.' She could feel tears rolling down her cheeks and brushed them away impatiently as she held her son steady.

When they had been driving for a few minutes, she asked, 'What do you think they'll do?'

'Nothing. What can they do? He's your son and you didn't give permission for him to be taken to that place.'

'Dr Herbert said Dr Browning-Baker might report me to the police.'

'Then we'll report *them* for kidnapping.' Peter scowled as he drove along because the sight of those poor children lying so still had upset him.

A little later Polly said quietly, 'Do you think that man often does this sort of thing?'

'I don't know. But Toby said it's not the first time it's happened. How does the fellow get away with it?'

'Because people are frightened and think doctors know better than *they* do – and because no one else has a brother-in-law as lovely as you.' She was sobbing now, hugging her child to her as she sat on the floor of the van and letting the tears drip down on his face.

'Are you all right?' asked Peter, worried sick about her.

'Not yet. But I will be when I get my son safely home.'

She would have to be.

CHAPTER SEVEN

May 1920

Polly spent a restless night worrying about Billy. But although she got up several times to check if he was all right by the soft light of an oil lamp she had left burning, because there were no gas lights upstairs, he seemed to be sleeping soundly enough. Too soundly? How did you tell if it was normal sleep?

In the morning, she cleaned him up carefully, then fed him on the runny porridge Dr Herbert had recommended. Billy had always liked porridge anyway, with cream and treacle on top. And was it her imagination or was he opening his mouth before she tapped it with the spoon, then swallowing the food willingly?

Afterwards she installed him on the sofa and quickly cleared up the kitchen. Her first attempt to stimulate the child was by singing to him, lifting up first one arm then the other in time to the music. Her voice wavered because it was the first time she'd tried to sing since Eddie's death, but after a few bars it steadied.

She thought nothing of it when someone knocked at the door – people were always popping into one another's houses in Bobbin Lane. Wedging Billy in a corner of the sofa, she dropped a quick kiss on his cheek and went to see who was there.

Outside stood Dr Browning-Baker, looking down his nose at her as usual. With him were a woman and man who looked like officials.

'Mrs Scordale?' It was the woman who spoke.

'Yes.' Polly's heart began to thud. What did they want? Dr Herbert had hinted that his colleague was vindictive. Had he brought these people to take her son away from her? If so they were in for a fight because if she called out her neighbours would come running. No one in this part of town liked nosey officials. In spite of her fear, she straightened her spine and stared right back at them.

'May we come in?'

'No. I'm busy.'

The two men exchanged meaningful glances, then the woman stepped forward. 'I'm afraid we have the right of entry, Mrs Scordale.'

'Not without telling me who you are, you don't. And proving it.' Mrs Pilby's housekeeper had taught her that. You always asked officials to prove who they were. If nothing else, it shook their confidence a little. She folded her arms and stayed right where she was.

The woman next door had come out on to her step. 'You all right, Polly, love?'

'No, I'm not all right. I'm trying to look after my son and these people from the Town Hall want to come visiting. Will you stay within hearing, please, Meg? I might need some help.'

Meg glared at the trio and moved forward. 'I certainly will.'

'My good woman . . .' Dr Browning-Baker began, frowning at Polly.

'Don't you "my good woman" me!' she told him. 'You're just trying to bully me into doing what you want. And I'm not going to let you.'

The man with the briefcase cleared his throat. 'My name is Maslam. I'm from Overdale Town Council Children's Welfare Department and I'm authorised to check on cases like your son.'

'My son's fine. And you still haven't *proved* who you are. Where are your identification papers?'

Meg, who had known her as a child, cackled loudly. 'I never

thought of that one, Polly girl. But you're right. You can't be too careful who you let into your house. They may be thieves trying to rob you.'

Mr Maslam turned a dull red and began to breathe deeply, but fumbled in his pocket and produced a business card with his name on it and the Town Council insignia.

'You're being very silly, Mrs Scordale,' the woman next to him said in a low voice. 'Let's do this quietly, shall we?'

'Let's do what?'

'Inspect the situation.'

Red rage was now humming through Polly's veins, unusually for her. 'Why? How would you feel if three strangers turned up and wanted to come into your house when you had a sick child to look after?' She glanced quickly over her shoulder to make sure that Billy was all right.

There was the sound of a car and Dr Herbert's black Humber swung round the corner with its hood up against the showery weather.

Relief made Polly sag against the door frame for a minute, then she straightened up and said quietly, 'Billy's doctor has just arrived. We'll wait for him, if you don't mind.'

The woman looked quickly round at the car, then back at Polly, frowning. 'I thought Dr Browning-Baker was the child's doctor?'

'No. I informed him that I'd found another doctor three days ago.'

'The letter must have gone astray,' he said quickly.

Polly lost the last of her fear of him at this blatant lie. 'It couldn't have done because I took it to the hospital myself and gave it to your secretary. What's more I have a receipt for it and a date stamp on it. I went to visit my son soon after that and found out you'd sent him away without even telling me!' Her chest heaved with both anger and pain at that memory. 'You had *no right* to do that!'

Dr Herbert arrived at the door, calm and smiling but with a

watchful expression in his eyes. 'Is something wrong, Mrs Scordale?'

'I don't know. These people turned up and insisted they could just walk into my house.'

He moved to stand beside her. 'I'm afraid Mr Maslam and Miss Withers can do just that. However, I don't see why *you* are here, Browning-Baker. You're not the child's doctor now.'

'He *was* my patient and as Senior Medical Officer at the hospital, I consider myself still responsible for him until I can ensure that he's being properly looked after. The mother is too young and ignorant to know what she's doing.'

The looks exchanged by the two doctors were not friendly.

'I disagree with that. And in any case, *I* am neither young nor ignorant,' Dr Herbert said firmly. 'Billy Scordale is my patient now and has been ever since Mrs Scordale rang up to let my secretary know that she'd delivered a letter to you to that effect.'

Polly moved back a couple of steps. 'You'd better come in, then, Mr Maslam, Miss Withers. I'll take Dr Herbert's word for what rights you have. You too, of course, Dr Herbert.' Then she fixed the other doctor with a glare. 'But I don't want *you* inside my house or anywhere near my son — not ever again! I don't trust you.'

There was dead silence then Miss Withers said doubtfully, 'Well, I suppose Dr Herbert will do just as well.'

'Do for what?' Toby asked.

'To judge whether *this woman* . . .'

'If you mean Mrs Scordale, it would be more polite to use her name.'

Miss Withers flushed. 'Er — yes. To judge whether Mrs Scordale *is* a fit mother.'

He raised his eyebrows at her. 'You can't be serious? She's an excellent mother.'

Miss Withers looked uncertainly at the man still standing on the doorstep.

'I'll leave them in your hands then, Herbert,' Browning-Baker said, his voice tight and plummy-sounding. 'See that you put the child's welfare first, though, however pretty the mother.' He swung on his heel and stalked off down the street.

'I consider that an unprofessional remark,' Toby said to the two officials, 'and I deny its implications absolutely – especially as I've only met Mrs Scordale twice before today, both times in the company of other people.'

'Er – yes.' Mr Maslam moved further into the room.

Polly closed the front door and went over to Billy. She straightened him up, brushing his hair out of his eyes, then sat on the edge of the sofa, holding his hand, and gestured to the other chairs. 'Please sit down.'

'We might as well examine the house first for cleanliness,' the man said to the woman, as if Polly were not there.

'*What!*' she bounced to her feet. 'After three years of working as a maid at Redley House, I think I know how to manage a small place like this.'

'We have to do this,' Miss Withers explained quickly. 'It's standard procedure.'

Polly jabbed one finger towards the kitchen door. 'Go on, then. Go and poke your noses in! And I hope you're proud of what you're doing.'

They walked out in silence, the man looking angry, the woman uneasy.

'Go with them, Polly,' Toby said softly. 'It'll be better if you do. I'll stay with Billy.'

So she showed them round – which didn't take long – making remarks like, 'Don't forget to look under the bed! Just have a feel along the top of the door frame. You haven't looked behind the wardrobe for dust.'

'It's – er – you keep it very nice,' the woman said as they walked back down the narrow stairs. 'It's clear that you've been – well trained.'

Polly sniffed, not even turning her head to acknowledge the remark.

In the front room Toby was playing with Billy's fingers, though the child was staring blankly in front of him. 'Look at me, Billy!' he said loudly at intervals.

But the boy just lay there, eyes empty.

At the sight of him Polly had to stop and blink back tears. Sometimes it was hard to believe her little lad would ever recover.

The woman glanced sideways at her, but the man ignored her and went across to stare down at the child. 'Is she looking after him properly, Doctor, and will you be continuing to supervise her?'

'Of course she's looking after him properly, and naturally I'll continue to supervise my patient. However, it wouldn't hurt to have the health visitor look in now and then, in case Mrs Scordale needs any help. Mrs Laksby is very good with such cases, don't you think?'

Their faces brightened.

'Yes. That would be an excellent idea.' The official turned to Polly. 'We shall be back in a month for another check.'

'Well, you still won't find any dirt in my house.' She showed them to the door, shut it as quickly as she could, then half fell into a chair since her legs now seemed to be made of cotton wool. She saw the doctor looking at her in concern. 'I'm all right. It's just,' she swallowed hard and confessed, 'I've never stood up to anyone like that before.'

'You were magnificent,' Toby said, smiling.

But tears were standing in Polly's eyes, blurring her vision, and she still felt shaky. 'I didn't *feel* magnificent. I had to stay angry to keep going.'

'Remind me never to make you angry, then.'

Polly managed a watery smile at the thought of anyone being afraid of her. When she had calmed down a little, she asked, 'Why did you suggest the health visitor calling in?' She had felt hurt by that.

'For two reasons. First, in case you need help. There are things that can and should be done to assist you. Secondly, so that they'll feel satisfied someone is keeping an eye on you.' He raised one hand when she would have protested. 'I know you don't need that, but we don't want to give Browning-Baker another chance to cause trouble, do we? And besides, Mrs Laksby is kind and practical. She really knows her job and wants to help people, not upset them. She's been helping me with one of my adult patients who has just gone home. You'll like her.'

'Oh.' Polly would welcome some help if it was genuine. She knew she had a lot to learn.

'How about making us both a cup of tea? Then I'll show you a few tricks for looking after Billy – who is recovering well physically, by the way. Look at his colour and his clear eyes.'

She nodded and went out to the kitchen, glad to have something to do.

As he sat sipping the tea, Toby said thoughtfully, 'If you can afford it, I have a man who makes special feeding chairs and playpens, where the child can be propped up in such a way that he can't fall but can watch what's going on around him.'

She turned to study her son. 'Only he's not watching anything, is he?'

'Not yet. You'll have to try to get his attention any way you can at this stage.'

'I have some money from the insurance, but it won't last for ever. Just for a year or two. If nothing happens by then, I don't know what I'll do. Still, you'd better order those things for me because he's too big for baby things. It'll help me get on with my housework.'

'And give you time to relax, too. Read a book. Do some embroidery. Don't forget your own needs.'

'I don't matter.'

'Yes, you do. And with the wheelchair you can take him out. You'll both be better for some fresh air and exercise.' He sat there thoughtfully for a while longer, then said, 'There would be no charge for my services if you'd help me by taking notes about Billy, detailed notes.'

Her voice was sharp. 'I don't need charity.'

'It isn't charity, actually. I'm making a study of such children and your notes would be invaluable.'

She searched his face. Was he telling the truth?

'I wouldn't lie to you, Polly.'

'Oh – well – all right, then.'

'I'll get my secretary to send you the full details of what I need to know. I'm doing this with a few clients, you see, not just you.'

She nodded, feeling better about it.

When he'd left there was only silence till Polly started singing to Billy. She began to play little games with his fingers in time to the music as she had when he was a baby.

It seemed a very long day. Billy lay there as helpless as a new-born infant, rarely moving. When Lizzie came round in the evening to find out if she needed help, Polly could have wept for joy to see her sister, who had brought more food and promised to send the delivery lad every day to see what was needed.

'I'll be able to do the shopping myself when they deliver his special wheelchair,' Polly said. 'How much do I owe you?'

'Nothing.'

'Either I pay or you take it back.'

'You're my sister! I'm *not* charging you!'

Polly folded her arms. 'Dearden's is there to sell groceries, not give them away. And I don't need anyone's charity.'

Lizzie heaved an exaggerated sigh. 'Oh, very well. I'm only charging you cost, though. Is that all right, madam?'

'Yes.'

Lizzie's voice grew softer again. 'Will you be all right, love?'

'As much as I can be now.'

'Oh, Polly!'

'D-don't be sympathetic. It makes me cry.'

Lizzie blinked the tears from her own eyes. 'All right, you horrible woman!'

They both laughed, but shakily.

*

Richard went to a domestic employment agency in Lancaster and asked them to find a trained nanny to care for his daughter, taking care to stress the fact that Stenton was a fairly isolated place.

The result was Miss Priscilla Leyton, a thin woman with excellent references, who fairly crackled with starch and authority. Under her care Connie became even quieter, but still protested if pressed to be more active. Richard didn't really take to Miss Leyton, but he was desperate to find proper care for his daughter and some modicum of education as well. At least now he knew Connie was being looked after properly while part of his time was still taken up with making arrangements for the rest home.

Florence came home for a visit but only, he soon found out, because she'd run out of money. She pulled a face at 'Miss Prune' and the strict regime in the schoolroom, but made no attempt to interfere and saw little of her daughter. She also made no secret of the fact that she was not in Stenton by choice and would be off like a flash if any of her friends invited her to stay with them.

'Are you not ashamed to sponge off people like that?' Richard asked one day when her complaints were even more shrill than usual.

'Yes, I am – especially knowing that you're sitting on all that money like the miserable old miser you are.'

'Times are hard and getting harder. And I can do a lot of good with that money. Besides, I'd much rather use it to help my men than let you waste it on – on riotous living.'

Florence nearly choked with laughter. 'Riotous living? You wouldn't know the first thing about that. All you know about is sober, boring living. You're so dull! And I'm bored senseless already in this place.'

'Then go elsewhere!'

Her eyes flashed with anger as she shouted, 'I would do if I could afford it. Haven't I just been telling you that?'

Knowing that everyone in the house could hear their quarrel, Richard went to shut the door.

'That's right. Pretend the servants can't hear us.' She threw back her head and screamed.

He took a step towards her, thinking for a moment that something was wrong. Then she gave him a triumphant smile and he realised what she was doing. 'Be quiet!'

'Or you'll do what?' She threw back her head and screamed even more loudly.

He could hear footsteps pounding up from the kitchen in the basement and Connie weeping upstairs, so he opened the door and yelled, 'It's all right, everyone.'

Florence sucked in her breath as if to make another of those dreadful noises, and he surprised both of them by slapping her across her face.

For a moment everything in the room seemed to stop, not just the noise but even their breathing. He stared at her in horror, seeing the mark of his fingers on her cheek, then he looked down at his own hand, surprised that it seemed no different. As he took an involuntary step backwards, she began to laugh. And the harsh sound was just as bad as the screaming.

'For heaven's sake, can you not keep quiet!'

Which only made her laugh more.

It was the thought of Connie that did it. 'I can let you have fifty pounds if that's any use to you.' He hated himself for caving in.

'A hundred.'

He shook his head. Even fifty would mean appreciably less to spend on his men.

She held out one hand. 'Prove it.'

He went to the library to unlock his desk, looking up to find her standing in the doorway watching him.

She smiled sweetly as she asked, 'Do you hate me as much as I hate you?'

He was done with pretending or trying to be polite. 'Probably more.'

'If you'll give me half the money you inherited, including the value of this house, you can have your quiet divorce tomorrow.'

So that was what she was leading up to. He shook his head. 'I'm not giving you that much. Besides, you'd have spent it before the divorce came through, then you'd be back for the rest. I know you.'

Her smile turned to a scowl. 'In that case, you're saddled with me, my *dearest husband.*'

Wordlessly he held out the banknotes.

She sauntered across and took them from him. 'Can you give me a lift to the station in Knott End? Suitcases are such heavy things.'

'Yes.'

'In an hour?'

'Yes. Do you want me to look up the train times? Where are you going?'

She turned at the door to say sarcastically, 'It's none of your business where I'm going. Just have the car ready in an hour. I can't get out of here quickly enough.'

'Wait!'

She paused, saying nothing, looking at him as if he was the lowest creature on earth.

'Go and say goodbye to Connie first or you don't get the lift.'

'I will if you give me ten pounds extra.'

He could only stare at her wordlessly. 'You are a heartless bitch.'

She shrugged. 'Well?'

He wanted to tell her to go to hell, but the thought of Connie's tears made him say instead, 'All right. But not till I've seen you say a proper goodbye.'

'I'll call you up for the performance.' With an airy wave, she strolled out.

When he went upstairs to get ready, he heard her come down and pick up the telephone in the drawing room. For some reason, the acoustics of the house made conversations held near the bay window in there echo clearly up the stairs. He hesitated then moved back to the top of the stairs to listen. He had never willingly eavesdropped on anyone before in his life and felt guilty until he heard what she was saying.

'. . . I'll be there tonight, Georgie, so better have a restful day!' Her throaty laugh betrayed the relationship between his wife and cousin as well as any words could have done.

Shock transfixed Richard. He simply could not move. He hadn't realised. Dear God, he hadn't realised it was George she went to. All sorts of minor details suddenly fell into place.

'. . . no, he didn't grab my offer of an uncontested divorce and half the money. But he will. I'll make him so bloody uncomfortable when next I visit that in the end he'll pay anything to get rid of me.'

Closing his eyes for a moment, Richard clutched at the handrail. George, of all people. Then he realised his wife had stopped speaking and he forced himself to move on, walking across the landing as quietly as he could. He didn't care that she was unfaithful – but he did care very much, for some reason, that it was with his cousin George.

He could hear Florence in her bedroom next door, humming as she opened and shut drawers. Coathangers clicked along rails as she selected frocks, walking to and fro to pack the suitcases.

He hadn't heard her go and say goodbye to Connie yet, but he would not pay for that until he saw it happen. For some reason the child needed desperately to feel that her mother cared about her, that this perpetual quarrelling was not her fault.

In the car Richard kept silent, listening as his wife hummed, checked her nails, filed one carefully and beamed at the world as he got her suitcases out of his car and carried them on to the station platform.

As soon as he got home, he went into the sitting room and picked up the telephone to call the private detective. Then he put it down again. A divorce gained this way would be so ugly, and he absolutely hated the thought of it. Surely he could talk Florence into doing the thing in a more civilised way, for Connie's sake? He'd make a big effort the next time she came home. He'd made a mess of it this time, but he wouldn't the next. He couldn't afford to. Not if he ever wanted to be happy again.

CHAPTER EIGHT

May–June 1920

Again Polly's morning was interrupted by an imperative knock on her front door. Neighbours knocked and then simply came in, as did her family, so as she went to open it, she felt apprehensive. At the sight of her mother-in-law she held the door open wider and tried to sound pleased. 'How lovely to see you. Do come in.'

Once inside Hilda Scordale made no attempt to sit down, but set one hand against the wall as if to hold herself steady. 'So it's true,' she said in the hollow tone of a doomsayer.

'What do you mean?' Then Polly saw where her mother-in-law was looking.

'You *have* brought him home.'

'Where else would I bring my son?'

'I couldn't believe it when they told me.' Her gaze shifted to Polly's face and her voice took on a sharp accusatory edge. 'How can you do this to my Eddie's lad? Billy could have been *properly* looked after at St Jude's. We could all have had our minds at peace about him. But no, you have to think you know better than Dr Browning-Baker, don't you?'

Polly sucked in her breath, taken aback by this accusation, then stiffened as the implications sank in. 'Who told you about this?'

'Why, Dr Browning-Baker himself did. He was that worried about Billy – and he knew we were the grandparents.'

Polly felt hot anger start to rise in her again. Why was someone as important as a doctor hounding her like this? Could a man in his position really be so vindictive? For Billy's sake, however, she didn't speak until she could control her voice. 'That man had no right to contact you. Did he go all the way out to the village just for that?'

'No, of course he didn't, someone as important as that. He sent us a letter. It came by first post today. So I decided to come into town and try to talk a bit of sense into you, because your own family don't seem to be doing it. Apparently they aided and abetted you to take the lad away from that nice home in Manchester.'

Polly shot a resentful look at her mother-in-law. 'Well, you'll not change my mind, so maybe it's best if we agree to disagree about this. Now – you haven't kissed Billy yet, and you surely aren't going to stay by the door?'

Hilda's voice broke as she said, 'That poor creature can't tell whether anyone kisses him or not. He's not *our Billy* any more, and the sooner you face that, the happier we'll all be.' But she did cross the room and sit on the edge of what had been Eddie's armchair.

Polly propped Billy up with pillows and went to put the kettle on. She felt she was handling the situation well. Even her clever sister Eva couldn't have done better. However, when she sat down her mother-in-law started to harangue her again, trying to make her promise to do as Dr Browning-Baker wanted. Polly offered explanations in response to her unkind comments and questions, but the tirade continued without abating in the slightest.

In the end, Polly gave up any attempt to reason with her visitor and stood up. 'I don't want to hear any more of this. Billy is *my* son and I'll do as I think best for him. If you don't like it, you'll just have to lump it. And what Eddie would say about you taking that horrible man's side against me, I don't know. It's not as if I haven't got Billy another doctor, because I have.'

Hilda slammed her cup down on the little side table, splashing tea on the doily. 'Our Eddie would want someone to talk sense to you. It's for *his* sake I've come over.'

'Someone *is* talking sense – Dr Herbert, our new doctor. What we're doing gives Billy a chance. Not,' Polly's voice faltered for a moment, 'not a big chance, but something at least. What you want me to do will leave him lying in St Jude's a hopeless case for the rest of his life. So you can . . . you can just save your breath because there's nothing any of you can do to change my mind.'

The older woman stood up, snatching her handbag from the floor and slinging it over her arm. 'I'm not staying here to be talked to like that by an ignorant young piece like you! What my son ever saw in you I don't know – and neither does anyone else in the family.'

This additional insult made Polly rush to hold the door open. 'Don't let me keep you, then.'

In the doorway her mother-in-law paused to glare at her and say loudly, 'I'm not coming back till you apologise, mind.'

'Good! Then don't come back. Better no grandmother for Billy than one like you.'

Bright red colour flooded Hilda's face. 'I shan't forget that.'

'Nor shall I forget what you've said. I don't deserve it from you. I've been hurt enough by what's happened.' Slamming the door behind her visitor, Polly tried to calm herself, but her eyes were blinded by tears as she fumbled her way across the room and flopped down on the sofa beside her son. Still sobbing, she held him in her arms for the comfort of a warm human body against hers, rocking him slightly as she wept.

When her tears dried up, she looked down at him and the words she had been going to say froze in her throat. A sunbeam was reflecting off the lustres of an ornament her sister Eva had given her as a present, making little rainbows dance against the back wall opposite the window. Billy was following them with his eyes, he really was. A shadow of a smile flickered on his face, then as the sun went behind a cloud and the rainbows disappeared, the light faded from his eyes and he sagged against her. But she knew she had not imagined it.

More tears began to flow, but this time they were tears of hope. It was surely a sign that she was doing the right thing.

'We'll prove them wrong, my little love,' Polly muttered into his hair as she cuddled him close. 'I don't care what anyone says, you're going to get better. And if the Scordales don't want to come and see us, they can stay away. There's your Auntie Lizzie, Uncle Percy and Uncle Johnny only a few minutes' walk away. We'll go and see them often. We shan't be on our own.'

Even as she spoke the postman poked a letter through the door which turned out to be from her sister Eva, saying she was coming over on Sunday to see her little nephew.

The feeling that she was not alone stayed with Polly all day, keeping her cheerful as she spooned mashed food into her son. She chuckled as she wiped his face, then began to tickle him and play clap hands with him as she had done when he was a baby. He might be three years old, but she was going to think of him as a baby again.

Richard spent the first part of the morning with his daughter, to the evident disapproval of her new nanny who followed him out of the schoolroom.

'It makes things very difficult if you interrupt my schedule, Mr Mercer. Children like your daughter benefit from order and knowing what to expect.'

'I'm sorry if it disturbed your routine, Miss Leyton, but I'm going to stay away overnight so I wanted to spend some time with Connie before I left.'

'You come and go quite often, don't you?'

'Well – yes.'

'Does that mean you'll be interrupting us regularly?'

There was a pause during which she folded her hands together and continued to look at him as if expecting the worst.

'Well, I do like to see her before I go and—'

'I really cannot improve matters here if I'm to be disturbed all the time.'

He could sense the underlying threat and did not like it, but was worried at the prospect of yet another change. It had seemed so simple: find someone to look after a quiet child who was a semi-invalid. And yet in practice it had proved almost impossible to find someone steady who would like living here – and whom he and Connie would also like.

'I'll try not to interrupt you too much,' he said at last, hating himself for giving in to her.

Miss Leyton inclined her head. 'Thank you, Mr Mercer. It's best for Connie.'

But he had seen the gleam of triumph in her eyes and it worried him. Damn it, he had no reason to dislike this woman who kept everything in immaculate order – but he did dislike her. And he didn't think Connie looked happy with her, either. If he had any alternative . . . but he didn't.

The following week Dr Herbert brought the special equipment to Overdale in his car and stayed to show Polly how to use it, as well as playing with Billy himself to assess the child. He listened to her story of how Billy had focused on the patterns of light and said carefully, 'I hope you're right, Mrs Scordale.'

She had been kneeling by the couch as he played with her son. Now she sat back on her heels, staring up at him in dismay. 'Don't you believe me?'

He hated to dampen her hopes. 'If it happens several times, I'll put some credence in it. But my dear Mrs Scordale, one swallow doesn't make a summer – nor does one event prove anything. I won't offer false hope to you – not now, not ever.'

She seemed so young and vulnerable he had a sudden urge to take her in his arms and comfort her. He could not understand why he found her so attractive because she made no attempt to gain any man's interest. Today she was wearing a wraparound pinafore in a faded print pattern over a simple skirt and blouse. Her face was scrubbed clean and her hair was just pulled back into a simple knot from which a few wisps had escaped. And yet, the mere sight of her had made his heart lift.

He turned hurriedly back to the child. What was he doing, feeling like this about a woman so recently widowed? A woman who hadn't shown any sign of interest in him. He'd known when he first met her that she was going to be special, but had not expected this sudden reawakening of feelings that had mostly lain dormant during the gruelling war years.

'Well, if everything is all right, I'll leave you now,' Toby said quickly. 'I'll be back next week. Telephone my rooms if you encounter any problems.'

After he'd driven away, Polly walked mutinously up and down, then went to look at the new wicker wheelchair standing near the front door. She'd seen other invalids wheeled out in these contraptions but had never thought that her son would have to ride in one. It was big enough for an adult. Oh, heavens, would Billy still need it then? She wouldn't be able to carry an older lad around, or care for him properly on her own.

For a minute or two, despair flooded through her, then she pulled herself together. She had been cooped up indoors for too long. The doctor was right. Not only would going for walks be stimulating for Billy, it'd be good for her, too. 'We'll go to the park,' she decided, speaking her thoughts aloud to him because it might help – and also because it broke the silence of the little house. She looked out of the window. 'Yes, a walk.' It was sunny outside and perhaps she would meet some other mothers in the park, make a few new acquaintances.

In the park she went across to sit near the swings with other young mothers. Some of them nodded a greeting, but no one came over to talk to her. Indeed, they looked sideways at her son, as if what was wrong with him was catching. Within minutes most of them had moved on so Polly sat there alone, jiggling the chair about, trying to take pleasure in the sunshine and colourful flowerbeds. But she felt lonely. People walking past smiled at the child till they saw the blankness in his face, the way saliva was running out of the corner of his mouth, then the smiles would fade and pity take their place.

She got up and walked slowly home where the silence of the house closed around her.

'We'd better do some more exercises,' she told her son.

But although Polly worked carefully with him there was no sign of another response, and when he fell asleep, she left him and sat down by the front-room window, staring down the street.

There simply wasn't enough to do here. This was nearly as bad as living in Outshaw, so quiet and still was the house during the daytime. Billy hardly made any noise at all. Was he ever going to speak again? Was she really doing the right thing? For herself as well as for her son? How could she even begin to judge?

In London, Florence was enjoying herself hugely. Georgie was in a particularly good mood because he'd been on a lucky streak lately. This time he let her stay openly with him at his flat which should make her money last considerably longer. In the evening he took her out to parties which provided most of their food. At some of them he gambled and she sat tensely behind him, willing the dice to fall his way or the cards to give him a good hand. At other parties they danced or chatted to people. Not once was she bored as she had been in Stenton.

For a time Georgie continued to have modest success. For a time Florence was as happy as she'd ever been in her life. And she thought that he was, too, she really did.

But it didn't last. Things never did with him. When he started to lose money, he grew morose, leaving her alone more often at night. But at least he didn't turn her out of the flat. Florence bought food for them, though she was not a good cook and hated housework of any sort.

One evening he set down his knife and fork, leaving half the food on his plate uneaten. Picking up her hand, he dropped a kiss on her wrist. 'You aren't made for a frugal life, Flo my pet. And neither am I.'

She sighed and kept hold of his hand. 'I'm not made to go back to Richard, either, but that's what I'll have to do eventually when my money runs out.'

'Yes, I suppose so.'

'What do you mean by that?'

His voice was gentle, his breath warm on her hand as he raised it to his lips. 'Wouldn't it be wonderful if we could get married and live together openly?'

She sighed – too loudly – betraying her relief that he wasn't ending their affair. 'I can't think of anything I'd like more.' But then it occurred to her that he knew it was quite safe to say such things because he couldn't marry her.

When she said as much, he clicked his tongue between his teeth. 'Tsk, tsk! So cynical. Well, proof of the pudding, my love.' He held out a small box.

She opened it and looked at him in puzzlement. 'It's an engagement ring.'

'Yes. Yours one day, I hope.' He didn't tell her that he had found it lying around at one of the houses they'd visited and had stolen it without compunction. He had smiled all the way home that night. It was a valuable ring and had come to him so easily.

She stared at it for a minute, 'I hope so, too, but I doubt it. Richard will probably outlive me. His Uncle James was nearly ninety when he died. They're a long-lived lot, the Mercers.' She snapped the box shut and shoved it back towards him.

'What if—' George hesitated, still unsure of how she'd react. Oh, well, he could always pretend he was joking. 'What if there was a way to,' he paused delicately, 'get rid of him?'

Florence's brow wrinkled as she tried to understand what he was getting at.

'Get rid of him *permanently* – and in the not-too-distant future,' George said very softly, his eyes on hers.

Her mouth dropped open. 'You can't mean – kill him!'

'Can't I?'

'You *are* serious, aren't you? Oh, my God!' she gasped, and covered her mouth with one hand.

He shrugged, watching her more carefully than she realised. 'You can't blame a chap for being tempted – especially a chap who's pretty good with firearms and weapons of all sorts.'

She got up and walked across to stand by the fire, one hand on the mantelpiece.

He went across to join her, putting his arms round her, letting her lean back against him. 'I would marry you if you were free. And if Richard no longer existed – well, we'd have his money, wouldn't we? It'd solve everything.'

'You'd only lose it as you lost all the money you inherited from your parents.'

'All the money!' His laughter was harsh. 'There was hardly anything left by the time they'd buggered about with stupid investments. I had to sell the house to pay off *their* debts, not mine.'

'Oh, Georgie! How dreadful for you!' It took her only a minute to ask the next logical question. 'Then how have you been managing since you got out of the army?'

'On my wits.' His smile was a mere baring of the teeth. He began to tick the ways off on his fingers. 'I've gambled, stolen, taken money from women of a certain age for services rendered.' He let those words sink in before adding, 'And I'd kill quite willingly if it'd make me financially secure. Why do you think I haven't asked you to leave Richard for me? Because I couldn't afford to keep you, that's why.'

She let her breath out in a long, slow stream. 'No wonder you were furious when he got all your uncle's money.'

'Yes – I was extremely angry.'

'I hate him,' Florence admitted. 'I can hardly bear to look at him sometimes. But Georgie—'

'Yes?'

'I don't think I could agree to kill him. Think of the risk. They hang murderers – and their accomplices. I wouldn't dare risk that.' She shuddered.

'If I decided to do something about your *encumbrance*, I'd plan it rather carefully, my pet.' He pulled her round to face him. 'Let's not talk about him any more. Let's not even think of him.'

After Florence had fallen asleep, he lay there, hands behind his neck, staring into the darkness. He was definitely going to kill his cousin one day. The thought was oddly comforting and George eventually fell asleep with a smile on his face.

CHAPTER NINE

June 1920

The following Sunday, Lizzie knocked at and opened the front door, beaming at Polly as she stepped inside. 'Look who's come to see you!' She waved one hand like a magician and their sister Eva followed her into the house.

'Oh, Polly love, how are you?' Eva asked as they hugged. She held her sister at arm's length to study her face. 'You look thinner. I'm sorry I haven't been able to get over to see you before. I feel awful about that.'

'Well, you're here now so that's all right. How's Alice?'

'She's ill. Really ill.' Eva bent her head and her next word came out muffled. 'Dying.'

After exchanging startled glances with Polly, Lizzie left Billy's side and came to put her arms round both her sisters. Their own mother had been a spiteful woman, and Alice had taken her place with Eva. The other two knew how happy the middle sister had been in recent years living with her former schoolteacher. For a few minutes the three of them stood close together, not saying anything, simply sharing their unspoken love for one another.

Later, when they were sitting down with cups of tea, Eva studied Billy. 'He looks better than I'd expected.'

'He's all right physically now. He just – isn't there in his head any more.'

But even as Polly spoke, the miracle happened again. Billy focused on something, this time his Auntie Lizzie who was never able to sit still for long and had gone to kneel beside him and tickle him. His mouth curved into a half-smile and he stared at her, really stared. As the smile began to fade, she tickled him again and he made a sound – such a small, soft sound, but it brought tears to his mother's eyes.

None of the women spoke for a moment, then Lizzie turned to stare at them. 'He definitely looked at me.'

'He hasn't made any real sounds before,' Polly whispered, her voice coming out choked because of the emotion welling inside her. 'He hasn't made a single sound until now. And I've missed his voice dreadfully. He used to chuckle a lot, you know.'

Eva, uncertain what was going on, looked from one to the other.

'He looked at the sunlight making rainbows from your ornament the other day,' Polly explained, pointing to the mantelpiece. 'It was the flickering light patterns that caught his attention. But Dr Herbert said not to set too much store by that; it had to happen regularly for it to mean anything.'

'And it just happened again – we all saw it.' Lizzie tugged Polly to her feet and waltzed her round the room, then did the same to Eva. 'He's going to get better, I know he is!'

Polly didn't spoil the moment by wondering to what extent Billy was going to recover. She did not dare hope for too much. Just let him learn to recognise her again, and to speak. It would make such a difference.

Later they went for a walk in the park, as they had done when they were children, the three of them taking turns to push the unwieldy chair along.

'We ought to get our Johnny to look at this stupid thing,' said Lizzie as she helped Polly shove it up the kerb on to the footpath. 'It needs a proper brake on it, for a start. He's a dab hand at making things work better, Johnny is. He does most of the jobs around the house for Emma and Percy now. They're going to get him an engineering apprenticeship at Pilby's.'

It seemed to set the seal on the morning when they met Percy and Emma in the park, also taking a stroll with their young family.

They all went to sit on the grass near the children's play area and when Lizzie put Beth down to crawl, Polly looked at her son thoughtfully. 'Let's put Billy on the grass, too. We have to do as many different things with him as we can, Dr Herbert says.'

So they set him down carefully, with his head on the pillow from his chair. Around them other children were running and shrieking, sometimes coming quite close to him, but he lay perfectly still, showing no signs of noticing anything. Polly swallowed hard as she watched her niece crawling about so quickly that Lizzie had to keep rushing after her and hauling her back. She reminded herself that there was at least some hope for Billy now. She was lucky in so many ways – especially today, when she had all her family about her.

When Eva got home again after the short train journey to Rochdale, Alice was lying on the sofa looking white and exhausted. In the kitchen the food Eva had left for her was almost untouched.

'I shouldn't have gone and left you. You'll never recover if you don't eat properly.'

Alice smiled. 'You needed to go and see Polly. In fact, you should have gone sooner. When it's a sister who's in trouble, you can't stay away.'

'Well, I shouldn't have stayed there all day. I'll get us some supper now and—'

'I'm not hungry. And Eva,' she hesitated, but it had to be said, 'don't you think it's about time we stopped pretending that I'm going to get better? Food won't make any difference so I'm not going to force any more down.'

Eva burst into tears. For years Alice had been the mainstay of her life. It was she who had helped persuade Eva's mother to let her stay on at school, who had helped her protégée to become a student teacher, then a fully trained one. And when Alice had inherited this comfortable house, they had come to live here together, as much a family as if they were blood kin.

'It's not fair,' Eva sobbed, sitting on the floor by the couch with her head against Alice's leg.

'No, but it's happening and we can't change anything. So we need to discuss what you'll do – afterwards.'

'What does that matter? Let's just pretend it's not happening and make the most of – of what time we do have.'

'No. No more pretending. We need to start planning. I want to know that you'll be all right after I'm gone.'

'Of course I'll be all right. I'm a trained teacher, aren't I? I can always earn a living.'

Alice sighed. A gentle girl at heart, her Eva. Kershaw family lore said that Lizzie was the lively one, Polly the quiet one and Eva the clever one. It didn't say anything about Eva's shyness with strangers which sometimes made her seem stand-offish, though she could control an impertinent child at school without any difficulty. 'I'm leaving everything I own to you, my dear, so you won't even have to work for your living if you don't feel like it. But I want to be sure you have something to keep you busy – afterwards. You're not to sit around moping.'

'I don't want to talk about it. Please. Not yet. Let me tell you about Billy instead.'

Alice let her change the subject this time. The doctor thought she might have a few months to live yet, perhaps even a year. During that time she would have to persuade Eva to accept the inevitable and together they would make plans because she knew how vulnerable the girl would be after her death.

Richard put the telephone down with a sinking feeling. He didn't want Florence to come home. She upset Connie, she upset the servants — and she set his teeth on edge at times with her selfish ways and interminable complaints.

However, the following day he dutifully picked her up at Knott End railway station, noting her downturned mouth and generally unhappy demeanour. 'Good journey?'

'Hell, no! Having to change trains to get to this dump is a dreadful bore.'

'Did you have a good time while you were away, at least?' He started the car, then got in and drove off.

'Yes, I had a wonderful time till the money ran out.' Florence scowled out of the window. 'How dreary this place is! I always forget the scenery's flat and uninteresting.' After a minute's pause she asked, 'How's whatsername working out? The new nanny. Is she still here?'

'Yes, but I'm not happy with her. She's too strict.'

'They say strict nannies are good for children.'

'I don't think so. And Connie doesn't seem any better under Miss Leyton's regime, either. She still hates to go outside.'

'I suppose it'll take time. Leave the woman to do her job. She's the expert, after all.' Florence tossed one shoulder pettishly as she always did when fed up of discussing their daughter.

Richard was relieved to see the house come into sight. When Florence let out a long, exaggerated sigh and muttered something, he didn't bother to ask what she had said, but parked the car and helped her out.

Florence barely noticed, just walked slowly inside. She could think only of George, who had told her plainly the day before that he was out of luck and out of money. His only avenue of survival now was a rich society woman who had taken a fancy to him, because he hadn't even enough money for a gambling stake. Florence would have liked to scratch the old hag's eyes out! The woman was willing to pay George for his favours and as he said ruefully, beggars couldn't be choosers, and they must both accept that.

So here she was, back in the house she hated with a husband and child who meant less than nothing to her. As Richard carried her suitcases into her bedroom, she sniffed and made no attempt to hide it as she wiped away a tear.

Even when Connie came down to see her, she found it hard to hide her impatience with the child and was glad when Miss Prune took her away again.

All Florence cared for now was George and if he was no longer available to her, then life was not worth living. If only they had some real money! Why should Richard have so much when he did nothing to enjoy it? It just wasn't fair. George was right about that.

The health visitor turned up a few days after Eva's visit, ostensibly to see if Polly needed any help with Billy. Mrs Laksby examined the child and said sympathetically, 'It must make a lot of extra washing for you to keep him so clean.'

'Yes, but I don't mind.' Polly stroked Billy's cheek, wishing he'd look at her again.

Mrs Laksby hesitated then said, 'Dr Browning-Baker wants me to check the whole house to . . . to see if it's still clean. Will you show me round, love?'

Polly stared at her in shock. 'Has he the right to ask this?'

'We-ell, he's very influential. Has friends on the Council. It's better not to go against him.'

'It's too late for that now. I have gone against his wishes and if looks could kill, he'd have me six feet under by now.'

'Yes. He's known for his spitefulness.' Mrs Laksby sighed. 'Look, I know you're looking after your son properly – well, you only have to look at him to see that – and I'm sure the house is clean as a new pin. It *feels* right as soon as you walk in. You can always tell. But I still have to be able to say I've looked.'

She hesitated again and added, 'I'd better warn you that they'll probably send the sanitary inspectors in to check the drains soon, and don't be surprised if they find something wrong and say the child is in danger. If I were you, love, I'd move to another town, I really would. I've seen this happen before when patients openly went against that man's advice.'

'But I was right to do that. Billy's starting to respond to Dr Herbert's approach!'

'That'll only make things worse. Dr Browning-Baker absolutely hates to be proved wrong.'

'I can't move away. My family are all here in Overdale! I'd be on my own in another town.' The thought of that terrified Polly.

As Mrs Laksby left, she repeated her warning. 'Mark my words, he'll find another way to get at you. You really would be better getting away from Overdale.'

Her visit left Polly feeling extremely depressed. Only the fact that Billy smiled again when she tickled him and made a few more noises helped her through the day.

There was nothing at all to help her through the evenings. They seemed very long. She wasn't a reader, like Lizzie and Eva. She preferred to do things, to keep herself busy.

When she was next in town, she saw a gramophone in a shop and went inside to ask for a demonstration, leaving Billy in his wheelchair outside. Listening to the music and marvelling at the wonders of this modern miracle, she forgot her son for a minute, to be jerked abruptly out of her enjoyment by a voice shouting in the street.

Rushing outside she found Dr Browning-Baker standing beside the chair talking to a policeman. The words '. . . unfit to care for him' struck terror into Polly, but she swallowed her fear and walked up to them both.

'Is something wrong, Constable?'

The doctor answered her triumphantly. 'Indeed there is, young woman. You have left your son untended here while wasting your time listening to music inside a shop. Yet another proof that you're not a good mother – as this officer will testify.'

Polly saw the deferential way the policeman looked at him

and the onlookers stared at her as if she was a criminal. That robbed her of any ability to think straight. 'I didn't – Billy's perfectly all right,' she stammered.

Behind her a voice said, 'There are five prams outside shops in this street. Go and count them. Are you going to go and shout at those mothers, too, you old bully?'

Polly swung round and found an old woman standing beside her, leaning on a walking stick and glaring at the doctor and policeman impartially.

Before anyone could reply, Polly's defender was off again. 'What are you doing wasting your time looking into wheelchairs, Constable? Have you police nothing better to do with yourselves than bully young women? This child is well cared for, as anyone can see. Look at his clothes. Nicely ironed, clean – and it can't be easy to care for a poor little crippled lad. It's hard enough with normal children.'

The policeman went red and started to back away.

The old woman came up to stand right next to Polly and glare at the doctor. 'Well, what are you staring at, Thomas Baker? Haven't you any patients to look after?'

He breathed in so deeply his whole chest seemed to swell up. 'My good woman—'

'Don't you "good woman" me. I knew you when you used to pinch my father's apples, only you were Tommy Baker then, not *Dr Thomas Browning-Baker.*'

'I am merely—'

'Poking your nose in where it isn't needed. I don't know what your mother would think, I really don't. *She* wasn't a snob, and she didn't bring you up to bully people, either. She must be turning in her grave.'

He swung round on his heel and marched back to his car, so that his chauffeur had to scurry to open the door for him. The policeman was trying to hide a grin and even the chauffeur was having a hard time not smiling.

The old woman chuckled and gave Polly a nudge with her

elbow. 'You just have to face up to them, lass. It's the only way with bullies.'

'I've never had to deal with anyone like him before. And someone told me recently that he never forgets a grudge.' Polly felt the tears well in her eyes. 'I don't know what I'd have done today if you hadn't come along, I really don't.' She held out one hand. 'Thank you so much for helping me. I'm Polly Scordale.'

'Mrs Nelly Baker, widow – thank goodness.'

As they shook hands Polly could not hide her surprise at this remark.

'I married a Baker myself, a cousin of this one. My Paul grew tetchy as he got older, and spiteful with it. All the Bakers do. So I don't miss him at all and I'm not going to pretend I do. If I'd taken the trouble to look at what his father was like, I'd not have married him in the first place. What did you do to upset Tommy, then?'

'Took my son out of his care and went to another doctor, one he doesn't like.'

'Ooh, he'll hate that.' Mrs Baker stared down the street. 'I live in Blackpool now and only come back to Overdale to visit my sister. Why don't you move away from here? I won't be around to protect you next time – and there will be a next time. Anyway this isn't the prettiest town in England, not by a long chalk. I don't know why anyone would live here by choice. Get some good sea air into your son's lungs. That'll help him recover more quickly.'

'My family all live here.'

'So does Tommy Baker.'

Polly sighed and looked down at her son, then clutched her companion's arm as she saw that Billy was staring at the moving shadows from a gently swinging shop sign. Really staring at them. 'He's doing it again,' she whispered, delight filling her. 'Dr Browning-Baker said he'd never be aware of anything and tried to shut him away in home, but already Billy's starting to stare at things and he's beginning to make noises again, too.'

Mrs Baker patted her shoulder. 'Then you have some hope. If you're ever in Blackpool, come and see me.' She fished in her handbag, pulled out a notebook and scribbled down her address, then tore the page out. 'Now, give me yours. I'll come and see you next time I'm in Overdale.' Afterwards, she walked with Polly to the end of the street and gave her a smacking great kiss as they parted.

That chance encounter warmed Polly's heart all evening as she sat knitting a new jersey for her son. She would definitely have to learn to stand up to people and not panic like she had done today. Her new friend was right. The doctor *was* a bully and you had to face up to them. Polly had learned that the hard way as a child.

But as for moving away – never! All her family lived here and she intended to stay here, too.

CHAPTER TEN

July 1920

On his next visit Toby Herbert saw Billy focus briefly on a toy dangled in front of him. Exchanging a quick excited glance with Polly, the doctor clapped his hands and again, for a short time, the little boy looked towards the sound and stared at the hands in front of his face.

When he had finished his careful examination Toby said carefully, 'There seem to be some small signs of progress.'

Polly nodded, unable to speak for joy.

'It's no guarantee that your son will ever become normal again,' he quickly warned.

'I know,' she managed. 'I do know that. But at least it's something, isn't it?' She hesitated then asked, 'Is Dr Browning-Baker – does he try to . . . annoy you? Because of Billy.' She couldn't think how to phrase it more tactfully.

'Does he try to pay me back for helping you, do you mean?' She nodded.

'Not exactly. The thing is I'm related to,' Toby hesitated and finished lamely, 'a few important people.' He didn't like telling others he was related to the Earl of Berston, especially people like Polly, because it put even more distance between them. 'Browning-Baker is such a snob he doesn't want to offend them and that helps protect me from the worst of his spite.' Eyes narrowed, he studied her, watched her smooth her apron unnecessarily with her work-roughened hands. 'Is the man still troubling you?'

She shrugged. 'A little.'

He felt anger run through him as she explained. It was just like Browning-Baker to attack those weaker than himself. 'If it continues, let me know, will you?'

But as Polly watched him drive away, she knew she wouldn't ask his help against Browning-Baker, not unless she was absolutely desperate. She had already put him at risk the day she'd taken her son from St Jude's. It would not be fair to ask more of him.

She went back inside to play with her son and tell him what a clever boy he was, then sang a few children's songs, moving his arms about in time to her singing.

After a while he fell asleep and she got on with her mending, but remained thoughtful. How long was it going to take for Billy to recover, and would her money last?

During the next month Polly watched her son begin to notice more of the world around him. There were tears of joy in her eyes when he made small noises, though not proper words yet, and she laughed out loud one glorious day when he moved his arms of his own accord as she began to sing. These might have been tiny signs of progress to outsiders, but to her they were beacons of hope for the future.

Dr Browning-Baker had been wrong and so had the nuns, though at least *they* had been trying to be kind.

But the month had its bleak spots and irritations, too. A sanitary inspector turned up one day to examine her drains, because of 'complaints about smells'. Not looking her in the eye, he said they must all be cleared out properly. It would have cost her ten shillings for the job if Percy hadn't heard about it and sent a man from Cardwell's, the builder's he ran, to do it free.

'Why me?' Polly asked the inspector when he returned for a second time. 'This house is no dirtier than the others in Bobbin

Lane, and if there are smells — which no one round here has noticed or complained about, because I've asked them — why have you picked only on me?'

He stared at her unhappily, moving his shoulders uneasily. 'I — um — can't answer that love. You've made a powerful enemy, it seems.' Then he switched back to the matter in hand, as if afraid he'd said too much. 'Whoever you got in did a good job and you won't have any more trouble with my department, I promise you.'

The following week the rodent inspector came to check out her house after more 'complaints', but could find no sign of mouse or rat droppings so gave her a warning to keep her yard clear and turned to leave.

She felt almost on fire with anger as she saw him to the door. 'You can just tell Dr Browning-Baker that my house is perfectly clean — always has been and always will be.'

'I work for Overdale Council, not the doctor,' he said, but he flushed as he said it and hurried off down the street without looking back.

Mrs Laksby came round regularly and each time made an inspection of the whole house. 'I'm sorry, love,' she would say, 'but it's as much as my job is worth to miss doing this. I know how clean you are, but I have to fill in a form each time to say I've made an inspection and then sign it in the presence of my supervisor.'

The following week Miss Withers returned.

When Polly opened the door and realised who it was, she glared at her visitor. She had had enough of this harassment, more than enough. 'What do you want now?'

'May I come in, Mrs Scordale?'

Polly flung open the door. 'Oh, feel free! Shall we check upstairs first or downstairs? I haven't dusted for at least an hour, mind.' She did not offer her visitor a seat.

'Your son — um — he looks well.' Miss Withers stood biting her lip, seeming uncertain how to start.

Polly had no intention of exchanging small talk. 'Look, I've got some washing soaking so you do whatever you need to then I can get on with my work.' There was always some washing soaking for Billy, who had no control over his bladder yet.

Miss Withers clasped her hands and took a deep breath. 'The Council has a programme to send children in special need to the seaside for a few weeks' holiday. Your son has been included on it. They'll be leaving next week and coming back in a few weeks – we're not sure how long exactly.'

'No, thank you.'

Miss Withers bit her lip, hesitated, then said, 'It might be wise to agree to this.'

'Why is Dr Browning-Baker doing this?' Polly asked. 'You all know that I look after my son properly. I have no need of help and I'm not going to send him away.'

Miss Withers swallowed hard. 'It – um – might not be your choice. Other parents refuse and the Council sometimes asks a magistrate to make a ruling so the child may be given the opportunity of a healthy holiday. Dr Browning-Baker has already said that if you don't agree, he'll arrange for this – out of concern for the child, of course.'

Polly stared at her and felt her heart begin to thump in her chest with sudden fear. 'You mean, you're going to let that man do this to me? And you call yourself a Child Welfare Officer?'

Miss Withers' whole body was hunched and tense. 'I don't have any choice, Mrs Scordale. My boss is a friend of his and he – my boss, that is – won't take my word against a doctor's about – about how you're caring for your son.' She hesitated again, then said in a low, hurried voice, 'There is one way you can get round this . . .' Her voice trailed away.

'How?'

'You can take him away for a seaside holiday yourself. Then they won't be able to use that as an excuse for taking you before the magistrate.'

Polly stared at her in bafflement, unable to believe what she was hearing. 'Why should I do that? We're settled her. I have everything set up to look after him. How could I care for him properly in a lodging house?'

'I realise that, but there's nothing I can do. They'll just – send him away. And I shouldn't even be telling you this.'

'Where would they send him to, anyway?'

Miss Withers moved uneasily from one foot to the other. 'It's a convalescent home near Blackpool and it has a special ward for children who can't move about. Children like Billy. They lay them outside on a verandah every day to get the benefit of the sea air. He'd be properly looked after, I promise you.'

'But he's just starting to move. He can wave his hands and arms now.' A dreadful thought suddenly struck Polly. 'If they stop doing the exercises with him, he might not start moving again.'

'I'm sorry. You won't say I told you about taking him away yourself?'

Polly pulled herself together. 'I'm grateful. And of course I won't say anything.'

After her visitor had gone, she sat down by Billy and hugged him fiercely, cuddling his warm little body to hers. 'I won't let them take you away from me, love, even for a so-called holiday.' She had not realised that anyone could be as spiteful as Dr Browning-Baker, could not understand why he was persisting in this when he had so many patients to deal with who genuinely need his help.

She remembered the old lady who had intervened on her behalf saying, 'My Paul got tetchy as he grew older, and spiteful with it. All the Bakers do.' Maybe that was it. Some people did go funny as they got older. Her own mother certainly had.

But how was she to prevent them from taking Billy away from her? And whatever she did, she'd have to do it quickly.

Richard stared at Miss Leyton in shock. 'You can't mean that!'

'I'm afraid I do, Mr Mercer. I pride myself on my moral

standards and I really cannot work in a household where such coarse language is used and where the mistress of the house is *no better than she ought to be.*'

'You can't possibly know anything about my wife's behaviour. You've just been listening to gossip.'

She folded her arms and gave him a chilling glance. 'I had already intended to give notice, but today I overheard a telephone conversation conducted by your wife — and I did not listen willingly, I assure you. Sounds carry up the stairs from the living room, as you must know.'

He could feel himself flushing. 'Yes, I have noticed that. It's — unfortunate.'

'It's more than unfortunate, Mr Mercer. What I heard today shocked and disgusted me. I'm not staying here another minute! I pity that poor child, brought up in such an atmosphere, I really do. You don't see the half of it because you're away quite often but that friend of your wife's comes round, then the two of them go out driving in cars with rackety young men. And Mrs Mercer,' the governess lowered her voice but it still throbbed with outrage, '*drinks!*' She shuddered theatrically. 'Gin, and who knows what else?'

He could not defend his wife. Florence's behaviour seemed to be getting worse by the day lately. 'I'm sorry you feel like that.'

The governess folded her arms. 'I'm sorry I've been so misled about the moral standards in this household. I was told it was a gentleman's residence.'

Richard was beginning to grow angry. 'Aren't you exaggerating somewhat? You're surely not accusing *me* of immoral behaviour?' Hell, he'd been living like a monk for the last two years!

'I can't say what you do while you're away, but I can see that you and Mrs Mercer live *separate lives* even when you're at home. It's not what I'm used to, nor do I intend to grow used to it.'

'You owe me a month's notice, Miss Leyton.'

'I'm leaving tomorrow and if you try to stop me, I'll tell the world why. *"He that toucheth pitch shall be defiled therewith"*.'

He was feeling angry with her now. 'I hope you won't be asking for references from me, then, because I should feel obliged to say that you had abandoned your responsibilities on a whim.'

She folded her arms, implacable in her righteousness. 'I'm leaving for reasons of morality. I have no reason to be ashamed of that. And I have plenty of excellent references from people I respect, thank you very much.'

He closed his eyes, then opened them to ask wearily, 'You'll keep an eye on Connie for the rest of the day, at least?'

She inclined her head in assent, but her mouth was screwed up as if she'd just drunk a cupful of vinegar.

When she had gone upstairs, Richard sat down behind his desk and rested his forehead on one hand. What the hell was he going to do now? A small sound made him look up to find Florence leaning against the doorpost.

'Good riddance to the old sourface!' She put the cigarette holder to her lips, smiling as she inhaled deeply and began to blow smoke rings.

'Were you aware of Miss Leyton's feelings?' he asked abruptly.

'She makes no secret of her disapproval of me. I didn't realise the telephone can be heard all over the house, though.'

'Just in the stairwell, actually.'

Florences eyes narrowed and she stared at him. 'Does that mean you've been listening in, too?'

'I have caught snatches of conversation on my way upstairs from time to time, but I hope you'll acquit me of deliberately eavesdropping.'

She tossed her head, the gleaming black hair whipping back and then falling against her cheeks again. 'Oh, yes, you're far too goody-goody to do that. Anyway, what is there to overhear?'

'Your conversations with my cousin, primarily.'

There was a very long pause before she spoke again, then

she said slowly, 'I haven't been speaking to Georgie.'

'Not lately, no. Anyway, your next quarter's money is due next week. I'm prepared to pay it early if you want to leave tomorrow.'

Her voice took on a pleading tone. 'If you'd give me half of your uncle's money, you and I could divorce and you could find yourself a goody-goody wife to look after Connie.'

'And if you had the money, George would marry you, I suppose?'

She shrugged, worried that she had revealed too much. 'Maybe.'

'Uncle James particularly asked me not to give any money to George. And I won't.'

Florence swung round and left him, her shoes clattering on the stairs and the door to her bedroom slamming hard.

Still frowning Richard got out his address book, lifted the receiver from its stand and dialled the same number he'd used before. 'I wish to place an advertisement . . .' From there he went on to ring various domestic staffing agencies, but it seemed there was still a dearth of maids willing to devote themselves to a young invalid and the agencies were reluctant to deal again with a man whom several maids had left at short notice.

George watched the cards fall every way but towards him. Steadily, he pushed some more chips forward and tried to bluff his way through another poor hand. Behind him stood Amelia, her hands on his shoulders, fingers gripping more tightly each time the cards were dealt. He could feel her excitement, see the age spots on her right hand if he turned his head a little, smell her cloying perfume.

He glanced up at her and forced a smile. 'Blow some luck my way!' he whispered.

She blew a kiss at him.

When he had used up the last of his chips, he sat motionless, his whole body rigid with despair and anger. He didn't know which of those emotions was the stronger. Anger at what he would have to do now, probably. If Amelia was willing. If not – hell, better not think of that. She was his only hope now.

'George, darling!'

She had to repeat it twice before it sank in that she wanted his attention, then he turned round and gave her his best smile.

'Aren't you going to place another bet?' she asked with a pouting look that was not becoming to a fleshy older woman.

'Nothing left to bet with, I'm afraid. And I don't intend to get into debt.' He pushed his chair back suddenly. 'Let's go and dance instead, eh?'

'But—'

He cut her words off short by tugging her arm under his and pulling her towards the dance floor. 'Unlucky at cards, lucky in . . .' He let the words trail away suggestively, watching the eagerness flare in her eyes.

Much later, when they had found a discreet hotel and made love, he lay with her head on his shoulder and said quietly, 'I'm going to have to find a job, I think. Won't be able to squire you around so often from now on.'

His words were greeted by silence.

'There aren't many jobs going these days,' Amelia said at last. 'Even for a man like you.' She splayed her fingers across his chest in a possessive gesture. 'Maybe . . .'

When she paused, he knew she wanted him to ask what she meant, but he wasn't going to. It was one thing to be a blasted lapdog to women like this, but quite another to be a tame lapdog.

In the end she gave in, as she always did, and finished her sentence. 'Maybe *I* can help you instead.'

'Amelia, that's very kind, but I can't—'

She interrupted eagerly. 'Listen to what I'm proposing first. I've been invited to the South of France. A house party. I can get you an invitation, too.'

'I don't even have the money for a taxi home, let alone the fare to France.' He could hear the harsh edge to his voice and tried to soften it. 'Look, Amelia, you're a darling, but—'

'I don't want to lose you, George, and – and I have plenty of money.' She leaned on one elbow and looked at him with that ugly, avid expression on her face. '*Do* say you'll come! Frank can't and I wasn't looking forward to going on my own. My friends would understand our – arrangement. We'd have a wonderful summer together! And if you needed any money, well, it'd be there for you.'

He forced a wry smile to his lips. 'I've been available whenever you've needed me without that. You don't have to pay me to—'

'George,' her voice was suddenly sharper, a warning tone behind it, 'don't look a gift horse in the mouth. There's no need for silly pride between us.'

He steeled himself to put his hands into the golden shackles. 'Of course I'll come, my darling. And – thank you.'

He knew that she would have him dancing attendance on her all day long while they were away, would be flaunting him like a trophy in front of her friends. He hated her for it already, but it was much better than selling shoelaces on a street corner. He had to keep that thought very firmly in mind from now on – until he could work out another solution.

CHAPTER ELEVEN

July 1920

All the Kershaws gathered at Percy's house that evening for a powwow about Polly's new problem. 'So I need to get away from Overdale because that man will keep trying to take Billy away from me for as long as I can stay here, I can see that now.' She looked round despondently. 'Surely if I take Billy to the seaside myself, they won't be able to say I'm depriving him of anything this time? And then after that I'll just – go somewhere else. Only how can I go to the seaside? I can't use ordinary lodgings.'

'Can't that doctor friend of yours help?' Percy asked.

Polly sighed and began to play with her son's hair, smoothing it back from his forehead as if it were the most important thing in the world. 'I've asked too much of Dr Herbert already. He says Dr Browning-Baker won't try to get back at him for helping me, but I don't believe him. *That horrible man* will do anything to get his own way.'

'We'll have to find you somewhere to stay at the seaside, then,' Lizzie declared.

Everyone immediately offered an opinion on where exactly she should take Billy.

Not until the hubbub had died down again did Peter say quietly, 'It won't be enough.'

'What do you mean?' Polly asked.

'I mean, Browning-Baker will say you're putting Billy in

danger by looking after him on your own. You'll *have* to bring your own doctor into this, love. And I'm sure Toby won't mind. He's a good chap.'

Polly stared at him unhappily, but realised he was right. 'I suppose so. I'll ring Dr Herbert up tomorrow, then, if you don't mind me coming round to use your phone, Peter and Lizzie?'

'Of course we don't mind,' Peter said at once. 'And in the meantime, I'll ring up my friend Richard as well. He was in my regiment and lives at Stenton-on-Sea. He may know of some lodgings there.' He saw from Polly's face that she didn't recognise the place name. 'It's a small village near Fleetwood. You might be better going to a place like that than somewhere big and busy like Blackpool.'

'I don't like you going away on your own, though,' Lizzie worried.

'I don't want to go,' Polly confessed. 'I'm going to miss you all dreadfully. But I'll do anything to prevent them from taking Billy away from me. Anything at all.'

With Lizzie beside her, she rang Dr Herbert's rooms next day and explained her dilemma to his kindly secretary because he was out.

'He'll want to ring you back,' the secretary assured her.

'I don't have a phone, but I'm ringing from my sister's and you can leave a message for me there.'

That afternoon Lizzie came round to see her. 'Your doctor rang up,' she said before Polly had even closed the door behind her. 'He's coming over to see you tomorrow, first thing in the morning.'

'That means he'll have had to change all his appointments,' Polly fretted. 'Oh, dear! I'm causing him so much trouble.'

'He wanted to help. He was very angry when I explained what had been happening lately. You should have told him about the other things.'

Polly shook her head blindly. 'I kept thinking it'd stop once they'd run out of excuses to get at me.'

Lizzie thrust a handkerchief at her. 'Use that and cheer up, you dope. We'll find a way round this.'

'I hope so.'

'Is Billy asleep?' Lizzie looked round.

'Yes. He sleeps quite a lot, even in the daytime.'

'It's very quiet for you in the evenings. I wish I could get round to see you more often, but we don't close till eight, and by the time we've cleared up . . .'

Polly shrugged. 'It was quiet at Outshaw, too. I've joined the library and started reading.' That was something which had never interested her before. Even so, the hours dragged sometimes.

'Eh, love. You must be really desperate if you've started reading!' When Polly didn't even smile at that, Lizzie gave her another hug, then held her at arm's length, studying her face. 'Maybe a change of scene will do *you* good as well. You've had a hard time these past few months.'

'I don't matter. I just want to help Billy get better and stay near you all.'

'You do matter. We all care about you.'

After her sister had left, the house was so quiet that Polly was even glad when the man across the road came home drunk and had a row with his wife. But although she had felt better in her sister's bracing company, as the evening passed she could not help wondering what Dr Browning-Baker would try next. Mrs Laksby was right. She would have to move away from Overdale permanently if this went on, for Billy's sake – only that would mean leaving her family as well. It simply wasn't fair!

Dr Herbert turned up just before nine the next day and Polly, who had been watching for him, opened the door before he even had time to knock. 'I'm so sorry to trouble you again,' she said before he'd stepped across the threshold.

'Mrs Scordale, I'm only upset that you didn't contact me sooner. Billy is my patient and I care very much about his welfare.'

But what she saw on his face seemed more than concern for Billy. Was that fondness in his gaze? Surely not? Toby Herbert was about thirty-five, rather plump with thinning, gingerish hair, grey-green eyes and a face that radiated kindness – only she wasn't interested in men, and anyway she'd never liked that colour of hair which reminded her of Lizzie's first husband's. Besides, Polly had more than enough on her plate looking after her son. She didn't want or need another husband.

She realised he was waiting for her to speak and tried to keep her mind on the present problem. 'I'm a bit worried about finding somewhere suitable to live. Ordinary lodgings won't do so I think I'll have to rent a house. And – can they come after me and keep checking up if I move away?'

Toby frowned. 'I don't know, but I'll find out. In the meantime, you should start thinking what you'll need to take with you. We'll find you and Billy somewhere suitable to live, don't worry. I'll go and see the child welfare people myself after my visit to the hospital to explain that you are already planning to take Billy away and that I'm supervising the arrangements.'

But even as he spoke, there was a knock on the door, a brisk sort of knock, not a neighbour's tap. Polly was beginning to dread that sort of knock and had to force herself to open the door.

'Good morning, Mrs Scordale. May I come in?' Mr Maslam didn't wait to be asked, just moved confidently past her, stopping in surprise when he saw the doctor, then looking from one to the other and frowning.

The doctor nodded in greeting, but said nothing.

Mr Maslam hesitated, then held out an envelope. 'This details the arrangements for Billy's stay at the seaside, Mrs Scordale.'

Polly couldn't move for the fear that was shivering through her.

Toby looked sideways at her and stepped into the breach. 'May I see this, Mrs Scordale?'

She nodded, afraid her voice would wobble if she tried to speak. She didn't even want to touch the thing.

Toby read the official letter quickly, then shook his head. 'Not suitable, I'm afraid.'

Mr Maslam gave him a smug smile. 'The Child Welfare Department thinks otherwise.'

'Do they indeed? Or is this more of Browning-Baker's interference?'

'Billy is resident in our area. Dr Browning-Baker acts in a consultative capacity to my department. It's very generous of such a busy man to give so much of his time and we value his opinion highly.'

'Well, you can tell him that I'm making my own arrangements for Billy to stay at the seaside. That's why I came here today – fortunately for Mrs Scordale. Do you people enjoy bullying widows?'

Mr Maslam flushed and drew himself up. 'Our concern is for the child, not the mother. We have a *duty* to supervise his welfare.'

Toby glared at him. 'Well, *my* concern is for them both, since she is the one who cares for him – and does it well, too. Indeed, where would he be without her?'

'In the care of professionally trained nurses. And personally I find it surprising that you have so much time free to spend with one patient.' Mr Maslam's eyes flickered towards Polly then back towards Dr Herbert. 'Or perhaps you have other interests here?'

Toby took a hasty step forward, his face flushed with anger. 'If you even hint at that again, you will receive a letter from my lawyer. I would do the same for any patient and their family.'

'I – um – meant no offence,' Maslam said hastily, then turned back to Polly. 'You will need to have the child ready next Monday morning at—'

Dr Herbert stepped forward. 'She'll do no such thing. And I think it's time you left now.'

Maslam fell back a step, but his expression was smugly triumphant. 'If you don't comply with these instructions, Mrs

Scordale, we shall have to bring this matter before the magistrate.'
He glared at Toby. 'And since a local doctor sees so much more
of the whole picture than one who comes over occasionally from
Manchester, I don't think we'll have any trouble proving our case.'
He fixed Polly with a glacial stare as he repeated, 'Monday next!
The ambulance will come to the door for your son at ten o'clock.'
Then he left, his footsteps echoing down the street.

Not until they had faded in the distance did Polly plump
down in the nearest chair and burst into tears. 'It's no use. That
man's got them all on his side.'

'We'll work something out.' But Toby was also beginning to
worry. Who was the magistrate here anyway? Another of
Browning-Baker's friends? He'd have to find out. If all the
officials colluded, it would be very hard to win against their
combined powers.

When he'd gone Polly sat and thought about it. She didn't
see what Dr Herbert could do. She only knew one thing: she
wasn't going to have Billy ready next Monday. In fact, she didn't
intend to be here even. She would go and stay with Eva for a few
days. She didn't need to ask if her sister would help her. She knew
she could rely on her family doing everything in their power for
her and Billy. Only – would it be enough? Would that horrible
man even pursue her to Rochdale?

As soon as Richard paid Florence her next quarter's allowance,
she packed her bags and left, not caring that he had not yet found
someone to look after Connie. He did not ask her to stay and
help. What was the point? She was not good with their daughter,
either spoiling her or ignoring her. Doris said she would keep an
eye on Connie, and Mrs Shavely said the child could sit in the
kitchen if she got lonely.

Richard drove his wife to the station in silence, helped her on
to the train with her luggage and left with a curt nod, not even
waiting for the train to depart.

Only when he got home did he realise he had omitted to find out where Florence was going. She hadn't looked quite as eager or happy this time, though, and he was pretty sure it wasn't to George. If it had been he'd have set the detective on to her.

To take his mind off all that, he spent the morning with Connie, persuading her to go for a gentle walk along the short street to the sea front with him.

'Where's Mother gone?' she asked, as they sat in a shelter, staring at the beach.

'London.' It seemed as good a guess as any.

'Other mothers don't go away so much.'

'No. But yours has a lot of friends and she likes to visit them.'

'That's because Mother doesn't like living in Stenton. She's always saying how horrible it is here. Couldn't we move somewhere she does like, then she wouldn't go away so much?'

He saw the disappointment on her face and decided to prepare her gently for the worst. 'She'd still want to go and see her friends, I'm afraid. It's nothing to do with you – she doesn't like living with me.'

'*You* won't ever leave me, will you?' Connie begged suddenly. 'Promise me, Daddy!'

'Only for a day or two.'

She nodded. 'To see your poor injured soldiers.'

For some reason she seemed to accept his little trips quite easily. It was as if, chronically unwell herself, she felt sympathy for other invalids.

'Tell me how your soldiers are going, Daddy.'

So he told her again about the men who couldn't see and those who'd lost limbs – though he spared her the worst details of their injuries.

'And when you find a house for them here in Stenton, I'm going to go with you to see them, aren't I?' she finished, as she always did.

'Of course you are. They'll love to see you. It'll cheer them up.'

When they got back home the agency had called. Richard rang them back and to his relief, they had found him a woman to care for Connie.

'Do you wish to interview her?'

'Has she got good references?'

'Excellent references.'

'Qualifications?'

'No. She's a war widow who needs to earn a living. She nursed her husband until he died of his wounds, and has gone on to look after others in similar situations.'

'Has she nursed any children?'

'No. But she says she's very fond of them.'

He chewed his lip, wondering what to do, then took a quick decision. 'Could you please ask her if she'd come on a month's trial? I'll reimburse all her expenses.' He couldn't afford to be picky at the moment.

When they phoned back later to say Mrs Jean Roulson would be happy to come to Stenton the following day, Richard sighed in relief.

The next day he went to meet her at the station, but his heart sank at the mere sight of her. She was wearing too much make-up and her clothes were a cheap imitation of the fashionable styles his wife wore, rather than the sensible ones maids and nurses usually chose. And not only were her hemlines too short, she seemed to enjoy showing a lot of leg as she got into the car.

As he drove her home to meet his daughter, he began to worry about the way she was eyeing him.

'I thought *Mrs* Mercer would be coming to meet me,' said Mrs Roulson. 'It's usually the wife who hires the nurse.'

'My wife is away at the moment.'

'Oh, yes? Goes away a lot, does she?'

'Occasionally.'

'Must make it very hard for you – sir.' Her eyes lingered on him in an assessing way.

'Not once we find someone suitable to look after our daughter. You – um – realise that this is just a month's trial on either side?'

'Of course. But I'm sure you'll be satisfied with my work. I've never had any complaints before, and I'd like a job that was more – permanent.'

He wished he was even half sure about her. It had been stupid to take her on without an interview, but he still had so much to do to set up the nursing home – and a girl needed a woman's company. Damn Florence!

CHAPTER TWELVE

July–August 1920

When Dr Herbert had gone, Polly stood for a moment in the silent house then went to stare at herself in the mirror. 'Pull yourself together, Polly Scordale!' she said out loud. After making sure Billy was all right, she went upstairs for a clean handkerchief because she had wrung hers into a rag.

As she was taking one out of her top drawer, a piece of paper fluttered to the floor and she picked it up. It took her a minute to decipher the scribble. 'Oh, yes. Mrs Baker.' She smiled at the memory of the lively old woman, so unlike her nephew by marriage, then she stilled, repeating, 'Mrs Baker,' slowly and thoughtfully. Was it possible – could there be a source of help here?

Tears forgotten Polly hurried down to the kitchen, scribbled a quick note and got Billy ready for a walk. By that time she was in two minds as to whether to send the letter. Why should Mrs Baker help a near stranger? But she decided she had nothing to lose, so took a detour past the post office and popped the letter into the box, then went to sit on a park bench and watch people pass by.

From time to time she spoke to Billy or played a clapping game with him. He seemed to be watching what was going on around him today and once or twice he made a mumbling noise.

When a light rain began to fall, Polly pulled up the hood

which she had made for Billy's coat since his restless movements dislodged a cap so easily and moved on. She called round at Dearden's to buy a few groceries, registering vaguely that her hat was dripping water down her nose but not really caring. She needed to ask her sister's help to get herself and Billy across to Eva's house. It was awful to keep asking for favours and she worried about getting her family into trouble with the law, but she simply could not get Billy to Rochdale on the bus.

'I don't think you should do this, Polly,' Peter said when she explained the latest developments to them in the back room.

'What do you mean?' Lizzie demanded. 'She can't just sit and let them take Billy away from her. I certainly wouldn't.'

'Yes, but if we go against the law it could be very serious for all of us.'

Polly stared at him in dismay because this was her own fear, too.

'Look,' Peter said in a gentle voice, putting his arm round her shoulders, 'Richard was going to ring me back tonight about finding lodgings in Stenton. Let's wait until then before making any definite plans, shall we? You get yourself home and change into some dry clothes. It won't help Billy if you catch your death of cold.'

Polly looked down at herself, mildly surprised by how wet her clothes were. When she went into the packing area, the girl who had been keeping an eye on Billy was playing with his fingers and he was watching her.

'He is improving,' Polly murmured.

'He certainly is. Don't you ever doubt it.' Lizzie walked her to the door, helped her push the chair out on to the path and whispered as they exchanged parting hugs, 'Peter won't refuse to help you, love, I'll make sure of that.'

'I don't want to come between you. And I don't want you to get into trouble over this.'

Lizzie got that stubborn expression on her face. 'We're not letting them take Billy away from you.'

Although it wasn't a cold day, it was raining even harder outside. Polly hurried home, rain dripping down her face and neck, shivering now. Thank goodness Billy had such a thick coat. She got him changed into dry clothes as quickly as she could, then changed herself. Then they both sat in front of the fire, with him watching the flames and her watching him.

She wasn't fooling herself about his progress. She wasn't! It was worth fighting for her son.

Remembering how noise carried up the stairwell, Richard closed the sitting-room door before he made his telephone call. 'Peter, I've had a quick look at some of the boarding houses in Stenton. None of them is at all suitable for your sister-in-law and the child, I'm afraid. And there aren't any houses to rent. This is quite a small place, you see. Sorry I can't help.'

'Oh, hell! I was hoping you could come up with something. That damned Child Welfare Officer has threatened to take her to court if she doesn't let them send her son away to the seaside. It's Browning-Baker's doing, of course, but all the officials seem to be hand in glove with him.'

'She could come here for a few days if you were desperate and—'

'Thanks, but we need some long-term accommodation for them outside Overdale to get the boy out of Browning-Baker's clutches. Nice of you to offer, but we won't trouble you.'

'Well, let me know what happens.' Richard put the phone down and went to stare out of the window. He felt sorry for Peter's sister-in-law, of course he did, be he had his own problems to sort out. When he went upstairs, he found Mrs Roulson humming along to a record on the gramophone and Connie looking bored. He'd rather his daughter was taken out for walks on fine afternoons and said so. Mrs Roulson had suggested taking her to see the latest Charlie Chaplin film at a cinema in

Blackpool, which he would do, but not on a fine day like today.

'Righty-ho.' Mrs Roulson bounced to her feet. 'Why don't you come out with us, Captain? You look a bit down in the mouth today yourself.'

'I'm afraid I have to drive into Lancaster.' He turned to his daughter. 'Will you be all right, Connie darling?'

'I suppose so.' Her voice was sulky. She seemed indifferent to her new companion, neither disliking nor liking her.

Richard cast a quick eye over the room. It was tidy and his daughter nicely turned out, but as far as he could see Mrs Roulson had no expertise whatsoever with children and hadn't initiated any activities.

He got ready to leave, sighing as he started up his car. He couldn't imagine a woman like that lasting more than a week in such a quiet place, for her talk was all of the films she'd seen and of dancing or clothes. But it was too soon to get back to the agency and far too soon to dismiss her.

Florence smiled brightly at her friend Phyllis and agreed to take a toddle into town, which meant the West End and a tour of the shops. Once there, however, Florence did not dare give in to the temptation of buying any new clothes or cosmetics because she was quite determined to make her allowance last longer this time. The mere thought of going back to Stenton made her feel sick.

'I was surprised you didn't buy the evening dress you tried on,' Phyllis commented as they sat sharing a pot of tea in a café. 'It really suited you and those chiffon overdresses are all the rage. You're slim enough to look good in a high waist.' She looked down ruefully at her own plump figure. 'I'd look like an over-stuffed bolster if I wore a dress like that.'

Florence decided on the truth. 'I shouldn't even have tried it on. I'm having to watch the pennies rather carefully, I'm afraid. Richard grows meaner as he gets older.'

'Poor you. You really ought to find someone else and get a divorce.'

'Know anyone – preferably rich?' She wasn't leaving a man with money for a man without in these troubled times. Only this morning the newspapers had been full of pictures of men queueing for the dole.

'I thought you and George Mercer had a thing going?'

'Unfortunately he's as penniless as I am, so we've agreed to go our own ways for a while.'

'Ah. The word is that he's running tame with Amelia Ferbington.'

'Yes, I know. He's – um – very fond of her.'

'And you're not just a teeny bit broken-hearted?'

Florence tried to smile, but didn't think she'd made a good job of it. 'Well, I do miss him, actually. He's really good company, if you know what I mean. I'm sorry he and I couldn't be together, but there it is. Money, money, money! From now on I'm not falling for anyone unless they're simply oozing banknotes all over the place.'

'I'll have to see if I can introduce you to someone suitable, then.'

'You do that. In the meantime, I'm really grateful that you're letting me stay with you.'

Phyllis giggled. 'Well, I was rather hoping you'd help me. Arthur can be so stuffy and I do like a spot of dancing. If the two of us go out together, he'll be perfectly happy to stay home and fall asleep over his newspaper, and once we're out you won't try to spoil my fun, will you? I'll make sure you have an escort, too, naturally. But if I were to – well, vanish for the evening, you'd not say anything?'

'You're a darling and you know you can count on me,' Florence declared at once, hand flattened against her chest in a mock vow. 'Anyone in particular you're seeing?'

Phyllis smiled. 'Yes. Someone very particular. I'll introduce you.'

'And Arthur?'

'Is showing his age since the war. But what he doesn't want, others do.'

'I know exactly what you mean.'

Early on Sunday morning, Peter and Lizzie turned up in Bobbin Lane in the delivery van to find Polly ready and waiting anxiously. Peter felt as worried as she looked about what they were doing, but Lizzie insisted on treating the whole thing as an adventure and her high spirits helped a little. In no time they had everything packed in the van and set off.

However, when they reached the end of the street, a policeman stepped into the road and held up his hand.

'What the . . .' Peter braked hard and wound his window down. 'Can I help you, Constable?'

The man looked ill at ease. 'I couldn't help noticing that you had Mrs Scordale and her son in the van with you. Could you tell me where you're going, sir, please?'

'None of your damned business!'

The constable shuffled his feet. 'Well, sir, I've been told to keep an eye on Mrs Scordale. The child welfare people are afraid she'll try to take her son away.'

'As she has every right to do. We fought for a free country, did we not?'

The man's face turned a dull red. 'Well, sir, that's as may be, but I'm told there's some question of her not caring properly for her child.' He stared through the window of the driver's side disapprovingly. 'And I must say, I think it's a bit hard on a poor little crippled lad to have him lying on the floor of the van like that. Can't be good for him, can it?'

'It's no use, Peter. Take me home again, please,' Polly said tiredly. It was one thing for her to go against authority, another to drag her brother-in-law into it.

He turned round to eye her searchingly. 'Are you sure?'

'What choice do I have?' she asked in a low voice. 'I won't drag you two into trouble with the law.'

'I'm sorry, love.' He stared the constable in the eye. 'I hope you're proud of yourself, harassing a widow like this.'

'I can't disobey orders, sir. It's as much as my job's worth. If you like, I won't mention this, but that's as far as I dare go.'

Back at the house they all sat in the van for a moment, then Peter shook his head. 'I've never heard of anything like this. It's persecution. That man is a megalomaniac. Who does he think he is, interfering in your life? Corrupting officials.'

Polly didn't have the energy to argue. 'If you'll help me carry Billy inside . . .'

'Are you going to let them take him tomorrow?' Lizzie asked in a hushed voice as she helped move Billy.

'Not if I can help it. They'll have to break the door down to get him.'

'I'll come round and help you,' Lizzie offered at once.

'No! You're to stay out of it. You two have a living to make and who knows what they'll do to your shop if you get on the wrong side of them? There are all sorts of regulations they can use to make your life miserable.' As Polly herself had found out.

'Do you have a lawyer?' Peter asked. 'If not, you should get one.'

'I could see the lawyer who drew up Eddie's will, I suppose.'

'Promise you'll do that.'

'All right.' But what did she know about lawyers? And how much would that cost? Her money was being used up faster than she had expected. It seemed like a fortune when she first got the insurance payment, but it would only last a year or two, however careful she was, and then what would she do?

When the others had gone, Polly sat beside her sleeping son for a while then roused herself to check the locks on her doors. The back door lock was wobbly so she sent the lad from next door round to Percy's with a note, asking him if someone could fix it today as the matter was urgent. She also asked the lad to check whether there was still a policeman stationed at the end of Bobbin Lane and he said there was.

Percy came round to help her himself, having already received a visit from an indignant Lizzie to share the bad news. He couldn't think what else to do, apart from making all her locks more secure, because like the Deardens he had a business to run and could not afford to fall foul of the law. His wife Emma owned a quarter share in Cardwell's and he was managing it till the son of the former owner, who had been killed in the war, was old enough to work there.

When her brother had left, Polly got Billy ready for bed, but didn't go upstairs herself until quite late. Even then she couldn't sleep and the night seemed very long. She lay staring into the darkness, feeling helpless, but determined to fight until the last. They'd have to smash their way into her house and tear her son from her arms if they wanted to take him away from her.

Beyond that she couldn't seem to think. She tried to pray, but couldn't think why a God who had let all this happen would interest himself in her now.

She didn't know whether she wanted morning to arrive or not, but eventually it started to get light. I can only do my best, she thought. If they took Billy away from her, she didn't know how she would bear it.

In the South of France that night George Mercer stood motionless outside the opulent villa in which he was staying, waiting for his eyes to adjust to the darkness. Then he made his way slowly along the road, keeping to the shadows as much as possible. He'd already decided which house would be his first target, a place where the owners seemed very careless about locking doors or windows and the gates were never closed.

Luck was with him. It had been a really hot day and at the back of the house someone had left a pair of French windows wide open to let in the cooler night air. He crept quietly along the edge of the drive, waited for a few moments to be sure no one was around, then simply walked into the house, grinning at how easy it was. He'd visited this place a few days previously with Amelia and had decided that Mavis Heatherby was a fool – though a rich one – and that fools like her were usually the easiest to part from their money. Of course it helped that Mavis was slightly deaf and her maids quite elderly. 'I always bring my own staff,' she had declared to Amelia. 'I don't trust these locals – except for the gardener, of course.'

George moved noiselessly through the house, enjoying that specially 'alive' feeling he always experienced when facing danger.

In the little sitting room at the rear he found a desk. Locked. There must be something valuable inside it if that silly woman had bothered to lock it. Did she really think a flimsy precaution like that would keep anyone out? It didn't take him long to force the catch, though he could not help making a bit of noise. He stood still, listening, ready to run for it, but there was no sound of anyone getting out of bed.

He turned back to the desk and began to search. There was a small cash box at the back of one drawer, but nothing else of value.

He stared at the box, then grinned and took a gamble. Swinging it carelessly in one hand, he strolled out.

A short distance down the road, he paused under a tree to jemmy it open and chuckled quietly. It was crammed full of English banknotes. Dear Mavis was even more of a fool than he had thought. She ought at least to have hidden this under her bed. He riffled through the notes, pursing his lips in a soundless whistle when he realised how much money there was.

Within the hour he had thrown the box into the sea and was lying in his own bed, smiling up at the ceiling, too full of high spirits to sleep. The money was safely stored in the false bottom to the shabby suitcase he'd used during the last year of the war to store bits and pieces he'd picked up at the front. Well, dead men didn't need their money, did they? Or their signet rings. It'd been a bit risky looting the dead, but the only time he'd been discovered had been by a ranker intent on the same quest. They'd stopped to glance furtively at one another, then moved on without a word.

It was all right for those with money or those who didn't mind doing without. Any fool could live an honourable and upright life in poverty, but George was no fool and he wanted every penny he could lay his hands on.

Mid-morning he heard the outcry about the villa being robbed and went to join in the shocked comments and speculations.

He waited a full week before making another foray – this time taking an hour's cycle ride in the opposite direction before breaking into a house. It was kind of his host to leave bicycles lying around beneath a tin shelter for the use of guests. Very kind indeed. No one would even notice that one had been used during the night.

He gained rather less from this outing – well, you couldn't expect to be lucky every time, could you? – but he did find a little cash and a few rather nice pieces of jewellery which he would take back to England with him and dispose of at his leisure.

When he had a decent stock of valuables Amelia could whistle for his services. She was growing increasingly possessive and demanding, publicly embarrassing him sometimes. Who did she think she was, the fat old toad?

Not until it grew fully light did Polly get up. Anxiety was weighing like lead on her stomach even before she got out of bed, but she performed her usual morning tasks with grim determination that they should not find one speck of dust in *her* house. Then she went and got Billy up.

As she was washing him he stared at her, opened and shut his mouth a few times, then said, 'Ma-ma-ma-ma!' quite clearly.

She stared at him in delight before burying her face in his chest, blowing air out softly to tickle him and saying his name over and over. At that he laughed, and even when he'd stopped laughing and making noises, his face seemed less empty, it really did.

That sign of progress carried Polly through the rest of her early-morning tasks and she even managed to play a few games with him, though she kept listening, sure someone would come banging at her door before long.

As it grew near ten o'clock, however, the hour specified for her son to be picked up, she found herself unable to play, unable to do anything constructive. Locking the house up, she sat and waited, sitting beside Billy on the edge of the sofa because it helped to touch him.

The knock did not come until twenty-past ten.

She went to the window, looking out at Mr Maslam. 'What do you want?'

He turned to stare at her. 'You know what I want. Open the door, please, Mrs Scordale.'

'No. You're not taking my son away from me.'

'You aren't going to be silly about this, are you?'

'I don't think it's silly to want to look after my son myself.'

She watched him rattle the door, as if testing the lock, but she had a solid bolt on it now. When he realised he could not just push it open, he beat on it with a clenched fist and shouted, 'I demand that you open this door at once. Do you hear?'

'No. I'm not giving up my son.'

By this time Meg Evans from next door had come out and was watching what was going on. She knew what they were trying to do because Polly had told her closest neighbours.

Her voice shrill, Meg yelled, 'You leave her alone, you great bully. She's a good mother, Polly Scordale is.'

Mrs Thomas from across the way came out next, eyes popping. She slopped across the street in her house slippers and a dirty apron, asking what was up.

'They're trying to take her lad away from her,' Meg explained loudly.

Mrs Thomas gaped at the officials then asked, 'Whatever for? You couldn't find a child as is better looked after anywhere.'

Mr Maslam ignored the two women and thumped on the door again. More neighbours came out and gathered in a circle around him, adding their voices to the chorus of complaints.

Miss Withers came hurrying along the street and whispered something to Mr Maslam. He scowled at the house, but nodded reluctant agreement and stepped backwards.

'You there! Mrs Scordale!' he shouted.

Polly moved closer to the window again. 'Yes?'

'This is your last chance. If you don't open that door, you may expect a legal summons later today, so if you have any sense—'

Someone from the back of the crowd threw a piece of coal at him, knocking his hat off, then a piece of horse dung followed it, hitting him squarely in the neck. A tomato splattered on the pavement beside Miss Withers. With a muffled squeak, she turned and ran towards the ambulance that had once carried injured soldiers and now carried crippled children, scrambling inside with more haste than dignity.

Mr Maslam followed her more slowly, but speeded up as another piece of dung found its mark between his shoulder blades, leaving a smelly wet patch on his jacket.

He turned to shake his fists at the crowd and was greeted by a chorus of jeers and a yell of, 'Here's something to help your rhubarb grow!' He ducked inside the ambulance just in time to avoid another malodorous missile.

When the vehicle had driven away, Meg came to hammer on the door. 'It's safe now, love.'

Polly opened it cautiously.

'They've gone and we'll set the kids to watch out for them coming back.' Her expression was full of sympathy. 'Look, if you want any shopping doing, you just let me know over the back fence and I'll get it when I go out for mine. Interfering devils! They want to mind their own business, that lot from the Town Hall do.' She frowned. 'They don't usually take children with parents as can look after them, though. Why do they want your Billy so particular?'

So Polly invited her inside, made a cup of tea and explained exactly what was happening.

'Well, I never!' Meg was both scandalised and delighted to be in the know. 'The mean old sod!'

Polly watched her go, knowing the news would spread down Bobbin Lane and the surrounding streets. It was nice to have the support of your neighbours, but there was not really much they could do to help. The problem had only been postponed.

Later that day a policeman knocked on her door. Again she did not open it, but went to the window and called, 'Yes. What do you want?'

'Open the door, please, love.'

Again the other doors in the street opened and people poured out, coming to stand in a circle around the policeman, something that clearly made him uneasy.

'What're you doing trying to take her lad away from her, Matt Waterton?' one neighbour demanded.

'I'm just following orders, Mrs D. And I'm not here to take her child. I'm just here to deliver this.' He waved an envelope.

Meg plucked it out of his hand. 'What is it?'

'A summons.'

'You promise you'll not try to take her son, because if you do you'll have all of us to reckon with?'

'I promise.' He eased his collar with one fingertip, then pulled out a pale blue handkerchief and mopped his forehead.

'You can open up, love,' Meg yelled. 'He's not come for your Billy.'

So Polly opened up, accepted the summons and took it inside to open, accompanied by her neighbour. Only she couldn't open it, just sat staring at it.

'You want me to do the honours?' Meg offered.

'Please.' Her neighbour was excited by the morning's events, but Polly felt weighed down by them.

'Matt said it was a summons to appear at the magistrates' court – yes, see, it says here – Wednesday morning at eleven o'clock. Special hearing about . . .' she frowned at the words, mouthing the syllables to herself '. . . about your com-pet . . . competence to care for your child. The rotten sods! What do they know about it? They haven't asked me how you look after him and I live right next to you. Who could tell them that better than me? Anyone who knows you could. Ah, love, don't take on!' Meg patted the shaking shoulder next to her, muttering, 'We'll find a way. We'll all help you.'

Polly bit on her forefinger, trying not to weep. She cried too easily, she knew, and it wouldn't help. 'I'll need to ring Billy's doctor and let him know. And I ought to speak to my lawyer. Only I'm frightened to take Billy out of the house in case they try to take him off me.'

Meg drew herself up, chins wobbling, arms crossed beneath her overflowing breasts. 'You get off about your business, love. Me an' Ada Thomas from across the road will look after your lad. Just let anyone try to take him away from us. They won't know what's hit them. I'll nip across and tell her now. Won't be a mo'. Hang on!'

'But you've got your own work to do.'

Meg turned at the door to grin. 'Not today we haven't. Besides, if they take your Billy away, whose child will they take next, eh?'

So Polly made her way into town to the office of the lawyer who had drawn up Eddie's will.

But Mr Finch got a sour expression on his face when she explained what was happening and she guessed he must be another friend of Dr Browning-Baker's. 'I can see you don't believe me,' she said quietly, standing up even as she spoke, 'so I won't trouble you any further.'

He didn't say a word to stop her leaving.

Polly walked round the corner and leaned against the wall, legs shaking. She ought to have a lawyer, but how did you find one who didn't know the town's leading medical man?

Seeing that people were eyeing her, she pulled herself together and went along to Dearden's to phone Dr Herbert's rooms and leave a message for him. And, of course, Lizzie's sympathy made her want to burst into tears again so she had to leave abruptly and walk home at top speed, breathing in deeply and telling herself to keep calm.

After that the only thing she could do was look after her son and wait for Wednesday morning. And she was torn even about that. She wanted the hearing to come quickly because she hated living in suspense – but she didn't want it to come because she was terrified they would take Billy away from her. She hadn't slept well for several nights, and Monday night was no different.

She felt more alone with her troubles than she ever had in her life before, in spite of the support of her family and neighbours. Sooner or later they left her to go to their own homes and then the silence in her little house would press down on her.

The two evenings she spent alone staring into the fire seemed to last an eternity. What would she be doing on Wednesday evening? Would she be totally alone? Would they have taken Billy?

CHAPTER THIRTEEN

August 1920

—————◆—————

Wednesday dawned overcast and Polly was awake before dawn yet again. She lay in bed for a while, but when she heard the mill sirens wailing, got up. Billy was still asleep so she went and made herself a cup of tea. On a sudden impulse she took out her wedding teaset, which they had always kept for 'best'. She wished now that they'd used it more, never mind whether it got broken, because Eddie had really loved it. The fine china seemed to give her heart and she stroked the delicate cup as she waited for the tea to cool a little.

Poor Eddie! He seemed a very distant memory now, though it was only just over four months since his death. She could not believe sometimes how her life had changed.

When she had drunk the tea, she washed the pieces of china carefully and put them away, then went up and shook Billy till he woke. 'Come on, love. Time to get started. We want to look our best today, don't we?' He stared at her and his lips moved, but he didn't say anything. She missed his childish babble and noisy play dreadfully. The house could get horribly quiet with just her pottering about.

After she'd fed him, she got him partly ready then put on her best clothes, the ones she'd got married in: a dark brown skirt, with a matching three-quarter-length coat in the same material. Polly had shortened the hem a little because fashions had changed since the war, grown simpler in some ways, even for the wealthy ladies like Mrs Pilby. With the suit she always wore her cream blouse, but she had changed the ribbon trimming on her matching brown hat recently to a soft orange-pink. She wasn't sure about the colour now. Brown was very practical, but it always made her look pale, and however fashionable the hat might be still – because hats didn't seem to go out of fashion as quickly – when she looked in the mirror the narrow brim seemed to make her face look fatter. And she wasn't plump now. She'd lost a lot of weight in the past few months.

It would have given her confidence to look more up to date, but she couldn't afford to waste her money on a new outfit, not even a hat, because the insurance money had to last as long as possible. Anyway, who was there now to care whether she looked her best or not? It was more important to look respectable today.

Lizzie and Peter came to pick them up at just before half-past ten, with Peter wearing his medals pinned to his jacket, something he didn't normally do. Percy turned up soon after, with Johnny in tow, and Polly knew that if Eva lived closer, she'd have been here, too.

She felt better surrounded by her family – better still when she found Dr Herbert waiting for her outside the Town Hall.

But the relief was short-lived. Dr Browning-Baker was already sitting in the magistrate's office, looking smug, as if he already knew he'd won. He was flanked by Mr Maslam, who gave her a dirty look, and Miss Withers, who avoided her eyes completely.

As the hearing began the magistrate, a Mr Nichols, began asking Polly questions about herself and her son in a loud, slow voice as if she might find it hard to understand him. This attitude annoyed her so much that she held her head up defiantly as she answered in a clear steady voice.

'I don't understand why you've brought Dr Herbert along,' he said after the preliminaries were over. 'Surely Dr Browning-Baker can deal with the medical aspects of this case?'

'But Dr Browning-Baker isn't my son's doctor,' Polly told him.

Mr Nichols turned a questioning gaze on Browning-Baker.

'I dealt with the boy in hospital,' he said in his posh, sneering voice, 'until the mother took him away from me on a whim. She must have realised I'd begun to wonder about her competence to care for him even then.'

Polly gasped in shock. 'That's not true!'

'Please do not interrupt, Mrs Scordale,' the magistrate said in a severe voice. 'Go on, Dr Browning-Baker.'

'That was when I began to make inquiries which made me feel even more uneasy about her. She is very young, you know, only just turned twenty-one.'

It was Toby who interrupted then. 'I have never felt at all uneasy about Mrs Scordale's ability to care for her son. Age has nothing to do with that sort of thing.'

'Sir, you have not yet been asked to speak,' the magistrate snapped.

'I apologise for speaking out of turn, but it is very hard to listen to such blatant untruths,' Toby retorted angrily.

'Are you calling me a liar, sir?' Dr Browning-Baker asked, drawing himself very upright.

'In a word, yes.'

There was silence as the two doctors glared at one another, then the magistrate cleared his throat. 'Please continue, Dr Browning-Baker, and I would be grateful if no one else interrupted.'

'We have had to have the rat and drain inspectors into Mrs Scordale's house, and since we continued to worry about the boy, we've been sending a health visitor to check on her regularly,' Browning-Baker continued.

There were gasps of indignation from Polly and Lizzie, low rumbles of anger from Toby and Peter, but they did not openly voice their indignation.

When it was Polly's turn to be questioned she denied what

the specialist had said, but could see that the magistrate did not believe her. Indeed, he did not seem to be listening to what she was saying. It was as if he'd already made up his mind.

Dr Herbert was questioned only briefly.

Then Peter stood up and said he wished to speak on his sister-in-law's behalf, but was refused permission.

'This matter does not hinge on whether Mrs Scordale is a competent housewife,' Mr Nichols said. 'It is a question of getting the best care for the boy.'

'You haven't even looked at my son,' Polly said angrily. 'None of you care anything about *him*.'

There was silence, then Mr Nichols came out from behind his desk to look down into the wheelchair. 'A very sad case. Completely incurable.'

'He is not!' snapped Polly.

As she spoke, Billy reached out his right arm towards her and began to mumble, the sounds 'Ma-ma-ma' coming out quite clearly.

'He's starting to speak again,' she insisted. 'Dr Herbert's system is working. But if Billy's sent to lie in a ward of children who can't move or speak, with no one to do his exercises or play with him, he'll get worse again.' When she looked down, Billy had lost his alert look and relapsed into his dull state. Her heart sank. Couldn't you keep that look in your eyes just a minute longer, Billy love? she pleaded silently, but he didn't move.

'The child is following a typical recovery pattern,' Dr Herbert said quietly. 'He has brief periods where his attention is caught, and the noises he's making show a new and very promising development. There is no doubt in my mind that he is starting to recover.'

The magistrate and Dr Browning-Baker exchanged disbelieving glances. 'If he is improving,' Mr Nichols said, 'and we've only seen the slightest sign of that, then I can only conclude that there is even more need for proper help for him. A holiday by the seaside in the care of trained nurses is just the thing to set the child up after what he's gone through, so I hereby—'

'No!' Polly shouted. 'You can't take my son away from me! I'll take him to the seaside if you think that's so important, but I'm the best person to look after him.'

'It's a very sad case, but this might be for your own benefit as well as your son's,' the magistrate continued. 'You are young enough to remarry, instead of wasting your life caring for a permanent invalid. I therefore rule that the child should be taken to the seaside and that afterwards—'

The door was flung open, slamming back into the wall and making everyone jump in shock. A voice said, 'You can stop this nonsense right now!'

Everyone turned round to stare.

When Polly saw who was standing there, she could not hold back a sob of relief. If anyone could deal with Dr Browning-Baker, this woman could.

'I've had to come all the way from Blackpool today so I apologise for being a bit late,' Nelly Baker said to the magistrate, then turned and gestured outside the room.

A man carrying a briefcase followed her in, inclining his head to the magistrate and moving forward to stand in front of the desk. 'I'm a lawyer, acting on behalf of Mrs Scordale.' He held out a business card. 'Phillip Saverly, at your service. I also tender my apologies for being late – the car had a puncture – and would crave your indulgence in repeating what has passed so far.'

'The hearing has concluded and I am about to deliver judgement,' the magistrate said frostily. 'I really can't be expected to—'

Mrs Baker, who had been staring at him, interrupted, 'Aren't you Reginald Nichols?'

There was a pause before he answered, 'Yes.'

'Don't you recognise me?' she said. 'I'm Thomas's Auntie Nelly. Eh, I remember you as a child, Reggie. Are you and Thomas still best friends? You two were as close as brothers in those days, if I remember right.'

The magistrate flushed and cast a quick sideways glance at

Dr Browning-Baker who looked as if he had just swallowed something very unpleasant. 'I – um – am acquainted with your nephew still, yes. But that is of no concern in this matter.'

Mr Saverly smiled sardonically. 'I find it of great concern. In fact, given the connection between you, I'd have thought you'd have declared an interest and asked someone else to hear this case.'

'It's an open and shut matter. There was no need to trouble anyone.'

'How did you know that before you heard what my client had to say today?'

The magistrated opened his mouth, then closed it with a snap and swallowed hard.

'However, since you've already started, we might as well continue – if you'd be so kind as to summarise what has happened, Mr Nichols?'

The magistrate hesitated then ran quickly through what had been said, with the lawyer stopping him every sentence or two to ask for more details or simply to wonder if this was the full truth and to ask that it be noted that he'd like to re-examine the witness on this point afterwards.

The third time he did this, Mr Nichols snapped, 'This is not a court hearing, merely a request from the Child Welfare Department for permission to remove this woman's son from her care.'

Mr Saverly smiled, his teeth very white and his eyes gleaming behind his round spectacles. He reminded Polly of her mother-in-law's fierce old cat when it was about to pounce on an unsuspecting mouse. She waited for him to continue, her hands clasped tightly at her breast, hardly daring to breathe in case she missed something.

'Should you decide to grant that request, we are giving formal notice that it will immediately become a court hearing because we shall appeal.'

'On what grounds?' demanded Dr Browning-Baker.

'We are rather concerned as to the procedural approach taken

here, as well as the magistrate's impartiality – and I'm sure we'll
have no difficulty in arranging for a fresh hearing before a demon-
strably impartial judge.'

Silence reigned for a moment or two, during which the sound
of Dr Browning-Baker's heavy breathing seemed to fill the room.

Beside Polly, Billy woke up from his doze and began
mumbling to himself. The words 'Ma-ma-ma' came again, more
loudly this time. She felt Lizzie squeeze her hand and turned to
exchange hopeful looks with her sister before focusing on the
lawyer and the magistrate again.

'In order not to waste everyone's time,' Mr Saverly went on,
'I'd like to tell you what we're proposing, Mr Nichols. Do I have
your permission to do that, Mrs Scordale?'

Polly nodded. Whatever he said, she'd go along with it
because he was her only chance. She saw Mrs Baker wink at her
and hope grew strong in her.

'Mrs Baker, whom I also represent, has been away from home
and has only just heard about this alleged problem with the
boy. She agrees that sea air would be good for the child, and feels
that the mother would benefit from it, too. Since Mrs Baker has
a large house in Blackpool, she has invited Mrs Scordale and
her son to stay with her for a few weeks – or for however long
the child's doctor, Tobias Edward Herbert, considers necessary.
Mrs Baker has two maids who can assist the mother in the care
of the boy, and her neighbour on one side is a doctor who has
agreed to make himself available if there are any emergencies –
though of course Dr Herbert will remain in overall charge of the
child's medical care.'

Dr Browning-Baker muttered something and glowered at his
aunt by marriage. When she grinned at him, he snorted audibly
in disgust.

The magistrate threw him an unhappy, apologetic glance, then
turned back to Mr Saverly. 'That – um – sounds like an excellent
solution. As long as the young woman is not unsupervised, I am
happy to allow this. Dr Herbert, do you wish to say anything?'

'I think it's an ideal solution,' Toby said, beaming at Polly. 'Dr Browning-Baker?'

The doctor stared towards the window as he spoke. 'My concern is, and always has been, for the child. I still feel that an institution with properly trained nurses would be far better for him.'

'But you are not now his doctor,' Mr Saverly said smoothly, 'so this is not really your decision to make. Indeed, I can't understand why you are so involved in this matter. It is a question I'd like to pursue . . . *shall* pursue . . . if the matter goes to appeal.'

'There is nothing secret about the fact that I am employed as a consultant by the Child Welfare Department.'

'Who are now, I'm sure, satisfied that Master Billy Scordale will be well cared for?' Mr Saverly cocked one eye at Mr Maslam, who nodded slowly, then turned back to the magistrate, who also nodded.

'On your own heads be it, then. I wash my hands of the matter. I just pray that the child does not suffer from this.' Browning-Baker stood up and began to walk out, not once looking at the boy he had claimed to care so much about. He paused briefly in front of Polly, saying nothing, just scowling, and the way his eyes narrowed said as well as words could have that he still bore her a serious grudge.

Mr Nichols cleared his throat. 'Dr Herbert, I shall ask you to – um – report to me every two weeks, to ensure that the child is being looked after properly.' He stared at Toby with every appearance of intense dislike as he spoke. 'How long would you suggest he needs to spend at the seaside?'

Toby turned to Mrs Baker who grinned at him, clearly enjoying herself hugely.

'Two months?' she offered.

'Perfect,' he agreed.

'After which we shall reconsider the matter,' the magistrate said.

'If there are grounds,' Mr Saverly interjected. 'Circumstances may change and the child may be out of your jurisdiction by then.'

The magistrate stood up and walked out of the room, closely followed by Mr Maslam. Miss Withers paused to look at Billy, the only one who had bothered to do that.

'I wish you luck,' she whispered to Polly.

Feeling shivery with relief, Polly sagged back against Lizzie. She wanted to shout or weep, do something physical to get rid of this dreadful tight feeling in her chest, but she knew she must still remain calm.

'Good thing you wrote to me, love,' Mrs Baker said, going to tickle Billy's chin and winning a stare and a gurgle from him.

Polly could only nod. She didn't think she could speak without breaking down.

'Come on, love,' Mrs Baker said bracingly. 'What you need is a nice, strong cup of tea – and I wouldn't mind one myself.' She looked at Lizzie, a question in her eyes.

'I'm Polly's sister. And these are our brothers, Percy and Johnny.'

'Nice to meet you all, but if you don't mind I'll take your sister away now. She'll need to pack her things and then she can ride back to Blackpool in the car with us. It's a big one. I do like my comfort. Can I leave you to close the house up for her? Is there somewhere to store her things? I wouldn't advise her to come back to live in Overdale. Tommy Baker always was a bad loser.'

Mr Saverly came up to them. 'I'm afraid I agree with that, Mrs Scordale. You should get out of Overdale while you can. Nasty piece of work, that Browning-Baker fellow. Can't believe he's a nephew of yours, Nelly love.'

Polly stared at him in surprise, for his accent had changed entirely now and had lost its upper-class tone.

He winked at her. 'I wasn't born among the nobs, Mrs S. I wormed my way in, you might say, via university. And they don't always like that.'

'I can't tell you how grateful I am for your help.'

'Tell Nelly here. It was her idea – not that I didn't enjoy myself today. I did. Very much. I take great pleasure in tweaking the noses of arrogant sods like those two, if you'll pardon my language.'

Mrs Baker nudged Polly. 'Come on, then. Better look smart. Phillip here has a nose for trouble. Let's get off round to your house and pack your stuff as quickly as we can before they think of something else. My chauffeur is waiting outside.'

Within two hours Polly had gone, leaving Lizzie and Percy to pack up her things and take them to Cardwell's to be stored until and if she decided to return to Overdale.

It wasn't till the big car was humming along the road towards the coast that she burst into tears. Mrs Baker at once produced a flask of gin and insisted she take a swig, jollying her along until the tears had stopped flowing.

But Polly had never felt so exhausted in her whole life. She would have liked to lie down and sleep for a week. Had she really escaped from Dr Browning-Baker's clutches? And how would she manage without her family? She couldn't stay with Mrs Baker for ever.

In the South of France, George Mercer began to hint delicately that he'd like to join the serious card players. When Amelia tried to dissuade him, he coaxed her to support him. 'Look, darling, I've just received a bit of money from home and I'm feeling lucky.' When this didn't work, he said frankly, 'I'm getting bored, if you must know. I wasn't made for lounging around. I like a bit of excitement in my life.'

She pursed her lips, studying him for a moment as if she'd never seen him before, then said, 'I can't afford to pay any gambling debts, George.'

'I shan't play beyond my means.' He'd meant to add 'my dear' but couldn't force the words through his lips.

Amelia clearly wasn't happy, but she took the hint and had a word with her friend Violet Sibley who arranged for George to join the card-playing group that very night.

The first time he simply observed the play, sitting quietly to one side of the room and taking in the players' styles. He made himself useful replenishing drinks and later agreed to play a hand or two, choosing to win a little money, then lose slightly more than he had won. Exultation was surging up in him. These men were good. But he was better. By hell he was!

This was more like it!

The following evening one of the major players was absent, having met a sweet young thing who had tempted him into her bed. There was much laughing speculation as to whether the elderly Lothario would survive the encounter, and George found himself included in a few more hands of cards.

Again he played modestly, losing just a little in total. He listened with every appearance of gratitude as one of the older men analysed his play and offered him some sound advice.

Next time they played, he won a little overall and made a point of thanking his mentor for his help. The mentor, smug in the knowledge that he himself had won again, nodded and stood chatting to George as drinks were served.

Drawing on his almost inexhaustible store of jokes, George entertained the group for a while after they had finished playing, and followed the humour with some carefully chosen anecdotes from the war, promoting himself to Captain. These gained him the usual respect of men who had not left their own firesides except to make more money from supplying goods to the armed forces.

By the time the group broke up, it was assumed he'd join them the following evening.

He took great care to keep Amelia happy during the daytime, teasing her about how careful he was being not to exceed his pockets. His plans didn't include alienating her at this stage.

Richard Mercer stared at Jean Roulson who had come downstairs again after settling Connie in bed. The so-called nanny had changed her clothes, put on fresh make-up and was giving him what could only be described as come-hither glances.

'I have work to do in the library,' he said, feeling very uneasy. Mrs Shavely and Doris had gone on their weekly outing to the cinema and he was alone in the house with Mrs Roulson – and a sleeping Connie.

'Oh, surely you don't need to work in the evening as well as in the daytime?' Her voice sounded huskier and she was wiggling her hips in a way which reminded him of a raddled and ageing Mary Pickford. Florence had dragged him to see *Poor Little Rich Girl* on one of his leaves towards the end of the war, and even he had admitted that Mary Pickford had a charming personality – an attribute not shared by Jean Roulson.

'Yes, I do need to work tonight.' He started to back towards the door.

'All work and no play . . .' With a swift move she blocked his way, then moved forward to place her arms round his neck. 'Don't be shy,' she breathed into his ear.

And, heaven help him, he was tempted. Not because he wanted this woman particularly, heavens no! But because lately his body had come back to life again and he had started having erotic dreams, waking in the night wanting – someone special. Not Florence, never Florence again, but someone young and fresh to wipe away the last gloomy legacy of the trenches from his mind and body.

'No!' His voice came out with a strangled gruffness and he saw her smile, realising in disgust that she thought she had won. That stiffened his spine. In the voice which had made new recruits and even careless lieutenants tremble, he roared, 'Stop that at once, woman!'

She let out a gasp of protest, then stood watching him with an angry expression on her face. 'There's nothing wrong with two grown-ups having a bit of pleasure.'

'If both of them want it,' he said pointedly.

She stared at him and suddenly her face lost its last trace of prettiness and showed a shrewish spite that matched her shriller tones. 'No wonder your wife left you if you can't get it up!'

'What the hell makes you say that?' Was there gossip in the village? Had the servants said something to her.

'It's obvious. Separate rooms, and Doris said you never went visiting hers, neither.'

He was aghast. '*Doris* has been gossiping about me?'

Jean threw back her head and laughed. 'No, not her. Thinks the sun shines out of your backside, she does. It's what she's *not* said that gave the show away.' She swung round, wiggling one hip in a parody of sexual allure and pausing at the door to stare over her shoulder. 'Well, if that's how things are, I'm giving my notice right now. As of tomorrow. It's a right old dump, this place is. And your daughter's a proper misery, too. Takes after her dad. Can't get a laugh out of her whatever you do.'

'I'll make up your wages in the morning and drive you to the station.'

'You'll not get suited easy, you won't. Modern maids don't enjoy working for stuffed shirts like you. They warned me at the agency that you'd had a few goes at finding someone. That's always a bad sign, but I was at a loose end so I thought I'd give it a try. I doubt they'll send anyone else.'

She flicked her hand in a dismissive gesture that encompassed him and the house. 'You should learn to relax, Captain Mercer. It's 1920 now, not 1900. Queen Victoria's long dead – but you wouldn't think it to look at this place.'

Not until she'd closed the door behind her did he allow himself to sink into an armchair, shuddering at the way she had behaved. Shuddering, too, at the thought that he had been tempted, just for a second, to take her up on her offer.

Only – now he had to find someone else to look after Connie, and how the hell was he going to do that?

CHAPTER FOURTEEN

September–November 1920

—————◆—————

The next two months passed quickly for Polly. Nelly Baker made her welcome in the three-storey, double-fronted terraced house just off Waterloo Road. It was a busy area, but Nelly said she liked to see a bit of life around her. She gave Polly and her son lovely rooms next to one another, and they even had their own bathroom. However, her hostess was often away visiting friends, so Polly was even more lonely than she had been in Overdale, with no family to visit. Nelly's two maids were helpful, but much older than her and had been close friends for a long time. She felt like an outsider if she sat with them, even though they were nothing but polite.

She missed Lizzie most and wrote long letters to all her family to help pass the evenings. But what helped her most of all was the way Billy was improving. It proved she had been right to keep him out of the convalescent home. He had lost that blank look completely now. It had happened quite suddenly, between one day and the next, a couple of weeks after her arrival in Blackpool.

Nelly found her weeping for joy another evening a few days later because Billy had suddenly started talking – disjointed fragments, but they made sense and showed he could understand what was happening around him. Nelly insisted Polly share a glass of port and lemonade with her to celebrate, though Polly didn't really like drinking alcohol, which made her head ache, and would much have preferred a nice cup of tea.

After that, Billy seemed to show new signs of life every day, especially in speech and understanding. Dr Herbert said sometimes people with head injuries weren't able to control what they said or did and it was like that with Billy. His arms and legs would jerk about at times as if he were a marionette and someone was pulling the strings carelessly. Or he would open his mouth and be unable to say exactly what he wanted, getting very frustrated about it and going red in the face with the effort he was making.

But even so, the child's movements were still restricted and that worried Polly. When Dr Herbert came for his fourth fortnightly examination, he checked the boy's progress, then said, 'Could you get one of the maids to keep an eye on Billy while we have a chat?'

'I think Babs will look after him for me. She has done before. They're all very kind here.' But kind or not, Polly was tired of living in someone else's house, of never feeling she could truly relax in case she upset someone. She wanted to have her own home again and see her family regularly. Her two months' stay was sliding gently towards three and now, as October came to an end, winter was setting in, with the occasional storm or rough sea sending salt spray over those brave enough to walk out. The miners were on strike so they were all trying to economise on coal. Polly's sympathies were with the men, but Nelly was indignant that they should want two whole shillings a week more when there were thousands of men who'd be glad just of a job. Polly had seen a poster explaining how much a ton of coal cost at the pit head, and a miner's wage of twenty-four shillings and three pence sounded reasonable until you thought about the danger they lived with and working in cramped conditions in the dark so far under the ground. You'd not get her down a mine, not for anything.

With the magistrate continuing to demand written reports from Dr Herbert each fortnight, even though he had been told of Billy's excellent progress, Polly did not dare return to Overdale. That upset her because she had hoped to spend Christmas with her family. She sighed and tried to pay attention to what the doctor was saying. When you were on your own so much your thoughts tended to wander all over the place.

'Polly? Are you all right?'

'What? Oh, sorry, I was just thinking about Christmas.'

'Go and get your hat and coat and come out for a walk with me. It's a shame to waste a lovely sunny winter's day like this and they tell me you don't get out much. Wrap up, mind. There's a chilly wind.'

Toby chose to take her along the sea front, striding out and not burdening her with small talk. She found herself enjoying the exercise, breathing deeply of the bracing air. Eventually he stopped at a shelter. 'Let's sit here for a while. We'll be able to talk privately.' He gestured to her to be seated, then sat down beside her and removed his gloves. When she glanced sideways she could see that he had his lips pressed together and was staring down at his hands.

Whatever he wanted to talk about could not be good news, then. Polly's heart gave a thump of apprehension. What was he going to tell her? Surely things were going well for her son? At least, she had thought so.

'You must have noticed that Billy's left side is not responding as well as his right,' he said eventually.

'Yes, I have. I just thought it was taking longer for that side to recover.'

Toby shook his head. 'I don't think so. Of course it's early days yet, but I suspect there is some permanent damage in the part of his brain that controls that side of his body. It does happen that way sometimes.'

She stared blindly at the beach as she listened to the soft voice continuing its careful explanation.

'Billy's left leg seems to be affected as well, though we shall know much better how things are when he begins walking again.

It's a good sign that he's rolling about now, though, and when we get back I must show you some new exercises to strengthen his legs.'

'Can't we – do anything to help the weak side?'

He sighed. 'We can do a little, but if there's permanent damage there will always be a – a problem with movement. Billy will probably limp and have trouble with his left hand all his life.'

'Oh.'

Below them waves rolled in towards the beach, with sand hissing beneath them. In spite of the cold, there were a few hardy souls throwing a ball to and fro, and a large wet dog was rushing from one to the other in a mad, futile chase to get it away from them. It helped Polly to watch them because they looked so normal. And her Billy – if Dr Herbert was right, her son would never be normal, never be able to throw and catch properly again like the young lad down there.

'We have to be thankful for what we've got in cases like your son's,' Toby went on gently. 'Billy is using words regularly now and he looks quite alert so I'm hoping his brain function has not been damaged, that he might in fact be a perfectly normal boy mentally.'

She managed to force a word out. 'Yes. That would be – good.'

'Oh, Polly, I—'

There it was again, that warm personal tone. She got up abruptly and walked over to stand by the little railing that separated the promenade from the beach, with her back to the shelter. She didn't want him getting personal, didn't want anything from him but his care of her son.

'I should be grateful for what progress we have made,' she said when he joined her a minute or two later. 'I *am* grateful, and to you most of all, Dr Herbert. But, it's hard to see a healthy child turned into a – a cripple overnight.'

'It might only be a slight limp.'

'Yes. But still . . .'

As the silence continued he risked saying, 'Couldn't you call me Toby?'

She shook her head. 'It wouldn't seem right. You're Billy's doctor.'

He sighed. 'And at that moment you only have energy to deal with your son.'

She nodded. It was as good a way of putting him off as any. 'I'll continue taking notes for you, but shouldn't I be paying you? I mean . . .'

'No. You're helping me enormously by letting me work with Billy. One day, I might ask you to bring him to Manchester and let me demonstrate my methods with him to a group of doctors so that they can help other children like him. Would you do that? And will you keep taking notes about the details of his progress?'

'Yes, of course. I like to think we're helping others with what we do.'

Toby smiled wryly. 'I might even get a paper published about it. That would really annoy Browning-Baker.'

'He deserves annoying, that one does.' As long as it didn't make him come after her and Billy again.

Florence tipped out her purse on to the bedspread, then up-ended her handbag and shook everything out of it. But there was very little money left. She'd made her allowance last better this time, much better, but what Richard gave her still wasn't enough to keep her away from home for a whole quarter and Richard knew it. He did it on purpose so that she'd spend time with their brat.

She went to find Phyllis. 'I'll have to leave soon, I'm afraid.'

Her friend's face fell. 'Oh, must you?'

''Fraid so.' She hesitated, then decided on honesty. 'The money's nearly run out, you see.'

Over dinner that night, Phyllis was very thoughtful. As they sat sipping gin and its after Phyllis's husband had retired for the night, she said abruptly, 'I don't want you to leave yet, Flo.'

'You don't think I *want* to go? I've really enjoyed being here.'
They were two of a kind, hedonistic and cynical. It was funny,
Florence reflected. She'd never had a close woman friend until
now, but she and Phyllis continued to enjoy each other's company
and there had been no quarrels or even minor disagreements to
mar the stay. 'But I can't trespass on your hospitality for ever.'

'You could stay another week or two, though. Look, I have
plenty of money – Arthur's not stingy, I'll give him that – so
won't you reconsider? Please?'

Florence bowed her head and forced tears into her eyes, a skill
she had perfected as a child. 'I can't sponge on you, Phyll.'

Her friend chuckled. 'Spare me the tears, love. You told me
once you could cry on demand.'

Florence looked up in shock.

Phyllis grinned. 'Oh, hell, we don't need to pretend with one
another, surely? I need you and it's worth it to me to slip you a
few quid. Please stay a bit longer.'

'What about Arthur? Won't he mind?'

'He won't know about the money. And he enjoys your
company, as well – says having you around keeps me in a good
mood. All the poor old thing wants now is a peaceful life.' Her
expression grew bleak for a few moments. 'That's what you get
when you marry a much older man. Money and a cold bed.'

Florence went and hugged her. 'I can't resist accepting. I
loathe it in Stenton. And as for Richard, he's so holier than thou
about life that I can hardly force myself to be civil to him any
more. Thanks.'

Phyllis leaned back and blew out a series of perfect smoke
rings. 'Bet you can't beat these!'

'Bet I can.'

They didn't mention the problem again. Florence found a few
bank notes on her bedside table the next afternoon, and Phyllis
paid for everything when they went out.

✻

Richard found a maid who was prepared to look after Connie temporarily. Aggie was planning to get married in a few months and the higher wages he was offering would surely keep her with the Mercers until then. The woman wasn't really what he wanted; she wasn't very well educated, and when Connie began speaking some words with a thick Lancashire accent he had to bite his tongue sometimes. But at least Aggie was a kindly woman who looked after his daughter carefully.

Though he tried to spend time with Connie each day, he still managed to organise the purchase of a house on the sea front for the incapacitated men from his regiment, something which gave him immense satisfaction. It was a former boarding house right at the other end of the promenade with plenty of space for their purposes. The main structural change needed was the installation of a lift big enough to hold a stretcher, which they did by building a little tower to one side, opening on to the landing on each of the three floors. However, he had difficulty getting the workmen he needed to modernise the house because all the local tradesmen were swarming over the Bella Vista hotel just beyond it, which was also being modernised and extended by yet another new owner, including an 'Italian Garden' at the rear complete with statues.

Richard wasn't sure he liked the amenities in Stenton being expanded like this and would infinitely have preferred it to remain a sleepy little village for ever, but the hotel would bring some much-needed jobs into the area so you could not protest, not in times like these with jobs vanishing all the time and bankruptcies becoming common. His own income had been reduced by the fall in returns on shares, but he felt that his inheritance was safely spread over a variety of conservative investments so did not expect any serious setbacks. He let out a snort of laughter at the thought of Florence and how she wanted always to be spending money. If he followed her ways in times like these, he'd be bankrupt himself within a few years.

He had a bit of luck in that he was approached by his former

Sergeant, Ted Foster, still known to one and all as Sarge. The man's wife had died of influenza and he was without work at present. He'd heard about the home and thought he'd enjoy working there with 'the lads'.

'I shan't marry again,' he said quietly. 'There's no one can touch my Madge. But I'd like to think I was doing something useful. You don't need to pay me much, just my keep and a bit of tobacco money.'

Richard wrung his hand. 'You're on. And of course we'll pay you. What's more, you can start right away supervising the final work. That'll take a load off my shoulders. If you don't mind roughing it, you can move in there as soon as you like.'

Sarge blinked rapidly then saluted and said, 'Pleased to report for duty, sir!'

What with his trips into Manchester, his work with Toby Herbert, and occasional dinners with members of his old regiment in Fleetwood, Richard was kept pretty busy.

As the quarter was drawing to a close, he kept expecting to hear from Florence – and dreading it. She seemed to be enjoying herself with her friend Phyllis and had even sent a couple of cheerful postcards to Connie with a return address, which had delighted the child.

But although he shuddered when he remembered Jean Roulson, Richard knew there was something missing from his life: a proper relationship with a woman. After he divorced Florence, he hoped to remarry. He had always wanted to have several children, had seen himself sharing a happy home life with a wife and had certainly never wanted to live like a bloody monk.

He was lonely. For human warmth and intelligent conversation. For someone to share the day's events with, and maybe a little laughter, too. Very lonely indeed. And he refused to spend the rest of his life like this.

With that in mind, he bit the bullet. He had hesitated for far too long. He no longer cared about the social stigma. He would do his best to protect Connie, but he had come to see that however he and Florence divorced, their daughter would be hurt. He contacted the private detective and set matters in train to have his wife watched carefully. The detective, a nondescript little man called Joe Rainer, was to spend a few days observing her while she was at her friend Phyllis's, and would then report back so that they could decide what to do next.

If his wife gave him the slightest evidence, Richard was ready now to sue for divorce. This haphazard way of living, with one temporary maid after another looking after his daughter, galled him. He wanted stability and comfort. All the things he had dreamed of in the trenches.

As autumn waned and even the South of France grew noticeably cooler, the gambling group began to break up and Amelia talked of returning to England. By now George had won some useful money, but he wanted more, hungered for it, was excited by the thought of taking it from these rich sods. So when he heard that Armand Rivaine, a noted gambler, was staying nearby, he led the talk towards that man's exploits, speculating as to how he played to have gained such a reputation.

'He's no better than you or me, but he has phenomenal luck,' George's mentor said sourly.

'You know him?'

Felix smiled. 'We're distant cousins.'

A pause, then George said softly, 'I'd really like to see him play, even try my luck against him.'

Because he had lost too much money to his so-called protégé, Felix gave a thin smile and said, 'Then I'll introduce you, old fellow. But I warn you, the play is always pretty high when Armand is around.'

The following afternoon Amelia's husband turned up suddenly, come to take her home again. George kept himself more or less out of sight, but it made him even more eager to try his luck with Rivaine, because he knew it was his last chance of a big win. His hostess had tolerated his presence for her friend's sake. He wasn't going to give her the chance to chuck him out. He'd have to leave fairly quickly of his own accord.

The game was arranged for that evening. As George shuffled the new pack of cards, he looked round the table, meeting the eyes of the other players, but not smiling or nodding to them. Excitement was pulsing through him. If he'd ever believed that luck was with him, he believed it now. He doubted any of this showed in his face, any more than feelings showed in the faces of the other players. Those who could not control their faces did not play poker – or not successfully and definitely not in this league.

Without any flourishes, but with an ease of movement that spoke of long acquaintance with cards, he began to deal.

Within two hours tension in the room was acute. Armand Rivaine did not enjoy losing and was showing it. When he threw down his cards and muttered something, George asked, 'Ready to stop now?' Although his tone was mild, the suggestion was an insult.

Armand jerked upright and glared at him. 'Certainly not! But I want a new pack of cards.'

'Do you really think that will make a difference to your skill?' George murmured, keeping his voice so low that the others could not hear him.

Breath hissed into the other man's mouth, but he clamped his lips together and did not respond to the jibe.

George flipped the new pack towards him. 'Want to check them?'

With a scowl, the other man did just that.

Then they started playing again. George felt supremely confident that he would win. He could feel it throbbing through him – luck, skill, confidence, call it what you would. And he could almost see the same feeling oozing out of Armand, leaving him visibly depleted of his winner's aura.

The other players dropped out, leaving him and Armand to

continue their duel, for that was what it had become.

For a time, Armand clawed back some of his money, playing with such ferocious concentration that the sweat dripped from his forehead.

Then the cards began to fall George's way again. He won several hands, but not conclusively enough. 'Double the stakes?' he asked casually, drawing deeply on his cigarette and letting the smoke curl around him.

There was a concerted sigh from the men watching him. He ignored it, watching Armand. No change in the other man's expression, but his little finger was tapping impatiently.

After a long pause, he nodded. 'Why not?'

The cards did not fall George's way that time, but he managed a smile, as if he had a good hand, and saw his companion's little finger begin to move more quickly.

When he discarded two useless cards, George didn't pick up anything really useful, but he let himself give the tiniest of nods as if he had.

Armand noticed. Reacted. Threw down his cards and walked out, tossing, 'You win!' over his shoulder.

George sat there in amazement.

'He does that sometimes, Armand. Just storms out. Never could stand to lose,' Felix commented. 'Want to play again tomorrow?'

'Not with him.'

'Oh, no. Armand will hole up on his estate for a while till he recovers, then come out and start playing again. You've fleeced him good and proper tonight, but he's rich enough not to care.'

They heard the next day that Armand had gone back to his lodgings and shot himself. He had not been as rich as everyone had thought and had lost what he did have through his gambling.

George whistled softly when Felix passed the news to him. It was a lesson, really. The luck didn't stay with you for ever.

He took a graceful leave of his host and hostess and arranged to depart the following morning. He had plenty of money for the moment because he had won a rather decent amount from Rivaine. It was time to return to England. And to Flo. He not only wanted her, he needed her. He was quite sure she'd come to him now that he had some real money. About time they made a more permanent arrangement, really.

And it'd be such fun rubbing old Richard's nose in it. That would give George the most satisfaction.

CHAPTER FIFTEEN

December 1920

Having reluctantly decided that she'd better return to Stenton, Florence told her friend and went to pack her suitcase. When the phone rang she thought nothing of it until she heard Phyllis yelling from downstairs.

'It's for you!'

Muttering in annoyance at the interruption, in fact annoyed with the whole world today, Flo walked slowly down the stairs, mouthing, 'Who is it?' as she reached the bottom.

Phyllis shrugged and handed over the earpiece.

'Hello. Florence Mercer here.'

'Flo, my pet!'

'*Georgie!*'

Phyllis paused in the doorway of the sitting room to raise one eyebrow questioningly. Florence beamed at her and made shooing motions with her free hand.

'Now don't pretend you're glad to hear from me,' George teased.

Flo had to swallow hard before she could speak. 'I don't know whether I'm glad or not. It's been a long time. You didn't even send me a card. How's your old lady going on? Still doting on you?'

'She's back with her husband. And,' he hesitated, then admitted, 'I missed you.'

It was out before she could stop herself. 'Did you really?'

'Of course I did, you fool. Come and find out just how much.'

Florence pulled a face at herself in the mirror and forced herself to refuse. 'I can't. I'm going home tomorrow.'

His voice grew softer, lower, and sent shivers down her spine. 'You know you don't want to go back to old misery-face. Come and stay with me for a few days instead.'

She did not want to say yes straight away, but couldn't force herself to say no, so kept silent.

He chuckled. 'Don't play games with me, Flo. We've never done that to each other before and I don't want to start – especially now. How soon can you get here? I'm still in the same place.'

She couldn't resist the chance to see him again. 'Oh, damn you, Georgie! I can get there this afternoon. But only for a day or two. I really do have to go home soon.' She glanced up at the hall clock, calculating train times, for she and Phyllis had often gone into central London shopping or to a matinée at the theatre. 'Meet me at Euston at two.'

He was waiting for her. Florence stood looking at him, feeling as if she had never seen him before, taking in his bronzed face and broad shoulders, the air of rakish charm that always surrounded him. She felt her whole body go soft with longing. He and Richard resembled one another physically, though Richard was thinner, not quite as tall and the scar on one cheek did not add to his appeal. Dropping her bags, she flung herself into George's arms and when he picked her up and swung her round and round, she threw her head back and laughed, not caring who saw them – not even noticing the balding middle-aged man who had got off the same train and was tying his shoelace a few yards away.

As George picked up her suitcase and put his free arm round her shoulders, the man picked up his own luggage and followed them to the taxi rank, hurrying at the last minute in order to listen to the address George gave.

'Caresby Terrace,' he told the taxi driver. 'And hurry.'

The man watched them drive off. 'Caresby Terrace,' he told the next driver. 'I can't remember the number, but I'll recognise the house when I see it. And I'd be grateful if you could hurry. I'm running a bit late.' He allowed himself one tight smile as he pulled out his notebook and scribbled down what he had just seen.

After paying off the taxi, he stood in an alleyway opposite the house into which George and Florence had disappeared. When a man's naked torso appeared at the window of an upstairs room and drew the curtains, the watcher smiled broadly, then withdrew to a nearby park to change his own clothes behind a tree.

An hour later, someone knocked at the door of George's flat. 'Damn!'

'Don't answer it.' Florence passed him the ornate silver cigarette lighter which he hadn't owned before his trip and which she'd just been admiring.

The knock came again.

'Coming!' George slipped into his pyjama bottoms and an overcoat and padded out into the living room, opening the door a crack. 'Yes?'

A man in overalls stood there. 'Very sorry to disturb you, sir, but there's been a report of a gas leak.'

'Not in here, there hasn't.' George tried to shut the door in his face, but the fellow had his foot in the way.

'If I might just check the kitchen and bathroom, sir? We don't want to risk an explosion, do we? You can get some very nasty injuries if it blows up on you.'

Florence peered out of the bedroom, wrapped in George's dressing gown. 'What's wrong?'

'They're looking for a gas leak.'

She pulled a face. 'I can't smell anything. Tell him to hurry up. I want that cup of tea.'

The man made a quick inspection, said it must be downstairs, then apologised again for disturbing them. He grinned as he ran lightly down the stairs and shut the front door very quietly behind him.

When he had gone, Florence stared at George, not attempting to hide the anguish in her eyes. 'Oh, hell, it'll be even worse going back to Stenton now. If only I weren't tied to your bloody cousin. If only we didn't need his money.'

'I don't need it at the moment, actually. I've got plenty of my own.' He came to lie beside her.

She stiffened. 'What do you mean?'

'I won a rather large sum from a certain gentleman whose luck ran out.' George lay staring up at the ceiling for a moment or two, reliving that night, then he smiled at her. 'And as a result, I'm inviting you to come and live with me openly.'

She stared down at him and like a child began chewing on one lock of the sleek dark hair that swung forward across her cheeks. Her eyes were huge and there was fear in them as well as hope. 'Do you really mean that?'

'Yes, I do.'

She swallowed hard. 'But what about when the money runs out?'

'I'll get us some more – but it'll be a long time before that happens. It was a big win. And I've developed a few other talents as well.'

She surprised him and herself by bursting into tears, sobbing loudly as she slid down and twisted round to nestle against him.

It was a new side to her, this vulnerability. He was not sure he liked it. 'Hey, what's happened to my sharp, sexy Flo?' he teased.

She flung one arm across her eyes. 'She just nearly died of shock, that's what.' She removed the arm to stare at him. 'You do mean it?'

'Of course I mean it, you fool. I don't lie to you, my pet.' Then he smiled as the Flo he loved returned.

Her face brightened with sheer glee. She laughed aloud and stretched exuberantly, not in the least bothered that she was stark naked. 'Oh, wouldn't I love to see Richard's face when he reads my letter?'

He gripped one arm and shook it slightly to get her full attention. 'Don't write, don't say anything to him.'

'What do you mean? How can I not tell him if I'm not going back to him? He'll be expecting me to go and collect my allowance.'

'Just let him wonder and worry. It isn't wise to put things down on paper. And surely you don't want to phone him up and listen to one of his lectures?'

She lay quietly, frowning, trying to understand his motives. 'But Richard *wants* a divorce. I refused to give him one. We could let him divorce me now, though. He said he'd supply the grounds. He'll let me have some money, too, if we do that.'

'No!' George's voice came out more sharply than he'd intended and he repeated more softly. 'No, my pet. Sometimes it's better just to leave people wondering.'

'But – don't you want to marry me?'

'I don't want all the fuss of a divorce, that's all. And I can't see that being married would make much difference to us, can you?'

She didn't feel it was wise to argue about that just then.

The detective rang from London. 'Mr Mercer? Can you speak freely?'

'Yes.'

'It's Joe Rainer here.'

Richard stiffened. 'Yes?'

'It's about your wife. She's moved from her friend's house and is now living openly with your cousin George Mercer in Caresby Terrace. I called at the flat and pretended to be the gas man.'

'Can you prove anything?'

'Oh, yes. They'd clearly just been making love. He was only wearing pyjama bottoms and an overcoat and she was wearing a loose dressing gown with nothing on underneath.'

Richard pursed his lips and stared up at the grey sky. For a moment he couldn't think what to say, could only let the relief pour into his body in a great big flood.

'Mr Mercer? Are you still there? Do you want me to continue watching them for a day or two, just to be sure?'

'Yes. You do that, Rainer. I'll consult my lawyer, find out what I have to do next.'

He put the phone down, sat staring blindly at it for a couple of minutes, then donned his overcoat and trilby and went for a walk along the beach. An icy wind was blowing and it was threatening to rain so he had the place to himself. Which exactly suited his mood.

What the devil was he going to say to Connie, who kept asking when Mummy was coming back?

'Hell and damnation,' he muttered, then shouted the words into the teeth of the wind. *'Hell and bloody damnation! What a mess!'* Which didn't make him feel much better. It was all so sordid.

To cap it all, when he got home Aggie came to see him.

'I'm very sorry, sir, but I'm afraid I have to give notice straight away. My Norman wants us to get married at once so that I can help him look after his mum who's had a seizure.'

He stared at her, aghast. 'But what about Connie? I was relying on you to look after her.'

Aggie began to sob into her handkerchief. 'I'm that sorry, sir. I'm going to miss her, I really am. But Norman is relying on me, too, and you have to put your family first, don't you?'

This immediately made him feel guilty. 'Yes, you do, Aggie. I'm sorry I spoke sharply. It was just so sudden. When do you have to leave?'

'As soon as I can, I'm afraid. There's a lot do do. I'm to move in with Norman's mother straight away and he'll stay with his aunt till we can get married.' Her eyes grew dreamy. 'Just a simple wedding will do us, we're not ones for fuss.'

Once she'd gone, Richard sighed and unhooked the

ear-piece of the phone. 'I want to place an advertisement in the newspaper . . .'

Polly noticed the advertisement straight away because she'd seen it before.

Companion required for girl of 10, invalid. Other help kept.

If she didn't have Billy to look after, she'd go for a job like that. Or perhaps not that one. They couldn't seem to keep anyone for long, this family with an invalid daughter, so either the child was very spoiled or they'd had a run of bad luck with their staff. Children needed someone reliable in their lives. She glanced towards the couch. Billy was staring into the fire. He loved to watch the flames. Eh, he was coming on nicely now, but he still had a long way to go and she still had to make her money last.

She was beginning to feel guilty about staying so long here. Although Nelly said it didn't matter, Polly knew she should be moving on. Of course, she tried to help out whenever she could. Once Cook had had to go home when her mother died so Polly had stepped in and done part of her work. Another time Babs had taken a week's holiday when her brother got married, and again Polly had helped out as much as she could. Billy liked sitting in the kitchen watching her work. He was no trouble, the little love.

Nelly had tried to pay her for her help that time, but Polly had refused to accept anything. She and her son had had all their keep for free since they came here, and she liked to think she could give her benefactor something in return. But she didn't want to trespass on Nelly's goodwill indefinitely, and however quiet they were in the evenings, having Billy in the house did cause a few problems. So Polly had started looking at houses, finding out what there was to rent in Blackpool. Dr Herbert had discussed it with her. He thought that if she was resident elsewhere, the child welfare people in Overdale would not have any further excuse to pester her.

Nelly was going to ask her nice, young lawyer about that next time she saw him, just to be sure, only she had been away visiting friends and hadn't got round to it. She went away quite a lot.

What Polly really wanted was to go back to Overdale and be near her family because although Lizzie and Percy had been across to see her a couple of times, and both her sisters wrote regularly, it just wasn't the same. Eva couldn't be away for a whole day so she hadn't been able to come at all. She was stopping work after Christmas to nurse Alice who was doing better than expected, though it was only a matter of time. Polly felt sorry for the teacher who had been so kind to their sister after their father had been killed. They all liked Alice Blake.

Polly went to stare out of the window at the stormy weather. The roar of the sea seemed to fill her days at this time of year. The sea front looked cold and bleak, and the pier was deserted. On fine days a few people would be out walking along the promenade, but on days like this there was nothing to see. She turned to her son who was making sleepy little noises and starting to wake up.

When she'd changed him, she started playing with his fingers, singing a little tune she'd made up. She held her breath when he grasped her hand and started playing with her fingers in time to the tune. 'There's my clever little fellow,' she encouraged him. 'Do it again.'

And he did. When she'd finished he said, 'Again! Again!' himself and Polly forgot her worries completely. It was moments like this which kept her going, showing her that Billy was continuing to make progress.

That night she sat thinking it all over again and decided she'd stay here till the New Year then find somewhere else to live.

And after she'd moved she'd try to find some part-time work, too. There must be something she could do, if it was only ironing in her own home. She was a good laundress and a pretty decent cook, too. Well, she'd had excellent training in all aspects of running a house when she worked for the Pilbys. It seemed a waste sometimes not to use her skills, but Billy came first and he always would.

Christmas was very quiet that year for many people because there were more unemployed every month. There were those who could not afford to celebrate, who could barely keep bread on their tables, and outside the charitable organisations and soup kitchens there were long queues of people seeking help. They looked so hopeless when Polly walked past that she wished she could help, but the sight of them also made her determined to husband her own money carefully. The idea of looking for a part-time job grew firmer each time she saw the queues.

Although jobs were scarce, ladies were still writing to the newspapers complaining about the difficulties of finding good domestic help. Surely there must be something she could do part-time? Of course staying with Nelly had helped spin her money out because she had hardly any expenses here. But it couldn't go on.

Nelly was away for the festive season. She seemed to enjoy an active social life and usually spent Christmas with a favourite nephew. While she was gone, the two maids were going to take the opportunity to go home to their own families, leaving the house in the capable hands of Polly.

'You're doing us all a favour,' Nelly said as she left, pressing a little parcel into Polly's hand. 'Don't forget – the tradesmen know you're free to order from them.'

Polly waved goodbye then looked at the parcel. She would keep it till Christmas Day, putting it with the presents that had arrived from her family.

The house was very quiet once Babs and Cook had left as well. Too quiet. It was so big she felt a bit uneasy, especially at night. She propped a chair back under the handle of her and Billy's bedroom, laughing at herself for her fears but still taking this precaution every night. She would often wake up in the darkness with a start, thinking she heard a noise downstairs.

Polly had a weep when she woke up on Christmas morning because there was no one to celebrate with. She fumbled for the matches and lit the candle beside her bed. They had gas lighting downstairs and on the first floor, of course, but up here only candles. Nelly was going to have electricity put in come the New Year and both Babs and Cook were very excited about that, though apprehensive too. Polly looked at the candle, flickering in the draft from the window, and wondered what it would be like simply to turn on a switch and have as much light as you wanted.

The tears dried up and she grew angry with herself for giving in to this weakness. She still had Billy, didn't she? After all her fighting to keep him, she should stop feeling sorry for herself and get on with things. There was a lot to be thankful for, indeed there was.

So the two of them had a special dinner, with Billy's favourite pudding, then she ate some nuts and raisins, and gave him some chocolate. He kept saying, 'Mmmm, mmmm,' and opening his mouth for more which made Polly laugh. Afterwards she took him into the big front room and picked out some tunes on the piano, something she was learning to do when Nelly wasn't in. She sang as cheerfully as she could manage and Billy joined in with that tuneless humming noise he now made as his contribution to their sing-songs. Afterwards he laughed at her when she played games with him.

'Well, you're having a good time, anyway, my fine fellow,' she said, nuzzling his cheek, then jumped in shock as the telephone startled her. As its ring echoed up the empty hallway, she hesitated for a moment before going to answer it. 'Mrs Baker's residence,' she said in the lofty tone she had once used at Mrs Pilby's where she had first learned to use a telephone and been absolutely terrified the first few times she picked it up.

A faint chorus of voices started singing 'We Wish You A

Merry Christmas', among them Lizzie's flat toneless drone. Polly laughed and joined in, then responded as they came on one after the other to speak to her and wish her a Merry Christmas.

When the call was over, she hung up the earpiece carefully, watching it sway to and fro on the candlestick-like holder. 'Eh, that was nice of them,' she said softly.

'Nice, nice, nice!' said a voice behind her and she jumped in shock. When she turned, she saw Billy sitting on the floor. Now how had he got off the couch by himself?

He waved one hand at her, his right one of course, always his right one, and repeated, 'Nice, nice, nice.' Then he shuffled towards her on his bottom, a slow ungainly movement, but she didn't try to help him. Dr Herbert said she was to encourage him to do as much as possible himself. He had moved about a bit before, but had never got down of his own accord. She'd have to watch him more carefully from now on.

When he reached her feet and crowed with triumph as he grabbed hold of her slipper, Polly bent down, picked him up and smacked a kiss on each cheek. 'Who's my clever little lad?' she asked. Then she swung him round and round till they were both breathless with laughter.

And that was her Christmas. Plenty to be hopeful about, she told herself firmly. And there was. She fell asleep to the distant roar of the sea and the wind whistling along the promenade. Perhaps the new year would be happier than the last. It could hardly be worse. And at least she had prevented them from taking Billy away from her. Yes, plenty to be thankful for. But still, it was a lonely life. She missed her family so much!

CHAPTER SIXTEEN

January 1921

———◆———

Immediately after Christmas Polly started applying for domestic posts, detailing her experience and offering her services free in return for her own and her son's keep. She hoped to find someone short of money and trying to keep up appearances. However, she received blunt refusals from all the people she wrote to, except for one man who asked her to go and see him.

But when she got there, her heart sank because she had seen his type before. Not knowing what else to do, she pretended to discuss the position with him, but he soon started making suggestions about there being other ways for a comely young woman like her to earn her living in these troubled times. Indignation swelling within her, she stood up. 'No, thank you,' she declared and moved towards the door.

'You'll be back!' he called after her. 'And I might not be as kind next time.'

Polly turned round to face him then, hands on hips. 'No, I won't be back! I have family who will take me in any time rather than see me want. You should be ashamed of yourself for preying on poor young women. Can't you get someone of your own class?'

He jumped to his feet, his expression so angry that she turned and fled. As she walked back along the sea front, anger made her sensible shoes drum on the pavement and her breath come out in little puffs of indignation. At one stage she paused to lean on a railing looking out to sea and demand of the fitful breeze, 'Who does he think he is?'

The following week she once again saw the advertisement that had caught her eye. It had exactly the same wording and address:

Companion required for girl of 10, invalid. Other help kept.

So they've lost another maid, Polly thought. I wonder why? She hesitated, wondering whether to apply for the position. Why could this family not keep staff? She didn't want to work for nasty folk, not with her Billy to care for. Still, a job was a job. It could do no harm to write and offer her services. All she asked was that she be allowed to keep her son with her.

She knew she was a good worker and got on well with children because she always had great fun with her nieces and nephews. It might even cheer up the poor little invalid to see another child in a worse case than herself, or if the girl was a troublesome sort, it might quieten her down to spend time with a small boy who was making such huge efforts to move around and speak. And succeeding, too, though progress came in fits and starts — as she recorded in the notes she kept for Dr Herbert.

It took Polly most of the afternoon to write a letter she felt satisfied with. When she had copied out her final version in her best handwriting, she put on her hat and coat then got Billy ready for the outing. As she turned the corner towards the post office, her footsteps slowed down and a few steps away from the postbox she stopped walking and almost turned back. What if the father of the little girl was like the horrible man who had made such a dreadful suggestion to her? What if that was why people wouldn't stay with him? She'd have to insist on meeting him and his daughter before she took on anything, she most definitely would.

After a moment's hesitation, she slipped the letter into the postbox. As she heard it fall, she wished she hadn't. Only it was too late to do anything about it now.

Why did she think she'd get a job anyway? All around her

people were out of work and trying to live on the meagre assist-ance of unemployment insurance. Fifteen shillings a week wasn't much, and only for fifteen weeks, so what did you do if you still couldn't find a job? And why the Government thought women only needed twelve shillings a week Polly could never understand. Landlords didn't charge women less rent and food didn't cost less for them, either.

In her last letter Lizzie had said that Dearden's wasn't getting as much custom as before, so they'd had to cut down hours for their staff. In his last letter Percy had said people weren't wanting as much building doing, so Cardwell's was only employing men when there was an actual job, apart from Walter, their foreman.

How long could this state of affairs continue?

And how would she and Billy survive if times continued bad? That thought was keeping Polly awake at night.

In mid-January a letter arrived for Florence in the first post and she felt her stomach lurch in apprehension as she recognised Richard's handwriting. She could see that George had recognised it too.

'Well, go on! Open it,' he said with a chuckle. 'I'm sure the ink isn't poisoned.'

'What do you think he wants?' She held the envelope gingerly between finger and thumb, tapping it against the edge of the table, reluctant to read it. How she wished she need never see or deal with her husband again!

George plucked the letter out of her hand. 'Only one way to find out.' He tore the envelope and tossed the fragments aside as he studied the two pieces of paper it contained. 'Hmm.' He pulled a wry face. 'One's from his lawyer and the other's from him.'

Florence turned her back and went to gaze out of the window at the rain. 'You read them and tell me what he wants.' Dreary weather, dreary day. They should have just tossed the letter in the fire. She listened to the crackling of the paper and when

George said nothing, turned round impatiently. 'Well?'

'Just a minute.' He continued to read slowly, his brow furrowed in thought, then looked up. 'The lawyer's letter gives you formal notice that your husband intends to sue for divorce on the grounds of adultery.' He grinned at her, flourishing one hand in the air as he added, 'With yours truly as co-respondent. I didn't think Richard would get on to us so fast, or be willing to publicise his little problem. And I wonder who told him where we were?'

'How should I know? He's asked for a divorce once or twice, but I've refused. Well, good riddance. I hope this means I never have to see him again.'

'Yes, but it's a pity you won't be able to get hold of any of Uncle James's money!' George said, tapping the letters against the table and frowning.

'He probably sleeps with it under his pillow now that he's not capable of sleeping with a woman any more. Not that I ever saw much money. What does the other letter say?'

'Richard wants you to write to Connie who's apparently fretting for you.'

Florence made a rude noise.

He shook his head reproachfully. 'You ought to write to her, you know, my pet. If it comes to a court case, it won't look good for you to have ignored your daughter completely. You want to see if you can retrieve something from this marriage. A little cash settlement, maybe?'

'I don't *want* to write to Connie. And anyway, I shouldn't know what to say. She's as dull as her father, and that limp is so ugly! I hate even to be seen with her.'

'Nonetheless, there are ways of doing things that *look* better to the courts.' George waited, but she didn't turn or speak. 'I'll help you write the occasional letter to Connie, if you like.' When Florence still didn't answer, he went across and swung her round to face him, pulling her against his hard, muscular body. 'Don't be a fool about this, Flo. I don't like fools.'

Fear shivered through her then and she suddenly realised how vulnerable Richard's letter had left her. Since they weren't married, George could just dump her any time he wanted. He wouldn't, though, surely? But she might as well humour him in this since it wasn't important. 'Oh, very well. You dictate and I'll write. Let's get the first one over with now.'

As he dictated she looked up a couple of times, her interest caught. 'You know, it's you who should be a writer, not *him*. You make everything sound amusing. I could never write a letter like this and he'll know it.'

'It won't matter what he guesses as long as your daughter doesn't realise what's happening. Anyway, that should be enough, just put "Love, Mummy" at the end.' As he watched her sign her name with a flourish, George added with a sneer, 'I'd never try to write books. There's not enough money in that sort of thing.'

'Are you ever going to do anything besides gambling?' Florence ventured to ask, for it was something that had been occupying her mind lately. She didn't think she'd enjoy a life of permanent insecurity.

He yawned and gave a big stretch. 'Such as?'

'I don't know. Settle down. Buy a business. That sort of thing. It'd be nice to have a big house, a circle of friends, play golf regularly. This flat is a bit grubby and down-at-heel, don't you think? Rents have gone down lately. We could get something much better for very little extra.'

He looked round as if he'd never seen the place before. 'I suppose so. I never think about it.'

'That's because you hardly spend any time here.'

When he didn't say anything, she let the matter drop.

Toby Herbert gave Billy his fortnightly checkup and smiled at Polly. 'He's doing really well, making far quicker progress than I had expected. You must be working very hard with him.'

'Yes, I am.' She hesitated. 'But his left side — well, it's still not responding properly.'

His voice was very gentle. 'I don't think it's going to, Polly. As I said before, there is usually *some* damage after head injuries of that severity.'

'It'll make life hard for him, having a limp. Other children will shout after him in the street. They can be cruel little devils sometimes.' They had been cruel to her because she wasn't quick like Lizzie and liked to think before she spoke. She remembered them shouting, 'Dummy! Dummy!' after her as she passed. She also remembered Lizzie threatening to belt one girl if she didn't shut up. Dr Herbert's voice brought her out of her reverie.

'But Billy will have a life at least,' he said quietly.

'Will — you know — his brain be all right?' She hadn't dared ask this before.

'It's too soon to tell whether he'll make a complete recovery mentally, but he's doing so well that we can certainly hope for it. He seems to grow more alert each time I see him.' Toby looked across at Polly's neat head, bent over her clasped hands, as if to keep her thoughts to herself. Everything about her was neat. He felt a warmth rise in him because he had grown really fond of Polly Scordale but it was still only a few months since she had lost her husband. He must be patient.

He stood up. 'Well, I've got to go and see my friend Richard now. We've bought a house for our soldiers' home on the Fylde Coast — big old place — and it's nearly ready now. Sarge is going to run it for us. He's a sound fellow and very strong. He'll have no difficulty lifting the inmates.'

Toby whistled as he drove away. It wasn't far from where Polly lived in Blackpool to Stenton-on-Sea, though you had to drive in a roundabout way because of the River Wyre. He really liked the little Fylde village, and as he paid his toll and drove across the Shard Bridge towards it his spirits lifted. Richard usually provided a decent lunch, and once business was over they could settle into a good natter about the war and the old days, when they had all been so close.

On this visit, however, Richard seemed rather preoccupied, not his usual self.

'What's wrong?' Toby prompted over a fine apple pie and fresh cream.

'What? Oh, you might as well know, I suppose. Florence has left me and is living with – with someone else. I'm planning to divorce her. It's going to be a messy business, though.'

'I'm sorry, old chap.'

Richard gave a wry smile. 'There's no love lost between her and me, and to tell you the truth I'll be glad to be rid of her. It's Connie I'm worried about. She's going to be upset when she finds out.'

'Do you know, in all the time I've been coming here, I haven't actually met your daughter.'

'No. Well, she's rather shy. And she's had some bad dealings with doctors, so she won't come downstairs till you've gone.'

Toby didn't push the matter, but he'd have been glad to offer his opinion on the leg, if asked. Every year they were finding new ways to help people; the child might not need to limp so badly. Thinking of that, he changed the subject to his pet hobby horse of rehabilitation and how they could best help the inmates of their home.

That brought Richard out of his preoccupied mood and they discussed it in great depth, determined to help the men become as independent as possible. Both of them were surprised when the clock chimed and they saw it was time for Toby to leave.

Richard watched his friend drive away then went to study the strange letter he'd received offering to care for Connie. He'd meant to consult Toby about the practicality of it all, but they'd got so involved in their discussion that he'd forgotten to mention it. He frowned as he re-read it. The writer had a round, childish hand, but had spelled the words correctly and set the letter out in a proper way. Only – he wanted someone prepared to devote herself completely to Connie, not someone with a crippled child to look after as well. He felt sorry for this woman, of course he did, but he had to put his daughter first.

In the next day's post came another letter of application, this one ill-spelled and untidy. He frowned at it. This applicant might not have any encumbrances, but she sounded disorganised and slapdash. Why could he not get someone suitable? Was Florence right? Was Stenton just too small and too far away for modern young women to be happy there? He decided to give it a few more days before doing anything.

Three days later Richard pulled out the same two letters and sighed. He was definitely not hiring the poor speller. After reading and re-reading the letter from Mrs Scordale, he grimaced and pulled a sheet of notepaper towards him. It could do no harm to speak to the woman, at least. And – most important of all – see how she dealt with Connie.

My dear Mrs Scordale,

Thank you for your letter applying for the position looking after my daughter.

As you will understand, it is important to me to find someone who will both understand Connie's needs and encourage her a little, since she is very shy with strangers. I therefore suggest that you come here to meet us, staying overnight, so that we can all get to know one another. I keep a cook-housekeeper and maid who will see to your needs.

To be truthful, I am not at all sure how it would work having your son here, and whether you could fulfil your duties towards my daughter as well as caring for him. We would need to discuss the practicalities of that in much more detail.

I shall be happy to reimburse your travel expenses. Please let me know if you are still interested and when you could come. Some time during the next week would suit me.

Yours sincerely,

Richard Mercer

On a sudden thought, he took Mrs Scordale's letter up to the nursery and showed it to Connie before he posted his response. 'What do you think? Shall we ask this lady to come and see us?'

Florence used to mock the way he consulted Connie about things, but he thought the child ought to have a say in something so important to her. Indeed, it worried him at times that she was so passive, so accepting of whatever happened to her.

Connie frowned and read the letter carefully for a second time. 'She doesn't sound loud, does she?'

'That's a funny word to use.'

'Well, I don't like noisy people. Mrs Roulson talked loudly and she kept playing music on the gramophone till it made my head ache. Even her clothes were too bright.'

He could only stare at her for a moment, surprised at her amazingly mature analysis of the Roulson woman. 'You're right. This one doesn't sound loud.'

'We'll have to get someone, won't we, so that you can help the soldiers?'

'Yes, my little duck, we shall have to.' He was pleased that she took such an interest in the lads, while at the same time worrying that it was a strange whim for a child of her age. Perhaps it was fellow feeling. She had certainly experienced a lot of illness in her short life.

Connie smiled and wagged one finger at him reprovingly. 'I'm too old now to be called a "little duck", Daddy.'

'You'll always be my little duck, darling.'

She nestled trustingly against him on the bed and they sat there in silence, as they often did. He wished she would be naughty sometimes. She was quite frighteningly well-behaved, as if her lameness and being ill had given her a maturity beyond her years — or as if she was frightened of upsetting people.

When he pulled away a small sigh escaped her. 'Sorry, love, but I have some letters to write.' Her face fell so he added, 'Would you like to come and sit in the library with me while I do them?'

She brightened at once. 'Oh, yes. I love it there. One day I'm going to read every single book on the shelves.'

He shuddered. 'Don't even try. Some of them are so dull they'll bore your socks off.'

She giggled, for a moment looking more like a child of ten, then her expression became calm again and she limped across to pick up her book before following him down the stairs slowly and carefully. He knew she hated to be helped, but he always tried to walk in front of her in case she fell. He didn't want any more accidents.

If Connie's fall had been an accident.

He always tried to give Florence the benefit of the doubt about that, but he could not help wondering sometimes how a little child who had been ill for days, too ill to move, could not only have managed to leave her bedroom without anyone noticing, but then have fallen down the stairs with enough force to break her leg in several places.

CHAPTER SEVENTEEN

February 1921

———————◆———————

Polly stared at herself in the mirror, wishing she were not so plain and that her clothes were smarter. She turned to her sister and spread her arms. 'Do I look – you know, all right?'

Lizzie gave her a hug. 'Of course you do. Now come on. We have to get you off to Stenton.'

Polly nodded, took a deep breath and went to give Billy a final kiss. She trusted Lizzie to look after him, of course she did, and was grateful that her sister had come all the way from Overdale just to do this for her overnight. But she hadn't been away from her son since she'd brought him home from hospital and felt awful about leaving him.

Thankful that the rain had held off and the sea was calm, she took the tram to Fleetwood then the ferry to Knott End. From there she walked to the station, intending to get a taxi from there to Stenton. However, a bored-looking porter informed her that the taxi was 'out' and was not expected back for at least half an hour so she went to sit on a bench and wait. The porter vanished as did everyone else. When a slow three-quarters of an hour had dragged past by the station clock, she went back inside to ask if there was any other way of getting to Stenton.

There was no one to be found so she knocked on a door marked *Private*. No one answered. Shivering in the chill wind, Polly made her way back to the bench – and found that her suitcase had vanished. For a moment she panicked then tried to calm down and work out what had happened. Someone had made a mistake, that must be it, had thought the suitcase lost and taken it to the police station, perhaps. She had been reading in the paper about how crime had increased because of massive unemployment, but surely not in a small place like Knott End?

She hurried back into the station and called out, 'Hello! Is anyone there?' But her voice just echoed in the windy space and although she called several times more, still no one answered. At the sound of a motor car drawing up outside she rushed out again and found that the taxi had returned.

When she told her story to the driver, he gaped at her for a minute. 'Someone's stolen your suitcase? Here in Knott End! Nay, never. Folk aren't like that round here.'

He escorted her into the station and bellowed at the top of his voice, 'Reuben, get thysen out here, lad!' thumping vigorously on the door marked *Private* for good measure.

A man appeared, his hair tousled and his eyes dull, as if he had just woken up. By the time Polly had told her tale again and Reuben had sent a lad to fetch a policeman, she was beginning to feel angry. Reuben professed himself 'stumped' to think who could have taken her case and disappeared with it so quickly. As there was a train due to depart for Fleetwood, a small crowd began to gather, exclaiming and muttering when they heard what had happened, some of them looking at her as if she were the guilty one.

In the end, after reporting the matter to a young police constable, she decided to continue to Captain Mercer's house, explain her problem to him and then return to Blackpool before nightfall. She felt really upset to lose not only her clothes but a little picture of Eddie that always stood beside her bed and that she had brought along to give herself courage.

The taxi driver kept up a continuous monologue on the short drive, the gist of which was that the war had ruined the country, absolutely ruined it, and that he couldn't believe there was such a brazen thief in Knott End, no, not if you paid him a thousand pounds, he couldn't.

A few minutes later he broke off in mid-sentence to say, 'That's it, love. The big house at the end of Seaview Close.'

Polly sighed as they drew up outside. She now had to face a potential employer, the first possibility out of all those letters she'd written, and tell him she'd let her suitcase get stolen. He wouldn't want to trust his daughter to someone who couldn't even look after her own suitcase.

It was quite a large house but had a stern, closed look to it, as if it needed bringing to life. Three storeys high and built of deep red brick, it was surrounded by neatly trimmed hedges, inside which the garden was kept too rigidly neat for Polly's taste. There was no sign that a child ever played there and yet Captain Mercer's daughter was only ten. Wasn't there even a swing? Perhaps it was round the back.

She smiled as she remembered how her garden in Outshaw had looked before Billy's accident. She could still remember a day when he had dumped his pull-along cart on the small patch of lawn and started digging busily in a border, muddy bottom set skywards, bobbing up and down with his strenuous efforts. When she'd called out to him he had turned suddenly to look up at her with such a blissful expression on his dirty face that she had not had the heart to smack him, as her mother-in-law said she should have done. Billy *would* play outside again one day and get dirty, too. She would make sure of that.

When the driver stopped and opened the car door for her, Polly asked hesitantly, 'Could you – would you mind waiting till I check that it's the right place?'

'It's the address you gave me, love, and I've brought folk to Captain Mercer's before, but I don't mind waiting.' He folded his arms and leaned against the car.

Her stomach churning with nervousness, Polly mounted the

three steps that led to the front door. Just as she raised the knocker the door opened and she exclaimed in shock before she could stop herself.

The man drew back a little. 'I'm sorry, I didn't mean to startle you. I'm Richard Mercer and you must be Mrs Scordale.'

'Yes.' She grasped the hand he offered and shook it. Goodness, he was tall! But quite good-looking with nice wavy, dark hair – or would have been had he not had such a stern expression on his face. Or was it the scar that made him look severe? She realised he had spoken and was waiting for an answer. 'I beg your pardon? I didn't catch that.'

'I asked if your suitcase was in the taxi?'

She blushed. 'No, I'm afraid—' She broke off, then blurted it out because there was no easy way to say it. 'Someone stole it when I was waiting for the taxi at Knott End station.'

He stared at her, blinked incredulously and asked, 'Stole it? In Knott End?'

'Yes. I'd only left it for a minute, but when I came back it had just gone. I should have been more careful, I know, but there was no one around—' She realised she was gabbling and stopped abruptly.

The driver moved forward to join in. 'They're all amazed over there, Captain Mercer. No one can imagine who could have done such a thing. And in broad daylight, too. Eh, I don't know what the world is coming to, I really don't. I blame it all on the war. It would never have happened before – not in Knott End it wouldn't, any road.'

Polly closed her eyes for a minute, wishing he would not go on saying that.

'Are you all right, Mrs Scordale?'

She opened them to see Captain Mercer studying her and tried to pull herself together. 'Yes. I'm – I'm fine. Just a bit – well, annoyed. With myself as much as anyone, really. And I won't be able to stay the night now as we'd arranged. But if I can catch the last ferry back to Fleetwood, we could – I could still meet your daughter and — get to know her a bit. If you want me to, that is.'

Richard saw how tightly her hands were pressed together, how her lips trembled suddenly and then closed tightly together, and felt a sudden spurt of sympathy. He could imagine Florence in the same circumstances. She'd have been ranting and raving, blaming everyone but herself. 'Look, you go inside, Mrs Scordale and I'll pay the driver. Wait for me in the hall. I'm sure you'll feel better after a nice cup of tea.'

'It's I who should pay the . . .' But he had already run down the steps so she stopped trying to protest and studied him. He looked very fit and healthy with his military bearing, like so many who had served in the forces. Underneath it all, however, he seemed tense and unhappy. She realised he had finished paying the taxi driver and was saying goodbye, and since she didn't want to be caught staring at him, hurried inside.

The hall was rather dark. If it had been hers, she'd have painted the panelling a nice light cream or hung up horse brasses to cheer things up. A muffled sound made her look up and she saw a child's face bob hastily back from the banisters. That would be the daughter. She smiled. The child was normal enough to want to peep at her, anyway. Polly didn't wave or call out, though, because it must be daunting to have to face a series of new companions one after the other, as this little girl apparently had. Let her look her fill. Polly doubted there was anything about her to frighten a child.

When Captain Mercer came inside, he said firmly, 'Come into the sitting room. We'll have a cup of tea first, shall we?'

'Oh, yes, please. If it's no trouble.' Polly guessed he wanted to talk to her before she met his daughter. Well, she wanted to talk to him, too. She didn't intend to get herself and Billy into a difficult situation, so she was going to check everything she could think of very carefully indeed before she took up this or any position. After all, she had over a year's money left — as long as there were no major expenses for Billy — because it had been very cheap living at Mrs Baker's.

He shepherded her into a room at the front of the house and she glanced quickly round, assessing it with a housemaid's trained eye. It was a pleasant enough room, but there were no flowers and very few ornaments. The dark green curtains looked as if they needed a good beating and a blow on the washing line on a breezy day. And that suite needed new loose covers. Why, the armrests were quite threadbare. In fact, the whole place needed a woman's touch. 'Is your wife not at home today, Captain?'

It seemed such a simple straightforward question, but she saw his expression grow chilly and her heart thumped in apprehension at the change of mood.

'My wife and I are separated, Mrs Scordale. And you may as well know from the start that I intend to divorce her as soon as I can. So if that offends you . . .'

Polly could feel heat flooding into her face. 'Oh, I'm so sorry. I didn't mean to pry. It's none of my business, I'm sure.' She saw his hands curl into fists, then relax slowly. How grim his mouth looked!

'You were not to know.' He indicated a comfortable chair and rang the bell. When a maid arrived, he ordered tea and cakes then sat down opposite Polly and cleared his throat. 'I have some questions to ask you, Mrs Scordale, and I'm sure you must have things you wish to ask me. But first I must say that I am not at this stage offering you the job. It's Connie's needs which count, so it'll be as much her decision as mine.'

Polly nodded. 'That seems fair enough.' The thought of how Lizzie would answer this gave her the courage to add, 'I'm not at this stage asking for the job, actually, only finding out about it. I'm in a – a difficult situation as well.'

He raised his eyebrows and stared at her, then inclined his head as if accepting that.

She let out a long slow breath and when he didn't speak, asked, 'What exactly are the duties? Your advert wasn't very clear about that.'

'Then why did you apply?'

'I'd seen the advert before. I thought perhaps you were having trouble finding someone suitable and might consider an unusual arrangement. It's not going to be easy for me to find something, not with Billy to look after and I won't have him put in an institution. A child needs its mother's love.'

'Well, that's honest at any rate.' Richard ran one hand through his carefully combed hair without realising what he was doing. As a few strands fell across his brow, he let out a deep sigh.

Why, he's nervous, too! Polly realised, relaxing still further. It's usually a wife's job to hire someone like me and he's not quite sure what to say. 'Tell me about Connie first,' she suggested. 'That's the most important thing for both of us, I think. What's wrong with her?' She saw his eyes fill with sadness, but it was not something they could avoid talking about.

'She—' He hesitated, stared down at his clenched fists. 'She fell down the stairs during the war. Broke her leg in three places and hurt her hip. I wasn't home at the time but apparently the doctors didn't think it would affect her this badly, only it has. She complains that the hip hurts if she has to walk too far, and prefers to sit in her room and look out of the window rather than playing out.'

'Poor child.'

He added quickly, 'She's clever, mind, older than her years in some ways. You're not to think she's in any way mentally impaired.'

Polly sat considering the picture he had painted, glad that he was allowing her time to take things in and not rushing on with other questions. 'Does she have any friends of her own age?'

'No, she avoids other children. It's as if she's afraid of them. Quite frankly, that's the only reason I'm considering employing you, given your circumstances. If she can get used to your little son, maybe it'll help her lose that fear. She shows such sympathy when people have – well, physical problems. She's always asking me about the men who are to live in the rest home for returned soldiers that I'm involved in setting up.' Another pause, then, 'Perhaps now would be the time for you to tell me about your son?'

So Polly explained once again about the accident. She had done this so many times that she no longer felt like weeping. Eddie was gone now and her life was following a different path.

'I was surprised that you felt you could manage to look after your son as well as my daughter,' Captain Mercer said thoughtfully once she had finished.

Polly felt on safer ground here. 'Oh, I'm quite good at doing several things at a time, sir. I was a housemaid with the Pilbys – they own the ironworks and are the leading family in Overdale, where I come from – and they entertained a lot.'

'Yes, I know them slightly. I come from Overdale, too.'

Then it all fell into place. 'You're Peter's Captain Mercer!' she exclaimed, annoyed with herself for not realising before.

'Peter? Not Peter Dearden?'

'He's my brother-in-law.' Polly beamed at him, feeling greatly relieved. Peter thought the world of this man and she trusted her brother-in-law's judgement.

Richard was surprised by that smile. It lit up her whole face, revealing what seemed to be a natural warmth of character. He didn't know when he'd last met a woman like her, rather old-fashioned some would have said, but he preferred Mrs Scordale's open expression and the way she had of thinking about what she was going to say to his wife's quick answers and brittle modernity – infinitely preferred it. In fact, it was partly that smile which made him feel it might be worth giving her a chance. That and the fact that she was related to Dearden. Only if Connie took to her, of course. That was the most important thing of all, the deciding factor. But the business with the suitcase still worried him. Was she careless about things?

'And the other duties?' Polly asked. 'You haven't mentioned them.'

He was surprised she asked because the other women had

done nothing apart from looking after Connie. 'To tell you the truth, I'm not certain. I presume you would keep Connie's rooms tidy – she has a bedroom and a day room upstairs – and see to the room you would share with your son, of course. Really, you would have to fit in as best you could in the household. I inherited this house from my uncle and his staff have kindly stayed on. Though Connie's companion would be more like a member of the family than a servant.' He had determined to keep a better eye on things this time, which would mean the woman he appointed eating with them and sitting with them sometimes in the evening, too.

Well, Polly thought, that's another thing in his favour. In these times, to keep two servants for years is quite an achievement.

'Well, if you've finished your tea, we could go up and meet Connie now.'

'Yes, of course.' She liked his quiet voice, liked the polite way he ushered her out of the room. As she followed him up the stairs, Polly paused to look round the hall with a frown, then realised that he had stopped at the top and was watching her.

'Is something wrong with the hall, Mrs Scordale?'

She could feel herself blushing. 'I'm sorry. I just – I always think how I'd have a house if it were mine. Mrs Pilby kept things so beautifully. She'd have painted this hall cream. It's a bit dark and that feels gloomy on a grey winter's day like today.' Funny how she felt she could be honest with him. She'd not have dared speak out like that when she worked at the Pilbys'.

Richard stared round thoughtfully. 'You're probably right. I don't know much about that sort of thing and I suppose the house is old-fashioned. I kept hoping Florence would do something about that – my wife, that is. She never did, though. She hated living in Stenton.'

It wasn't Polly's place to comment, but the words escaped her before she could stop them. 'It seems a nice little village to me.

The taxi driver said they're extending the hotel at the other end of the sea front.'

'Yes. It's almost finished. Our rest home is also on the sea front near there.'

'It'll be nice for the inmates to be able to watch the sea. It's sad how so many men have been left crippled. My husband couldn't go in the forces because he had a bad limp from a childhood accident, but some of the lads I grew up with came back so badly hurt . . .' Her voice trailed away. Even two years after the end of the war, its marks were still everywhere. The men without legs were what upset her most, moving about on little wheeled carts, using pieces of wood to push themselves along with. And there were others who were missing arms, or blinded, or with their lungs ruined by the mustard gas. It was sad to hear them wheezing for breath. She sometimes wondered if England would ever be free of the war's shadow.

'It's a dreadful price to pay,' Richard agreed. 'They were so young, most of them. There is one who . . .' He broke off. 'I'm sorry. I shouldn't bore you with my stories.'

'It doesn't bore me. It would be worse if we forgot such people, wouldn't it?'

When she looked up again he was staring at her with an approving expression even though she was still keeping him waiting. She climbed the last few steps in a little rush and, as he turned without a word, followed him briskly along the landing towards a door at the end. She noticed that he rapped on it lightly before opening it. Courtesy again. Most parents would just walk into a child's bedroom. Her own mother always had.

Connie Mercer was sitting hunched up in a big chair in the bay window. She had a large book clasped against her chest, as if for protection. To Polly, the child looked terrified and her heart went out to her.

'This is my daughter Constance,' Captain Mercer said. 'Only we usually call her Connie, don't we darling? And this is Mrs Scordale.'

Connie nodded and gave him a quick relieved smile as he went to stand beside her, one hand on her shoulder.

Polly moved forward with her hand held out. 'How are you, Connie? My name's Polly, and that's a nickname, too. I was christened Mary, but no one has ever called me that.'

The girl looked surprised at being offered a handshake like a grown-up, but took Polly's hand and shook it briefly. 'I'm very well, thank you, Mrs Scordale.'

'I'd rather you called me Polly.' She kept hold of the little girl's hand and looked round, frowning. 'You feel cold. Do you want me to get the fire burning better? It's a raw day out there.' Without waiting for an answer, she went across and put some more pieces of coal on the fire, using the poker to set them to best advantage and watching in satisfaction as flames began to lick at them. 'There. I do like a nice fire.'

She turned round, saw them both watching her and blushed. 'I'm sorry. Maybe I shouldn't have—'

It was Connie who spoke. 'I like a nice fire, too,' she said, as solemnly as a little old woman.

'My son loves to watch the flames now that he's starting to get better,' Polly said. 'Would you mind him being with us here, Connie? If I came, that is. He had a very bad accident and he's only just starting to recover. He can't speak properly yet or move much, either.'

Richard watched in surprise as she drew up a chair – something he should have done, he thought guiltily – then chatted quietly to his daughter, not asking intrusive questions but speaking about her son to break the ice. To his surprise, Connie gradually began to volunteer information and ask questions about little Billy and the two of them continued to chat without the need for him to intervene.

Polly, he mused. The name suited her. Simple and straightforward, just like she was. He listened as she told Connie about her son and the accident which had nearly destroyed his life. He noted with approval that she listened carefully to what Connie said, responding to the remarks his daughter made, seeming instinctively to let the child take the lead in the conversation when she wanted to. If this was Polly Scordale's normal way of talking to children, it was a good sign.

Leaning back because he was feeling rather tired today, he continued to watch them both closely, contributing the occasional comment when Connie brought him into the conversation, but otherwise leaving them to it. He could feel himself relaxing and wondered at it. He had felt very keyed up this morning, thinking of the ordeal to come. Only it wasn't proving to be an ordeal at all.

'Do you like to go out for walks?' Polly was asking. 'I have to take Billy out each day if the weather's not too bad, you see. The doctor says if his brain is to recover we have to show him things and let him learn about the world all over again. And he does love his walks, bless him. He gets excited as soon as I put his coat on.'

'They're always wanting me to go out,' Connie said, a frown marring her face. 'I don't like it, though. People stare when I limp.'

'Yes, they stare at my son, too. But Billy and me don't let that worry us. People are always staring at others. If it's not for one thing, it's for another. They used to stare at me when I was at school and call me slow. Well, I am slow. I like to take time to think about things, not rush around before I know where I am. But I'm not stupid, and they called me that, too.'

Connie looked at her in surprise. 'Did they really stare at you?'

'Oh, yes.'

Richard stood up. 'I'll leave you two to continue getting acquainted, shall I? Connie, could you show Mrs Scordale her bedroom and the bathroom when you've finished chatting? She's had her suitcase stolen so she can't stay tonight after all, but she'll still want to wash her hands before lunch, I should think.'

He walked slowly out, wondering if Connie would find an excuse to call him back. He wasn't going to leave her on her own with Mrs Scordale unless she felt comfortable about that. But she didn't call. And as he stood outside, unashamedly eavesdropping, he heard her breathless little chuckle and the low murmur of voices continued.

Feeling much better about things, he walked down the stairs, thinking about Polly Scordale. She wasn't at all what he'd expected, but she was a very comfortable sort of person. He felt it and clearly Connie did too. But how would it be if her son were here as well? It was such a strange proposition – to work for nothing but her keep if she could have her son with her. He probably shouldn't even be considering it.

Was he considering it? Yes, he was. He definitely was. There was something rather likeable about Polly Scordale.

Later Polly and Connie went downstairs to have afternoon tea with Captain Mercer when the phone rang. Richard picked it up and heard Sergeant McWhey's voice, which always seemed much louder than necessary. He held the receiver a little way from his ear, grimacing.

'They've found the lady's suitcase, sir. A bunch of lads saw it and decided someone must have forgotten it. They were going to bring it to the police station, only on the way they stopped to play football and then forgot about it, just left it standing in the field. I gave them what for, I can tell you, and a good clout round the ear holes to din the lesson in. They won't pick up people's luggage again in a hurry, I can tell you.'

'That's good news. Excuse me a moment while I tell Mrs Scordale.' He turned to find Polly hesitating in the doorway. 'They've found your suitcase.'

She gave him a glowing smile and Richard found himself returning it before he turned back to the phone. 'Shall we come down to the station and pick it up, Sergeant?'

'If you would, sir. It'll have to be formally identified, I'm afraid.'

'We can be there in a few minutes.' He looked questioningly at Polly and she nodded agreement.

'I'm so relieved,' she confided as he put the phone down. 'You must think I'm every sort of fool. Only I was that nervous while I was waiting I couldn't sit still.'

'There was no need for that.'

She gave him one of her wide smiles. 'No, I can see that now. I couldn't be nervous of anyone who loves his daughter as you love Connie. But I hadn't met you then and, well, I'm not much good with strangers.'

He went into the sitting room to tell Connie what was happening before nipping along to the kitchen to tell Mrs Shavely that Mrs Scordale would be staying the night, after all, and would be joining them for the evening meal.

At the police station Sergeant McWhey himself came forward to deal with them and Polly could see from his attitude that he held Captain Mercer in high esteem.

On the way back she apologised again for troubling him like this and Richard found himself soothing her, as he would a new recruit. He hadn't made allowance enough for her being nervous, he decided. But actually he rather liked it. It showed she wasn't brassy. After Mrs Roulson he had a horror of brassy women.

He also liked the way Mrs Scordale took charge of getting Connie ready for bed, then lingered in the kitchen for a chat with Mrs Shavely and Doris afterwards. It was important that she get on with the staff. When he went to fetch her, they were all three laughing together and the newcomer was wiping the dishes for Doris.

In fact, Polly Scordale seemed too good to be true. She had told him that Toby Herbert was her son's doctor, so he'd be able to ring his friend up later that evening to ask about her. If Toby said she was all right, the job was hers.

'I like her, Daddy,' Connie whispered when Richard went up to say goodnight. 'She doesn't treat me as if I'm stupid and she makes me laugh.' She paused, head on one side, to consider this and amended it to, 'Not laugh, exactly, more chuckle or smile.'

'I know what you mean.'

'Isn't it sad about her son? But she says he's getting better. I'd like to help with him. Would that be all right?'

'You want her to look after you, then?'

'Yes, please.'

Toby had nothing but good to say about Polly Scordale, and explained how difficult her life had been made since the accident. Richard had met people like that Browning-Baker fellow in the army, petty tyrants who delighted in making their underlings' lives a misery. He hadn't allowed it in his company and he wouldn't allow it in the convalescent home, either.

When he nipped back upstairs Connie was still awake, so he went in and whispered the good news and she gave him an extra hug. 'Thank you for finding Polly for me, Daddy.'

She seemed to have no doubts about Mrs Scordale – and strangely enough neither did Richard.

In the morning he waited until breakfast was over and Connie had limped upstairs after exchanging a conspiratorial glance with him, then asked Mrs Scordale to join him in the library. He nearly called her Polly because that suited her so much better somehow.

She didn't say anything, just sat down and clasped her hands together in her lap, waiting for him to speak. Were her eyes pale blue or grey? He couldn't make up his mind. Anyway, what did that matter? What mattered was that Connie liked her – and so did he.

Richard came straight to the point. 'Do you want the job now you've met us, Mrs Scordale?'

'Yes, I do. I like your daughter.'

'She's definitely taken to you, but I still have my doubts about how you'll manage with both her and your son, I must admit, so I think we should have a month's trial before we decide anything definite. After all, *you* might not like working here. You might find it too quiet.'

She chuckled at that, a soft musical sound. 'It's downright

busy here in Stenton after Outshaw, Captain Mercer. I lived in a tiny hamlet on the edge of the moors after my marriage because Eddie worked on a farm there. Half a dozen houses and no one of my own age. No little children for Billy to play with, either. I was lonely there all right. And since I've been in Blackpool, I've found that I like living by the sea.'

She hesitated then added, 'My only worry is that if I don't suit, it'll take time to find somewhere else to live. So if you're not happy with – with how things work out, I'd ask you to give me enough time to find somewhere to go to before you turn – um, expect us to leave. It's not easy with a lad like my Billy.'

'That seems reasonable. Now, money. I would prefer to pay you for your services. I really don't like the idea of your working for nothing.'

Polly flushed. 'Let's wait and see how it all works out, shall we, sir? If I'm going to stay, we could discuss it later. I'm not short of money at the moment, just trying to be prudent and . . .' Another hesitation, then she said in a low voice, 'I've been a bit short of company, like. It's hard having no one to talk to, day after day. I shall enjoy being with Connie. Eh, she's good company, your daughter is.'

He smiled. 'A month's trial it is, then. And on a more practical note, how will you get your things here?'

'If we can wait till the weekend, my brother-in-law will come across from Overdale and bring us in his van.'

'Hmm. You couldn't possibly come to us earlier if I drove over to Blackpool and collected you myself, could you? Tomorrow, even? I have a meeting in Lancaster on Thursday, you see, and I have to see my lawyer afterwards. That'll take all day, so it'd be nice if Connie had some company while I was away. Not that Doris and Mrs Shavely don't look after her properly, but they have their work to do.'

'Well, I suppose so. Only there are some larger things to bring. Billy's special wheelchair and – and the other things he needs.'

'My car is quite roomy, and if there's anything which doesn't fit into it, there is a carter in the village.'

'Well, all right.'

'How soon do you want to leave?'

She looked at the clock. 'Lizzie will want to catch the earliest train home that she can. She's needed to serve in the shop, you see. The customers think the world of her. She came all that way just to look after Billy for me. She's a lovely sister.'

'I'll drive you to the ferry myself as soon as you're ready, then.'

Polly felt a little breathless as she climbed the stairs to say goodbye to Connie and pack. This was all happening too quickly for her. She wasn't used to making important decisions so rapidly. Well, until Eddie died, she hadn't had to make any important decisions at all for a few years, had she? With the wisdom of hindsight she had come to realise that her mother-in-law had made all the major decisions for them, and since Eddie had gone along with it, Polly had too because she didn't want to upset anyone.

I wonder if I'd have put up with it for ever? she thought. She might have done. She had always preferred a quiet life. But the accident had forced her to change, and now she felt a bit ashamed of the way she had let others run her life. Even a husband shouldn't decide everything.

She knocked on Connie's door and went inside to find the child looking at her expectantly. 'Your father has offered me the job. Well, a month's trial, anyway. Is that all right with you, love?'

Connie beamed at her. 'Oh, yes.'

Polly went across and hugged her. 'I'm that glad. I was getting a bit lonely looking after Billy on my own. He can't speak properly yet, you see. It'll be lovely to have someone to talk to, and perhaps you can help me teach him to speak again.'

'I'd like that. I'm going to help Daddy with the soldiers when they move into the home. One of them hasn't got any arms or legs, you know.'

'Eh, the poor lad!'

'You can come and visit them, too, if you like. Some of their families don't come to see them at all. Daddy says they love having visitors.'

When Polly got back to Blackpool she saw Lizzie standing by the window of the bedroom with Billy in her arms. Polly hurried inside, anxious to see her son, but Nelly stuck her head out of the front room and called to her to come in and tell her what had happened *this minute.*

After that it was rush, rush, rush to get Lizzie to the station in time for the one o'clock train, then Polly had to pack everything up for the next day's move.

In the evening, once she had got Billy asleep, she went and knocked on the front-room door. 'Nelly, I want to thank you properly for letting me stay. I've been here longer than you really wanted, I'm sure, but I don't know what I'd have done without your help.'

Her hostess grinned at her. 'It was worth it to stop Tommy bullying you – and, anyway, you've made yourself useful. And if you're ever stuck for somewhere to go . . .'

In the morning Captain Mercer turned up in Blackpool at nine o'clock as arranged, by which time Polly had been up since five and had everything ready. Nelly invited him in, but he said he'd rather get back quickly if they didn't mind so Polly took him upstairs to meet her son.

He stood looking at the child and his face had that glassy expression people assume when they're hiding their feelings.

'I hadn't realised how badly injured he was,' Richard said at last.

'He's a lot better and improving by the day,' Polly insisted.

Her new employer's expression said he didn't quite believe her.

She put up her chin and stared him in the eyes. 'Dr Herbert thinks he has a good chance of recovering his wits, though he'll probably always limp.'

Toby had said much the same thing to him on the phone, when he'd been asking about Polly Scordale. 'Well, Toby has worked miracles with some of our lads . . .'

While she was speaking to Captain Mercer, Polly was putting Billy's coat on and the tam o'shanter that she could pull down over his ears. He tried to grab it from her, saying, 'Ma-ma-ma!' and smiling at her.

She saw that Captain Mercer was smiling, too. 'Billy loves brightly coloured things,' she said apologetically, pulling some red and yellow mittens on to his hands.

Richard watched her, surprised at how efficiently she worked. She might be slow-spoken, but she moved with sureness from one task to the other. When he realised he was staring at her again, he looked round for something to do and saw several cases and bags standing ready by the door. 'Are those your things?'

They worked together to load the car and it was clear they were both used to working as a team. When he said as much, Polly smiled. 'If you don't work together in a big house, it makes life twice as hard. Our housekeeper knew her job and we were all very happy there.'

He'd have carried the lad out for her, because he seemed heavy for such a small woman, but Polly said it was best to leave Billy to her. He got nervous with strangers. The glow of love on her face as she talked softly to her son brought sudden moisture into Richard's eyes. It was such a contrast to Florence who hardly spent any time in Connie's company, though she was writing to their daughter now at least. Funny, he hadn't known she could write such amusing letters.

Then he stopped and let out a little growl of anger as he suddenly realised that people didn't suddenly turn into good correspondents overnight. George must be helping Florence with the letters. Or someone else, if she had moved on. Anger washed through him at his own gullibility. Unfortunately he wouldn't be able to tell them to stop the charade because Connie loved her mother's letters and kept them in her treasure box, re-reading them regularly.

Oh, hell! He wished it didn't take so long to get a divorce! Wished he didn't need to have his wife spied on – and as for the prospect of exposing her infidelities in court for the whole world to mock, it filled him with disgust every time he contemplated it.

If he had to do it, he wanted to win, though, so with great reluctance he'd asked Toby if he would be a witness, too. Apparently his friend had several times seen Florence cavorting around London with various officers during the war – though he hadn't told Richard about that at the time. Toby had apparently seen her sharing a hotel room with one man as well and she hadn't even attempted to be discreet about it.

Richard caught a concerned glance from Mrs Scordale and forced himself to smile. 'Sorry, I've been ignoring you. I was thinking about – um – a little problem I have.'

She nodded, not prying, just sitting there in the car, composed and alert, holding her son so that he could see out and occasionally pointing something out to him. And she was right, the boy did seem to be paying attention and following her pointing finger. Maybe there was some hope for him?

There was no hope for Richard's marriage. None at all. He didn't even want to try to retrieve it.

CHAPTER EIGHTEEN

February 1921

———◆———

Florence woke up with a start as George pulled off the bedcovers and demanded that she wake up. She squinted at him and realised it was very early in the morning. 'Have you been out all night?' she asked sleepily.

'I have indeed. I won a lot of money, enough to take us to the South of France.'

'Georgie!'

'You'll need to get up, too, and start packing, Flo, my pet.'

She became suddenly very wide awake. 'You mean it about going to France, then? You really do?'

He shot her a sideways glance, one eyebrow raised quizzically. 'Don't I always mean what I say?'

She nodded, irritation forgotten. 'Oh, Georgie, you're absolutely marvellous.'

He was not listening. 'We'll get rid of this place. Pack everything you want to keep and we'll simply abandon the rest. As soon as we've eaten I'll go and see about tickets and storage companies. I want to leave this afternoon.'

'But, George – it's not possible to pack our cloths and everything else so quickly.'

He swung round to fix her with one of his hard looks. 'It'd better be possible. I'll get tea chests sent round within the hour and *with or without you* I'm leaving this afternoon. Now, make me some breakfast then get to work, woman.'

Swallowing her annoyance, Florence pulled on a dressing gown. Unlike Richard, George would never help in the house, insisting that was a woman's job. Usually she didn't mind because they ate out a lot, but she was tired this morning and didn't at all feel like cooking bacon and eggs.

An hour later George walked out of the building pulling his trilby down to shadow his eyes and tugging the collar of his overcoat up. He didn't want to be too easily recognised. Last night he had won rather a lot of money and Lucky Palmer had been unhappy about that. Very unhappy indeed.

George grinned at his reflection in a shop window. Well, he *had* been cheating – though only during that last hand because he really preferred to win by his own skills. But with so much at stake, he had felt it worth the risk. Now, however, he'd made himself an enemy. Palmer was too good a player not to suspect, or else – George's smile broadened – perhaps he had been planning to cheat George! His luck in the final hands of close-run games was legendary. Maybe he also made a habit of helping things along from time to time.

George had decided that it was best to get out of the country for a while and let the other man's anger die down. You didn't cross Lucky Palmer, not if you could help it. The man had some rather nasty friends. Well, George could be very nasty, too, if pushed.

Later that afternoon, as he and Florence were escorted aboard the boat train by an obsequious porter, George thought for a moment that he saw Thad Baxter, Palmer's henchman, watching him from the other side of the ticket barrier. But when he glanced hastily back he could see no sign of anyone even remotely resembling the bull-like Baxter, just a nondescript fellow waving to someone.

He breathed out in relief and got into the train, annoyed with himself for imagining things. Mind you, he'd keep his eyes open. He didn't want Palmer's pet thug on his trail. Baxter had been a boxer and had the battered face to prove it, but he was better known nowadays for dealing harshly with anyone who crossed his boss. It was definitely the right thing to get out of the country quickly and stay away for a while. As long as Palmer didn't follow him . . . Well, George would deal with that if it happened. Palmer wasn't the only one who could use violence if the situation called for it.

Leaning his head back, George half-closed his eyes and studied Florence who was sitting staring out of the window, her eyes aglow. The poor bitch had led a very sheltered sort of life, what with the war and that old sourpuss she'd married. Well, they'd both have some fun while they were overseas. Lots of it. The war had taught him to seize the moment with both hands! It was the only way to live.

Captain Mercer gave Polly two of the second-floor rooms just above Connie's bedroom. They were quite decent-sized bedrooms, but she decided to have Billy in to sleep with her and use the other as a sitting room.

'The Captain likes things to be kept really tidy, mind,' Mrs Shavely warned her. 'Comes of being in the army, I suppose.'

'I'm a bit that way myself,' Polly replied. 'Are you sure he won't mind my changing things round?'

'I'm not sure he'll even notice. Sits staring into space for hours, he does, sometimes. The poor man's had a lot to put up with, he has that.'

On her first morning in Stenton, Polly woke early, while it was still dark. She could hear Billy breathing softly in the bed next to hers and outside the low hum of the sea rolling in on the small beach.

Well, no use lying here, she thought, easing herself quietly out of bed and fumbling for her dressing gown in the dark. She'd have a wash later, but she wanted to light a fire in the other room before she got Billy up and started doing his morning exercises.

And she usually had a cup of tea first thing. There was nothing like it for getting you going. Mrs Shavely had told her to help herself any time as long as she left things tidy – as if she wouldn't!

Feeling fairly certain that no one would be around to see her in her night things, Polly tiptoed down to the kitchen and got the fire in the old-fashioned stove drawing up a bit. After she'd set a kettle on the gas cooker to boil, she filled the second kettle and set that on the edge of the hob to heat up more slowly. Mrs Shavely would no doubt be glad to have things started for her. It was a big house for two elderly women to look after.

'You're an early riser, Mrs Scordale.'

Polly jumped in shock and turned round with one hand pressed against her breast. 'Oooh, sir, you startled me.'

'Sorry. I thought you'd have heard me coming down the stairs.'

'I was riddling to stove. Didn't hear a thing. Would you, um, like a cup of tea?' She pulled her dressing gown more tightly around her, feeling a bit embarrassed to be caught in her night-clothes by her employer.

He sighed and rubbed his forehead as if it were aching. 'I'd love one, actually.'

'If you always get up this early, I could bring a cup up to you regularly,' she offered. 'I'm always up at this time.'

'No, thanks. I don't usually get up until seven-thirty. I didn't sleep very well last night.' He was still worrying about how the divorce would affect Connie. Worrying about the rest home, too, which would be opening soon. But strangely enough, he had not worried at all about his new employee who was now flitting noise-lessly to and fro in the kitchen, humming under her breath.

'You've made yourself at home quickly, Mrs Scordale,' he commented, pulling out a chair and sitting down at the central table to watch her work.

'Oh, once a housemaid, always a housemaid,' she said, smiling cheerfully. As he yawned and stretched, she noticed how drawn his face looked. In fact, come to think of it, there was a permanent shadow of unhappiness in his eyes. Well, it couldn't be pleasant having to divorce your wife.

The kettle boiled at last and Polly poured the water on to the tea leaves in the warmed pot. 'There you are!' She placed the teapot on the table. 'Just give it a minute or two to brew.'

He'd expected her to sit down, but she busied herself getting another tray ready. When she saw him looking at her, she said, 'I might as well give Cook a start while I'm waiting. I think your tea should be ready now.' She walked round the table to deal with it for him.

He found himself watching the deft way she filled his cup. She didn't ask how he wanted it and must have remembered from the day before. When he took his first sip, he sighed in pleasure then saw that she hadn't poured herself any. 'Aren't you going to join me?'

'I didn't want to – to presume.'

'It's not presuming, and anyway I'm the one who interrupted you. Look, this is a small household and I don't stand on ceremony with my staff. Sit down and enjoy your tea.'

'Oh. Well. All right, then.' She poured some for herself and sat down across the table from him, cradling the cup in her hands to enjoy its warmth then sipping it slowly.

He realised he'd been staring at her and looked hurriedly down at his cup, swallowing another mouthful of tea before looking up again. 'Did you and your son sleep well?'

'Oh, yes. We always do.'

He watched her face cloud over and asked gently, 'What did I say to upset you?'

'Nothing, sir.'

'I did upset you and I'd rather know why.'

She hesitated, looked at him with those clear steady eyes, then said in a rush, 'It's the thought of Billy, not what you said, that upsets me. He didn't sleep like this before the accident, you see, but now he sleeps so long that I worry about it sometimes.'

'You're bound to.'

'Dr Herbert says we just have to accept the changes, but it's hard.'

'Yes.' Richard found that his cup was empty and reached out for the teapot.

'Let me!' she said at once.

Their hands met in mid-air and for a moment everything seemed to move very slowly, shifting around them as if the world was settling into a slightly new pattern, like Connie's kaleidoscope when you turned it. He drew his hand back, unable to think of anything to say, still caught up in the moment. When Polly reached out to take the teapot, he managed only, 'You do it much more efficiently than I do. I always seem to splash tea into the saucer.' Which was not exactly sparkling repartee.

When she pushed his cup back across the table to him, he nodded his thanks but found himself still lost for a suitable topic of conversation.

A glance sideways showed that she was staring down at her own cup, chewing on one corner of her lip as if unsure of something. Well, he felt unsure, too, because there was a current of feeling humming between them as if they were old friends. He didn't understand why that should be, but he liked sitting quietly with her, would enjoy starting every day like this. Perhaps it was because Polly radiated serenity and kindness more than anyone else he had ever met. He was sure Connie sensed that, too, or she would not have talked so easily to her new companion within minutes of meeting her.

'I can see you love your cup of tea, Mrs Scordale,' he murmured at last when the silence had dragged on for too long.

She glanced sideways at him, frowning slightly. 'I'd rather you called me Polly, sir. Scordale was my married name and it's never felt to be really mine.' Why she had told him this, when she'd told no one else, she could not work out. He'd think she was a proper old babbler.

But he just gave her a half-smile that crinkled the corners of his eyes and agreed that it must be difficult to change your name like that. She could not help staring at him for a moment because as his face softened, he seemed younger – and very attractive, too, in spite of the slightly puckered scar. She continued to watch as he put three heaped spoonfuls of sugar into his cup, stirring it with great concentration.

'You like your tea very sweet,' she teased.

'Yes. We couldn't always get sugar in the trenches, or milk. Now I can't seem to have enough sweet things.' He laughed self-consciously. 'You'll find that I like cakes, too. Mrs Shavely makes delicious sponge cakes and,' he glanced over his shoulder as if about to reveal something shameful then whispered, 'I have a real weakness for bars of Fry's Milk Chocolate Cream.'

She chuckled. 'Me, too! Eddie used to buy me a bar sometimes for a treat.'

'You speak about him comfortably, so you must have coped with your loss now.' It was a statement, not a question.

'Well, you have to, don't you?'

'Some people never seem to manage it. Do you have any other family apart from your sister Lizzie?'

'Oh, yes. There are five of us, three girls and two boys.' Tears welled in her eyes and she could see that he'd noticed. 'They all live in Overdale and you might as well know that I only moved away from them because I had to.'

'Because of this Browning-Baker person? Toby has already explained something of that. But you were right to trust his methods. I've seen what he has achieved sometimes with men who've been badly wounded. Miracles, some people call them. But there's a lot of hard work goes into those miracles.'

Polly nodded, surprised at how comfortable she felt confiding in him. 'Yes, but I'm still frightened the child welfare people from Overdale will come after me.'

Richard stared at her in astonishment. 'Surely it's none of their business now that you've left the town? Why ever should they do that?'

'Because Dr Browning-Baker keeps finding ways to get at me.'

'Well, if they come after you here, they'll have me to deal with, Mrs Scordale, I promise you.'

'But I can't ask you to—'

'You didn't ask, Polly. I volunteered.' He watched as a smile slowly replaced the anxiety on her face.

'Thank you, sir. I'm grateful.' She realised she had lost her nervousness of Captain Mercer already. He wasn't like any other employer she had heard of. Mrs Shavely had already told her how he refused to stand on ceremony, popping into the kitchen to ask for a piece of cake rather than ringing the bell, or going outside to help the elderly gardener dig up the vegetable bed.

'Polly really suits you as a name.'

She grimaced. 'Ordinary.'

'No, not ordinary – warm and friendly.' He wondered whether this remark was too personal and said hurriedly, 'Goodness, look at the time! I'd better go and get dressed. I have a busy day ahead of me. I'll see you at breakfast, Polly.'

She frowned. 'Are you still sure you want us to join you, sir? Billy's a rather messy eater still.'

His voice became firm again, taking on the tone of someone used to making decisions and giving orders. 'If you're looking after Connie, you'll eat with us. I like to have my meals with my daughter.'

Still she hesitated.

'You think I'd be upset by your son's disabilities? I've seen far worse, believe me, and have often helped feed men who can't feed themselves. No, my mind is made up. You'll both join us for breakfast – and for all meals when we don't have guests. And that's only because I think Billy himself will be more comfortable not having to deal with strangers.'

'You're very understanding.'

'I've always found that if you look after your people, they look after you.'

Feeling optimistic about his new employee, though he couldn't have said why, Richard walked up the stairs, whistling softly, not hurrying, enjoying the morning quiet before the day got going. He hadn't felt this good for a while. It was probably because he'd got Polly now to look after Connie. He'd been very worried about his daughter.

Later, as Polly was carrying Billy down for breakfast, finding him heavy and awkward on the broad shallow lower staircase and wondering how she was going to manage when he got bigger, Richard came out of his library and hurried across to relieve her of her burden. She was worried about how Billy would react to a stranger, but he made some of his strange crowing noises at the strange face so close to his and moved his arm towards it.

The Captain laughed and said something to him, then carried him into the dining room, where a carver chair had been set up with cushions. 'This is not a very satisfactory arrangement for you, my lad, but it will have to do for now.' He looked at Polly. 'Later, if things go well, we'll get a more suitable chair for him.'

'Or maybe he'll keep improving and not need one,' Polly said.

'We'll *help* him get better!' Connie said firmly, going to sit next to Billy at the opposite side from Polly.

When the little boy turned his head towards her and made the sound Polly recognised as a greeting, she smiled to see the two of them, then felt the smile fading. It was all going so well. Too well, perhaps. After the troubles of the last few months, she had come to expect problems, not pleasant smiles and food placed on the table for her, as Doris was doing. Even at Nelly's, she and Billy had usually had a tray in their own room.

As she ate and intermittently fed Billy, she thought at first that Captain Mercer was watching her and it made her feel a bit clumsy. Then she realised it was Connie he was watching, looking as if he approved of the interest his daughter was taking in Billy.

He insisted on carrying the boy up to Connie's sitting room after breakfast and then brought the special playpen and chair into the room for him.

When Polly went out, intending to run up and fetch some of Billy's toys, he caught hold of her arm, saying, 'Just a minute.'

Her heart thumped in her chest as she looked at him. Was something wrong?

'I wanted to say that I haven't seen Connie look so animated for a long time,' he said softly. 'Let her help you with your son. It's bringing her out of her shell already.' He didn't wait for an answer but called to his daughter, 'I have to go out now, darling.'

The child rushed out to hug him and Polly watched the tenderness in his face as he hugged her back. Why, he adores her, she thought, pleased to see that.

After he had left, Polly spent a pleasant day with the two children, the only problem being Connie's point-blank refusal to go out for a short walk. I'll give it a day or two, Polly decided, but I'm not having this. Let alone my Billy will suffer. That child is far too pale. She needs some fresh air. And I'll speak to Captain Mercer about getting her a swing in the garden, too. You're never too old for a swing.

Polly smiled guiltily at that thought. She loved swings herself and had been known to have a quick go on them in children's playgrounds when there was no one around. Adults weren't supposed to do that, but she wasn't heavy enough to damage them and she did enjoy it.

As she got ready for bed that night, she reviewed her day and decided that things had started off well. She did hope it would work out all right. Surely it would? She had got very fond of Connie in the short time she had known her. And Captain Mercer was nice as well.

CHAPTER NINETEEN

February–March 1921

———————◆———————

On her second morning at Stenton, Polly didn't visit the kitchen in her dressing gown. She was longing for a cup of tea, but got fully dressed and waited till she heard Doris moving about the house before she went downstairs.

At breakfast time Captain Mercer greeted her with a smile and bent over to greet Billy as well. The child looked up at the man's face and stretched out one hand, saying, 'Da-da-da.'

Connie laughed. 'Billy thinks you're his father! I'm going to teach him to say Connie next.' She clapped her hands together and Billy turned at the sound, gurgling happily at her while the two adults exchanged amused glances.

When breakfast was over Richard walked over to Billy's chair. 'Let's see whether it is a coincidence or whether he does recognise me now.' He crouched down so that he was on eye level with the chair.

The little boy focused on him and at once said, 'Da-da-da.' Then he breathed noisily, as if trying to say something else, and began to wave his arms around before managing, 'See you. See you.'

Polly closed her eyes for a moment, joy pouring through her. She often said this to Billy when they were playing their little games. When she went over to her son, she was greeted by 'Ma-ma-ma,' followed by, 'See you.'

'Your turn, Connie.' Richard stood up and moved backwards.

Once the little girl came close, Billy started waving his arms about again and beamed at her.

'Connie,' she said solemnly. 'I'm Connie.'

Silence, then 'Con-Con-'was followed by more noisy breathing and arm waving, then again, 'Con-Con-'.

Polly did not try to hide her joy and when she turned to Richard, he said simply, 'You were right. Your son is making progress every day.' He turned back to the boy, who did not respond until he had bent down, then asked thoughtfully, 'Um – have you had his eyes tested, Polly?'

'There's never been anything wrong with his eyes.'

'Well, there might be now. It seemed to me that he only got excited when we were really close to him. It was as if he couldn't really see us clearly before that. And I've seen him squint a few times.'

Polly realised her mouth was open, a habit she knew she had when surprised and one which embarrassed her greatly for she was sure it made her look like an idiot. 'I never thought . . . Oh, I'll definitely ask Dr Herbert about that next time we see him.'

Connie, who was standing next to Billy, took his little hand in hers, patting it and saying, 'Clever boy!'

Polly looked up at the tall man beside her. 'I hope you're right. This could make a big difference.'

He looked down at her and smiled. 'I hope I'm right, too.'

Again, there was that warm feeling between them. She didn't want to move away from him, because he felt so solid and strong beside her, but then she reminded herself that she had to stand on her own feet now and, anyway, Captain Mercer was her employer not a friend. She went to pick Billy up.

When she looked back over her shoulder, however, Captain Mercer was still gazing intently at her, a faint frown wrinkling his forehead. Eh, she didn't know what to think of this man. He was kind, certainly, but disturbing too. And although he looked severe most of the time, when he smiled, he looked – she struggled to find a word – lovely. He must have been quite handsome before that scar.

It was not for her to find her employer handsome, though, so she dismissed that thought and concentrated on the children. This morning she was determined to get Connie out for a walk.

They went upstairs and she waited until they had cleaned up Billy, something Connie didn't seem to mind at all when other girls would have been backing away from the messes he couldn't help making. 'Right then,' Polly said firmly when they had finished, 'you and I need to have a serious talk, my girl.'

Connie looked at her warily. 'What about?'

'About going for walks.'

The girl's face closed into an expressionless mask. 'I don't like going outside. And walking makes my hip ache.'

'But you do like helping me with Billy. And he really needs his walk. Watch!' Polly moved over to her son, bending so that he could see her face, watching his eyes come into focus when she was very close. Excitement filled her. She was sure Richard Mercer was right about the need for spectacles. As a smile appeared on her son's lips she said loudly and clearly, 'Walk, Billy. Shall we go for a walk?'

Immediately he began to wave his arms around, his left arm as usual lower than his right one and making much feebler movements.

'See how excited he is,' she said softly. 'Only we can't go out and leave you alone here, Connie. Are you really going to deny him a treat?'

The girl's eyes filled with tears. 'That's not fair.'

'I think it is because not only do I need to take Billy for walks, they'll do you good as well.' Polly glanced out of the window. 'The clouds are building up and we won't be able to go out this afternoon, so it's now or never.' She looked at the scowling child pleadingly. 'For Billy's sake. Please, love, won't you make an effort?'

Connie was studying the floor, rubbing her toe along the patterns in the carpet. 'People stare at me because I limp.'

'They'll be staring at Billy today, not you.'

'Well, that's not fair to him, either, is it?'

Polly shrugged. 'He doesn't mind. He does love his walks, though. You should see the way he turns his face up to the sun.'

Connie hesitated, said, 'All right!' in a gruff voice and turned away.

As they pushed Billy's chair out of the gate, two elderly ladies came out of the next garden. They both nodded a greeting, then stared at Billy openly, hardly even glancing at Connie who had stopped walking and moved closer to Polly as soon as she caught sight of them.

'Is the dear little boy hurt?' one of the women asked in a falsely sympathetic voice.

'He had a bad accident last year, but he's starting to recover now,' Polly said. If these were the local gossips she might as well give them the correct information.

'What's your name, little boy?' one of them cooed.

'He can't talk properly yet,' said Polly. 'He's starting to say words again, though.'

The two women moved back a little.

'He learned my name this morning,' Connie burst out, going to take Billy's hand.

The women looked at her dubiously, then even more dubiously at Billy. When they said goodbye and moved on, they put their heads close and began to whisper. After a few steps one of them looked round and shook her head.

'Who are they?' Polly asked.

'Miss Barton and her friend Miss Clough. They're horrid. They're always staring at me and whispering.'

'Take no notice of them.' Polly led the way slowly towards the beach, making allowances for Connie's limp which was bad today. Even in the short time she'd been at Seaview House, Polly had noticed that the limp seemed to vary greatly. Did the hip only hurt Connie sometimes or was it perhaps not as bad as the child claimed?

There was a wall along the sea front and a short promenade. Not many people were around since it was too cold for holiday-makers, but those who were said hello, and as Polly had predicted, it was Billy they stared at not Connie. She stood for a moment looking longingly at the narrow crescent of firm yellow sand, but the tide was quite high and anyway she couldn't push a wheel-chair on the beach. While she'd been staying in Blackpool she'd been longing to walk barefoot on the sand and paddle in the sea, things she'd only read about. She'd not been able to do that, of course, because there was Billy to look after, and anyway the water was too cold at this time of year. But one day, she promised herself, one day she'd have a proper paddle. Even a swim, maybe. Not that she could swim, but she could buy a swimming costume and play about in the water, couldn't she?

With a sigh, she set her little dream aside. She had no money to spend on swimming costumes, or even on more modern clothes. She'd get her sewing things out and take the rest of her hems up, though. Most of her skirts were so long they looked dowdy. That wouldn't cost anything to change.

Today she kept the walk short, for Connie's sake, though she'd have loved to stay out for longer.

When they got back, the little girl was sulky and claimed that her hip was hurting, but Billy was full of himself. He said 'Connie' quite clearly whenever she was close enough for him to see. He also waved his right hand vigorously when Polly approached him with a biscuit and a drink of milk. Experimentally, she put the biscuit near his hand and he grabbed it, trying to cram it all in his mouth. Laughing she moved the hand away from his face. 'Just a bite at a time, love.'

Connie was very quiet, but as they were getting ready for lunch, she said in a small voice, 'He did love going out, didn't he?'

'Yes. And so did I.'

*

Dr Herbert was coming across to Stenton to confer with Richard two days later, so he arranged to see Billy at the same time. When he arrived in mid-morning, Polly detailed her son's progress and told him about Richard Mercer's theory that Billy couldn't see clearly more than about a yard away. He looked much struck by that and did some experimenting.

Several times Billy brightened as Toby drew close and came out with an excited stream of gibberish.

'It seems Richard is right. I can't think how we missed that. Were his eyes bad before?'

'I don't think so, though we never even considered getting them checked because he was too little to read, you see.'

'We'll have to get Billy to an optician's, see if they can help him. Now, let's see how well he can move.'

Afterwards, Toby accepted Polly's notes on her son's progress and thanked her for helping him in his research.

'It's not enough. I ought to be paying you for all these consultations,' she worried.

'Certainly not. I had to come over here anyway, to see Richard, and you're acting as an unpaid research assistant which is truly useful. I don't want any payment – especially from *you*.'

She was startled by the emphasis he put on that word and was glad when she heard Captain Mercer come in.

Toby looked closely at her and with a sigh of resignation went out on the landing to call, 'Come up and join us, O Noble Captain.'

There was a laugh and footsteps came running lightly up the stairs. Polly was surprised when Richard came in with a broad smile on his face.

'Something good happened?' Toby asked.

'Something very good. We've got another big donation. We can bring the first four men over here as soon as the place is ready. And with Sarge in command, it's going to be very soon.'

'That's wonderful!'

'If you've finished here, come down to the library and I'll

tell you all about it.' Richard nodded politely to Polly and led the way out.

She could hear them chatting as they went down the stairs. She had never seen her employer as relaxed as this. She bent over Billy and played a silly little game with his fingers, singing in time to it, but her thoughts were in a turmoil. Had she misread what Toby Herbert had implied? No. You couldn't mistake that look in a man's eye. But surely she had given him no encouragement? He was a lovely man, but somehow she just could not fancy him. She didn't think she'd fancy Eddie, either, if she met him now. She liked tall men with dark hair . . . Realising whose image had just come to mind, she dismissed it firmly and concentrated on the two children.

Only when Dr Herbert had left the nursery did Connie come out of her bedroom to join Polly. The child had clearly been avoiding meeting him. What had doctors done to her in the past that made her so afraid of them?

'I heard you singing,' Connie said. 'You have a lovely voice.'

'Thanks, love. I do like to sing, I must admit. I'll teach you some of my songs if you like.'

Connie nodded, but she was avoiding Polly's eyes as she added, 'I don't feel hungry today so I'm not coming down to lunch. I think I'll just have another lie down. That walk tired me.'

'I'll get Mrs Shavely to send up some sandwiches, then,' Polly said at once. 'You're not going without food.'

'All right.'

When she went down, Polly apologised for Connie's absence and was surprised when both men chuckled.

'It's all right,' Richard said cheerfully. 'She always hides when Toby is here. She doesn't like doctors.'

'What happened to make her feel like that?'

Richard's smile disappeared. 'Your friend Browning-Baker, that's what. She's never forgotten how much he hurt her.' It was yet another thing which had made him take Polly's side instinctively when he found out who was hounding her. He saw the two others looking at him in concern and shook the memories away. 'Sorry. Did you say something?'

'I said Dr Herbert could perhaps win her round,' Polly ventured. 'If she hasn't seen a doctor for a while, maybe she ought to have a check-up?'

'I'd be happy to examine her next time I come over,' Toby offered at once.

Richard's voice was firm. 'Only if she agrees. I won't force her.'

'Yes, well, I'd prefer to know how far I should push her,' Polly said. 'Should we be going for these walks, for instance? It's not natural for a child to live so quietly, but if moving around is so very painful . . .' She let the words trail away. It was too soon for her to insist on anything. She allowed Richard Mercer to help her to meat and vegetables, then concentrated on eating and feeding her son, leaving the two men to chat freely. It didn't seem right for her and Billy to be here, but they both insisted Dr Herbert was not a visitor in the normal sense.

Polly was now worried that if she openly discouraged the doctor's attentions toward herself, he'd stop looking after Billy. No, surely he wouldn't? He was a kind man, none kinder. She glanced down the table, saw that he was watching her and concentrated on her plate, feeling a hot blush creep up her neck. What was she going to do about him? Why did life have to be so complicated? She didn't want to marry again, let alone he was a doctor and she only a farm labourer's widow, without much education.

Besides, she had enough on her plate with Billy. And now Connie. That girl was too quiet. There was something wrong and Polly intended to find out what.

CHAPTER TWENTY

March 1921

———◆———

The next day Polly didn't insist on Connie's accompanying them for a walk but chose a time to take Billy out when the girl was with her father. As she walked briskly along the promenade, she noticed that the two ladies who had fussed over Billy the previous day ducked into a shelter to avoid her and her son. Well, let them. She didn't care about them or anyone else.

At the end of the short promenade she stoped to stare out over the windswept sea. It must be lovely in summer here. She was looking forward to it. Then she reminded herself that she didn't yet have the right to look forward to anything. Richard Mercer might not want her to stay on. Funny, she mused, as she started walking again. She didn't think of him as Captain Mercer any more. Richard was a lovely name. Dignified. And thank goodness he didn't insist on calling her Mrs Scordale any more. She hated that name now, thanks to her in-laws, none of whom had made any effort to get in touch with her since she'd left Overdale. Well, she was managing perfectly well without them. Eddie would be proud of how she was coping.

She sighed at the memory of her husband, remembering the way he used to toss Billy in the air or smile at her when she sang to him, but did not allow herself to dwell on her sadness. Instead, she walked briskly up and down, enjoying the exercise and Billy's pleasure in his outing. After half an hour she turned back towards the house, ready for a quiet hour or two. She was teaching her charge to sew and both of them were enjoying that very much. It must be nice to have a daughter, to share women's things with as she grew up.

As if to prove that it wasn't safe for her to feel happy, a letter arrived for Polly at the end of the week which made her gasp at the mere sight of the envelope. It was from Overdale Council. When she opened it she found a peremptory demand from Mr Maslam to know why she had omitted to let them know about her change of address. It was followed by the threat that if this happened again, they would 'take action'. She swallowed hard and clutched the letter to her chest. Surely they couldn't do anything else to her? Not at this distance?

'What's wrong?' Connie demanded.

'What? Oh, nothing.' Polly stuffed the letter into her pocket and began to tidy up some of the toys they'd been using to gain Billy's attention.

'You look worried.'

'Just a silly letter. Nothing to upset you.'

But the thought of it continued to perturb Polly all day so after she had got the children to bed, she went to show Richard Mercer the letter.

When he had finished reading it she said, 'I can't see why I'm any concern of theirs now. Do they have the right to pursue me like this? Well, it isn't the Council, really, it's that Dr Browning-Baker.'

He read it again. 'I'm fairly certain you and your son are outside their area of responsibility now, but I'll have a word with a friend of mine who will know for certain. I'll show him this letter and explain the situation, if you don't mind?'

'I'd be very grateful, sir. I don't know what to do, and that's the truth.'

'I hope you're settling in all right?'

'Oh, yes. I absolutely love it here.' Then she worried that

she'd sounded too pushy, but when he smiled at her, she relaxed again. He had such a lovely smile.

'You look happy. You get on well with Connie and you don't seem to mind how quiet it is in Stenton. In fact, I don't think we need continue on a trial basis any longer, if that's all right with you, so will you please stay on here, Polly?'

She beamed at him. 'I'd love to, Captain Mercer.'

'Good. Maybe now Connie will stop nagging me about you.' He chuckled at Polly's expression.

'Has she been doing that? Eh, the little minx!'

'The only other thing we need to sort out is your wages. I really must insist on paying you for your efforts.'

'That isn't fair. You have two of us to feed and—'

'Billy hardly eats enough to keep a sparrow alive, and you're not exactly a huge eater, either. He shares your bedroom and Mrs Shavely says you help out in all sorts of ways – which none of the others used to do.' Even after such a short time, his housekeeper spoke very positively about Polly, as did Doris. Both of them seemed to like as well as respect her. 'Everyone thinks you fit in really well here.'

Polly had never known what to do when someone gave her a compliment. She looked away, shuffled her feet and managed, 'Well, I – um – like to keep busy.'

He hid a smile at her embarrassment. 'I'm going to insist on paying you a pound a week as well as your keep.'

Polly gasped. 'It's too much!'

'You've been working seven days a week. That's the other thing – we must arrange for you to have some time off.'

Polly smiled at him. 'And what would I do with it? Go out and walk up and down the promenade all day? I like looking after Connie. She's good company. I was a bit lonely on my own with just Billy.'

Polly had a lovely smile, he decided. 'You could visit your family, perhaps?'

She shook her head decisively. 'Not with Billy, I couldn't. I couldn't take him on a train on my own. Though Lizzie and Percy might come and visit me here later on, if that's all right with you? Eva too if Alice gets better. But Connie could stay with us when they come. And actually,' she frowned thoughtfully, 'if they brought one of Percy's older children with them as well as their own little ones, it might help her get used to being with other young folk.'

Richard spoke without thinking. 'I'm beginning to think you're an absolute treasure, Polly Scordale.'

She could feel the heat rising in her face again and grew annoyed with herself. Why did she always get flustered by compliments? 'I just like to give good value and keep busy.'

He leaned forward and said softly, 'And you don't like receiving compliments, do you?'

'I never know what to say to them,' she muttered, avoiding his eyes.

'Just say, "Thank you for your kind words, Richard," then give me a little smile.'

She found herself giving a big smile at that, then realised what he had said. 'I can't call you *Richard!*'

'Why not?' He hadn't thought about it when he'd used his own first name just then, but now he realised that he'd far rather she called him Richard. No one else used his first name. To Connie he was 'Daddy' and to Mrs Shavely and Doris 'Captain Mercer' or 'sir'.

'It wouldn't be right. You're my employer.'

'I lost the habit of being stiff and formal when I was in the trenches.' He closed his eyes for a moment against sad memories then opened them and forced a smile. 'I don't even like being called "Captain Mercer" any more, to tell you the truth, but people will do it.'

Polly's expression was sympathetic and she didn't pretend not to understand. 'They say it was bad out there.'

'Very bad. A living hell. I still get nightmares about it

sometimes. Most of us do. And yet we're the lucky ones who survived in one piece.' After a moment's silence, he said, 'So you'll stay with us, then?'

'Of course I will. I've got really fond of Connie already.'

'I'm delighted, Polly.'

'I'm delighted, too, Capt——'

He put one fingertip on her lips. 'Richard.'

'I can't,' she whispered, enjoying the warmth of his fingers. There was something rather special about a man's touch.

His voice was low and amused. 'Have a practice.'

She looked up into his eyes, smiling again, and suddenly the name came easily to her lips. 'Richard, then. But only when there's no one else around.'

'It shall be our secret,' he said with mock solemnity.

She chuckled and left, smiling all the way up the stairs. She went into Connie's bedroom first to check that all was well because she knew Billy would be sleeping soundly. She found the girl sitting on the window seat, her arms round her knees. 'Connie Mercer, what are you doing out of bed without even your dressing gown on?'

'Did he – did Daddy say anything – about you staying here? I've been as quiet and good as I can. Do say you'll stay, Polly.' Suddenly she was sobbing.

Polly rushed across to gather her into her arms and sat down on the bed, rocking Connie to and fro and making shushing noises. Gradually the storm of tears abated and then she produced a handkerchief. 'Here, wipe your eyes and nose, young lady.'

Connie mopped her face. 'Did he ask you, though?'

'Yes. And of course I'm staying. Why should I want to leave? And, Connie love, you don't have to be quiet to keep me here. In fact, you're too quiet. It's normal for children to be noisy sometimes and to run about. Even if I have to tell you off, it won't make me go away. Eh, you should have heard my Billy before his accident! Talk about noisy. And dirty. He was for ever finding mud to fall into.'

This drew a watery chuckle from Connie, who then allowed Polly to help her get into bed. As she lay staring up, there was such a desperate longing in her face that Polly gathered her into her arms again and gave her another long hug, then smoothed the hair back from the flushed forehead.

'My mother doesn't like cuddling,' Connie whispered. 'I sometimes wonder if she doesn't really like me. Only she writes me such lovely letters.' Memories of that dreadful day when she had fallen down the stairs hovered suddenly at the edge of her mind and she shivered. Her mother had assured her it had been an accident, yet her memories of that evening were all tangled up and she still had nightmares about someone pushing her down the stairs, someone with a bony hand that *hurt*. She couldn't understand it, didn't want to understand it.

'I'm sure your mother loves you. And I do, too,' said Polly. 'I've really missed cuddling since my husband died. So you can give me as many hugs as you like.'

'Daddy likes cuddling, too.'

'I should think so. Who wouldn't with a daughter like you?'

Polly was very thoughtful as she made her way to her own bedroom. She felt happy here, really happy. Richard – she smiled as she used his name in her thoughts without feeling guilty – was a nice man, if a bit stiff with people sometimes. And as for Connie, that poor child seemed to have been tossed from pillar to post during her short life.

Eh, it all seemed too good to be true. Polly picked up a book she had borrowed from the library downstairs, but it was too full of long words. She'd never been much of a reader though now she was beginning to enjoy stories as long as they weren't too sad. Perhaps there was a local library she could join and get some easier books. And Connie could join it, too.

Oh, she was going to enjoy making a life for herself here, really enjoy it!

*

In the South of France, Florence was not enjoying life nearly so much as she had expected. After the first few days, George had turned very chancy-tempered, and seemed unhappy about something. She had learned not to disobey him in any way because he could become so furiously angry and she was becoming quite nervous of his darker moods.

She blamed this on the group of men he was gambling with now, men whom she disliked intensely, so cold were their expressions when they looked at her. The only thing that made those chill eyes gleam was the fall of the cards. And they treated their own women very scornfully.

Florence was terrified that George would grow like them, and was hoping things would change when they moved on as he kept threatening to do. He took her along to the games sometimes, and she would sit and talk to the other women in a nearby room, finding them as on edge as she was. As George had forbidden her to reveal anything about him or their life together, beyond the merest everyday details, she hardly dared open her mouth on these occasions, let alone enjoy a frank gossip. She was not surprised to find that the other women were similarly reticent. She didn't know whether they were married to their escorts, but they didn't look like wives and none of them ever mentioned children.

Another letter from Richard had been forwarded to George's club by their landlord, and then forwarded again to Poste Restante here. Her husband said it was more than time she wrote to Connie again. She'd have to see if she could catch Georgie in a good mood and get him to write a letter for her. She couldn't think of half the things to say that he did, let alone make them amusing. Of course, she didn't mean any of them, but that didn't matter if it would look better in court.

Sighing, she stared across the street to the little café where they sometimes ate dinner, then leaned forward to peer at the dark corner at the back which wasn't as well lit as the front of the café. Surely that was the funny little man again? As he turned toward a waiter, his face caught the light. Yes, it was him. He was the most ordinary person she had ever seen and she wouldn't have noticed him at all if she hadn't heard him swear in English once when the waiter tripped up and splashed beer over him.

'Look, Georgie, that funny little man is back sitting in the café, on his own as usual. I haven't seen him for weeks. I'm sure he's English. Do you remember the waiter spilling beer all over him?'

George was by her side in an instant. 'Oh, hell, what's *he* doing back here?'

'What do you mean? Do you know him? Does it matter whether he's here or not?'

'Of course it matters, you stupid bitch! Haven't you realised yet that he's been following me for quite a while now?'

Shock held her silent for a moment. 'But why should he do that? If anyone's being followed, it's me, surely – only Richard already has evidence for the divorce so why should he still have me watched?' To her exasperation, George ignored her question completely.

'I think it's time I had a word with him,' he muttered. 'I need to find out exactly what's going on. Come over here and give me a kiss so he can see our silhouettes, then you go into the bedroom, fiddle around for a minute or two and put the light off as if we're making love. Meanwhile I'll nip across the road.'

He slipped downstairs and waited near a quiet alley for the little man to leave the café. But the fellow seemed to sense his presence and put on a sudden turn of speed, disappearing round the corner so rapidly that by the time George reached it, he'd vanished.

From then onwards the watcher was more careful, keeping out of sight most of the time so that it was only very occasionally they saw him – just often enough to keep George anxious. It couldn't be Richard doing this, only Palmer. Damnation!

Two days later they moved on from Nice, leaving their lodging house very quietly at dusk with Madame helping George orchestrate the removal of their luggage through the back door where her brother-in-law's taxi was waiting for them. They were driven to a secluded side entrance of the station where George made Florence sit in a quiet corner while he checked that the watcher hadn't followed them.

Florence couldn't understand the suddenness of their departure or George's anxiety, but she didn't mind too much. She'd grown tired of Nice anyway. It would have been different if they'd had their own villa and done some entertaining or if they'd been staying in a luxurious hotel. But they hadn't, and she was getting bored.

On the train George relaxed a little and she ventured to ask, 'Where are we going now?'

'Where else but Monaco, my pet?' He smiled, looking his old self again.

Florence beamed at him. 'Oh, I shall like that. I've heard it's very exciting there. Shall we be visiting the Casino?'

'Undoubtedly. And they put on opera performances there, too. They must be getting back into the swing of all that sort of thing now, after the war. But you, my lamb, will not be doing any gambling. You do understand that, don't you?'

She pouted. 'Not even a little bit, just for fun?'

'No. We shall tell everyone you don't gamble. And you won't talk about *my* gambling, either. That's something I like to do very discreetly.'

She sighed but nodded her acceptance of this fiat. 'Did you do well in Nice?'

'Well enough.'

'Oh, Georgie, you never tell me *anything*.'

His voice took on a hard edge. 'I tell you what I want you to know. Do you have any other complaints about me?'

She let out a sniff of annoyance and didn't try to answer but stared out of the window at the passing scenery for a time. Growing bored with that, she turned back to him and said, 'I wonder how long the divorce will take.'

'Years.'

She sighed. 'I wish we were married now. It feels better to be married.'

'As far as anyone knows, we are. And as your passport says "Mercer" on it, like mine, let them prove otherwise.'

Florence brightened. 'Yes. There is that.' But she wished he'd said something about wanting to marry her. He hadn't for a long time. Now wasn't the time to confront him about that, but she didn't intend to spend the rest of her life living in sin. She wanted a proper social life again, a house of her own, servants. Not boring, old-fashioned ones like Mrs Shavely and Doris but lively younger folk who knew how to cater for parties and serve cocktails. She hoped Georgie would win a great deal of money in Monaco and then – yes, she was beginning to agree with him on that – take her back to England. It had been fun at first, but she now realised that she wouldn't want to be a foreigner in some overseas country for the rest of her life.

George could tell what was going through Flo's brain and it gave him wry amusement. When would she realise that he wasn't going to marry her without the money? She'd simply assumed he would do so. How angry she would be when she did realise! She would come round eventually, though, and accept what he was offering, he was quite sure. Well, what choice did she have now? Besides, she was his and only his, not his cousin's any more. He had only to touch her to prove that.

He watched her doze off a short time later and was glad to be left to his own thoughts. He was not doing as well as he'd expected with the gambling. There were some superb card players around, damn them, and he didn't want to risk being caught fudging the cards and get a bad reputation. No, better to save those little tricks for a crucial moment like the one in England. Still, his nest egg was building up, even if more slowly than he wanted. A wolfish grin etched itself briefly across his face. Maybe he'd do a bit more burgling and add to it that way. He had a few good pieces of jewellery stashed away, just in case. And it had been exciting creeping through darkened houses, robbing his chosen victims then sometimes commiserating with them the next day.

He was starting to feel restless again, growing tired of the gambling life. Yet he didn't know what else he wanted to do with himself. Truth to tell, he still missed the excitement of the war, though that wasn't the sort of thing you could say to people.

Anger vibrated in him. Why had Uncle James left all his money to Richard? Why had George's parents been so careless with theirs? This situation was all the fault of those old fools. He wouldn't have had to turn thief then. Well, he didn't intend to leave all that money in Richard's hands. He'd find some way to get his share. He was a bit busy with other things just now, but one day . . .

Only even if he did get the money, what the hell was he going to *do* with the rest of his life? He'd be bored silly in a place like Stenton and wasn't interested in charitable works, even for former soldiers. Perhaps he'd go travelling – though even that could pall on you. *Everything* palled on you. He looked around sourly as the train pulled into the station, then shook Florence awake.

'Oh. Are we there already?'

'Of course we are, you fool! Why else do you think the train has stopped?'

Richard drove into Poulton to consult his lawyer and together the two of them drew up a letter which Mr Havershall would send to the Overdale Council Children's Welfare Department on Polly's behalf. When Richard brought it home to show her, she read it carefully, keeping it overnight to be sure she understood it, then asked him at breakfast how much it cost to employ a lawyer to write such letters.

'You don't need to worry about the cost, Polly.'

She lifted her chin and said very firmly, 'Yes, I do. I'm not having you pay for this as well as everything else you've done for me.'

'It's very little — and it ensures that I keep your services for my daughter.'

She had to force the words out because she hated to argue with anyone. 'I'm sorry, but I think it's *my* business to pay for my son's protection. So I'd like to go and see this lawyer for myself, if you don't mind. I have something else to discuss with him anyway. Doris can keep an eye on Billy for me and I'll be as quick as I can. I can catch the bus into Poulton and . . .'

'I'll ring Havershall up and make an appointment for you, then drive you over to see him — you'll surely allow me to do that much?' He saw that stubborn look come over her face again and said hastily, 'I have to go in anyway as there are some papers to sign. You can bring Billy with you, too, if you like. The outing will do him good.'

She stared at him, eyes narrowed, then decided she could not call him a liar to his face. 'Very well.'

The visit was arranged for the next afternoon and Polly had the happy idea of asking if Connie would go along with them and sit with Billy in the waiting room while Polly saw the lawyer.

They both watched Connie hesitate.

'I really need your help today,' Polly pleaded as the silence lengthened.

'Well — all right, then.'

Richard breathed out slowly and avoided Polly's eyes. He knew what she had just done and was hugely grateful. Connie hadn't been out of Stenton since their arrival.

They set out with quite a festive air, Polly wearing her best clothes and sitting in the back holding Billy on her lap with the wheelchair strapped on behind.

When they parked outside the lawyer's office, which was just off Church Street, she could see that Connie looked terrified and was slow to get out of the car, so she enlisted the child's help with Billy and somehow they were all inside the lawyer's office before Connie could have second thoughts and take refuge in the car again.

'Thanks,' Richard mouthed as he manoeuvred the wheelchair through the door of the building, past the shiny brass plate saying 'Havershall & Deeversby'.

Quentin Havershall, alerted by a phone call from Richard, had agreed to deal with the case in person. Richard went in to see him first, ostensibly to sign his own papers, but really to ask Quentin to keep the charges very low and let him make up the difference.

When she was ushered in, Polly found Mr Havershall to be a kindly old gentleman and had no trouble telling her tale to him.

'This is blatant persecution,' he declared. 'And if they don't stop, we shall sue them. I know Dr Herbert and would trust his opinion on your son absolutely.' He knew Richard, too, and was amused to see him helping this little dab of a woman, so plainly dressed, the antithesis of his own wife. However, when Mrs Scordale smiled at him, he acknowledged that she was attractive in her own quiet way. Did that wholesome look appeal to Richard now? If so, he had better warn his client very strictly to do nothing to suggest that the two of them were having an affair.

'My clerk can type the letter now, if you will wait a few moments, Mrs Scordale,' Quentin said. 'It's very straightforward.'

'If that's all right?' She looked at Richard, who nodded, then Polly opened her mouth, closed it and hesitated.

'Do you want me to leave you alone with Mr Havershall?' Richard asked.

She pursed her lips and tried to decide. Richard watched her and Quentin continued to watch him just as carefully.

'No, it's all right. You'd have to know anyway.' Polly turned to the lawyer. 'I want to take my old surname again – Kershaw – and to change Billy's name to it as well. Is that possible? You see, my husband's family have been very hostile to me since his death and I no longer feel like a Scordale. And they . . .' her voice wavered for a moment '. . . they've disowned Billy. Their own grandson! They don't deserve him to carry on their name. Can I do that?'

'Nothing easier.' He explained what she must do. 'I can help you with this as well, if you'll trust me?'

She nodded, her face clearing.

Richard watched Polly indulgently. Such a transparently honest face she had – and a smile like a gentle sunny day, warm but not overwhelming. Indeed, everything about her was gentle and loving. Why could he not have married someone like her?

'You should start calling yourself Kershaw from now on,' Quentin said. 'Establish a precedent of common usage.'

She screwed up her courage to ask, 'How much will that cost?'

Without blinking he said, 'Five shillings – but that will not be payable until everything has been legally attended to.'

She glanced suspiciously at Richard, then back at the lawyer. 'That doesn't seem enough. Are you sure?'

Quentin smiled. Not stupid, little Mrs Kershaw. 'It isn't an onerous job, my dear young lady, but it does take time. We shall need to write a letter or two and then we shall all have to wait for the due processes to be carried out. And there will be a further ten shillings for the other matter, of course.'

The suspicion cleared from her face and she beamed at him. 'That's wonderful! Thank you so much, Mr Havershall. I can't tell you how happy this makes me.'

As he watched them go out, Quentin smiled to see Richard fussing over them all and wondered why anyone would want to harm this young woman or take her son away from her. Well, this Browning-Baker person would soon be receiving a very stiff letter about that, with an implied threat to pursue the matter in court and report the man for professional misconduct if the harassment continued. But Quentin doubted it would. Even bullying doctors thought twice about taking such minor matters to court. It could not only be expensive, it could damage their good name and standing in the community if they lost.

Richard then took Polly and her son to an optician's and after some tests they ordered spectacles for Billy.

'We'll be able to do this better once he can speak again,' the optician said as they left. 'But I'm sure these lenses will help.'

As they came out, Richard suggested they all celebrate in a nearby teashop where they served excellent ice cream.

When Connie shrank against her, looking up pleadingly, Polly shook her head. 'Not with Billy,' she said quietly, her eyes flickering once to Connie and back to Richard's face in a silent plea for him not to pursue the matter.

So they got back into the car and instead took a drive along the sea front into Fleetwood and then to Blackpool.

'Thank you so much for taking us,' Polly said when they got back.

'Thank *you*,' he said.

She didn't pretend not to know what he was referring to: the way she had once again, without any fuss, got Connie out of the house. Well, women were better at that sort of thing than men. And Polly was sure her charge had enjoyed herself today, which would make it easier next time.

Two weeks after Polly's position was made permanent, Toby came over again to consult Richard and set a date for the first four invalids to move into the rest home. Connie was continuing to take a great interest in all this and for once agreed to join them for luncheon. She listened to the discussions like an adult and had already confided in Polly some of her childish plans to go and visit the poor soldiers.

During the meal she treated Toby very warily, almost as if she expected him to snap at her, but he merely included her in the general conversation and made no attempt to talk about her own problems, so she began to relax a little.

'Another visit or two,' Polly told Richard after the children were in bed, 'and she'll let Toby examine her leg.'

'Polly Kershaw, what did we ever do without you?' he asked. That name came far more easily to his tongue than the ugly-sounding Scordale and everyone in the household had started using it without any difficulty.

Polly tried to do as he had suggested when offered compliments so gave him a half-smile and murmured something in such a low voice that he could not make it out. But she could still feel herself flushing. She often did when she was with him. He must think her very silly.

When she went up to her room, she sat for a while staring thoughtfully into the fire. She couldn't remember feeling so happy for a very long time. It was a fragile sort of happiness, because she wasn't a member of the family here. But Richard made her feel as if she belonged and as if he really valued her help.

Eh, he was the kindest man she had ever met, and good-looking, too. She was glad of the dusk and shadows that hid yet another of her blushes. And she didn't admit, even to herself, why she was blushing.

CHAPTER TWENTY-ONE

March 1921

———◆———

Lizzie and Peter were to come over to see Polly one Sunday with their two children. She asked Connie to join them, but the child began to fiddle with the edge of her book and eventually said, 'They won't want me around. I'm not family.'

'They *will* want you. They like children. Anyway, I'd really appreciate some help with Billy. He's used to you and he's not to them. Now that he's got his spectacles and can see better, he gets nervous of strangers.'

Connie studied the floor, then shrugged. 'All right. If you really want me.'

'I do. And thanks, love.' Polly immediately changed the subject and suggested getting ready for their morning walk.

Connie sighed but went for her coat and hat. She was used to going out now, but hung back when Polly stopped to talk to anyone and made no attempt to chat to other children on the promenade, though some of them looked as if they wanted to make friends.

The Deardens arrived just before noon and the two sisters didn't even wait to get inside the house to hug and exclaim over one another. Richard came out to greet Peter and although Polly had intended to take her family up to her own room, they somehow wound up in the big downstairs sitting room.

While they were all getting settled, Richard stopped beside

her and drew her into the hall, saying in a low voice, 'I didn't mean to intrude on your family reunion. You'll have more room down here, but I'll make myself scarce in a minute or two.'

'So long as me and Lizzie get some time together, you're welcome to stay.' Did she dare ask for his help? Yes, why not? 'And actually, if you chatted to Peter that'd help me. We could send the children out to play in the garden and you two could keep an eye on them through the window, then I could take Lizzie for a quick stroll along the promenade.'

'Sister talk?' he teased.

She nodded, smiling at him.

'I'd be glad to do that, Polly. And no need to make it a quick stroll, either. Dearden's a decent chap. He was a very reliable junior officer and if the war had continued he'd have risen higher. I shall enjoy his company.' Richard smiled faintly at his own stupidity in saying that. As if anyone would have wanted the carnage to continue. He really was bad at small talk. 'I'll, um, ring for lunch to be served here, shall I?' He saw worry lines wrinkle her forehead. 'Is something wrong with that?'

'I'd arranged to make us some sandwiches in the kitchen,' Polly confessed. 'I didn't want to make too much work for Doris and Mrs Shavely.'

'No need for that. I'm happy to offer your family some hospitality.'

'Well, you must let me pay for the extra food, then.'

'Don't be silly. The food's there already and Mrs Shavely loves catering for people. I bet she's secretly made you a cake.'

Polly smiled. It was true. She wasn't supposed to know, but Doris had let the information slip.

'I thought so. Now you go and talk to your sister and I'll sort out lunch before joining you. You're more than due some time off.'

So Polly caught up with the Overdale gossip, then when Richard gave the signal, led her family into the dining room and sat there like a lady at the head of the table. She didn't think she did too bad a job of keeping an eye on everyone's needs, either, if she said so herself. She was so enjoying having everyone there and Richard seemed to fit in well. But of course he knew Peter already, and Lizzie was easy to get on with, so lively and outgoing. Polly enjoyed listening to them all, putting in a word occasionally, but not worrying about keeping the conversation going or taking a major part in it. She preferred listening to others talk and always had.

Richard did not prevent her and Lizzie from helping clear the table so she was able to introduce her sister properly to Mrs Shavely and Doris, which she knew they'd like, and they all had a little natter in the kitchen.

After that the men shooed the two women out for a walk and it was just like old times when she and her sister had gone strolling in the park on Sunday afternoons. There was so much to catch up with. Lizzie never stopped talking and asking questions, and Polly had always been able to talk easily to her eldest sister.

'He's rather good-looking, isn't he?' Lizzie said suddenly while they were leaning on the railings watching the waves roll gently in.

'Who is?' Polly looked round, expecting to see someone walking past.

'Your Captain Mercer.' Lizzie gave her a nudge and grinned.

Polly didn't know what to say to that one. 'He's my employer,' she managed at last, worried that Lizzie should talk like that.

'That doesn't stop him being good-looking – in a severe sort of way.'

'It's the scar which does that.' Polly had a think, then shook her head. 'He's not at all severe. He's lovely to work for and ever so considerate.'

Her sister's grin broadened. 'He's your employer and yet I heard you call him "Richard". What's going on here my girl?'

Polly could feel herself turning red. 'I just – he likes to keep things friendly for – for Connie's sake.'

Lizzie threw back her head and laughed. 'Ooh, Polly Scordale, what a fib! It's me you're talking to, not a stranger, you know.'

Polly tried to divert her attention. 'I don't call myself Scordale now, actually. I've gone back to calling myself Kershaw. I've got a lawyer sorting it all out for me so that it's legal. And he's doing it for Billy, too.'

'Well, I never did like the name Scordale. Or Eddie's family, though *he* was pleasant enough and definitely loved you. I saw your dear mother-in-law in town the other day, by the way. She looked very thin and unhappy, but that didn't stop her giving her husband what for about something. She pretended she hadn't seen me so she didn't have to stop and talk. He's aged a lot, too, since Eddie died.'

'She nags him something shocking. Nags them all.' Polly was glad to have a change of subject. She didn't like the knowing expression still lingering on her sister's face.

When they got back, Lizzie watched Polly avoiding Richard Mercer's eyes. She also saw the way he smiled down at her as he spoke to her quietly near the door when she was taking the tea tray out. Lizzie drew her own conclusions and hoped something would come of it, though she couldn't really see what, not with him being so well off and Polly, much as they all loved her, only an ex-housemaid.

She wished she knew Richard Mercer better because she didn't want her sister getting hurt. She'd have to find out more about him from her husband, though Peter seemed to like the captain and to be at ease with him. And of course Richard was still married to that wife of his, and it'd be ages before he could get a divorce – but still, his gaze seemed warmer when he spoke to Polly. And her sister watched him quite a bit when she thought no one was looking.

As Richard said goodbye to the Deardens, he assured them that they'd be welcome to visit any time.

'You could bring Polly over to see us one weekend, if you like,' Peter suggested. 'And Connie. Give everyone an outing. We can manage any Sunday.'

'I may take you up on that.' Richard's gaze lingered on his daughter for a moment. 'It's good for Connie to be with people. Until your sister-in-law came to us, she avoided all visitors to the house.'

They both watched the girl helping Matt into the car, smiling down at him. And the little boy had obviously taken to her because he planted one of his sloppy kisses on her cheek which made Connie smile and she wiped the moisture off surreptitiously.

Lizzie could have killed Peter. Didn't he see what might happen here if they encouraged those two to spend too much time together? However, when he gave her a nudge, she said quickly, 'Yes, do bring them all over to see us sometime. There's always someone popping in on a Sunday.'

Richard could see that both sisters had over-bright eyes and noticed Polly trying to wipe away a tear without letting anyone see as the car drove away. 'Thank you for letting me share your family, Polly,' he said as they turned back towards the house.

'It was nice of you to let them come and visit me.' She put an arm round Connie. 'Did you enjoy yourself today, love?'

Connie nodded and nestled against her, a gesture which pleased Richard and yet saddened him immensely. His wife had never encouraged the child to cuddle her, didn't even touch her daughter unless she had to. And yet within a few short weeks Polly had made Connie feel free to hug and touch her, as if she were part of the family.

And he was jealous of his daughter, he realised, for he, too, would have liked to cuddle up against Polly's soft curves. Hell, that would never do! What was he thinking of? The last thing he needed now was to become involved with a woman and harm his chance of getting a divorce.

'I have some business matters to attend to,' he said hastily and left them standing in the hall.

*

In the van, with the children lying sleeping in a nest of blankets and pillows in the back, Lizzie was so thoughtful that Peter asked, 'What's wrong?'

'What? Oh, nothing, love.'

'Then what are you thinking about?'

'Our Polly. She seems a lot happier, doesn't she?'

'A lot.'

'And Billy has definitely started to recognise things.' She chuckled suddenly. 'Fancy him calling Richard Mercer "Da-da-da"!'

'He knew Connie's name, too. And lots of simple everyday words. He was quite alert, taking everything in.'

'He looks funny with those spectacles perched on his nose, doesn't he? Like a little owl.' Lizzie began to fiddle with the strap of her handbag. 'What's Mrs Mercer like?'

Peter pulled a face. 'Sharp. Doesn't care for anyone but herself. Very fashionably dressed and so thin she looks as if she'd break if the wind blew too hard. He was very unhappy with her and you couldn't have thought of a worse wife for him. None of us liked her. We wanted better for our Captain.'

She sighed. 'I wish divorces didn't take so long. And there's still a stigma attached, isn't there, whether you're the guilty party or not? I've heard people talking in the shop.'

That caught his attention. 'Lizzie, you're not starting match-making, are you? Because if so, you can just stop. Richard Mercer will never marry again, I'm sure of that. And much as I love Polly, she's not exactly – well, his class.'

Lizzie put her chin up and scowled at him. 'Our Polly's good enough for anyone. She was far *too* good for that nobody, Eddie Scordale. If she hadn't been so shy, she'd never have married a soppy little man like him. And if I hadn't been stupid enough to marry Sam Thoxby, I'd never have let her do it.' Only Sam had not let Lizzie see much of her family after they were married and then she'd run away and not come back for years. She shivered. She still had occasional nightmares about him, still dreamed he was thumping her. Then Peter would hold her tight and the world would come right again. They both had their demons in the night, she and Peter.

'If Polly hadn't married Eddie, she'd not have Billy,' Peter pointed out. 'And she'd probably still be working for the Pilbys. She's the stick-in-the-mud sort who doesn't change unless pushed into it.'

'Well, she's been well and truly pushed into it this time and she's making a good fist of it, too. And you know what? I think she'll surprise everyone yet, our Polly will. Still waters run deep. Look how she stood up to everyone to keep Billy. She's got courage, my little sister has.'

Matt suddenly began to sob and say he wanted to wee-wee so the conversation was interrupted while they stopped by the side of the road.

Lizzie didn't return to it. But she thought about it quite a lot. She couldn't decide whether she wanted Captain Mercer to be interested in Polly or not. In the end, she came to the conclusion that she was probably just imagining things. He was her sister's employer, after all.

Once inside the library, Richard stood by the door and listened to Polly and Connie fetch Billy from his special chair in the sitting room, then take him upstairs. Sitting down at his desk, he fiddled with the papers there, unable to settle to anything, though there were letters to write and the novel mocking him from a corner of the desk – such a small number of pages.

Seeing Polly with her family today – so at ease, so happy together – had made him painfully aware of all the things he had missed during his unhappy marriage, all the small, shared, daily activities. It had also made him want to make up for lost time. With a woman like Polly. He closed his eyes for a moment. Only he couldn't do anything about that yet. He didn't have the right. He was still a married man.

And would she even consider him? He gathered that her own marriage had not been unalloyed joy, though nothing like as bad as his, and knew how devoted she was to her son. He had heard her say several times that she didn't intend to get married again because Billy would likely always need her.

He stared blindly ahead, shocked at where his own thoughts were leading him, but once the thought of marriage had entered his head, he couldn't seem to drive it out. The trouble was, fate had brought Polly into his life at a time when he and his daughter needed her quiet warmth. Some would say she was beneath him – well, she wasn't an educated woman and she was slow-spoken. But she wasn't stupid. She was . . . A smile curved his lips for a moment. She was just Polly. A born homemaker who was healing his daughter and making the whole house feel a happier place. Since she had come, *he* had even started to feel that there was hope in the world again.

After the horrors of the war and the bitterness of life with Florence, Polly seemed like sanity incarnate.

But he had no right to approach her in any way!

Not yet, anyway.

CHAPTER TWENTY-TWO

April 1921

———————◆———————

'Did you lose much money last night?' Florence asked as she passed George the plate of brioches which she had just collected from the bakery across the road.

'None of your bloody business.'

'It's not fair telling me so little, Georgie! Other men tell their wives what they're doing and—' She broke off. He was staring at her as if he hated her this morning.

'But you're *not* my wife.'

'Well, I'm going to be, so it's the same thing.'

'Leave well alone, Flo.'

'But—'

He slammed his knife down, smearing butter over the table-cloth, then slammed both hands down as well, making everything on the table rattle and coffee slop from the cups. 'Look, you stupid bitch, not only are we not married now but we're never likely to get married.'

With a huge effort she held back the words of outrage she did not dare utter. She had never felt afraid of him before – well, not really – but she did now.

'Georgie, don't be mean,' she managed at last.

'Mean!' He rolled his eyes at the ceiling, grabbed a knife and stabbed it into the nearest brioche.

It was that gesture which set the seal on Florence's fright. It wasn't a random angry action but a powerful thrust and she had a sudden vision of him stabbing men like that during the war, killing them, relishing that act of ultimate power. She raised her eyes slowly to his face and what she saw there transfixed her with fear till she couldn't have spoken – not and made any sense. Thrusting the chair back, she stumbled to her feet and ran out of the room.

In the bedroom, she sank down on to the bed and stared bleakly into the mirror. If George did not want to marry her, she might just as well have stayed with Richard. *Fallen woman!* The stupid phrase echoed in her mind. She didn't want to be known as a *fallen woman*. She wanted a position of respect in the community as well as a husband who cared about her and was good in bed and made life fun.

That evening, when George got ready to go out, Florence went to sit in the apartment's tiny sitting room. He smiled and left her to her sulks. A man called Raoul Jarvin, with whom he had become acquainted recently, had booked a luxurious hotel suite for tonight's game. George intended to make a big killing.

When he arrived, he looked round in appreciation. These fellows didn't do things by halves! He took a chair, then leaned back and watched the other players fiddle with their cufflinks and shuffle themselves comfortable. They were all experienced gamblers and their expressions gave nothing away, the looks they turned on him coolly disinterested.

For the first time, a suspicion that he was out of his depth among these men whispered through George's mind, and certainly the pile of chips he had exchanged his money for on entering was lower than theirs – but then, it always was at the beginning. He dismissed those thoughts as he had always dismissed the worry that he might be killed during the war. You didn't get anywhere by thinking what might go wrong, only by making it go right.

He realised suddenly that Jarvin, who was sitting opposite,

was eyeing him with what looked like — was it? — yes, it was amusement.

What the hell was the fellow amused about?

A waiter offered him wine and George accepted a glass, but set it aside barely tasted.

He heard the door open, felt a draught swirl around the room and saw malicious anticipation on Jarvin's face. Feeling uneasy, he turned to see who had entered the room.

As the newcomer paused in the doorway George squinted in an effort to see better, because there was something familiar about the silhouette. But the lighting beyond the bright circle around the table was dim and it wasn't until the man took another step forward that he became clearly visible through the smoke haze. It looked like — George stiffened and shock made the breath hiss into his mouth. Oh, hell, it *was* Lucky Palmer! What was *he* doing here. If George had known, he definitely wouldn't have come tonight. In fact, he'd have left town. It all fell into place suddenly: the little man following him, even Jarvin's expression tonight. This was a set-up!

'*Bonsoir, Messieurs,*' Lucky said, his French marred by a frightful English accent.

It might have been amusing to hear another man mangle the language, but somehow you could not think of Palmer as a figure of fun. And his notorious henchman, Thad Baxter, was standing behind him, immaculately dressed, hands clasped in front of him, but still with that battered boxer's face and that air of being ready to punch anyone if his master so much as flicked a finger towards them. Oh, hell!

When Jarvin nodded to the newcomer as if the two of them were old acquaintances, George's anxiety increased. He was not a man prone to fear, but tonight something very like it was fluttering in his belly. He didn't like that. He was beginning to suspect he had lost his edge in the past few months and was concerned about that. When a man lived by his wits, he couldn't afford to go soft.

Having also swivelled round to inspect the newcomer and nod a greeting, the two other players turned back towards the table, one drumming his fingers impatiently on the green baize cloth.

Palmer strolled across to join them. As he sat down, he let his eyes run over the other players, but when they settled on George he said, 'Dear me!' in a distinctly mocking tone. 'I hadn't thought *you* were in this league, old fellow.' He glanced down scornfully at George's smaller pile of chips.

'Oh, I think I'll manage to hold my own,' he drawled. But he didn't feel as sure of that as usual. Damn Palmer! And damn Jarvin, too!

Lucky leaned forward. 'Well, a word to the wise – you should think twice about playing tonight, Mercer. The stakes might be a little high for you.'

There was dead silence at the table. By now everyone was staring at George. If he left the room, he would never play in the big league again. Word would get out and doors would close in his face. It would be one form of revenge for Palmer, George realised, but there was no guarantee that such a humiliation would be enough to satisfy the other man, certainly not if the rumours about him were true.

Still, George was half-tempted to leave – only he had always prided himself on never turning tail so in the end he rejected that idea and said, 'But I'm looking forward to the game.'

Challenge. Response. Engagement commenced.

Adrenaline began to pulse through George and suddenly he felt more alive than he had for weeks – months, even. Of course he hadn't lost his nerve! He wasn't a milksop like his cousin.

'As you choose.' Palmer's voice was as soft as ever. It was said that no one had ever heard him raise it.

George inclined his head.

Palmer picked up the cards and shuffled them. 'Stakes?' He answered his own question. 'Minimum of a hundred francs in the first hand, hmm? We may as well start gently, then move up to more interesting sums.' Again his expression was taunting and it was George he was aiming the words at.

The game began. Everyone played conservatively, assessing one another, and for the first few hands the stakes were rarely raised above the modest starting levels.

George won some money, lost a little, much like the other players. But he was waiting for the real action to start. He was feeling fully alive, his senses sharp and alert, though like the others he kept his expression calm. But things seemed to be happening in agonisingly slow motion and something in him was wanting more — more excitement, more money, more everything!

As the game began to warm up, the players' voices remained quiet, waiters only moved to refill glasses or empty ashtrays in between hands — it was the cards which dominated the room. They slipped and rippled across the table, forming and re-forming, transforming themselves into an infinite variety of patterns. George had always enjoyed those patterns.

Until now. The cards had stopped falling his way, and his piles of chips were slowly diminishing, increasing again momentarily but never rising as high as they had been at the start — yet never vanishing entirely. It was as though the money they represented was being siphoned away very, very gradually. He noticed that the man beside him, whom he had never seen or heard of before, had also lost a great deal, judging by the few chips remaining to him.

Jarvin's pile had increased, however, and so had Palmer's.

After a few more hands, the man beside George muttered something and scooped his remaining chips together in a small pile. With a murmur of, *'C'est trop pour moi!'* he pushed his chair back and folded his arms.

For a moment George was tempted to do the same. But then he looked across at Palmer, saw the challenge on his enemy's face, and the impulse died still-born.

Palmer rearranged his own piles of chips in a way that minimised their appearance, but George wasn't fooled. The fellow was gaining steadily. And starting to raise the stakes much higher.

After the next hand, while the cards were being shuffled, Palmer murmured something to Jarvin who nodded slowly, his expression thoughtful. No one had spoken a word to George or even glanced in his direction since Palmer's arrival. It was as if he was sitting alone – at the table but not with the others.

Two hands later he was sweating on three sevens, bluffing well, he thought, but he still lost because Palmer tossed a pile of chips contemptuously into the centre and said, 'See you.'

Of course the bastard had four tens!

The other stranger dropped out after that, with an apologetic murmur, of *'C'est assez!'* He too pushed his chair back and continued to watch, his face more expressive than it had been all evening.

Which left three of them – Jarvin, Palmer and George.

Anger began to pulse in George's veins. He was not going to back down. He had never run away from the enemy during all the years of the war and he did not intend to start now.

A kind of madness seemed to grip him, the same feeling of wild exhilaration that had always taken him over the edge of the trenches and into battle. Others had told him that he always smiled as he went over the top and he rather thought he was smiling now. Well, he hoped he was. He knew he was losing a lot of money, but could not be bothered to count how much. There were still chips beside him so he went on. Fortune was a fickle lady. You could be losing one minute, winning easily the next.

All that really mattered was the duel between him and Palmer. The cards were only the weapons.

Eventually Jarvin also dropped out, taking a nice pile of chips with him.

'Do we continue?' Palmer asked, a taunting smile on his face, his voice so quiet it was almost a whisper.

'Of course,' George replied – speaking too loudly he realised in annoyance the minute the words had left his mouth.

'New pack, then,' Palmer ordered calmly.

George debated asking him why, then decided it wasn't worth it.

A new pack was proffered by one of the waiters and Palmer dealt.

George's hand was a good one: two pairs, queens high. He filtered breath into his nostrils, trying not to move a muscle, just concentrating on his cards. He won that hand and the next. The pile of chips increased dramatically because the stakes were huge now. It seemed that his luck had turned. If this went on he was going to win a huge amount of money, and wouldn't that serve Palmer right? He could almost taste how sweet the victory would be.

Seconds ticked by like years. Every move Palmer made seemed slower than the last till George wanted to yell at him to get on with it. Then between one hand and the next the cards stopped falling in his favour. The piles of chips began to diminish again and he felt sweat break out on his brow.

The next hand nearly wiped him out as the stakes tripled then tripled again, both players bluffing on quite good hands. But Palmer won, damn him!

Desperate situations needed desperate measures. George stared across the table and tossed out a challenge just as Palmer was about to scoop up the pile of chips from the centre. 'Why not double that lot for the next hand?' If he didn't win it he was finished, anyway. Well, so be it.

'There is just one small problem about that,' Palmer said, pursing his lips and waiting a moment before he continued. 'If you lose, how are you going to pay your debts? You haven't got enough there.'

George stared down at the chips beside him, surprised by how few were left. He'd thought he had more than that. There had been more a few minutes ago. He looked up and saw Jarvin smirking. Reckless anger boiled up in him. 'I have other money with which I could meet an IOU.'

The room was totally silent. Even the cigar smoke seemed to

hover, as if waiting to see how Palmer reacted before it rose and joined the haze near the ceiling. Not a glass clinked, not a foot shuffled.

Palmer said calmly, 'Very well.'

George nodded, then dealt. As he picked up his cards, he could have wept. They were not good. A pair of tens and three assorted cards. But a quick glance sideways showed him a flicker of – what? Dismay – yes, dismay – on Palmer's face. He clearly wasn't pleased with his hand, either. So maybe there was still a chance of winning.

Play began. George discarded only one card to make it appear that his hand was a pretty good one. He was dealt the ace of diamonds which paired with the ace he already had. So now he held two pairs, aces high. Exultation shot through him. He *was* going to win, after all!

Palmer hesitated and George became more and more certain that his opponent had a worse hand than he did. Palmer signalled for another card and turned up its corner quickly before letting it drop.

George didn't miss the fact that his opponent pressed his lips together for a moment. He held himself still only with a huge effort. Palmer must have picked up a useless card. George had won!

There was another of those long pauses, then Palmer began to smile, very slowly letting triumph glow in his eyes – and scorn, too.

George froze. It couldn't be a hoax. Surely not?

No one else in the room spoke or moved.

The silence went on for one more minute then Palmer gave a short laugh and laid down his cards, one by one, extremely slowly. All four were hearts. He turned over the one lying face down. It also was a heart.

Oh, hell, the bastard had a flush!

There was a spontaneous shout of glee from the other men and a quick buzz of whispering from the waiters.

Palmer looked across the table. 'That, my friend, is why they call me "Lucky". I usually manage to win when it counts unless something – shall we say? – takes me by surprise?' Another pregnant pause, then, 'Shall we go somewhere and discuss payment of what you owe me?'

George felt numb. He still could not take it in that he had lost, but when the other men got up, he began to push his chair back as well. He glanced at the table and stopped moving, only now registering how very many chips there were piled haphazardly in the centre.

Sick disgust at his own stupidity in not finding out exactly who would be playing tonight welled in his throat.

Sick disgust at his own pride, too. He should have walked out when Palmer came in, accepting the minor defeat and keeping his money. He'd been growing tired of gambling anyway. What had it mattered if he wasn't able to continue playing with the big boys afterwards?

Most of all, he was disgusted because this proved that he'd lost his edge – lost his ability to assess a situation.

He stiffened his shoulders and looked across at Palmer, but inside something was crumbling, whimpering, bleeding away. 'Do you want to count the chips?' At least he'd kept his voice steady.

Palmer waved one hand in a casual gesture. 'No, you can do it, old fellow. I want you to be quite sure of exactly how much you owe me. Thad will help you.'

Baxter, grinning broadly, moved forward to stand next to George, who took a deep breath and began counting. As the piles of chips formed up in neat little rows, bile scalded his throat. He felt like vomiting when he'd finished. He hadn't thought they could add up to so much.

When the last chip had been pushed into place, he counted the piles carefully again before clearing his throat and calling across the room to Palmer to check.

The voice was as soft as ever. 'I'm sure you wouldn't try to cheat me, old fellow.'

Thad Baxter was grinning as if his master had said something witty. And he was easily as big as George, with muscles that made the formal collar and tie look ridiculous on his thick neck and broad shoulders.

No chance of doing a runner with that ape keeping guard, George decided. He'd have to pay up. If he could.

He waited till Palmer had accepted the congratulations of the other players and drunk a glass of champagne. He even downed a glass himself, though it tasted like acid, not wine. When Palmer beckoned he followed the winner outside, trying to decide whether to make a run for it.

A car was waiting, a big black Hispano-Suiza. As the chauffeur opened the rear door, George tensed, but Baxter took a quick step forward and Palmer reached out to take George's arm in a grip of surprising strength.

'Don't do it, Mercer. I'm in a good mood now. Don't make me angry.'

So George got in. He had, after all, lost. And he didn't think Palmer had fudged the cards. So he would have to pay.

One way or another.

'Very wise.' Palmer got in beside him and leaned back, smiling but not saying anything.

They travelled in silence up the hill, then along a winding side road that ended at a walled villa. All that registered with George was that the building inside the walls was large and white, gleaming in the moonlight. Numbly he followed his host inside, hearing the front door close quietly behind them. Such a small noise, but it echoed in his head like the door of a prison cell slamming shut.

He was shown into a sitting room and asked to wait. As soon as he was alone he checked the window, found it locked and began to pace up and down, unable to sit still, furious at his own stupidity. The room was exactly three and a half strides each way. He confirmed that many times before the door opened again. He never did remember what the room looked like, not a single detail.

Baxter, face expressionless, gestured to him to follow.

This time George was shown into a library where Palmer was sitting sipping whisky. The henchman took up a position by the door, arms by his sides.

'Help yourself!' Palmer gestured towards a drinks stand.

George hesitated, shrugged and did so, gulping a large mouthful of brandy then struggling not to choke as it burned its way down his throat.

Palmer set his own glass down and clasped his hands loosely, the very picture of relaxation. 'How soon can you pay me what you owe, Mercer?'

'As soon as I contact my bank in England.'

'You can do that from here in the morning.'

George frowned. Did that imply what he thought?

Palmer's grin matched that of a wolf George had once seen in a zoo somewhere. Predatory. Aiming to rip the guts out of someone – and enjoying the thought of it. 'You don't think we'd let you slip away without paying, do you?' he asked softly.

His henchman was also grinning.

The man who had gone unscathed through the war years would have fought his way out of there. The man George had now become shrugged, accepting the inevitable, fading a little in his own eyes. His response, 'Then I hope you've got a comfortable bed for me!' sounded like bravado.

'Reasonably comfortable. Though I'm afraid you'll find the wine cellar a bit dark. But it's a very secure place. You will be quite safe there. And if you get thirsty, there's plenty to drink at least.'

At the thought of being locked up, George wondered again whether he could take both of them on and escape. He hated confined spaces, absolutely hated them. He took a hasty step forward.

'We can do this the easy way or we can do it the hard nasty way,' Palmer snapped, stiffening. 'Thad has a gun and is quite prepared to use it. You weren't the only one to go to war, you know, Mercer.'

'I wasn't thinking of running.' George tried to sound calm, but even he could hear the sharp edge in his voice. 'I just don't like confined spaces.'

'We'll leave the light on for you.'

'And I'll have to ring my wife.'

'Your mistress, you mean. Same name as you but married to your cousin – the war hero.' Palmer picked up a fat cigar that was alight in an ash tray and flicked the ash from it into the hearth, not speaking till the fine grey dust had floated right to the ground. 'We checked up on you. You can phone her from here, though I'll be on the extension when you do.'

George picked up the phone and told Florence he'd not be back for a day or two.

Her voice was shrill with suspicion. 'Where are you? Who are you with?'

'He's with me,' Palmer interrupted. 'I'm so sorry to take him away from you, Mrs Mercer, but we got caught up in a card game. We're out at my villa and it's a bit late for George to get home so I suggested he stay for a couple of nights. We have unfinished business still. He was worried about you, but I'm sure you'll be all right now you know he's safe.'

'Who are *you*?'

'Oh, didn't I introduce myself? Sorry, Mrs Mercer. I'm known as Lucky Palmer – and I'm afraid I've just won rather a lot of money from poor old Georgie. He's fine, though, and will be back with you as soon as he's paid up. Just a few days or so.'

He broke the connection.

Baxter had to remind George to hang the earpiece up. And he knew he wasn't fine. Not only had his confidence been shaken by this encounter, but he would be cleaned out financially as well.

As the cellar door closed on him, he sank down on the make-shift bed and fought his demons. The space was only dimly lit and at first he had difficulty breathing. Even when he calmed down, he was so sick at heart about this fiasco that if he'd been a woman he'd have been weeping his heart out.

The night seemed to pass very slowly and he never really slept, just dozed. At times he wished he had a gun and could simply shoot himself and be done with the whole sorry mess of living. He'd had black patches in his life before but nothing to compare to this.

At other times, he felt he could learn from this and do better in future. Only what if he didn't do better? What if things simply went from bad to worse? He didn't think he would stay around to face that. Definitely not.

On the second day, however, he felt a bit brighter and began making some plans to recoup his losses. Shit or bust this time, he told himself. So he made his plans very carefully indeed. And it seemed as if they might work. He'd give it all a damned good try anyway.

Florence was putty in his hands, she'd do as he wished. And he'd get back his old edge. He would. He had to. Without it, he didn't want to live.

It was two days before George returned to the flat and although he looked as immaculate as ever, his grim expression made Florence's heart lurch.

'Did you lose very much?' she asked.

He flung himself down in a chair. 'Most of what I'd saved.'

She sank down into the chair opposite. '*Oh, no!* Georgie, how *could* you risk it *all*?'

That remark made his task easier. Stupid bitch! What did she know about anything? 'I was tricked into the game. Palmer was the reason we left London so hurriedly. He's definitely not a man to tangle with.'

'Could you not have stopped playing when you started losing?'

What the hell did she know about the madness that gripped a man sometimes? 'No. It's not done. But I'm not going back to it. I was getting fed up of gambling and it didn't bring in nearly as much money as I'd expected.'

The silence was broken by sounds from the street and from the flat above them. Florence didn't speak again. George deliberately let the pause drag on for several minutes.

After a while she asked hesitantly, 'What are we going to do now then?'

'What we should have done in the first place. Go back to England, find jobs and save our pennies. We'll find a flat somewhere cheap and keep our heads down for a while. Earning money by playing cards was a nice dream, but it didn't work out. I've enough left to pay for you to take secretarial training and I can try various avenues. I still have a few useful contacts.' He almost laughed out loud at the horrified expression on her face.

'I'm going to need to be flexible for a while,' he went on when she seemed unable to speak. 'I'll keep my options open, can't have any encumbrances. You'll have to pay your way. We may even have to go out to the colonies and . . .'

'Is that all I am to you – *an encumbrance?*'

He could see the tears forming in her eyes and a sudden feeling of pity took him by surprise. Poor bitch! She didn't deserve this. Then he hardened his heart. He couldn't afford to pity her now, not if he was going to get her to do what he wanted. 'You would be an encumbrance if I had to support you, Flo. So it's either go back to Richard or get yourself a job. And I know you don't want to go back to him.'

She gaped at him. '*Get a job?* What do I know about earning money? There are thousands of men out of work and things are getting worse by the month. You know I couldn't get a job, even if I did take some secretarial training – which I'd loathe. I've no experience.'

'Then you can go whoring. There's always a call for that. I think I might make a rather good pimp. We'd certainly earn more that way because you're good in bed.'

She began to weep and his feeling of pity vanished. 'Be

sensible, Flo! We need money and two can earn more than one.'

'How can you even say it. *Go whoring!* What do you think I am?'

'My mistress. There's not much difference, really. And you know you enjoy having sex.'

'Because I love you, Georgie, and always have. I didn't enjoy it with Richard and I'm certainly not going to do that sort of thing with strangers!'

'You did it with a few strangers during the war – for free! Love doesn't put bread on the table.'

Her voice rose to near hysteria. 'You've just been using me! You don't care for me at all.'

'As much as I can love any woman, I've loved you.' And that, he realised in surprise, was the absolute truth – though he hadn't meant to say it. He had to keep sounding harsh and unyielding if he was to drive her away.

'Love! What sort of love is that? *What do you think I am?*'

'I know exactly what you are, my pet. And I've already told you that I won't marry you.' A sudden memory of walking through a darkened villa and stealing money from under its owners' noses made a shiver of excitement and anticipation run through him. He felt the first lifting of his spirits since the game. Burglary. Selective burglary of the rich anyway. He'd been rather good at it before. It wasn't what he wanted to do with his life, but it had its compensations. He still had some of the jewellery from the last few jobs. A few careful burglaries would fund him for a while if he was on his own, though you didn't get what the stuff was worth when you fenced it. He'd managed to pay Palmer without touching his jewellery reserves, thank God.

'You're going to have to decide what option you want to take,' he said, knowing exactly what she'd choose. She was a lazy little bitch everywhere but in bed.

As the sobbing continued, he pulled her into his arms and held her close. 'Shh, now. Shh! We've been good together. Let's not spoil things now, but part friends.'

'I don't want to be your *friend*,' she said, her voice sharp as a wasp's sting, her expression sour.

He pushed her away and tossed the idea at her again. 'Sure you wouldn't like to help me get hold of Richard's money? I would *have* to marry you then.'

She jumped backwards, taking another step away from him. 'No. You can't mean that, Georgie. You wouldn't murder him – you *couldn't*!'

He would do whatever it took to make himself secure, including killing his cousin Richard with his bare hands if necessary. Killing someone was easy enough as he'd found during the war. But she had to be on his side to make it worthwhile. She'd be the one to inherit Richard's money, after all. 'I could if it meant setting ourselves up for life – getting married.' He watched her fidget, twisting a handkerchief round and round in her hands. 'Well, if you won't do the obvious, what *are* you going to do then?'

'What choice do you leave me? I'll have to go back to Richard.'

'Will he have you, do you think.'

'I'll *make* him take me back. There's Connie, you see. She's always wanted me to go back – you've seen her letters – now she's going to get her wish. I'll become a devoted mother for a while. But damn you for driving me to this, George Mercer!'

He let her rant on for a minute or two before standing up and catching hold of her arm. 'Come on then. Let's go to bed and say our farewells properly.'

'You don't think I'm going to let you—'

He had to tug her into the bedroom and put his hand across her mouth when she threatened to scream for help. But after he got her undressed and began to play with her body, she proved as co-operative as ever.

'What am I going to do without this?' she moaned against his chest afterwards.

'It's your own choice.' He kissed her bare shoulder and whispered, 'Ah, there's no one like you in bed, Flo, no one in the whole world.' Which was, unfortunately, the truth.

But in the grey light of morning, he made no protest as he watched her pack her things. After giving her money for the journey, he took her to the station and booked her a third-class ticket.

As he leaned forward to kiss her farewell, she turned away from him and flung herself down on a seat, snapping, 'Cheapskate!'

He shrugged then tossed a piece of paper at her. 'If you ever need to contact me, send a letter to my club. This is the address. It might take a while, but I'll get it eventually.'

He spun on his heel and walked off, not waiting for the train to leave, already starting to plan his next week or two. She'd contact him. He was quite sure of that. Even Richard wasn't stupid enough to take her back now.

Florence stared at the piece of paper, screwed it up and tossed it to the floor. A few minutes later, she picked it up and smoothed it out, studied the address and shrugged as she stuffed it into her handbag.

It'd take something desperate to make her contact George again, she decided bitterly, but there was no need to burn all her bridges.

Now she had to work out how best to approach her husband. Oh, if only she didn't have to! But committing murder? No, that was too high a price to pay. She simply couldn't do it.

CHAPTER TWENTY-THREE

April 1921

The trip to Overdale was one of the happiest days Polly had ever enjoyed in her whole life. Everything went well from the minute they left Stenton in the comfortable big car till they drove back across the Fylde.

'It's been wonderful,' she said to Richard, keeping her voice low because both children were sleeping.

'I've thoroughly enjoyed visiting your family. It was one of the happiest days I've ever spent,' he said with a quick smile in her direction.

It took her a minute to digest that. Hadn't he had a happy life before? She'd have thought a man like him would have had many happy memories from his childhood.

'I had elderly parents,' he explained, seeing her puzzlement. 'They spent most of their time telling me to be quiet – or at least that's what I mainly remember. The only other child at family gatherings was my cousin George and I hated him desperately even as a child.' Hated him still, but with an adult's understanding of why.

'You poor thing!' She might have lost her father at the age of nine, and had a bad-tempered mother who grew very strange after her husband's death, but she had always had Lizzie, and to a lesser extent Eva, not to mention Percy and Johnny. It was so comforting to know that your brothers and sisters were there.

'I didn't want the same loneliness for Connie.' Richard sighed and his fingers tightened on the steering wheel. 'I wanted several children and a happy home. Just like the one we saw today.'

She could hear the rough edge in his voice as he said that. For a moment, her hand touched his, then was hastily withdrawn.

Richard tried to find a more cheerful topic, not wanting to spoil the mood. 'I really like Lizzie. Is Eva like her or more like you? It's a pity she couldn't join us today. I'd like to meet her.'

'She wanted to come, but her friend Alice is very ill and not expected to get better. And Eva isn't like either of us, actually. We're all very different, though it doesn't stop us getting on well. Eva is the clever one, *really* clever! She's a teacher.'

He could hear the pride in her voice and also the tinge of envy. 'Cleverness isn't everything, Polly. You have something I value far more: the gift of making a house feel warm and friendly, of making a child happy. I think that's much more important.' He glanced over his shoulder to check that his daughter was still asleep before adding, 'And I can't thank you enough for what you've done for Connie. She really enjoyed herself today once she'd settled the other children.'

'And didn't seem to limp as much as usual,' Polly mused.

After a moment's startled silence, he eased his foot off the accelerator and stared at her. 'You're right! She didn't limp as badly.'

'I think she has a problem with the leg, don't mistake me, Richard, but perhaps it's not as bad as you fear. If she'd just let Toby work with her . . .'

In the back Connie stirred and mumbled something in her sleep.

'We'll discuss that tomorrow,' he said hurriedly.

'All right.' Polly snuggled down under the rug he had thrown across her lap, feeling drowsy and content. 'Thank you for taking us out today.'

He took a risk. 'I like spending time with you.'

She jerked round to look at him, opened and shut her mouth,

then swallowed hard, not knowing what to say. Did he mean what she thought he did?

He didn't say anything else, let alone anything personal, but his words had made her face her own feelings. How she felt so comfortable with him. How she thought about him when he wasn't there. How she considered him so much more attractive than other men.

Only she couldn't imagine someone like him getting fond of a woman as ordinary as her. No, he just meant that literally. He enjoyed her company – as his daughter's companion.

When he kept his attention on the road for the rest of the way back, she decided that she must keep a better guard on her emotions. She didn't intend to make a fool of herself or to jeopardise her position in his household.

Lizzie prowled round the crowded first-floor sitting room when everyone except herself and Peter had gone to bed, not feeling tired at all. It had been a splendid day, absolutely splendid, but it had left her wondering.

She paused in front of her husband. 'Do you think your friend Richard is a bit gone on Polly?'

He held out one hand. 'Sit down, you restless female, and talk to me properly.'

So she plonked herself down on his lap and snuggled up to him. 'Well, do you?'

'He seems to like her, but I don't think – look, love, I value your sister Polly as much as anyone and admire what she's doing for Billy as well. But she's not exactly his class, is she?'

Lizzie frowned. 'No, but he gets a soppy smile on his face when he's watching her.'

Peter sighed against her hair. 'I'll admit he likes her and he told me she's doing wonders for Connie – but don't forget that he's still married.'

'Separated and planning a divorce, though.'

'Yes, but that'll take a while. I hope he'll be careful. Indeed, I hope he doesn't care for her in the way you mean. We don't want Polly involved in all that muck-raking. You should warn her not to get involved when you write to her next.'

'Is there much muck to rake?'

'I should think so. Florence Mercer was rather well known for her – um – generosity to officers on leave. We all hoped that the captain wouldn't find out, but of course he did.'

Lizzie sighed. 'Poor Richard.' A minute later she added, 'I will warn Polly. In fact, I'll write tomorrow. She's been hurt enough.'

'Life isn't easy for any of us. But there are some compensations.' He nibbled her ear, then trailed kisses across her face. 'And you're one of mine. Are you tired, love? You've been on your feet all day.'

She gave a loud mock yawn. 'Oh, dear me, yes. I'm absolutely longing to get to bed.' But her dancing eyes belied her words. And it was quite a while before they got to sleep.

As the car drew up in front of Seaview House, Polly noticed that the lights were on in the sitting room and wondered why.

Richard got out and opened the door for her, then they each took a child and carried them towards the house.

Connie stirred in Richard's arms and began to yawn and rub her eyes.

The front door was flung open and Florence came rushing out, crying, 'My baby! My dearest child!'

For a moment no one moved, then Connie shouted, 'Mummy! You're back!' She struggled to get out of Richard's arms.

When he put her down, still too stunned to think what he was doing, she ran to fling herself at her mother.

Florence held her daughter close, not sure what to do with her next, but pleased with the success of her opening gambit. 'You've grown, darling,' she managed after some frantic thought. 'And you look – wonderful!'

Connie beamed up at her. 'You look wonderful, too. You always look nice in red.'

Florence patted Connie's shoulder and looked at Richard, trying to gauge his reactions.

Polly muttered some excuse and tried to move past Mrs Mercer into the house.

'Who's she?' Flo demanded, not giving ground. Had Richard got a mistress? Surely not? Not living in the house!

'This is Polly – Mrs Kershaw, that is – who looks after our daughter. And her son Billy.' He stepped forward and pulled Connie away from her mother. 'You've had a long day, love. Go up to bed, now.'

'No! I want to be with Mummy!' She tried to tug away from him, but he was holding her very firmly.

'Your mother and I need to talk, darling.'

Connie turned pleadingly to her mother. '*You* put me to bed, Mummy, and tuck me up. You said you wanted to do that in your letters. I have them all in a box, tied with blue ribbon.'

Florence swallowed and then said, 'Perhaps if you go up and get started. Your Daddy and I *do* need to talk.'

Polly moved forward. 'Come and help me with Billy, Connie love. I'm sure your mother will come and kiss you goodnight later.'

Flo moved out of the way, frowning at the sleeping child the woman was carrying. What the hell was going on here? You didn't usually let servants' brats come to work with them.

As the trio climbed the stairs, Florence waved to her daughter then turned back to Richard, attempting to thread her arm through his.

He pushed her away and held her at arm's length, staring at her coldly. 'You'd better come into the library.' Not waiting to see if she was following, he marched off across the hall.

She followed more slowly. This was going to be the trickiest part.

Leaving the door open and indicating a chair, he went to sit behind the desk, hardly waiting for Florence to sit down before demanding, 'What do you mean by turning up here like this uninvited? We're separated, in case you've forgotten. You don't live here any more.'

'I wanted to – to see if we couldn't try again to live as man and wife.'

'I suppose that means George has chucked you out.'

She glared at him. '*I* left him, if you must know. I found I wasn't cut out for that sort of wandering life. And besides, I missed Connie.'

Richard leaned forward, anger on his face. 'Don't bring her into this! We both know how little you care for your daughter and you're *not* going to use her to worm your way in here again.'

'I *do* care for her. Didn't I write her all those letters?'

'One every month or so is hardly a lot, and after my own experience of you as a correspondent, I'm prefectly well aware you couldn't have written them unaided. I didn't tell Connie *that* because they comforted her, but I will if I have to. Who did write them for you? George? I didn't think he had it in him.'

She had to struggle to contain her anger, but didn't deny his accusation, just muttered, 'He helped a bit, but that doesn't change the fact that I *do* care for her.'

'Oh, no. If you did, you'd have made an effort to rebuild our marriage immediately after the war. And you didn't. What's more, if you did care, I'd make the effort, too, even now. But *you*,' his voice was thick with disgust, 'you don't care for anyone but yourself. And you never will.'

She looked up quickly. This was it. The way to hook him. 'But I do, I promise you. That's why I've come back. For Connie's sake.'

'Why do I not believe you?'

'Let me stay and prove it.'

'You can prove you love Connie by seeing her regularly and being kind to her, but we're not going to try to rebuild our marriage. I want other things from a wife — things you couldn't give me even if you tried.'

She laughed, a harsh bitter sound. 'What do you want? It isn't sex, that's for sure. You were never really interested in it. That's one of the reasons I left you — because I'm a normal woman.'

'What I want from a wife is none of your business now. And I'm definitely not having you back, Florence, so you can just get your bags and leave.'

'And go where? With what? I don't have any money.' She debated pulling out a handkerchief and dabbing at her eyes, but she'd never been the weepy sort and he knew it.

'I'll pay for your accommodation at the Bella Vista Hotel and give you some money. After that, you'll have to find yourself a job and somewhere to live. Preferably not in Stenton!'

Florence leaned back and tossed a wild card at him, as Georgie would say. A pang ran through her at the thought of him, but she pushed that to the back of her mind. 'Who is she?'

'Pardon?'

'That woman, the one carrying the little boy. Who is she?'

'She looks after Connie.'

'That's not what I asked and you know it. Let me rephrase it: *what is she to you?* And who's the little boy? Surely not yours?'

'Mrs Kershaw is nothing to me. She's Connie's companion and a damned good one, too. The boy is her son. He was injured in an accident, in which her husband was also killed, and the poor lad can't walk or talk, though he is getting better slowly.'

'He's a dummy and a cripple, then! Fine companion a child like that is for *my* daughter! She may have a limp, but at least she still has her wits.'

Fury pierced him at this callous dismissal of little Billy and he remembered suddenly how Florence hated crippled people and had always flinched from disabled ex-soldiers such as those he was helping now. 'It's thanks to Polly that your daughter is starting to come out of her shell,' he said coldly, 'and I'm not having you do anything to drive her back into it — as you did before.'

Florence had not missed the softening of his voice and eyes as he spoke of the nondescript little woman or the way he had used her first name this time, as if that was what he normally called her. 'What did I ever do to Connie?'

'It must have been your fault she fell down the stairs because they told me she was not well enough to run around, as you claim.'

She avoided his eyes. 'I admit I was careless, but it was an accident.' She made a dismissive gesture with one hand, lacquered nails flashing, exactly matching her bright red gash of a mouth, and repeated, 'It *was* an accident, Richard. One I've always regretted.'

He hoped his disgust for her showed on his face, hoped to persuade her once and for all that he was not having her back. The contrast between her appearance and Polly's only made him more sure of that. Florence was wearing a very smart red suit, the skirt coming only to mid-calf and the jacket belted just below the bosom – a stupid fashion, to his mind, when a woman's waist was naturally lower than that. And he had seen how she'd tried to avoid Connie's sticky hands touching her. Beneath the suit jacket, which was hanging open, Florence wore a black silk blouse, an expensive garment if he was any judge and not one he'd ever paid for. He'd also seen a small black hat with feathers sweeping backwards from it tossed carelessly on the hall table. A nasty little thing, he considered it, the sort of confection you'd mistake for a dead bird if you didn't know it was a hat.

In fact, Florence had already made herself at home, scattering her belongings around as she always had done and leaving them for other people to tidy up. Well, she wasn't going to make herself at home in this house again. He couldn't bear to think of her sharp voice punctuating his days, demanding this, that and the other of the servants. And he didn't intend to watch Connie's disillusionment grow as she realised how little interest her mother really had in her. No, his daughter needed protecting from that.

And there was Polly, too. He simply wasn't going to have his wife hurting her, perhaps driving her away. He paused mentally on the thought. Definitely driving her away. Florence would hate Polly, hate her son even more, would make their lives a misery. And without Polly, Connie would become withdrawn and unhappy again. No, he had to prevent that.

Florence leaned forward, stretching one hand across the desk, long varnished nails groping for his hand. 'Please, Richard, let's just try. For a few days. I've nowhere else to go and—'

He leaned back out of her reach. His lawyer had warned him against having her stay in the house under any pretext, as that might be seen by a judge as condoning her immorality.

'No.'

She sat bolt upright and folded her arms. 'I warn you, you'll have to drag me out of here screaming. I intend to stay with my daughter and I'll fight for that quite literally.'

He stood up, shoving his chair backwards so hard it fell over. But he didn't care about that. Suddenly all he cared about was getting her out of his house and life again. 'If that's what it takes, that's what I'll do.'

She stood up and dodged behind a chair, shrieking, *'I'm not going!'*

His voice boomed out over hers. 'It was your choice to leave in the first place, Florence, and your choice to go and live with another man. I'm not taking you back, not under any circumstances.'

'Oh, aren't you?' Her face a mask of viciousness, she threw back her head and began to scream. Shrill piercing sounds.

It seemed to Richard that the whole household converged on the library in one minute flat: Mrs Shavely, enormous in curlers and dressing gown; Doris, visibly bursting with curiosity; and Polly, quiet and watchful as ever. To his horror Connie was there too. He could have wept to see how much it upset his daughter to see her mother scream like that.

But even that didn't change his mind. He'd learned his lesson hard during the war. Better a short, sharp pain than a lingering illness.

He got rid of the servants with a few terse words, then asked Polly if she would mind helping him with Connie.

She nodded and he turned back to Florence who was still sobbing wildly and wielding a handkerchief, but without any tears showing on her rouged cheeks.

'If you don't shut up, I'll slap your face,' growled Richard in a voice he barely recognised as his own.

She moderated her sobbing, not even seeming to notice that Connie was trying to cuddle her, was weeping with her and demanding to know what was wrong.

'Connie, go back to bed,' he snapped. When his daughter turned a look of loathing on to him, he could have wept too, but he steeled himself. Easy enough for Florence to fool a ten-year-old child, easy for her to undo all the good Polly had done in the past few weeks. But it was not as easy to fool him, who knew what his wife had been doing while she'd been away – and with whom. As if he'd ever take George's leavings!

He spoke more loudly. 'Connie! Do as you're told at once.'

'No!' the child screamed and clung to her mother.

This time Florence noticed and clutched at her daughter, shooting a quick, assessing glance sideways at Polly as she did so.

Fury boiled up in Richard, and the thought of being tied to this woman for the rest of his life made that anger overflow in a wave of red rage such as he had never felt in his whole life before.

He dragged Connie away from her mother, pushing Florence aside so violently that she overbalanced and fell. Without hesitating, he shoved his daughter towards Polly and flung open the door. 'Get her out of here, for God's sake!' he begged. 'It's all a sham. My ex-wife cares for no one but herself.'

Polly had been watching closely and had already come to the conclusion that Mrs Mercer was play-acting because her own mother had been exactly like that, throwing hysterics at will to get her own way. If anyone knew how to recognise false hysterics, it was the Kershaw girls. She nodded and was glad to see Richard's expression lighten for a moment or two.

Florence scrambled to her feet and tried to get to the door to bar Polly's way, but Richard held her back.

Polly could not make Connie listen to her, so dragged the screaming child out of the room and up the stairs. Anger at how that woman was using the child helped her do it. She might be quiet but she wasn't stupid. There were no tears on Mrs Mercer's face, no real anguish in her expression, and nothing but calculation in the glances she had kept darting from behind her handkerchief.

It seemed a long way up to the bedroom and when Doris peered over the banisters, Polly called, 'Come and help me, will you? Mr Mercer wants me to take Connie to her room but she's fighting me all the way.'

Doris nodded and came running down. Between them the two women got the struggling, kicking child up the last few stairs and into her room.

Once there, Polly whispered, 'You can leave her to me now, Doris. But will you wait outside, please? Just in case.' She pulled Connie across to the bed and simply sat there holding the sobbing child in her arms.

Connie tried to turn away but Polly held her close, making shushing noises and rocking her slightly. She intended to stay with the child until Richard got rid of the mother, if it took all night.

Downstairs she could hear voices shouting. Although Connie had stopped sobbing and shrieking now, Polly knew the child was listening carefully as well. She continued to sit and hold the little girl close, murmuring, 'Shh, love!' from time to time.

After a few moments, Connie had calmed down enough to ask in a voice that broke in the middle of the words, 'Why won't Daddy let Mummy stay with us?'

'I don't know, love, but I'm sure there must be a very good reason. We can ask him about that tomorrow.'

'But I want my Mummy to *stay!*'

'I know, I know.'

'She came back to us, so he should let her stay.'

Polly could see the tears still trickling down Connie's face. A child this age shouldn't have to face such scenes. 'In cases like this, love, when it's between a husband and wife, it's best to let them sort out the quarrel themselves.'

'But if Daddy knows I want my mummy . . .'

'He knows.'

'Then why is he sending her away?'

Again Polly repeated, 'I don't know his reasons, but they must be good ones. He would never do anything to hurt you, you know that.'

Something was happening downstairs. There were bumps and bangs in the hall, more shrieks and yells, then Florence Mercer began to curse at her husband, using words that most men would shrink from.

Polly looked down at the dark head lying limply against her breast. Connie, poor little Connie, could hear it all. Oh, that woman should be taken out and shot, she really should. How could such a fiend be the mother of a child as lovable as this?

The two of them heard Richard drag his wife bodily out of the house and after a while Polly could not resist the temptation to detach herself gently and look out of the window. She was relieved when Connie stayed huddled up on the bed.

Hand pressed against her mouth, she watched as Richard thrust his wife into the car and slammed the door on her, then went back for her luggage and hurled it into the rear seat.

By that time Florence had wrenched the car door open again and was trying to get out, hampered by her tight skirt. He pushed her back, shoving her feet in roughly and slamming the door again, then ran round to the driver's side, but by now she had got the door open again. There was a flurry of arms and legs inside the car, clearly visible in the light spilling out of the open front door as he fought to keep his wife from jumping out.

Face grimly determined, Polly marched across to the door. 'Doris, keep an eye on Connie, will you? Don't let her watch out of the window, whatever you do.' If Florence was going to struggle like this, how was Richard going to get the car started?

Polly ran down the stairs and out to the car.

Richard turned a despairing face towards her.

'You get her into it and I'll hold the door shut while you start the motor,' she said, noting the scratches on his face.

He closed his eyes for a moment, then nodded. 'Thanks.'

It took him more than one go to start the car and Polly could see that he was upset when he let the starting handle swing back and hit him. That must have hurt. Inside the car Florence was still shrieking and mouthing curses now at her, now at Richard. Polly let them flow past her, giving a groan of sympathy as the engine caught for a moment, then sputtered to a halt.

When at last it began to fire properly, Richard rushed round to the driver's seat and slid in quickly, shouting, 'Stand back, Polly!'

With a clashing of gears and a screech of wheels, the car pulled away.

Polly could see Florence hitting him as they drove out of the gates and him holding up his arm to fend off his wife's blows. The car swerved as it accelerated down the street towards the sea front, then turned the corner with a further clashing of gears.

Polly let out a long shuddering breath then looked up to the bedroom window, upset to see a white face staring out. Squaring her shoulders, she went back into the house, closing the door quietly behind her and hurrying back up the stairs.

Connie was still standing beside the window, staring out into the darkness. Doris was wringing her hands.

'I couldn't keep her away from it, Polly. I just couldn't.'

'All right. You get back to bed now, Doris.'

'Will you be all right?'

'Yes.' She waited for the maid to leave then closed the door and said, 'There's nothing to see now, Connie. You might as well get ready for bed.'

The child turned round to glare at her. 'Why did you go

and help him? You could see how she wanted to stay here.'

'She went away. It was her choice. He doesn't want her back. He'll explain it all to you in the morning.'

Connie trailed back to the bed and collapsed on it as if she hadn't the strength to stay upright, asking brokenly, 'Where is he taking her, then?'

'I don't know, love.' Polly tried to cuddle her.

Connie pushed her away, yelling, 'Don't touch me! I hate you! You helped him.'

'Connie, love—'

The shrill young voice screamed, 'Don't call me love! You don't care about me at all! And *you* aren't my mummy. I don't want you. I want her.' Then the sobs began again, though quieter now and despairing in tone.

Polly waited until they had begun to die down before saying, 'I'm going to tell you again and you must listen to me carefully this time, Connie. There are some things which adults have to settle between themselves. This was one of them. And I *do* care about you. Very much.'

Silence.

'But she wrote to me. And then she came back to be with me! She said so.'

'Yes, but – but maybe she and your father aren't happy together. Do you want him to be unhappy for the rest of his life just so that you can be with your mother? Does he deserve that? After all, there will be nothing to stop *you* seeing her from time to time, will there? I'm sure he wouldn't prevent that once – once things are settled.'

There was a long silence while Connie digested this information, then she asked. 'Were you happy with your husband?'

Polly took a deep breath then answered honestly, 'No. Not always.'

Another silence. Then, 'But you stayed with him.'

'Yes. Him and Billy.'

'If he hadn't died, would you still be with him?'

'Probably. But I wouldn't have been happy. I got married without thinking what it'd mean to live his sort of life. Most girls do.' And she had been stupid enough then to accept a life of boredom and frustration. When she looked back on it now, she couldn't believe all she had put up with – especially from her mother-in-law – or how much she had changed since Eddie's death! Grown up really. She'd been a girl when she'd married him, but she wasn't a girl now.

Connie's voice was very faint as she said, 'I don't understand.'

'I don't understand everything, either. I just know that we have to let them sort out their problems themselves, just the two of them.'

'But I w-want my mummy back!'

'Since the war ended, your father's the one who's stayed with you and looked after you, hasn't he? You have to remember that and trust him now.'

There was no answer. Fully dressed as she was, Connie climbed into bed, turning her back on Polly and dragging the covers up so that her neck and part of her head were covered. 'Go away.'

Polly sat on beside her, not attempting to make her undress and not saying anything. She had thrust Billy into his bed fully dressed, too. It didn't matter. Nothing mattered except getting through this terrible night and helping the child she had grown to love so much.

As the silence dragged on there was a movement in the bed and Connie asked in a surly voice, 'Why are you still here? I want to go to sleep.'

'I'm here because I love you and I'm worried sick about you.'

Then Connie was sobbing again, but this time reaching out to Polly, wanting to be held and comforted and shushed until she fell asleep from sheer exhaustion between one sob and the next.

Only when she was sure that Connie was fast asleep did Polly leave her, to go up to the floor above and stare down at her son.

She would never understand how Florence Mercer had been able to leave her child, never.

Billy woke up suddenly and stared at her in the moonlit room. 'Ma-ma,' he said tentatively.

She moved forward. 'Yes, my little love.'

'Wee-wee.'

And for the first time since his accident, he did not simply wet himself. It was a funny sort of consolation, Polly decided later as she lay in bed. But then life had a way of treating you in funny ways, didn't it? She could hear nothing from Connie's room and there was no sign of Richard returning. What was he doing?

She knew she wouldn't get to sleep until he returned.

The Bella Vista Hotel was dark when Richard drew up in front of it.

'I won't go inside!' Florence declared in a harsh voice. 'You'll have to pull me from the car screaming and carry me.'

'I'll do that, if you make me.'

'I'll run away as soon as you've left and stand outside your house shouting.'

'In which case I'll call the police. And the village constable knows me very well. Jim Bulmer is a returned soldier like me.'

'You're all against me! All of you!'

This time he could see real tears on her cheeks, but he was utterly certain they weren't for Connie. He got out and banged on the front door of the dark hotel until a light came on inside, all the time keeping one eye on the car. But as he had expected, Florence did not attempt to leave it.

When the door was opened by a sleepy night porter, Richard apologised for disturbing them, explaining that his ex-wife had arrived rather late to see their daughter and had nowhere to stay. He'd be really grateful if they could give Mrs Mercer a room.

By that time the manager had come down and Richard had to explain everything again. When the man stared at him, clearly wondering why his wife wasn't staying at Seaview House, Richard said tersely, 'We're in the middle of a divorce. She can't stay with me.'

'Ah. Yes, sir.'

'I'll pay for a room and three meals a day. But not for anything else, no luxuries or drinks from the bar. Is that clear?'

Having difficulty hiding his astonishment at this blunt speech, the manager nodded. 'Er – yes, sir. If you'll bring the lady in and ask her to wait, I'll just call the housekeeper.'

Florence folded her arms and declined to leave the car.

Richard hauled her out and thrust her towards the hotel, upon which she assumed a distressed mien, handkerchief to her eyes, weeping loudly.

Feeling too angry for embarrassment, he dumped her on a sofa in the hall and went outside again to bring her suitcases in. Then he stood near the reception desk keeping a wary eye on her.

The housekeeper arrived in her dressing gown, offering profuse apologies for keeping them waiting.

'Captain Mercer requires a room for his wife. One on the third floor would be best.' The manager mouthed the words, 'I'll explain later.'

She nodded, staring at the woman sobbing on the sofa. 'Number thirty-four is ready.'

'That'll do.'

After a moment's hesitation, the housekeeper went across to Florence. 'If you'll come this way, madam?'

Florence did not attempt to move, just sat there with her head in her hands.

Richard strode across to join them. Without attempting to lower his voice, he said, 'I'm quite prepared to carry you upstairs if necessary, Florence.'

She hesitated for a moment then got to her feet, glaring at him.

Richard followed them towards the lift. Florence halted outside it so he shoved her in and got in behind her, pulling the iron grille across before pressing the correct button.

By that time the porter had started to stack Florence's suit-cases near the lift. 'If you'll send the lift down for me, Mrs Naizley, I'll bring the lady's things up.'

The metal cage rose slowly with a faint clanking sound. Richard didn't even look at his wife. He had never felt fury like this. How dared she use Connie, make a scene that would leave their daughter with painful memories for ever?

The lift wheezed its way up to the third floor. The house-keeper cleared her throat and made a move towards the grille. Richard pulled himself together and opened it.

He did not have to push Florence out. She moved of her own accord this time, keeping as far away from him as she could.

The housekeeper hurried along the corridor and opened a door.

After a quick glance round the room, Richard nodded. 'Yes, this'll do fine.'

Florence pulled a face. 'It's very small.'

'It's all I'm paying for. I didn't ask you to come back.' For the benefit of the housekeeper he added, 'As far as I'm concerned, the quicker we can get that divorce, the better.' He turned to the goggling woman and repeated his instructions about what he would pay for, ending up, 'Please make sure that nothing else goes on my bill, Mrs Naizley.'

Spots of red burning in her cheeks and showing through the layers of smudged make-up, Florence glared across the room at him. 'You always were mean, Richard Mercer. Even to your own wife, the mother of your child.'

He hated all this, hated exposing the shame of their marriage to everyone, but it was better to do that than let Florence find some way to make the courts think the two of them could ever be reconciled. 'Since you left me of your own accord to live with another man, I no longer consider you my wife or a fit mother for my daughter.'

The housekeeper gasped and gaped first at him then at

Florence, her mouth slightly open as if she couldn't believe what she was hearing.

'Oh, go to hell, you bastard!' Florence shrieked suddenly, making everyone jump. 'I hate you! Hate you, hate you, *hate you!*' She turned to the housekeeper and the porter who had just joined them with the suitcases. 'And you two can get out! I don't know why you're still here. You'll get no tips from me because I can't afford them and *he's* too mean to tip like a gentleman.'

Richard waited till they'd left the room then said quietly, 'I'll do whatever it takes to get that divorce, Florence.'

'Go to hell!'

As he shut the door he heard something thump against it. It sounded like a shoe.

They rode down in silence in the small lift. In the hall Richard turned to the porter and housekeeper. 'I'm sorry you had to witness this display.'

The manager was still standing behind the desk. The house-keeper joined him there. Richard had no doubt they'd be gossiping about what had just happened as soon as the front door shut behind him.

The porter escorted him out, wished him goodnight, then locked the door behind him.

Richard stood for a moment in the darkness because the main hall light had just gone off inside the hotel. The moon was behind some clouds and the whole world felt dreary and without colour. The happiest day of his life – and the worst evening he had ever experienced. The scandal would be all over the village by the following day, but he didn't care. Well, he did care, but that couldn't be helped. He had to make sure that nothing, absolutely nothing, put the divorce in jeopardy.

There was also Polly to consider. Whatever must she be thinking? Florence couldn't have fooled her because she'd come out to help him. He felt warmth rise in him at that thought. Polly had understood, supported him.

He groaned aloud and swung the starting handle with

unnecessary violence. This time the engine fired the first time. He got into the car, put his head down for a minute on hands that were shaking as they grasped the steering wheel. It was a few minutes before he felt steady enough to drive home.

He tried to plan what to do, but his thoughts were slow and stupid tonight. The only thing he could decide was that first thing in the morning he must phone his lawyer. No, first he must explain about the divorce to Connie.

He glanced up as he stopped the car outside Seaview House, but everything was dark except for a light in the hall. Was Polly still awake? And had his poor daughter cried herself to sleep?

The front door was unlocked. He went inside and shot the bolts, making his usual tour of the ground floor to check that all was secure. Only then did he go into the library and pour himself a large whisky. Even if he did go to bed, he'd not be able to sleep.

On the third floor of the Bella Vista Florence was also awake, leaning on the window sill, staring out at the dark sea and the quiet village. She felt herself burning with hatred for her husband. What had happened to change him? Once he'd have done anything to prevent Connie getting upset. Now – her lips curved into a parody of a smile – now there must be some reason he didn't want his wife back. Perhaps someone else he was protecting as well as his daughter? Yes, that was it. And that someone could only be the dowdy little woman who was probably exactly right for a fuddy-duddy like Richard.

Only she wasn't going to get him if Florence could help it. Florence was determined to find some way to pay him back *and* get some money out of him. There had to be a way. He had humiliated her, spurned her – oh, God, what on earth was she going to do now?

A little later the moon went behind some clouds and in the darkness Florence made her way across to the bed, slumped down on it and admitted at last what she was going to do. George had given her an address, said to write if she ever needed him. There was only one way to get him back now. It was risky, but she had no choice.

As soon as the hotel began to stir, she went down to the reception desk and sent a telegram to the address George had given her, telling them to make it 'Urgent'. The people at his club would forward a telegram quickly and Georgie would come as soon as he heard from her, she was quite sure of that, because she was giving him what he wanted. But her co-operation would come at a price. Nothing less than marriage.

The thought of what they'd have to do first terrified her, but it was the only way out of this mess. It was Richard's own fault, really. He had brought it on himself. In the meantime she'd spend a boring few days here because she hadn't the money to go elsewhere.

CHAPTER TWENTY-FOUR

April 1921

———————◆———————

When George received the telegram from Florence, forwarded from his club in London to Poste Restante in Toulon, he smiled in triumph, feeling in charge of things once again. 'I don't know what you did to her, Richard old fellow,' he said aloud, 'but whatever it was, thank you. You've made my task much easier.'

He sent a reply straight away and set off for England the same day. You had to strike while the iron was hot at times like these.

From his club George sent another letter to Florence, asking her to meet him in Blackpool two days later. He reckoned by that time she'd be so frustrated she'd do exactly as he wished. In the meantime, he sold some of the stolen jewellery, visited a couple of picture houses, drank some good English beer in a pub and decided he was never going abroad again.

Richard tried to explain about the divorce to Connie and only succeeded in upsetting her further. But when he went to see his lawyer, Havershall commended his speed in getting Florence out of the house and making it plain to the hotel staff that he hadn't invited his wife back and didn't want her staying with him.

'Can't we hurry the divorce along?' Richard asked.

Havershall shook his head. 'Sorry, old chap. The wheels of justice grind exceeding slow, especially when it comes to divorces.

And the fact that your wife has asked for a reconciliation for your daughter's sake is not good. She's been rather clever there.'

'I'm not taking her back.'

'You're certain of that?'

Richard gave a bitter laugh. 'Very. My only problem is: should I allow her to see our daughter? She keeps asking – and Connie wants to see her.'

'I think so. Supervised visits, however.'

'Supervised by whom?'

'What about that companion of your daughter's? Mrs Kershaw.' The name change had gone through quickly enough, but he still wondered why Mercer had helped the woman out like that. Did he have his own romantic interests? Was that why he was so adamant about not even trying for a reconciliation? If so, Havershall didn't want to know anything about the matter. 'Can't she go with them?'

Richard frowned. He didn't like to think of exposing Polly to his wife's petty spite. 'Do you think that's necessary?'

'I think it would be wise.'

'I'll see if Mrs Kershaw minds doing it. But I won't force her into it.'

When he got back, however, he found a note from the hotel asking if he'd settle his wife's bill as she had left that morning. He ran up to the nursery where a sulky Connie was making a token effort to embroider the pinafore she'd been very enthusiastic about only a few days before.

'Hello, darling!'

Connie scowled at him and turned back to her work without replying.

'Everything all right?' he asked Polly.

'Yes, of course.'

Billy waved his hands wildly and Richard went across to greet him and talk to him about the 'Teh-dee' he was holding, a golden furry toy that Richard had seen in a shop and bought on impulse.

Connie kept her back turned.

Richard grimaced at Polly, who returned a sympathetic smile, then he said he was going for a walk and strolled along to the hotel.

'Mrs Mercer left us rather suddenly this morning,' the manager told him. 'We – um – did as you asked and she has paid for everything apart from her room and meals. She was not very pleased about that.'

'Having settled the bill and left a generous tip for the staff, Richard walked slowly back. Florence had not left any word for him or – much more important – for Connie. His daughter was going to be upset all over again.

Which was an understatement. She flatly refused to believe him when he told her that her mother had left Stenton. After a hearty bout of weeping she glared at him and declared, 'I want to rest – on my own!'

Polly intervened. 'Very well. Billy and I will be down in the garden. You can join us there when you're ready.' She picked up her son and gestured to Richard to leave.

'Will she be all right?' he asked in a low voice once they were outside the door.

'I think so. She doesn't know what to believe. You'll just have to let her come to terms with it, I think.' But Polly knew exactly what *she* thought of a mother who abandoned her daughter without a word of farewell.

'Come and join me for a cup of tea.'

She frowned. 'I'm not sure I ought to, given the present circumstances.'

'Please. Billy can be our chaperone. Let me carry him down for you.' As he hefted the little boy in his arms, Billy crowed in delight and grabbed hold of his hair.

'Da-da-da! Go walk!'

Polly followed them downstairs into the sitting room and helped Richard prop up her son with cushions.

When Doris brought in the tea tray, Polly said to her,

'Connie's extremely upset. If you hear her come out of her room, would you please let us know, Doris?'

The maid nodded and went off to share this information with Mrs Shavely. The butcher's boy had seen Mrs Mercer being driven to the station that morning and had shared the information with them, but they hadn't felt it their place to tell the master.

'Proper shame, it is. That child is pining for a mother's love, absolutely pining. Only she won't get it from *her*.' Mrs Shavely cut them both a piece of cake and Doris poured the tea from their own special pot, then they sat down to enjoy some gossip and speculation.

Connie waited till everything was quiet in the house before getting out of bed, picking up her shoes and opening her bedroom door. After listening carefully, she tiptoed down the stairs. Through the sitting-room door she could see her father talking to Polly with Billy playing on the floor at their feet. They didn't care about her. No one did. Only her mother. And she didn't believe that her mother would just leave her. Her mother had come back specially to be with her. Why was her father lying to her?

She slipped out through the french windows in the library, keeping to the far edge of the lawn as she made her way round the garden and left by the side gate near the vegetable patch. It felt strange to be out walking on her own. She couldn't remember the last time she had done that.

Ignoring everyone she met, she made her way along the sea front.

The hotel seemed bigger than she had remembered and when she went inside everyone looked very busy. Only the thought of seeing her mother gave her the courage to move forward.

The man behind the desk turned, noticed her and looked behind her, then stared up and down the hall.

'I've come to visit my mother,' Connie said quickly before he could tell her to go away.

'And who would that be?'

'Mrs Mercer. I know she's staying here.'

'Mrs Mercer left the hotel this morning,' the man told her.

Connie stared at him, feeling angry. Why were they all saying this? 'I don't believe you.'

He frowned at her. 'I'm not in the habit of lying, miss, and if you really are Captain Mercer's daughter, then I suggest you get back home to your father. He's well aware that your mother has left us because he came and paid her bill only this morning.'

Connie burst into tears. She wept even more loudly when the man tried to shush her, then abandoned herself totally to her distress. It wasn't true. It couldn't be true! Her mother wouldn't leave her like this!

Florence made her way to Blackpool where she was to meet George at the railway station. There were hours to go yet so she put her things in left luggage then went out for a stroll. It seemed quite a long way to the front and these shoes weren't very comfortable for walking in. Only she wanted to look specially nice for Georgie. If he didn't take her back, she'd kill herself, she really would, because she was definitely not going to get some miserable job and slave away for a pittance.

When she stopped for a cup of tea, she watched the waitress and shuddered at the thought of having to do something like that.

She should have stayed in Stenton a bit longer because Georgie wasn't due until mid-afternoon, but once she'd got his letter she couldn't bear to hang around that dreary place a second longer. She looked in her purse as she paid the bill. The few measly pounds Richard had given her weren't going to last for long. Why were men so mean with their money?

Back at the railway station she sat in the first class waiting room, staring out at the people bustling to and fro.

Suddenly a voice behind her said, 'Well, well!'

She turned and threw herself into Georgie's arms and he gave her a big hug, to the patent disapproval of an elderly lady sitting nearby.

'Come on, Flo! Let's go and find somewhere to stay.'

I need to get my things out of left luggage.'

'I'll put mine in there, too, then come back and fetch them later.'

At the station entrance she stopped, expecting him to signal to a taxi, but he tugged her on. 'Let's walk. We can look at the hotels as we go.'

Only there weren't any nice hotels in that area and the place he eventually chose was dreadful, far worse than the Bella Vista. She didn't dare argue with him because he had *that look* on his face – and anyway, she didn't want to upset him. She just wanted him to take care of her – in bed and out of it.

It wasn't till evening, when he insisted on going for a stroll along the promenade, that they really managed to talk.

'So, my pet,' he said, sitting in a shelter and putting his arm round her shoulders, 'what are we going to do next?'

She watched the sea rolling up on the sand, then rolling back. What people thought was special about that she didn't know. Give her London and people and excitement any day! 'How should I know what we're going to do?' she muttered, not wanting to put it into words.

'You know what we have to do so let's not pretend, eh?'

She swallowed hard. 'I – don't think I can do it.' His arm was withdrawn and he moved along the seat. 'Georgie!'

'I thought you understood the situation, Flo. There's only one way we can get enough money to live comfortably together. Gambling is run by a set of criminals – just how far they control it I hadn't realised before, I'll admit. I'm not going to get another break there.'

She heard herself make a little sound in her throat like a kitten mewing, but couldn't think what to say.

He picked up her hand. 'Look at me.'

Slowly she raised her eyes. As he put her hand to his lips, a thrill ran through her and a stab of pure longing for him. She had missed him so much during those interminable days in that dreary hotel.

'Flo darling, this is the only way we can get married, be together, have a decent life.'

She managed to nod, but still didn't want to say the words.

He pulled her close again and kissed her, then whispered, 'You won't have to do it. I'll see to all that. And it's not as if you even like Richard.'

'Like him? I hate him! And he's got another woman, you know. *Already!* Fine one he is to talk about my being unfaithful! You should see her. Plain and ordinary. Doesn't even speak nicely. Definitely lower class. And she has a crippled son. The boy and Connie make a fine pair.'

'Dreadful. We'll send her packing as soon as we get rid of *him*.' George took her back to the hotel where they both enjoyed themselves enormously, shabby room or not.

'There's no one like you, Flo,' he told her afterwards.

'Or you. I shall enjoy being Mrs George Mercer.'

Which was, he realised, her way of accepting the inevitable. 'I shall enjoy being able to marry you,' he murmured, settling into a more comfortable position.

'Will you really, Georgie?'

But he didn't answer because he was already asleep.

She lay awake for a while, worrying about what they were doing, then consoled herself with the thought that George had promised that he would do *it*. She had already decided that if anything went wrong, she could always deny knowing what he had planned. That thought cheered her so much she was able to sleep.

Richard abandoned the car in front of the hotel, forgetting even to switch the engine off. Inside the foyer the manager himself came forward to greet him.

'The little girl is very distressed, I'm afraid, sir.'

'Where is she?'

'If you'll follow me, sir. The housekeeper has her in one of the upstairs rooms.'

The sound of weeping greeted them even before the manager opened the door. Richard's heart was wrung by the sight of Connie lying curled up on the bed, sobbing loudly.

As he moved forward the housekeeper and manager exchanged glances and left the room. 'Connie, my darling, stop crying!' But he had to pick her up and cradle her against him before she even became aware of his presence.

'She's gone,' sobbed the distraught child. 'And she didn't even say goodbye to me.' Then she noticed who was holding her and tried to push him away. 'Why did you send her away? It's all your fault and that stupid divorce thing. You don't love me any more!'

'I didn't know she was going, either. Connie, please listen to me!' He captured her flailing arms and gave her a very slight shake, which was enough to make her stop screaming at him, though her breath was still catching on sobs. 'Connie, I did not know she was leaving until this morning when the manager called and asked me to pay the bill.'

'But if you'd let her stay at home, she wouldn't have left. It's all your fault.'

'No, it isn't. And I've already explained why she can't stay with us.'

But she was beyond reason, just continued sobbing wildly.

Taking a sudden decision, he picked her up in his arms and carried her down the stairs. The porter rushed to open the main door. Guests moved out of his way with disapproving glances.

The car was standing there with its engine still chugging softly. Relieved at not having to tussle with a starting handle, he slid his daughter into the front seat where she slumped down, weeping inconsolably, not seeming to be aware of what was happening around her.

He drove home slowly, this time remembering to switch off

the engine when he stopped. It seemed very quiet then because Connie had stopped sobbing and was just a huddle of silent misery.

Damn Florence for doing this to the child!

He opened the car door, but Connie didn't attempt to get out. He stood there chewing the corner of his lip and wondering what was the best thing to do now.

'Carry her up to her room and let me speak to her,' Polly said next to him.

He turned to her with such a glowing look that she could only stand there for a moment, staring up at him. Then the child's needs took over.

As she followed them up the stairs, she heard Connie saying, 'Put me down. I hate you! It's all your fault.' How that must hurt him.

Once they were in the bedroom, Polly asked Richard to leave and went to get a damp face flannel and towel.

Sitting next to Connie, she pulled the weeping child upright and began scolding her softly, knowing it didn't really matter what she said, just that she spoke and continued to speak until the sobbing stopped.

'Just look at you! Getting yourself into a state like this. And what good will it do? Your father didn't send your mother away from you. You know really that he'd never do that without telling you.' She said the same thing over and over again using different words while at the same time sponging Connie's flushed face and then holding the shaking body close. 'Eh, you poor little love, what are we going to do with you?'

Eventually Connie flung her arms round Polly's neck. 'She left me. It's all Daddy's fault.'

'Now how can it be his fault when he didn't even know she was going?'

'He *must* have known.'

'No, he didn't. I was there when he got the phone call from the hotel. He looked surprised. I'd say he definitely didn't know.'

Another long pause, then, 'Really?'

'Would I lie to you?'

Connie swallowed hard and swiped away a stray tear. 'Then he must have said something to Mummy last night.'

Polly held her at arm's length. 'If he swears he didn't, will you believe him?'

'No. Yes. I don't know.'

'He doesn't lie to you. He doesn't lie to anyone. You know that.'

'But she left!'

'She's left before, love. Lots of times.'

The silence went on for some time. Polly didn't know whether to say anything else or not. But her instinct said to let Connie decide what happened next.

'Polly—'

'Yes, love?'

'You won't leave me, will you?'

'I'll try not to.'

Connie looked at her in shock. 'Promise me you won't leave me!'

'How can I promise when I don't know what will happen in the future? All I can promise is that I'll try my hardest not to leave you. I have Billy to think about as well as you. You know that.'

'You don't love me, either, then. Nobody loves me.'

'I do love you. So does your father. And Billy does, too. Eh, I haven't checked to see if he's all right. Will you come with me to look at him?'

After some hesitation, Connie wriggled off the bed. Before they got to the door, she slipped one hand into Polly's. And Billy was crying, too, in his room, because he had wet himself, something he now hated to do.

'I'm sorry, Billy,' Connie said solemnly. 'It was my fault. But I didn't mean to do it.'

Soon they had him changed, then they all sat together.

'Dinner,' said Billy into the fraught silence. 'Want my dinner.'

Connie blinked and stared at Polly. 'Those are new words.'

'Isn't that wonderful?' said Polly huskily. 'Oh, Connie love, he's getting better all the time.' And then she was weeping as well. But not for long. Laughing at herself, she wiped her eyes, persuaded Connie to keep an eye on the boy and went down to get some food.

When Richard came out into the hall, Polly whispered, 'She's looking after Billy now. Leave her to me for a while.'

He stopped her moving past him. 'You've been crying, too.'

Polly smiled. 'For joy. Billy just asked for his dinner ever so clearly.'

'That's wonderful!'

But she could tell that he was speaking automatically. His eyes were still on the stairs, as if he wanted to rush up them.

'Shouldn't I go up to her?' he asked, taking a step forward.

Polly tugged his arm and pulled him back. 'No. Definitely not. Let her come to herself in her own time. She's admitted this isn't the first time her mother has left her. That's a start. She'll gradually grow used to the idea of the divorce as well.'

He gazed down at her. 'You're very wise, Polly Kershaw.'

'Me?' She chuckled. 'I was always a dunce at school.'

'Wise where people are concerned,' he said firmly. 'I'm so glad we've got you.' He repeated her name softly, using the phrase her sister had used, 'Our Polly.'

She didn't know what to think of that, so told herself not to start imagining things, just because he was grateful to her. But she liked the way he'd said 'Our Polly'. It made her sound a real part of the family. Which she felt herself to be. However much she kept reminding herself that she had no right to stay here, that he was only her employer.

CHAPTER TWENTY-FIVE

Late April 1921

For a week nothing happened in Stenton. Connie recovered somewhat from her disappointment and began to speak to her father again, but was very subdued. She talked a lot to Polly, though, asking questions about grown-ups and love and families, and eventually about divorce. Once again she had to be coaxed to go out for walks and shrank from meeting people. It upset Polly a great deal to see how their careful progress had been spoiled by a selfish mother.

Billy was the main bright spot in these difficult times, making visible progress each day, which pleased all of them. He had regained his sunny nature and was now greeting people by name and describing his simple wants more and more clearly.

When Toby came on his next visit, he was delighted to see the progress his youngest patient had made. Billy laughed at him as Toby swung him up in the air, and the doctor laughed as well before putting the lad down. 'Well, now we can move on to the next step in my programme – making his limbs stronger and teaching him to walk again. I want to show you some more exercises to try. They've worked with some of the men so they may help Billy.'

'Could we bring Connie in to learn them, too?' Polly asked. 'It'll give her something to think about and she does like helping with him.' She hesitated then asked, 'Did Richard tell you that his wife turned up a few days ago?'

'Yes. Bit sticky for you, eh?'

'Very difficult for us all, but especially for Connie. When her mother went away again suddenly without saying goodbye, without even leaving a note . . . well, Connie was devastated. Which is why I want to distract her if I can. Also I'm going to *insist* she consults you about her limp. When she's happy, she limps far less because she forgets about it. Maybe there are some exercises she could do to strengthen her bad leg. What do you think?'

'I'm happy to have her here with us as we work on Billy, and I'll try to help her, too, if she'll let me.' But he was disappointed that he and Polly were not to be working alone together. She had greeted him with such a smile he had wondered if she was starting to grow fond of him. Surely she must have recovered from the loss of her husband by now? Surely he could start courting her openly?

Not only Connie joined them for a demonstration of the exercises, but Richard as well. When Toby saw how at ease he and Polly were with one another, his heart sank. They exchanged glances as if they didn't need words to communicate and seemed – together. Toby's dreams came crashing down around him and he had to struggle to conceal his disappointment by focusing on his patient. He should have known that no woman as attractive as Polly would want someone who was plump, red-haired and slightly balding when there was a tall handsome fellow like Richard Mercer around. He should have bloody well known!

But the little boy still needed him and the notes he was amassing on this case would help him with other patients. You could never quite tell how people with head injuries were going to turn out, but just leaving them to lie around helplessly was definitely not the best way to treat them.

Patiently he demonstrated a version of the exercises he had devised for the wounded soldiers and watched as even

Richard took turns at moving Billy's legs and arms correctly.

When Polly sang a little tune in time to the movements, Toby stared at her. 'I didn't know you could sing like that.'

She blushed and looked confused. 'Oh, I can hold a tune.'

Richard chuckled. 'Don't compliment her. It makes her come over all funny. But she has a beautiful voice and we all enjoy it when she sings.'

'Shut up!' Polly hissed, fiery red by now.

When they had finished practising the exercises, Polly gave Toby her latest set of notes and turned to Connie. 'Why don't you let Dr Herbert examine your leg while he's here, love? He might know some exercises which would help you as well.' She saw Richard looking at her in shock, but she was quite prepared to insist and was more interested in how her charge would react.

Connie didn't say anything at first, just glanced sideways at Dr Herbert once, then scowled down at the carpet. She even opened her mouth to say no when she suddenly remembered how her mother always flinched away from her leg and looked irritated if she limped too much. It occurred to her that even if her parents never lived together again, perhaps her mother would like her more if she didn't limp so badly. After another glance at Dr Herbert and Billy she muttered, 'All right.'

'Good. No time like the present,' said Polly briskly. 'Richard, would you mind keeping an eye on Billy while Dr Herbert checks Connie's leg?'

'I'd be happy to.' He had hardly dared breathe while his daughter was coming to her decision and now, as he watched Polly lead the way to Connie's bedroom, he turned to the boy and declared, 'She's a miracle. Your mother's an absolute bloody miracle.'

Billy laughed at him and shouted, 'Bu-dy meecle! Bu-dy meecle!' at the top of his voice, then chuckled again.

Richard could not help returning the smile. There was something very infectious about Billy's happiness now that there was life in his eyes again. 'You, young fellow, had better watch your language,' he ordered, tickling the small chest. His smile faded and his voice was almost a whisper as he added, 'We'll get those legs of yours working properly again. And perhaps Connie's as well.'

It seemed a very long time before Toby came back. Richard looked at him hardly daring to voice the questions that were welling up inside him.

Toby said casually, 'It'll take time, but there are definitely ways to improve Connie's walking.'

She didn't rejoin them but stayed in her bedroom. When Polly came back. Toby gestured to the door and she closed it.

'I don't know why she limps,' he said very quietly. 'There's not much wrong with your daughter's leg, Richard. A reaction to some trauma in the past, perhaps? The difficult thing will be persuading her to walk properly. The exercises will indeed strengthen her muscles, but their main purpose is to trick her into believing she can walk properly.'

Richard could only gape. 'Are you sure about that?'

'Pretty sure. What exactly happened?'

'I don't know, only that she fell downstairs. Florence was with her at the time and I've always assumed – well, that the accident was due to my wife's carelessness. She didn't deny that, either. By the time I came back on leave after the accident the limp was there. After the war I took Connie to see that Browning-Baker chap, but he made her scream with pain and said it was all in her mind. I didn't like to subject her to such an ordeal again. There seemed no point.'

'She didn't scream when I was examining her,' Toby said thoughtfully. 'And we learned during the war how men can recover from the most appalling injuries. But she won't recover as long as *she* is convinced there is something permanently wrong with that leg. For once I have to agree with Browning-Baker. I told Connie the leg would gradually get better if she did the exercises. I said that now she was older her bones were getting stronger so it was a good time to improve things.' He pulled a wry face. 'It's not really true, but if it gives her the confidence to try to walk more normally, I think I can be excused a small lie in a good cause, don't you?'

'I could forgive you a very big lie if it helped Connie recover and lead a more normal life,' Richard said fervently.

'Well, don't make an issue of it. Just wait and see if she makes any effort.'

The two men then went to have their usual drink in the library and Polly went back to see Connie, who looked at her resentfully, said she was tired and wanted to rest.

So Polly went back to her son – and her thoughts.

Downstairs Richard leaned back and closed his eyes for a moment.

'You all right?' Toby asked quietly.

'Yes. Just a bit tired.'

They both took a sip of whisky and Toby changed the subject. 'The first four men are doing so well in the rest home that we could bring in another two residents now, I think. How about that Adness chap, the one who had the bad head injury? I want to try some of the things on him that have worked on Billy.'

'All right. You start things moving to get him transferred here and I'll make sure the room is ready. And Parkley, perhaps? He's pretty unhappy in that hospital, however well they look after him physically.'

'Yes, why not?' After another pause Toby said, 'Polly seems to have settled in well here. She's very fond of your daughter.'

Richard's smile was warm, his feelings showing clearly. 'Yes. She's a wonderful woman. I don't know what we'd do without her now.'

'You love her, don't you?' Toby said abruptly, staring down into his drink.

'Hell! Is it that obvious?'

'It is to me. You see, I've grown rather fond of her, too.'

After one quick glance in his direction, Richard stared out of the window. 'I didn't know you felt like that. But I haven't said anything to Polly. I have no right to – to commit myself and won't have for a long time. She might not reciprocate my feelings.'

Toby's voice was quiet. 'I think she does.'

'What makes you think that?'

'You act – I don't know – like a married couple. As if you're already very close.'

Richard gaped at him, then frowned down into his glass. 'I'd better do something to change how I act, then. We don't want any counter-claims of adultery from Florence.' That might bring more trouble for Polly.

'I hope you're intending to do the right thing by her eventually, though. She's had a rough time this past year.'

'Of course I am.'

'You're a lucky chap.'

'In some ways.' In others he was very unlucky, or had been till Polly came into his life. One youthful mistake had led to more than ten years of deep unhappiness. He wondered if Florence had rushed back to George the other day? Why else would she leave Stenton so suddenly? There had to be someone with the money to support her. She would never be able to support herself, or want to. Well, Richard wasn't going to give her much more money. There were hard times coming, unless he was very much mistaken, and he wanted to husband his resources carefully.

It took two days for Polly to win Connie round again. 'We won't force you to do anything you don't want,' she said. 'But I don't think Dr Herbert's exercises would be painful. The ones Billy does aren't. And anyway, we could take things slowly.' She changed the subject entirely. 'Now, don't you think it's time we got you some new clothes? You've grown out of just about everything you own.'

Connie's face lit up. 'Oh, I'd love that! Mother said it didn't matter what I wore, since I only sat in my room.'

That mother of hers, thought Polly with unaccustomed savagery, had a lot to answer for. She decided to ask Richard about the new clothes over dinner, but he was so stiff with her that she stopped trying to talk to him. Maybe he'd had some bad news. She'd wait till morning to ask.

Richard watched her take Connie upstairs to bed, knowing she'd go and sit in her room afterwards or join Doris and Mrs Shavely in the kitchen. The evenings seemed very long to him sometimes. He ought to be working on his novel. It would be the wisest use of his time. But he couldn't settle tonight. He knew he'd treated Polly in a way that had puzzled her at dinner, but after what Toby had said, he didn't dare be too friendly. For her sake, as well as his own.

The following morning Richard was still very stiff, but Polly screwed up her courage over breakfast. 'Richard, Connie needs some new clothes. I wonder – could she and I go into Blackpool and do some shopping? I'm sure Doris will keep an eye on Billy and—'

'Yes, of course.' He glanced at his daughter, thinking of the difficulties of the trip and changing buses. 'Look, to save Connie getting over-tired, why don't I come with you? It'll be much easier with a car, then you can load your purchases into the boot.' An outing might also bring him and Connie closer again. He hoped so. As they stood up to leave the dining room, he noticed how tall his daughter was growing, nearly as tall as Polly now. Where had the years gone?

He caught up with Polly in the hall and tugged her sleeve to make her slow down. When his daughter had gone on up the stairs, he said quickly, 'Thank you. I should have noticed that she needed some new clothes myself.'

She nodded, looking sideways at him. 'You're a busy man. It's my job to notice such things now. And I'll enjoy helping her choose some more flattering styles. Those she has are too young for her, you know.'

'One more thing. I'm sorry, but I'd better call you Mrs Kershaw from now on – and – and you should call me Mr Mercer – or sir.' He hated saying that, absolutely hated it.

Polly drew herself up. 'Certainly, sir.' Then she walked quickly away.

He had meant to explain that it was because of the divorce, but as usual he'd messed things up, fumbling for words, upset by the sudden pain in her eyes. One day he would tell her why. In the meantime, he had to protect her not only from gossip but from his wife's spite. Maybe, on second thoughts, it was better that she didn't know, but continued acting stiffly with him. Just for the time being.

They left within the hour to make the most of the day after Polly had repeated instructions on looking after Billy to Doris, who nodded and said, 'I'll take good care of him, lass, so you stop worrying and enjoy yourself. We're all getting right fond of your little lad, we are that! Me and Mrs Shavely are going to take him for his walk along the sea front together this morning once we've got the place cleared up a bit. It'll be a treat for all of us.'

So the other three drove into Blackpool. As they went into one shop after another Connie lost her unhappy expression for once as she was encouraged to say what she really liked. She was thrilled with their purchases, Polly making sure she had some really pretty things, even her nightdresses. After buying enough clothes they went into a shoe shop.

Every time her opinion was not needed, Polly moved away and left father and daughter together. She was still angry with Richard and didn't want to presume on her close relationship with Connie. If her employer felt it necessary to tell her to call him Mr Mercer, when *he* was the one who had insisted she call him Richard, then he had only to tell her once. She knew what lay behind his words. She had been behaving like a member of the family and that was not permissible in a servant. Only *he* was the one who had made her feel like a member of the family, and now for some reason he had changed his mind. She could not understand why. Perhaps his wife had said something.

While he was trying on a pair of shoes in the men's section of the shop and Connie was putting her socks and shoes back on after they'd selected some for her, Polly moved to look out of the window in time to see an elegant couple walking past. She froze where she stood because it was surely – yes, it *was* Florence Mercer and with her was a tall man who resembled Richard. It could only be one person: his cousin George.

She kept an eye on Connie to make sure the child didn't see her mother, breathing a sign of relief when the couple were out of sight. Once the girl's shoes were fastened, Polly quickly led the way towards the rear of the shop where Richard was standing by the counter paying for everything.

She thought she'd hidden her shock, but he noticed immediately that something was wrong and opened his mouth to speak. She was so afraid he'd ask outright what the matter was that she shook her head and glanced towards Connie warningly.

When they got outside he sent his daughter to buy an ice cream from the shop next door. As soon as she was out of earshot, he said, 'Something's wrong, Polly. Don't pretend it isn't.'

'I just saw your wife go past with a tall man who – who looks a bit like you.'

Richard's face went white and he stiffened in shock. Even as she watched his eyes seemed to lose their colour and turn to ice.

'My cousin George. What's he doing here?' He glanced towards the ice-cream shop and muttered, 'We'll talk about this later.'

When Connie returned, Polly claimed to be tired and worried about Billy so as soon as the child had finished her ice cream they went straight home.

It was not until both children were in bed that night that Richard caught Polly on her own as she was going to the kitchen quarters at the rear to share a final cup of tea with Doris. 'I wanted to thank you for warning me about what you saw today,' he said.

'I felt Connie ought not to see her mother, sir.'

'Or the man she was with.' He smiled, but with a visible effort. 'Funny, isn't it? I don't want Florence back and yet it galls me that she's living with my cousin.'

The words suddenly poured from him right there in the dimness of the hall, his voice low but filled with pain. 'She's been unfaithful to me for years, ever since the war began, and not only with George. I married her purely because she was expecting our child. I had no idea what she was really like, hardly knew her at all. If I had realised . . .' He rubbed his temple as if his head were hurting, then shrugged. 'I don't know. You see, she gave me Connie and I'll always be grateful for that. And in those days it never occurred to me to provide for my child in any other way than by marrying the mother. It was the way things were done.'

Then he realised that he was doing what he'd promised himself not to do again, confiding in Polly, so he took a hasty step backwards. 'I'm sorry. I shouldn't be burdening you with my troubles, Pol— um, Mrs Kershaw. You have enough of your own.' He moved towards the library door. 'I shouldn't have – I don't usually – oh, hell!' He turned on his heel and shut himself away from her.

He wished very much he could sit in the kitchen with the three women instead of on his own. He had done that occasionally and enjoyed their cheerful company, but now he must keep his distance. He would never forgive himself if Polly was dragged into the divorce case. Anyway, he had to stay here. Polly only went to the servants' quarters when she knew he was around to hear if one of the children called. It was an unspoken agreement between them.

Unspoken agreements were dangerous.

He must not get into any more habits like that.

He went and sat at the desk but did no writing. He found his mind wandering and kept listening for Polly's quiet tread on the stairs as she returned to her own room. When he heard the door that led to the kitchen open, he even stood up to go and wish her goodnight, then sat down again quickly. Thank heavens Toby had given him a nudge. He'd been playing with fire, getting so friendly with Polly. Fire that could burn *her*.

Only – he could not forget that hurt expression on her face. He should have spoken more tactfully.

In Blackpool George found a place to live where he and Florence could cater for themselves – and most important of all – could come and go without anyone noticing.

She was not at all pleased by the accommodation. 'This place is a slum!' she said angrily the first time he took her to see it. 'How can you expect me to live here?'

He took a firm hold of her arm and swung her round to face him. 'We can live somewhere decent once we've got what we want. Until then we have to make some sacrifices – and this is one of them. Another is that you will stop wearing those bright clothes, which stand out like a sore thumb in this area, and dress more quietly so as not to be noticed.'

She looked at him apprehensively and tried to move away, but he wouldn't let go of her. 'You're *hurting* me, Georgie.'

He didn't let go but bared his teeth in a grimace that was not really a smile. 'You aren't changing your mind about what we decided, are you, Flo?'

She summoned up a picture of Polly Kershaw, queening it at Seaview House while *she* hadn't even been allowed to stay there for a few miserable nights, and said quickly, 'No, of course not.'

'Good.'

So they moved in. And Florence began dressing more quietly.

A week later, George ate his evening meal quickly then leaned back in his chair and fixed her with one of his stern gazes. 'I'm going out tonight. You're to stay here. Don't open the curtains or door. In fact, don't do anything which might show that I'm not here. If anyone asks later, you're to say we spent the whole evening together.'

She gazed at him in horror. Suddenly her stomach felt as if it was full of crumbling cardboard and her throat seemed too tight. Swallowing, she asked in a hoarse whisper, 'Are you – going to do *it* tonight?'

'Of course not. I'm just going on a little recce.'

'How will you get to Stenton?'

'Leave that to me.' He stood up, anxious to change into some dark clothes and be off.

'But—'

He turned at the door. 'Flo, you don't really want to know the details. Leave it, eh?'

She pulled her cardigan around her shoulders and sat closer to the fire. It seemed a very chilly night, though it was April now. She'd be glad when the summer arrived. She always felt better in warmer weather.

A few minutes later George left, dressed in dark clothes, with a common-looking grey cap on his head instead of his usual smart trilby. She stopped lying to herself then. The night wasn't all that cold, it was just that *she* felt cold inside because she was terrified of what he was going to do.

She grimaced and amended that mentally. Not afraid of something happening to Richard . . . heavens, no! Her stupid husband deserved all he got. But she was very afraid indeed of that something being traced to her, and of being tried for murder and hanged. Or even just put into prison. Only what other choice had she? She had tried to do the right thing and go back to Richard, hadn't she? But *he* already had another woman living there and had treated Florence, his wife still in the eyes of the law, abominably.

She could not settle to read so sat staring into the fire. Every time there was a noise, she jerked round. When two of the neighbours clumped past, talking animatedly, she sat rigid then realised she'd been holding her breath. Only she couldn't laugh at herself.

As more footsteps approached, she got up to peer out of the

window and check who it was, then remembered that George had told her not to do that. 'It's all right for him,' she muttered. 'He's *doing* something. I just have to sit here and wait.'

It seemed a very long evening.

George strolled along the street, turning down a back lane and then making his way to a shed at the bottom of a nearby garden. Inside was a neat little Singer Ten. The vehicle was light enough for him to roll it outside. There, with a huge extra effort, he pushed it a little further along the back lane, cursing the recent rain that had made the ground so soft.

When he had gone as far as he could, he managed to start the engine. It seemed very loud in the darkness and he stood there for a moment or two, listening intently, ready to run away if anyone came out to investigate. But no one did and with a smile he hopped on board and set off.

He enjoyed the drive to Stenton, but took the precaution of keeping the cloth cap he was wearing pulled down nearly to his eyes. As he paid to cross Shard Bridge, he tried to keep his face in shadow. He'd have sung as he went, something they'd all done in the Army, but didn't want to give anyone a reason to remember the car or anything about its occupant. Which was why he hadn't bought a car of his own. He didn't want people to recognise anything.

Ah, it felt good to be *doing* something again, really good!

By the time he got to Stenton most folk were in bed. He left the car under some trees just outside the village and made his way to Seaview House. As he approached it he saw that there was a light on in the library. Since the curtains were not drawn, he crept round the house and crouched in the bushes staring in through the window. Richard looked so at home and comfortable there that George felt jealousy scald him. His cousin didn't need to steal cars and go creeping round other people's houses in the dark – or to live in a slum, either.

'Make the most of it while you can,' he muttered. 'You've not got long left to enjoy it.' That thought cheered him up immensely.

He crept round to the kitchen but everything was dark there. The staff obviously went to bed much earlier than the master. The lock on the back door was old-fashioned and would be easy enough to pick for a man with George's skills. Or else there was a window he could open, wide enough even for his broad frame. He tested it and grinned. Stupid to leave it with such a simple lock on it. They should have put a bar across it, too.

A light went on upstairs and he moved quickly backwards. Another quick circuit of the house showed that Richard was still in the library. Who was awake, then? That light wasn't coming from the staff wing. George intended to get to know the habits of everyone in the house. Florence said Richard was having an affair with the maid he'd hired to look after Connie, but that sort of thing didn't sound his cousin's style at all.

Light came on in the hallway and Richard stood up, his expression eager, then sat down again, looking unhappy. Intrigued, George continued to watch. When he saw a light come on in the kitchen, he crept round to the back again to see who it was. A rather ordinary young woman was putting the kettle on. This must be Connie's maid. He reckoned Flo had got it wrong. Even Richard wouldn't have fancied this woman, surely? And she looked unhappy, not at all like a woman having a love affair with her employer.

The sound of the front door opening sent him hurrying back to the other side of the house. Richard came out wearing an overcoat, his shoulders hunched. When his cousin had walked down the street George crept up to the front door and tried it. It was unlocked. What a trusting fool! But it was useful to know this sometimes happened.

He turned and strolled along the street, nose buried in a scarf and cap pulled down. He doubted Richard would recognise him even if they met, but he'd prefer to keep out of sight.

At the end he stopped following Richard because there was

nowhere on the sea front for him to hide. But from where he stood in someone's front garden, he could see his cousin striding up and down the promenade like a man possessed.

When Richard returned to Seaview House half an hour later, George saw him coming and went to wait in the shrubbery again. The light in the library went on and didn't go off until nearly one o'clock. The light upstairs hadn't come on again. Hardly the behaviour pattern of a man having an affair, whatever Florence said.

George made his way back to the car, well satisfied with his night's reconnoitring. The vehicle started easily and he headed back towards Blackpool, humming quietly to himself again.

Halfway there the damned engine began to falter and he guessed it was running out of petrol. It limped along for another few hundred yards, then the engine cut right out and it slowly coasted to a stop.

He cursed and searched for a spare can of petrol. There was indeed a can in the holder at the rear, but no petrol in it. The owner was a fool. A total and utter fool. He deserved to lose his car. If there'd been a hill to push it down and crash it, George would have done so to teach him a lesson. But the countryside was very flat and he certainly wasn't drawing attention to himself by trying to wake someone up and buy petrol.

He set off to walk back to Blackpool. It took him an hour and a half, and proved that he wasn't as fit as he had been, but he used the time to good purpose, going over what he had seen in his own mind and working out how best to dispose of dear Richard. To hell with trying to arrange an accident! Too hard. Besides, he wanted his cousin to know who was killing him. So it would have to be murder by person or persons unknown – by gunshot. Not his own service revolver, but one that was not traceable.

He would get himself a bicycle. There was something very anonymous about a bicycle at night and they were nice and quiet as long as you kept them well oiled, not to mention being easily hidden.

At their accomodation, he found Flo in a state of panic. It took him an hour to calm her down again.

'You're going to have to learn to trust me,' he said after they'd made love. 'I know what I'm about. What do you think I was doing during the war? I made regular sorties behind enemy lines. I didn't get caught then, did I? And I won't now, I promise you.'

She stared at him in surprise. 'You never said anything about that before.'

'Well, we spies were told to keep our big mouths shut about the details of what we'd been doing when the war ended, weren't we? Just in case our side ever needs to use the same tricks and techniques again.' He waited for that to sink in and added casually, 'I've killed quite a few men, my pet. It's quite easy. You can safely leave all that to me.'

CHAPTER TWENTY-SIX

May 1921

———◆———

Feeling more confident in her pretty new clothes, Connie made a friend, something she had not dared to before. Or rather, she was befriended by Morag Drummond who was staying with her spinster aunts two doors away from Seaview House while her mother had a baby. Morag found life at her aunts' house very lonely, and was not afraid to make the first overtures towards the little girl along the road.

Although almost paralysed with shyness during their first encounters – too paralysed even to flee – after some earnest discussions with Polly, Connie began to play out regularly with Morag. At mealtimes she talked hesitantly about her 'friend' and behaved more like a normal child than she ever had done before. But she still limped badly and Polly had not seen her trying to do the exercises Toby had suggested.

Polly was delighted about the friendship and did everything she could to encourage it, inviting Morag round to tea and letting Connie pay return visits. At first these terrified the child so much that if Polly hadn't explained to Morag how shy her friend was and asked her to come across to collect Connie, the tea party at the Drummonds' might never have taken place.

Morag was fascinated by Billy and once the aunts had checked out exactly what was wrong with the little boy – for they took their responsibilities towards their niece very seriously – the two girls were allowed to play at being mothers to him. Soon Polly trusted them to take him in his wheelchair for walks along the promenade, letting them feed him and teach him new words as well.

Under their enthusiastic tuition Billy's rate of improvement speeded up and Polly went across the road one day especially to thank the Misses Drummond for allowing their niece to help. She had felt very nervous about doing this, but was pressed to stay for a cup of tea and enjoyed an hour's gossip while Doris and the girls kept an eye on her son.

After hearing about the poor injured soldiers that Captain Mercer was helping, Morag begged to be allowed to accompany Connie and her father on visits to the rest home and the aunts too signified their interest in helping cheer up 'our poor injured boys' once their niece had gone back to Oban. A down-to-earth, practical child, Morag did not seem in the least upset by the men's disabilities and they in turn loved seeing the two little girls. Sarge usually hovered nearby to make sure things went all right, acting like everyone's favourite uncle.

Even Polly was roped in to go and sing to the men, with Richard accompanying her on the piano (though he apologised for being a bit rusty). Although she was nervous the first time, they were so appreciative that she promised to come regularly.

'It's all going too well,' she worried to Richard one evening as they strolled along the promenade behind the children.

'What – Connie's friendship with Morag?'

'That and Billy. Everything.'

He smiled down at her. 'Don't you think it's possible for life to be completely happy?'

She was silent for the next few paces, then said, 'I haven't found it so.'

'Never?'

'No, never.'

He vowed to do his best to change that one day, but did not say so. Once they reached the far end of the promenade he excused himself and went into the rest home because he didn't want to look like a lover accompanying his mistress.

For some reason, though, Polly's words lingered in his mind. There was something that continued to worry him. Someone else from the village had also seen his wife and her companion, and had mentioned it to him. Why were Florence and George staying on in Blackpool when both of them preferred life in the south of England? He didn't care where they lived as long as they left Connie alone, but why stay so close to him? It couldn't be from maternal feeling because Florence had made no effort to contact her daughter. Should he employ that detective again to find out where exactly they were? But even if he did find out, what could he do about it? It was a free country. They had committed no crime and could live where they liked.

He tried to banish his worries, but they kept coming back to haunt him when he sat on his own in the evenings.

The village church which the Mercers occasionally patronised and which the Drummond sisters attended every Sunday was planning for its May Queen procession which, unlike those of other villages, always took place on the last Saturday in the month. In an ancient ritual the parishioners chose a May Queen, and then the little girls from the parish, all dressed in white, walked in procession to the church behind her as 'attendants' with a few decorated carts following them.

Once Morag found out about this festival she was eager to join in, and since the congregation was small and everyone knew one another, no one seemed to mind in the slightest if the little stranger became an attendant as well. And of course Morag wanted Connie to join in the procession, too.

'I can't do it,' she whispered to Polly, 'I'd die of embarrassment. And anyway, I wouldn't be able to keep up with the others.'

Polly busied herself with her mending because she'd found that Connie confided more if no one was looking at her.

'My limp is so *horrid*.'

'Get along with you! Nobody minds it. You try doing those exercises and one day you'll walk as well as anyone else.'

Silence. Then: 'My mother hates my limp, I know she does. I heard her telling a friend once how ugly it is.'

This made Polly so angry with Florence Mercer that she didn't watch what she was doing and stabbed the darning needle into herself, yelping involuntarily. 'Sorry. I pricked myself with the needle.' She sucked her thumb and tried to think what she could say to make Connie feel better.

'And the girls all wear long white dresses.'

'We can get you a white dress. Or I can make you one.'

'Morag says I'd look nice in white.'

'She's right. She's a sensible little lass, that one.'

Connie began tracing the pattern on the carpet with one dusty shoe. 'But I'd still limp and be slower than the others, so . . . Polly, will you please tell Morag I'm not allowed to go?'

'I don't see any need to lie to her. Besides, if you do those exercises, you'll not limp as badly.'

'I have been doing them.'

'Oh?'

'And I *can* walk a bit better – only I'm frightened my leg will hurt worse if I walk for so long.'

'You need more practice. You and Morag should go for a walk every day.'

'People will stare.'

'Not here in Stenton. They're quite used to you now.'

'Well, strangers will stare.'

'What do you care? You won't see them again.'

'I wanted to surprise my father.'

'He'll be delighted, love.'

Polly let Connie sit there quietly in case there were any other confidences, and sure enough, there were.

'Morag's mother's going to have a baby and after it's arrived she'll have to go back to Scotland,' Connie said a minute later. 'Then I won't have anyone to play with.'

'Well, now that you've learned how to make friends, you'll be able to find other children to play with — especially if you start going to school in September, as your father and I are hoping.'

Connie's gasp was followed by silence, then, 'I couldn't go to school. Polly, *please* don't ask me to do that.'

'You'll have to or you won't get a proper education. I'm not good enough at book learning to teach you your lessons. So if you don't go, your father will have to get you a governess, and in that case there won't be a place here for me any more.'

Connie stared at her in horror. 'But you said you wouldn't leave me!'

'I said I'd *try* to stay. And if you go to school, I might be able to do that — though even if I don't, I'll keep in touch by writing to you.' She hadn't discussed her future with her employer yet. He'd been so stiff with her lately, Polly was beginning to think he'd want her to leave once Connie started school. But she was quite sure he wouldn't stop her writing to the girl. Whatever his own feelings, he cared deeply about his daughter's happiness and knew that Polly did, too.

But why had he changed towards her? Had she done something to upset him? She just couldn't understand it. She realised Connie was still looking anxious and banished her own worries. 'When Morag goes home, you and she will be able to write to one another. She won't forget you, love, and she'll still be your friend. Why, she might even invite you to stay with her in Oban.'

'Do you think so?'

Honesty compelled Polly to temporise. 'I'm sure she'll write. Not sure about the invitation to stay.'

Connie began to weep. 'Why do I have to be so ugly? Why does everyone leave me?'

Polly tossed the darning aside and gathered the girl into her arms. 'You're not ugly, love. And your father isn't going to leave you, you know that.'

*

The next evening Connie heard Polly go across the street to discuss dresses for the May Queen festival. She and Morag had practised walking in procession the past few days, and Morag said the limp was hardly noticeable now. Mrs Shavely and Doris were in their quarters and Billy was asleep along the corridor.

Just as she was falling asleep, Connie heard her father go out for one of his walks. He'd been going out a lot lately, not with Polly any more but by himself. Perhaps he had gone to visit the rest home.

It was the smell of burning which woke her a short time later. It took her a minute to realise there shouldn't be such a smell. She got out of bed calling, 'Polly! Polly!' but there was no answer so she pulled on her dressing gown and peeped out of her room. The smell of burning was stronger here and there was a sort of flickering light upstairs where Billy's room was.

She shouted again: 'Polly! Daddy!' But no one answered. So she tried calling, 'Mrs Shavely! Doris!' Only their quarters were at the back of the house and she realised they couldn't hear her.

She hesitated, wondering whether to go and fetch them, but Billy's voice, crying out for his mummy, made her turn and run up to his room.

Inside flames were leaping around the window and he was coughing in the smoke.

Without hesitation, Connie went and tried to pull down the side of his special bed, only it seemed to be stuck. She shook it, frightened now, and again wondered briefly whether she should go for help. But the flames were licking right up the other side of the bed and by the time she got hold of Mrs Shavely and Doris, he could be badly burnt.

Leaning over the cot, she tugged him into a sitting position, saying, 'Come for a walk, Billy. Come for a walk!'

He reached out to her and she pulled him over the side of the bed away from the flames, struggling with his weight. They both fell to the ground. She sat up at once and looked for the wheelchair but couldn't find it, though it was usually left standing beside his bed.

She said, 'Hold tight, Billy!' an instruction he understood well. When he put his arms round her neck she half dragged, half carried him to the door.

The flames flared up higher than ever. There seemed to be a draft coming from somewhere. She glanced round and saw that the window was partly open at the bottom, which it wasn't usually. The smoke was making her cough now and Billy was crying again, so she didn't linger, just staggered out on to the landing and closed the bedroom door behind her because she had once read that flames spread more quickly if they got a good draft of air.

When she got to the top of the stairs, she left Billy lying there and ran screaming down the stairs, shouting for her father or Doris. She had to go right through the kitchen to the servants' wing before they heard her, then they came running in their night-gowns.

'The house is on fire,' she panted. 'It started in Billy's room. I got him out on the landing, but he's too heavy for me to carry down the stairs and I can't find his wheelchair.'

'Oh, my heavens?' Doris set off running towards the upstairs floor.

'What's that flickering light?' Polly asked suddenly as she stood at the door of the Drummonds' house saying goodbye.

'It's . . . oh, dear heavens, it looks like your house is on fire!'

Polly tore off across the street.

Miss Drummond gave her sister a shove. 'Go and telephone Constable Bulmer at once, Josephine! Don't just stand there.' She followed Polly.

Richard had reached the corner of the street on his way home when he saw the flickering light at the back of his house and a figure darting across the street. It was only a faint light, but he'd seen too many burning buildings in France not to guess that something was on fire. *Danger!* screamed a voice in his head and for a moment he was back in the field of war, seeing a farmhouse burn down. But only for a moment. He began running, praying it wasn't his home burning.

But it clearly was his home, and his child was inside. He burst in through the front door just as Mrs Shavely and Polly were shepherding the children through the hall. 'Get everyone outside and shut the front door!' he ordered. 'Polly, your son's all right. Go and knock up the neighbours and ask for help in forming a bucket line.'

'The fire's in Billy's room, Daddy,' Connie called. 'And we can't find his wheelchair.'

'My sister is calling the Constable,' Miss Drummond added.

Richard snatched a heavy rug from the hall floor and pounded up the stairs.

By that time he had laid it across the worst patch of flames, one of his other neighbours had arrived in pyjamas and overcoat. 'What can I do?'

'We have some barrels of rainwater out at the back. We need a bucket line and a ladder.' Richard went into his own bedroom for another rug and started beating at the other flames.

Within minutes four neighbours, perched precariously at intervals on a ladder, were passing buckets up to the window. Throwing the water on to the heavy woollen rugs seemed to stifle the flames.

Richard's arms were aching and when he turned to reach for the next bucket, he realised that the person who passed it across the room from the window was Polly – with smoke-blackened cheeks and forehead and a very determined expression on her face.

The Volunteer Fire Brigade arrived a few minutes later, pushing their big water tank and hand pump.

'Damned engine on the truck wouldn't start or we'd have been here sooner,' the Fire Captain panted as he and his well-rehearsed volunteer crew unrolled hose-pipes and started hand pumping water on to the remaining flames.

Within a few minutes the last of the flames in Billy's room were out. Richard closed his eyes for a moment in relief, then turned to Polly. 'Are you all right?'

'Yes.' She looked round at the charred furnishings and shuddered. 'Connie saved Billy's life, you know. She dragged him to safety.'

Her hair was a tangled mess, her face covered in smuts. For a moment they stared at one another, then she took a step backwards. 'I think they've got it under control,' she said in a voice that sounded hoarse. 'The Drummonds have taken the children in.'

'You did well.' The Fire Captain came to join them. 'Good thing you had those heavy rugs to throw over the flames. They held things till we could get a proper supply of water in here.' He frowned, studying the hearth. 'The fire wasn't lit, was it?'

'Of course not,' said Polly. 'It's been quite mild lately.'

'So how did the fire start, then?'

'And why had someone moved my son's wheelchair?' Polly added. 'I left it beside his bed as usual when I put him down.'

As her words sank in, Richard felt as if the ground shuddered beneath his feet. Someone must have started the fire deliberately. But who? And why choose the boy's room? It didn't make sense. This was Stenton not France, a peaceful Fylde village.

George had covertly watched the furious activity from behind the back garden wall. At first he had smiled, confident that the house would burn down and then Richard would receive a nice big lump of insurance money. He had checked in the library of Seaview House one evening while his cousin was out walking and had found the insurance policy, still current.

And he had made sure that the volunteer firefighters wouldn't be able to get the motor of the brand new fire engine started. But the stupid fools had managed to push the trailer bearing the water container through the streets anyway. That was the trouble with these little places, everything was close to everything else and people rushed to help if something went wrong. And how had the neighbours got organised so quickly to pass buckets up a ladder? Interfering sods!

It was a pity Florence's brat had not perished. He'd set the fire so that it would take hold in the cripple's room above hers once he'd seen Richard go off for one of those long strolls and the maid nip across the street. George had been inside the house a few times now while he was making his plans. He'd even contemplated smothering the girl in her bed while he was at it, but that would have been a bit too obvious. He wished he had done it now, though, because she was the one who'd seen the fire and started screeching her stupid head off. If it hadn't been for her, his plan might have succeeded. Those two doddering servants wouldn't have noticed a thing from where they slept until it was too late.

He should have used more oil – only he'd wanted the fire to appear like an accident, the sort of thing a child could have started by playing with matches.

Well, he wouldn't work as tentatively next time. He'd go straight for Richard and leave the brat until later. Once his damned cousin was out of the picture, Florence could take charge of everything and he'd make sure she trotted to the altar with him as soon as possible, handing everything to him on a platter.

Damnation! It'd have been so much easier to collect the insurance money on a totally gutted house than to wait for the repairs on a damaged place and then try to sell it.

Once the firefighters and neighbours had left, George made his way back to where he'd hidden the bicycle he'd stolen once he'd paddled across the river on foot at low tide to avoid being seen crossing the bridge. The water was higher now, but not too high for him to get across without being noticed after abandoning the stolen bike. Wet and angry, he retrieved his own bike and pedalled furiously along the road to Blackpool.

By the time he reached the flat he'd made up his mind to kill Richard as soon as possible. He was fed up of all this hanging around, fed up of trying to stop Flo from backing out of their little arrangement. He had to succeed this time, had to. If it didn't work out, he'd . . . he cut that thought off. No need to jinx things. There had been a small hitch today, that was all.

He'd be more careful next time. And once he had killed Richard his confidence would return and he'd be on top of the world. He was sure it would.

CHAPTER TWENTY-SEVEN

May 1921

———◆———

The part of the house where Billy had been sleeping was damp and smoke-ridden; the whole place stank to high heaven. The only rooms that were habitable that night were the downstairs reception rooms and servants' quarters. While Polly put together makeshift beds down there, Richard had a talk with the local constable, Jim Bulmer, and the Fire Captain, Don Greinor.

'I think that fire was set deliberately,' Don said immediately the three men were alone. 'Do you – um – have any enemies that you know of, Captain Mercer?'

Richard could guess who had done it, but he had no proof. It could only be George. Why the hell was his cousin trying to burn the house down?

'It's not as if that little lad could get out of bed or play with matches or anything,' Don went on.

'He's improving, but he can't move about freely yet,' Richard confirmed. 'And there weren't any matches in the room. Polly's very careful about such things.'

'And then there's the wheelchair,' Jim said in his slow, thoughtful way. 'Mrs Kershaw seems very certain she left it in the lad's room.'

'She leaves it there every night,' Richard agreed, 'and she's not given to forgetting things.'

'Well, there you are, then. Someone must have moved it. She'd have left the front door unlocked while she nipped across the road, I dare say?'

'Yes. And I have to confess that I often leave the door unlocked myself. I like to take a walk last thing at night.'

'Yes. Seen you myself walking along the sea front,' Jim Bulmer confirmed. 'Lovely time of year for it. Better lock up more carefully for a while, though. I'll ask around, find out if any strangers have been seen round here at night.'

When the two men had gone, Richard sat on, lost in thought. Surely Florence couldn't be involved in this arson attack? She wouldn't hurt her own daughter. And how would this have benefited George? His cousin only did things that would benefit him in some way.

Although his mind went round in circles, worrying at the problem, Richard could not work out what was going on. But he was going to be a lot more careful about locking doors in future.

Workmen were going to be swarming over Seaview House for the next few days so Richard arranged for everyone except the servants to stay at the Bella Vista, and hired a night-watchman to keep an eye on things.

'Me and Billy could use one of the downstairs rooms,' Polly protested. 'Hotels are expensive places.' She had never actually stayed in one and felt quite nervous at the prospect.

He debated with himself how honest he dared be.

But she had seen from his face how worried he was. Well, she was worried, too. She had nearly lost her son for a second time. 'That fire was deliberately lit, wasn't it?' she challenged him.

Richard nodded. 'Yes. So I'd be grateful if you didn't let Connie out on her own, particularly at night. Not even to cross the road to Morag's.

Polly sucked in her breath and stared at him as things suddenly began to make a bit more sense. 'You think someone was trying to hurt *her*?'

His expression was so bleak that she realised he did think exactly that.

'They weren't after my Billy, then?'

'Heavens, no! Why should you think that?'

'Dr Browning-Baker. He's gone to great lengths trying to take Billy away from me. If my son was killed, or even injured in a house fire, it'd show I wasn't to be trusted, wouldn't it?'

That idea had never even occurred to Richard. He considered it briefly and rejected it almost at once. 'No, this is more likely to be aimed at me.'

Another of Polly's thoughtful silences then she said slowly, 'But we can't be sure, can we?' She had lain awake for most of the night, worrying that she had brought this on the Mercers. 'I've been thinking that – well, if it's aimed at me, it'd be better for you and Connie if we left.' Though where she would go next, she couldn't imagine, with Browning-Baker still ruling the roost in Overdale. But she'd find somewhere. She couldn't bear the thought of Connie being hurt because of her.

Richard wasn't sure of anything except that he didn't want them to leave. 'I doubt it was Browning-Baker. It can only have been my cousin George's doing – only I can't understand why he wanted to burn the house down. What good would that do him?'

'Insurance money?' Polly hazarded. She had, after all, benefited from an insurance pay out herself.

'But *he* wouldn't get that. I would.'

'Your wife might get some, though, if there was a divorce settlement.' Every time Polly saw a divorce reported in the newspaper now, she read about it, trying to understand what you had to go through.

'I can't believe even Florence would agree to this.'

'Perhaps she didn't know what he was going to do?'

Richard shook his head and changed the subject back to the hotel, insisting she and Billy join Connie and himself there.

＊

The staff at the Bella Vista could not have been more helpful. Polly, standing wide-eyed taking it all in, saw her luggage brought in for her like a proper lady's. She then had her first ride ever in a lift while Richard spoke to the manager. As the metal cage clanked its way up to the second floor, she tried not to let her nervousness show. Billy, of course, was staring around him, shooting out words one after the other.

The housekeeper, who had accompanied them, smiled down at the child in the wheelchair. 'I didn't realise he could speak.'

Polly stiffened, but the housekeeper's expression wasn't disdainful. She explained her son's condition for what felt like the thousandth time since the accident.

'Well, I'll tell the staff to speak to him as much as possible, then,' Mrs Naizley said. 'He's a bonny little lad, isn't he?' She turned to Connie, looking a little more wary, remembering the hysterical child she had last seen. 'I hope you're keeping well, Miss Mercer?'

'Connie saved Billy's life last night,' Polly said quietly, putting an arm round her charge. 'We're very proud of her.'

When the housekeeper opened a door to show off a large sunny bedroom with two single beds and a view of the sea front, Polly tried not to show how impressed she was. It was a lovely room, with everything matching and, as she saw at a glance, properly cleaned and maintained.

'I've put the little girl next door to you.' The housekeeper showed them a connecting door. 'Captain Mercer suggested you should keep the outside door of his daughter's room locked and let her use this way through.'

Polly glanced quickly at Connie, but her young charge didn't seem to realise the implications behind this. This precaution ought to prevent any further attacks and would also safeguard Polly's reputation, since she'd be with Connie every night. But to make doubly sure of their safety she had already decided to place a chair back under the door handle every night.

'Captain Mercer's room is on the other side of his daughter's,'

Mrs Naizley went on. They had all wondered whether this woman was Richard Mercer's mistress but, if so, there was obviously nothing going to happen here in the hotel, with both children sharing Mrs Kershaw's accommodation. And anyway, now that she'd met Mrs Kershaw in person, Mrs Naizely had come to the conclusion that the rumours were wrong. She prided herself on being able to recognise a respectable woman when she met one.

Mrs Mercer, on the other hand, had not struck the housekeeper as at all respectable. She had dressed like a vamp and acted like one, too, sitting drinking alone in the bar like that.

'I hope you enjoy your stay with us, Mrs Kershaw. If you need anything extra for your little boy, just ask at the reception desk. We pride ourselves on making our guests comfortable at the Bella Vista. And you might all enjoy walking in our Italian garden at the rear. We're rather proud of it. The statues were brought from Italy 'specially.'

So later, Polly and the children went down in the lift and strolled around the garden, with its flowerbeds and statues of naked men with leaves festooned about them to hide their male parts, something which made Polly want to giggle. She preferred gardens overflowing with flowers to this neatness, but still, the place was sheltered from the sea breezes, which could be chilly, and was pleasant to sit out in.

That evening she had her first experience of dining in a large hotel. Richard suggested she feed Billy first in their room, then eat with Connie and him in the dining room.

'I can eat up here,' she protested. 'And anyway, I don't want to leave Billy on his own.'

'You deserve proper meals. And I want you to be with Connie if I'm not around any evening. I don't want Connie eating down here on her own.'

Polly looked at him and blurted out, 'But I'm not used to this sort of thing – hotels and public dining rooms.'

His voice became gentler. 'No, I know you're not. But you'll find it's not much different from dining with Connie and me at home. And I've arranged for one of the chambermaids to sit with Billy while we're at dinner.'

Polly couldn't think of any other excuses, but for all his re-assurances, she felt nervous as she put on her one good dress later that day. 'This still smells a bit of smoke and it's very old-fashioned,' she worried to Connie, who had got ready and come in to join her as she put the final touches to her hair.

'The navy blue's a nice colour, though. It suits you.'

Polly patted her hair into place, observing casually, 'You're not limping as much lately.'

'No.' Connie began to fiddle with the counterpane. 'Dr Herbert was right. The exercises have helped. Perhaps my bones really have got stronger. I've grown three inches this year, you know. That must have changed something.'

'Yes, that'll be it.'

There was a knock on the door. One of the chambermaids stood there. 'Captain Mercer's arranged for me to keep an eye on the little boy while you have dinner, Mrs Kershaw.'

By the time Polly had explained about her son and had checked again that Billy was sleeping soundly, it was time to go down to the dining room.

And it really was very similar to eating with the family at Seaview House. Eh, she'd been worrying about nothing! She'd better save her worries for keeping an eye on Connie from now on.

The following day, Richard received a phone call from Toby.

'Got a bit of news for you – or rather, for Polly.'

'What?'

'Browning-Baker has had a seizure. He can't move or speak.'

'Good heavens!' Richard shook his head in disbelief. If ever there were a case of poetic justice, this was it. 'I'll tell Polly later.'

'OK. Now, about that new fellow at the home . . .'

That afternoon, while they were strolling in the gardens with Connie pushing Billy in his chair, Richard told Polly the news. 'So, you see, nothing that's happened can have been aimed at you and your son. In fact, you're quite free now, which must be a relief to you.'

'Well, I'm glad he won't be able to hurt me any more but . . .' her eyes went to Billy '. . . I don't think I'd wish that on anyone. It's terrible.'

'Not even after all the people that man has harmed?'

Polly shook her head. 'No.'

Richard smiled down at her. He was not surprised she could not rejoice in someone's downfall. She had a forgiving nature. If there were more people like her in the world, wars such as the one he'd had to endure wouldn't happen. 'You're a wonderful woman,' he said softly.

'Me? I'm not. I'm just ordinary.'

'No, that's the last thing you are, Polly Kershaw.'

Two days after the fire, Don Greinor popped out of his public house to catch Constable Bulmer as he was walking past on his morning rounds.

'Got a bit of interesting news for you, my lad. The reason our fire engine didn't start was because someone had taken the rotor arm out of the distributor. Didn't show till we took it in to be looked at.'

Jim whistled. 'We'd better tell Captain Mercer. I'll have a quiet chat with him when I next go past the Bella Vista.'

'Funny business, this,' Don said thoughtfully.

'Yes. I'd never thought to see such goings on in Stenton.'

'I reckon that war ruined people, made them dissatisfied with their lot.'

'It's going to get worse before it gets better, too. Country's in a right old state.'

'Takings are down, that's for sure. People are making their drinks last longer.'

'Well, they'll allus need policemen, whatever the times are like, though I'm glad I don't have to deal with them poor devils who're on strike. I feel sorry for them'

'It's Captain Mercer and that little lass I feel sorry for at the moment. Someone's out to harm them.'

George waited a few days before going across to Stenton to check things out. He was angry with himself for failing in this first small operation. It would have been good to get the child out of the way before he dealt with the father, though – and to turn the inheritance into cash.

He hadn't told Florence what he'd tried to do and had been careful to keep her as cheerful as possible. He'd have holed up in the flat, but she fretted if she had to stay indoors too much, and of course there was food to buy. So he took her out for walks into Blackpool, or allowed her to ride on the trams or walk along the sea front. However, he insisted that she continue to dress quietly and do nothing to draw attention to them.

One night he took her to a show at the Opera House, which pleased her more than anything else, though they had the usual row about what she was to wear before they set out. When they got there, however, and she found out that he did not intend them to sit in the best seats, she protested angrily.

'Keep your mouth shut or we walk out of here this minute!' he said in a low voice, seeing heads turn in the foyer around them.

'But Georgie . . .'

He pretended he was about to leave and she grabbed his arm, whispering, 'All right, all right.'

Two days later Constable Bulmer took the opportunity to have a quiet word with Captain Mercer when he saw him leaving the rest home. 'Your wife's been seen again in Blackpool.' He avoided Richard's eyes and studied his own feet with apparent interest.

'Who saw them?'

'My sister's lass. Mabel works at the hotel as a waitress so she knew your wife by sight. She went into Blackpool on her night off and saw Mrs Mercer. Said she wouldn't have noticed her only there was some sort of fuss in the foyer of the Opera House. Mabel – um – thought you were with her at first, then realised it was that cousin of yours. He looks a bit like you from a distance.' Constable Bulmer didn't say that his sister had particularly mentioned the adoring way Mrs Mercer looked up at George and hung on his arm.

'Thank you for telling me.' Richard closed his eyes for a moment. He had hoped the failure of the arson attack would have made them leave the district. Damn George! And damn Florence, too! What else were they after? How could he protect Connie – and Polly – once they all moved back into Seaview House?

George cycled over to Stenton in the daytime to check what was going on, donning goggles and a leather flying cap pulled well down to hide his face. He didn't linger in Seaview Close itself, just rode past the house, but he did talk to an old man in one of the sea-front shelters and found out exactly what had been said in the village.

'It were set on purpose that fire, they say.' The old man spat with great accuracy through one of the gaps in the shelter.

'Never!' George had adopted a Somerset accent which he had learned from a fellow he'd known during the war. 'Fancy that, then. And in a peaceful place like this.'

'Oh holiday, are you? Folk'll be crowding into the village soon.' Another eruption of phlegm signified the old man's dislike of holiday makers. 'You're a bit earlier than most. It's going to rain later. I can feel it in my knees, I allus do.'

'I've just got a few days off so I chanced the weather. Anyway, cycling keeps you warm.' George got back on the bike and set off, riding slowly past Seaview House again and scowling to see so many men working on it.

Bloody Richard! He always had been lucky. Well, his luck wasn't going to last. By hell, it wasn't!

The following day a letter arrived for Connie. Recognising his wife's handwriting, Richard consulted Polly before giving the letter to his daughter.

The child stared at the envelope, then looked doubtfully at her father.

'You might as well see what she has to say. And Connie, if you don't mind, I'd like to read it, too.'

'All right.' She went into her hotel bedroom and stared at the letter, unable to work out why she was so reluctant to open it. Only, ever since her mother had vanished so suddenly, she had been thinking a lot about her parents. This was not the first time her mother had let her down. Memories had started to surface again of the day she had fallen down the stairs and hurt her leg so badly. And they had surprised her. Why had she not remembered those things before? And why was she remembering them now?

With a sigh she opened the envelope and began to read:

My dearest Connie
I simply had to write and find out whether you were all right. I'd come over and see you, but I'm not sure your father would welcome a visit from me. You might ask him and let me know what he says when you write back. You will write back, won't you?
I'm sorry I had to go away without saying goodbye. Did you get

*my letter? I left it on the desk in my hotel room. I said in it that I'd get
in touch and here I am, keeping my promise.*

Let me know if it's all right to come and see you.

Lots of love,

Mummy

Connie re-read her mother's words. There hadn't been a letter,
she was sure, because the hotel staff would have passed it on.
Everyone was very helpful at the Bella Vista. She re-read the letter
again, but didn't find it any more comforting – or believable –
the third time.

It was a full half hour before she went next door to find her
father and give it to him. She stayed in the room with him,
watching as he read it several times.

Afterwards Richard leaned his forehead on his hand and
sighed wearily. 'Do you want to see your mother?'

'No. She shouldn't have left without saying goodbye. And –
and I think she's telling lies about leaving a letter. I don't care if
I never see her again.'

He couldn't blame her and didn't try to change her mind. He
didn't really want Florence coming back here, either.

They decided to return to Seaview House the next day,
even if it was not completely finished. It was a strain keeping
Billy quiet in a hotel and they all preferred their home surround-
ings.

When Morag came to visit her at Seaview House, Connie
confided in her friend about the letter from her mother. Morag
said at once that she ought at least to hear her mother's side of
things. So the next morning Connie told her father that she had
changed her mind and now wanted to see Florence.

He sighed, but didn't protest. 'I'll need to see your letter
before I send it – and I'll be adding a note of my own.'

Connie scowled. 'I don't ask to read *your* letters. Why do you have to see mine?'

'I have my reasons.'

An hour later she slapped a piece of paper down in front of him. Richard read her short letter in silence, wondering if he was doing the right thing and wishing now that he hadn't even shown her the letter from Florence. 'Just one thing, Connie. I want to be with you when you see your mother.'

She scowled even more darkly at that. 'But you don't like her any more. It'll make it difficult for us to talk.'

'I want to make sure you're all right.'

'What do you mean "all right"?'

'Just what I say. Until we find out who lit that fire, you're not going anywhere on your own.'

Connie, who wanted to ask her mother privately whether her memories of the accident were true, said sulkily, 'Well, I don't want you with us. She's never as nice when you're there.'

'Connie, I mean what I say.'

She left him and shut herself in her bedroom, slamming the door behind her.

'Won't I do?' Polly asked. 'I've stayed with them before.'

'Not this time. I can't explain to you, either, but I have my reasons. Good ones, too.'

Richard's voice was so frosty that Polly did not say anything else. He had seemed friendlier while they were at the hotel, but since they'd come back to Seaview House, he'd been very much on edge. She hoped it wasn't anything she'd done.

She was beginning to think that once Connie started school she would give in her notice and go away somewhere. Not that she wanted to leave, but she knew she had got too fond of him, had 'forgotten her place', as Mrs Pilby would have said.

Why had he changed towards her? Had she betrayed her feelings for him? Or was it just because of the divorce and him needing to make sure he didn't appear to have a mistress? That was the only conclusion she could come to. And either way, maybe it would be better to leave.

Polly lay awake for a long time that night in the newly painted bedroom she shared again with her son, listening to his soft even breathing next to her, thinking about this and that. It was strange how your thoughts wandered during the night.

She kept coming back to the fire. Did Richard think Mrs Mercer had been involved? Surely not? That cousin of his sounded a real bad sort, but for a woman to do something like that to her own child – no, it was unthinkable.

If this cousin of Richard's could attack children, though, who would he come after next?

It didn't take her long to realise there was one person who was in more danger than anyone else: Richard. He was concerned about his daughter. Was he concerned enough about himself, though? Was he being equally careful about his own safety?

She didn't think he was, somehow. She had noticed before that men didn't look after themselves properly but left that to their womenfolk. Only Richard hadn't any womenfolk. Just two elderly servants – and her.

Could she help keep him safe? She didn't know, but she would certainly try. He might be beyond her reach, but she didn't want another man she loved being killed.

And then it hit her for the first time that she loved Richard Mercer far more deeply than she had ever loved poor Eddie.

'You're a fool, Polly Kershaw!' she whispered aloud in the darkness. 'A real fool. He'd not for such as you.' But that didn't change her feelings about him in the slightest. Or her determination to keep an eye on him when she could.

CHAPTER TWENTY-EIGHT

May 1921

———————◆———————

Florence felt the worries beginning to pile up on her and it wasn't *fair*. All she asked was a bit of fun, an active man in her bed and a comfortable life. But George was keeping her indoors most of the time and insisting she prepare meals and wash his clothes like a housemaid. He didn't make the slightest effort to help so why would he not let her get a charwoman in?

She didn't dare protest too strongly, however, because he was acting rather strangely. He sat up till quite late each night, staring into space, muttering to himself and ticking points off on his fingers. He went out mainly after dark and refused point-blank to say where he was going, let alone when he was coming back.

One day he studied her so carefully that she began to wonder whether she had a dirty mark on her face. Eventually he said, 'Get your red dress ready to wear tonight. The one with the low neckline.'

She felt better immediately. This was more like it! 'Are we going out? Somewhere nice, I hope, with dancing. I'm sick and tired of this place.'

He choked with laughter and was unable to answer her for a moment or two. When he stopped, he said, 'Actually, we're going into Fleetwood, to a rather rough area near the docks, where *you* are going to play the whore for real.'

She couldn't believe she'd heard him correctly. 'Pardon?'

He leaned forward. 'I said: you're going to play the whore tonight, my pet.'

'I've told you before that I'm not going to earn money for you that way.'

He spoke slowly, with an edge to his voice. 'Don't worry. You won't be expected to take your knickers off, just look the part. All we're going to do is meet a certain gentleman who will have a package for me. Only I don't want to be seen by him so I'm going to leave you at an agreed spot, pretending to be a street-walker. When he comes along, he'll say, Honour bound, then he'll hand you a package and you'll give him this envelope.'

She didn't like the sound of this at all. 'I still don't understand why it's necessary for me to — to dress like that just to pick up your package.'

He sighed and rolled his eyes at the ceiling, something she hated him doing. He could be so scornful at times, as if she had no feelings. 'I'm buying a gun, Florence, and you're going to pick it up for me. I still have my own from the war, but I don't want to use that. The police can tell what sort of gun a bullet comes from. And so that no one understands what's going on, tonight *you* are going to dress like a whore and do the picking up. Right?'

She shivered at the thought of what he'd be using the gun for. She didn't intend to be involved in *that*. 'No. I've done a lot for you, Georgie, but I'm not going to pretend to be one of those women. Or deal with guns. What if the man is late? What if someone else tries to — to pick me up? It's not safe down there at night.'

'You just tell them you'll see them later, that you're waiting for a regular. Anyway, I'll be keeping an eye on you from a distance. I can always play Galahad if necessary.'

'If you're going to be there, why can't you pick up the thing yourself?'

He shouted very loudly, 'Because the man passing it on mustn't see me, and because a whore is fairly anonymous round there. And to make you even less recognisable, I've got this for you to wear.' He flung a small drawstring bag at her.

She glanced sideways at him, saw that he still had that fierce expression on his face and decided it'd not hurt to look in the bag. It contained a blond wig. She looked at him for enlightenment.

'*To disguise yourself with*. It's easier for women to put on a disguise than men. If anyone ever does manage to follow the trail, all they'll know is that a blond woman of a certain sort met a sailor who supplied her with a gun for her own protection. Right?'

Florence folded her arms. 'I'm still not going to do it. You can pull the brim of your hat down to hide your face and – and just go and get the horrid thing yourself.'

He picked her up and shook her so hard that tears started in her eyes and her teeth snapped together. She thought he'd never stop and she couldn't even utter a scream, just gurgle in terror. When he did shove her away from him, she collapsed on the floor, sobbing.

George bent over her. 'Shut up, Flo, and listen. Do you want me to plan this so that we're not caught, or don't you?'

She didn't want him to plan it at all, but she no longer dared say that. In fact she didn't dare do anything after that but dress as he commanded, put on the horrid wig which stank of cheap perfume, and go out with him. He'd borrowed a car from 'a new friend' and she slumped down gratefully in the seat, trying to stay hidden from view.

At the docks he stopped the car and said curtly, 'Go down that way and try to act the part. Waggle your backside as you walk. I'll be behind you, making sure we're not being followed.'

Florence walked along the street in fear for her life. When a man with a scarred face approached her, she froze in terror.

'Looking for a customer, love?'

Richard came up behind her and said in a common sort of voice, 'She's got a booking. Maybe later, pal? We'll be around this area again in an hour or so.'

The man studied her. 'No. I prefer 'em plumper than her, really. I'll find my own tart.'

As he ambled off into the night, George gave her a shove and said, 'Get moving.'

Florence moved.

When George told her where to wait and then faded into the darkness, she stood trembling under a lamp post, hugging her arms round herself.

Another man approached her, but he didn't say the password so she told him she had a regular coming any minute now. She was so relieved that he went away without any trouble that she closed her eyes for a minute.

When she opened them, she saw a third man approaching her and took a step backwards.

'This way, me darlin',' he said, taking hold of her arm.

'No, I'm waiting for someone. I—'

He leaned forward and whispered, 'Honour bound,' then tugged her again and added loudly, 'Don't keep me waiting, pet. Haven't had it for a month.'

In the alley he pulled a parcel out of his pocket and slipped it into her hand. Then he looked at her, as she stood pressed against the wall, and burst out laughing. 'You can relax, dearie. You don't think I'd fancy a scrawny bint like you, do you? I can find someone more willing in any pub. He's really frightened you, this guy who's after you, hasn't he? Now, where's the bloody money? I've better things to do than stand round here all night.'

She handed over the envelope, the man checked the contents then strode off down the street without a word. When Florence turned round, she expected to see George but she was alone. Wind whistled past her. The alley was very dark. With a squeak of fright she ran back towards the street.

When she bumped into someone and realised it was George, she sagged against him, trembling.

'You're a coward, Flo, do you know that? Be careful. Don't knock the wig off.'

Her teeth were chattering. 'I wasn't brought up to – to do this sort of thing.'

'Come on, let's get you home, Mata Hari.'

She scowled at him. Comparing her to a traitor like that! 'Aren't you going to check the parcel?' She moved to pull it out of her handbag.

'Don't do that!'

She didn't speak on the way home and was at first glad that George didn't, either. Then she began to worry. He had such a strange light in his eyes tonight, was being so unkind to her. He had changed for the worse since he lost all that money in France. She had believed him so clever, but he wasn't. Where gambling was concerned he was stupid.

Florence wasn't looking forward to a lifetime of this sort of treatment. Maybe when she'd got Richard's money, she'd refuse to marry George, just offer to give him half. After all, he couldn't betray her without betraying himself at the same time. Only she'd have to be very clever about how she did it. He would make a dangerous enemy.

The procession which was the main focus of Stenton Gala Day was to take place the following week and Connie, who was walking almost without a limp now, begged her father to let her join in and walk behind the May Queen with her friend Morag.

'I don't think that would be wise, darling.'

'Why not? My leg's a lot stronger now. I won't get too tired.'

That was not what he'd meant, but he didn't want to frighten her unnecessarily. He looked across at Polly. 'What do you think?'

'There'll be lots of people about. I can't see any problem. And I'm sure she can do it. I thought I'd take Billy along to watch.'

'I'll come with you and . . .' He broke off in mid-sentence as he realised he shouldn't have said this.

'There's no need for that – *sir.*'

367

'I want to see my daughter in the procession, too.' And he wanted to keep an eye on all three of them. It made him nervous every time they left the house, and would do until he'd solved the puzzle of what his cousin and wife were after – and dealt with it.

George said thoughtfully, 'I think we'll go over to Stenton tomorrow. It's Gala Day and there'll be all sorts of people there. Your daughter's walking in the procession. Now's the time for that meeting with her. And make bloody sure you act the part of a loving mother this time! Go and watch her walk along the promenade as well.'

'How do you know that?'

'I just do.'

Florence scowled at him. 'I hate Stenton! And you can't call that pitiful affair a procession. There aren't enough people in the whole of Stenton to make a decent queue, let alone a procession. I'd rather go to the cinema any day.'

'Nonetheless, we're going to Stenton and you're going to watch the procession with a proud smile on your face. You can book in at the hotel and I'll slip into your room later and spend the night with you.'

'What if someone sees you?'

'I'll make sure they don't.'

'But accidents happen.'

'Then I'll make sure the person involved doesn't live to tell the tale.'

She froze, staring at him with eyes so filled with fear he could have slapped her stupid face. 'It's time to arrange our own little accident, Flo.'

She shuddered. 'But everyone will know I'm in town. What if the police suspect me . . . afterwards?'

'Stop making difficulties. I'll make sure you're seen doing something else before I strike. Now do you or do you not wish to become a rich widow?'

She gnawed her bottom lip and looked down at her feet, then whispered, 'I'd love to be a rich widow.'

'Leave it to me. You shall be. And take some fairly subdued clothes with you, nothing too eye-catching. Here, let's see what you've got.' He made a quick selection. 'Pack a change of clothes for me, too – but don't let the chambermaid unpack the case for you.'

When he looked at her again, she was pale and worried. He was worried, too. Not about the job in hand but about her and whether she'd hold up. Given how much she hated Richard, George hadn't expected her to go to pieces like this. Well, he'd *make* things go right. His luck might have turned for the worse in France, but it was about to return in full measure.

Toby decided to go over to Stenton for the Gala to help the men at the rest home get a good view of the May Queen procession. Those who could were to be brought outside to watch from the garden. Time the locals got used to the sight of battered faces and mangled bodies. Sarge was proving a tower of strength, but he would be glad of a bit of help. The men loved him and his banter, and he'd won the hearts of the elderly neighbours by doing odd jobs for them. A born leader, Sarge, and a strong man, who could lift any patient without bumping him.

Luckily the day was fine. Toby set off early, but it was just after nine o'clock when he arrived and he had to follow a couple of slow, horse-drawn charabancs down the narrow road. There were more charabancs standing empty in a farmer's field, with the horses grazing peacefully in the next one. He'd be able to leave his car behind the rest home so he drove on.

He had never seen so many people in Stenton, but then the Gala, he was told, marked the beginning of the holidaymaking season and from now on things would be a bit more lively – well, lively by local standards anyway.

He went to visit his smallest patient first and found Billy more communicative than ever and making a huge effort to drag himself around.

Polly didn't look her usual cheerful self, however, so Toby asked if something was wrong. She nearly snapped his head off, insisting she was fine.

When Richard came in to ask him something about the day's plans and Polly made a point of addressed him as 'sir'. Toby blinked in shock, glancing quickly from one to the other. Richard avoided his eyes and Polly turned her back and began playing pat-a-cake with her son.

Down in the library afterwards Toby didn't mince his words. 'What happened? It was "Polly" and "Richard" before.'

'I decided to keep my distance.' Richard saw the disapproval in his friend's eyes and added, 'I don't want Florence making any false claims about Polly's role in this household when the divorce is being heard.'

'I see.' Richard being over-protective again, Toby decided. But that still didn't explain why Polly had looked so hurt. Surely his friend had explained his reasons to her?

After Dr Herbert's visit, Polly helped Connie dress and her spirits lifted a little as her charge turned into a pretty little girl, tremulously proud of her appearance in her first long dress. Connie gave her a careful hug, then together they fitted on to her dark, shining hair the wreath of white roses Miss Drummond had made for her.

Connie walked carefully downstairs, holding up her long skirt and calling, 'Daddy! Look at me!'

He came out of his library, frowning, then stopped and stared for a moment before unashamedly wiping away a tear. 'You're beautiful today, my darling. Absolutely beautiful.' He moved forward, arms outstretched.

'Don't crumple my dress!' Connie moved backwards.

There was a knock on the front door. Miss Josephine Drummond had come to collect Connie and take her to the church with Morag so that the procession could form.

'We seem to have a larger crowd than usual this year,' she said brightly. 'Oh, my dear child, you look beautiful.'

Which made Connie glow with happiness.

After they had left, Polly went to finish getting herself and Billy ready. As she carried him down, Richard was standing in the hall.

'Are you ready? I'll just go and bring the wheelchair down for you.'

'You'd no need to wait for us,' she snapped as she settled Billy in place. 'We know our way into the village.'

'Polly, please. I didn't mean you to feel – to feel . . .'

The pain overflowed and for once she spoke without thinking. 'To feel what? Like a servant? But that's exactly what I am, isn't it, *sir*? So I have no right to feel resentful when you remind me of my place.'

'It's not like that!' He caught hold of her arm and, as she looked up, he groaned. 'Oh, Polly, it's not like that at all.' Gathering her in his arms, he explained that he had done it because of the divorce and the need for them to be careful.

'I thought . . .' She broke off.

'Thought what?'

Polly blushed and buried her face in his jacket.

'Thought I didn't care for you?' he asked, putting one finger under her chin and forcing her to look up at him. 'Of course I care.'

'But I'm only a maid.'

'You're Polly.' He let the words escape, just this once. 'The woman I love. The woman I want to spend my life with.'

'Oh, Richard!'

'I made a mess of it. I was so terrified of Florence involving you and I couldn't have borne that. It's going to be bad enough as it is. She can't deny the evidence, but I'm sure she'll make counter-claims. So until the divorce is over, you and I should go back to being careful.'

'Yes.' Polly smiled at him, feeling happiness welling up in her again. There was a big difference between being careful and feeling rejected.

Reluctantly they moved apart and she got Billy outside. They walked sedately along Seaview Close to the promenade, which was as packed with people as Polly had ever seen it. Her heart was so full of joy she could have danced along the street. She didn't dare look at Richard, not until she'd got herself under control, because she was afraid her feelings might show. 'Goodness, what a lot of people!'

'The sea front gets even more crowded in summer,' Richard responded quietly, as if sensing her need to get back to normal, 'though never half as bad as Fleetwood or Blackpool. We're smaller and we get a quieter sort of visitor.' He looked down at the excited child. 'By the time the weather gets hot, Billy should be walking well enough to paddle with the other children.'

She glanced fondly at her son. 'I hope so. I want to paddle, too. I never have.'

He chuckled. 'I'll make sure you get the opportunity, I promise you.' He looked along the promenade, searching for their neighbours. 'Ah, there's Miss Drummond. I'm going to leave you here with her and nip along to lend a hand at the rest home. Will you be all right?'

'Of course I will.'

Standing beside her neighbours, Polly calmed down still further as she listened in amusement to two old men talking next to her as they waited for the procession to start.

'They couldn't put on a better show at Poulton Gala, for all it's a bigger town,' one man said.

'Aye, you're right there. But the Police and Poulton Brass Band is better'n ours,' his companion said after judicious consideration.

'We haven't got a brass band in Stenton. We had to get one in for today.'

'That's right. So theirs is better.'

They both cackled at their own wit and Polly smiled with them.

At that very moment she saw a familiar figure strolling along the promenade, a thin woman with sleek black hair and heels so high she could only walk slowly. Her expression was disdainful in the extreme. Polly could not hold back a gasp as she realised who it was. Florence Mercer! What was *she* doing here on this day of all days! This was going to upset Connie. It wasn't fair. Whatever did the woman want?

Florence spotted her and came across. Without a word of greeting, she asked, 'Where's my daughter?'

'At the church, getting ready for the procession.'

'Will she be able to keep up with them? Who was stupid enough to let her join such a thing?'

Polly drew in a long, slow breath and did not allow herself to reply angrily. 'Connie's limp is hardly noticeable these days. She's growing out of it now.'

'I'll believe that when I see it.' Florence gazed briefly down at Billy. 'Your son's no better, I see.'

He proved her wrong himself by shouting, 'Funny hat! Funny hat!' and pointed to the big fluffy pompoms that graced the cloche hat pulled down low over Florence's brow. He chuckled loudly and said it again: 'Funny hat.'

Polly chuckled, too, couldn't help it.

Florence glared down at the little boy. 'It's time you taught your son a few manners.' As she swung round to leave, her foot caught on the brake of the wheelchair which stuck out at the side. She flailed about, but could not keep her balance and fell sideways, knocking into one of the old men before sprawling on the ground.

He gave her a disapproving look as he clutched his friend to keep his balance. 'You want to watch where you're going, missus! Them fancy shoes are a danger to everyone if they trip you up like that.'

No one offered to help Florence up. Stenton folk were like that, Polly had found. Made their disapproval very obvious. Florence's hurtful remarks about Billy had been loud enough to be heard by everyone in the vicinity, causing mutters of outrage.

She got up, brushing dust from her coat with one hand. Adjusting the fox fur round her shoulders, she glared at Polly again but lowered her voice as she said, 'I'll make you sorry for that! And sooner than you realise.'

But the old man had heard that too and he said, 'Nay missus, howd your spiteful clack! It were your own fault you fell, so there's no need to blame t'little lad's mother. You should look where you're goin'. Aye, an' you should wear decent clothes, too. You look like a whore on holiday, you do.'

Face scarlet, Florence stormed off through the crowd.

Miss Drummond touched Polly's arm gently. 'Are you all right, my dear?'

'Yes, of course I am.' She tried to pull herself together, but there had been such venom in Florence's voice that it worried her. How could that woman possibly hurt her? Then she realised how. As Richard had said, Florence intended to drag her into the divorce case, and that *would* hurt. She had done nothing wrong, but she didn't want her family or her son embarrassed, didn't want the stigma of being publicly referred to as 'the other woman'.

'I never did like that female,' Miss Drummond muttered.

Her sister nodded vigorous agreement. 'Yes, she's a dreadful woman. Oh, I do hope she won't spoil Connie's day. I've never seen the child looking so happy, or so pretty.'

Polly hoped so, too. Did Richard know his wife was here today? Should she go and warn him? No, there wasn't time. The procession would be starting soon.

She could not imagine why she should feel so apprehensive but she did, although the sun was still shining and people around her were having a good time,. Something was wrong, she knew it was.

Back at the hotel Florence went up to her room – a nasty little place at the back looking out over the gardens – and changed her torn stockings, muttering angrily to herself. If George hadn't made such a point of her finding Connie and being seen with her, she'd not go outside again. But he had made a point of it – and had repeated it so many times that she did not dare disobey.

Stupid little town! Stupid little woman, too. Staring at her own reflection with approval, Florence wondered why she was letting that dowdy female make her so angry. What did it matter anyway if those yokels had seen her fall over? After this visit the only things she'd come back here for were Richard's funeral and to take what she wanted from Seaview House before putting it on the market.

She went outside again, walking very carefully and avoiding the part of the promenade where *that woman* was standing.

As she approached Church Lane she saw a group of men in uniforms fussing about. Oh, heavens, a brass band! That was all the day needed. As the procession formed up behind the band she quickened her pace. At first she didn't recognise Connie, then something about the dark hair made her look again at the tall girl chatting and laughing with a much shorter child with red hair. Was it possible? Had Connie, awkward limping Connie, really grown into this lovely girl?

The procession started off just then and there was a further surprise as Connie moved along with only the slightest trace of a limp. Had Richard had her leg operated on? Florence felt aggrieved that no one had told her of the improvement. She tried to move to the front of the crowd so she could call out to her daughter, but a woman pushed her back and told her to come early and queue next time like everyone else had, instead of trying to push her way in.

Trying to keep an eye on her daughter, Florence began walking along behind the double row of spectators, looking for an opening so that she could attract Connie's attention. She didn't mind being known as the mother of a pretty child like that, and the slight limp added a touch of appeal, unlike the previous ugly, rolling gait.

When at last she found a gap between two women, Florence called out loudly, 'Connie darling! I've come specially to watch you.'

Connie heard the voice and grabbed hold of her friend. 'Oh, no! That sounds like my mother. I don't want to see her. Will you look for me? She's tall and thin, with black hair, bobbed, and she always wears bright red lipstick.'

'Aye, there's a woman just like that waving at you. You'll have to wave back.'

The voice called out again.

'I'm not answering her!' Connie said fiercely. 'If she thinks I'll come running whenever she turns up, she's wrong.' She dragged Morag forward to catch up with the others.

'Is your leg starting to hurt?' her friend asked after a minute or two.

'No. Why?'

'Your limp's worse.'

Connie stopped and stared down, then her face crumpled and she swayed as if she was about to faint. The noise of the band sounded very far away for a moment, then it roared in her ears. If it hadn't been for her friend's arm round her shoulders, she'd not have been able to keep going.

'Are you all right? Do you want to drop out?' Morag whispered.

'No, I don't want to drop out. I just – remembered something.'

'Remembered what?'

'My mother pushing me down the stairs when I was little. The accident was *her* fault! She pushed me!' Connie burst into tears as the memories overwhelmed her and a kindly woman on the opposite side of the road from Florence hurried over to draw the two girls out of the crowd and tell some people on a bench to make room for the poor child who'd been overcome by all the excitement.

Richard, who had been watching the procession from the

garden of the rest home, saw that something was wrong. He ran out on to the street and pushed his way through the crowd, daring to cross the street in between the last of the white-clad girls and a lorry loaded with flowers and young animals.

As the procession continued to file past slowly and the sound of the brass band thumped gradually away into the distance, he knelt beside Connie and asked, 'What's wrong, love? What happened?'

But she was weeping hysterically and didn't make any attempt to answer him.

Morag tugged at his arm and looked over her shoulder. 'Captain Mercer, she saw her mother and suddenly began to cry. She said she'd remembered the accident.'

As he listened, Richard stroked his daughter's hair. 'It's all right, darling. I'm here.'

He looked across the street but could not see his wife so stood on a nearby bench to stare along the promenade. A woman was standing behind a big family with several small children. She was staring in their direction and was dressed far too smartly for the seaside. As she looked across the road, their eyes met and she waved.

He did not return her greeting. What the hell was Florence doing here today? And why had her presence upset Connie to this extent? His heart was breaking for his child who had been so happy this morning and was sobbing so bitterly now that she could not even answer him.

Scooping her up in his arms and holding her close, he murmured, 'Shh, love. Shh. Let's get you out of this.' Not looking at his damned wife and with Morag in solemn attendance, holding Connie's wreath and bouquet, he carried his daughter along the back of the crowd looking for somewhere less public.

When he stopped for a moment to shift his burden into a more manageable position, Morag tugged at his arm and whispered, 'Captain Mercer, Connie said her mother pushed her down the stairs *on purpose.*'

He stared down at her in horror. 'Are you sure she said that?'

Before Morag could speak, Connie opened her eyes. 'She did push me. I'd forgotten. How could I have forgotten that, Daddy? Mother was always shouting at me when you were away, and that day she – she said she hated the sight of my ugly face and to get away from her. Then she pushed me. Hard. I was only little. I hadn't been naughty, just ill. Why did she do it?'

He hugged her close. 'I don't know how anyone could do that, darling.'

Just then Polly came hurrying along the sea front to join them, pushing Billy in his chair. 'What's happened?'

There was a shelter on the promenade and the side facing the sea was empty. Richard jerked his head in that direction and carried Connie over there, setting her down carefully.

The other side of the shelter was full of people oohing and ahhing, laughing and making a lot of noise.

Polly pushed Billy's chair into place at the side and put on the brake, then went to join Richard in comforting the girl any way they could.

'You go back to the procession, Morag,' she said gently. 'We'll look after Connie now. Thank you for helping her, though. You're a good friend. You can come across later to see how she is.'

As the little girl went away, a shadow fell across them and Richard looked up to see Florence reaching out towards their daughter.

Connie buried her face in Polly's shoulder and shrieked, 'Tell her to go away!'

'You heard her, Florence!' he shouted in a voice so harsh it cracked. 'Go away and don't *ever* come near her again!'

'You can't stop me. I'm her mother and I have every right to—'

'You have no rights from now on as far as Connie is concerned.' He paused then said slowly and clearly, 'She's remembered you pushing her down the stairs.'

Florence shrank back, her face going first red then chalk white. 'It was an accident. I didn't mean to – I was just pushing her away. She was being naughty and—'

His voice was thunderous. 'All those years of pain, and even now you're lying about what happened! Get away from us and don't come near us again.'

Florence walked away along the sea front, oblivious to the procession, the crowd, everything. When she got to her hotel room and found George there, she flung herself into his arms. 'The sooner you kill that man, the happier I'll be! Just tell me what to do and I'll do it. He's a monster. An absolute monster! I don't know how I could ever have married him.'

George smiled in satisfaction as he took her to bed and distracted her from her distress. His luck was turning all right. His main worry had now been taken care of. Florence had lost the last of her doubts and would work with him properly tonight.

CHAPTER TWENTY-NINE

May 1921

As evening started to fall, groups of laughing passengers climbed into their charabancs and began to make their way home. Many were singing, faces rosy from a happy day out in the early-summer sun, swaying in time to the music.

Holidaymakers of the more affluent sort were just finishing dining in the Bella Vista, which had quite a number of guests staying that night, and both of the public houses in Stenton were doing a roaring trade. Well, it was Gala Day still, wasn't it?

No one in the hotel noticed George as he made his way down the back stairs, though he had to dive behind a curtain and share a narrow space with some mops and buckets as a maid trod heavily up the stairs. Once outside the hotel, he blackened his face with dirt scooped up from behind a shed and left his jacket behind on a bench, so that it would look clean and smart for his re-entry into the hotel.

He could feel excitement throbbing through his veins as he made his way along the dark streets, slipping in and out of the shadows with the ease of long practice. It was just as it had been on sorties behind enemy lines. Tonight he was not only enjoying himself, but doing what he had been born to do: hunting prey.

Half an hour after George left the hotel, Florence made her way down to the foyer and ordered a gin and tonic at the bar. She saw the barman stifle his annoyance at such a late customer, but sat sipping it, then knocked it over and insisted on a replacement. By now all the other guests had left, but she took her time finishing her new drink. George had given full instructions for establishing an alibi.

When she got up to her room she pretended to fumble in her handbag in case anyone was watching, also as instructed, then made her way downstairs again to the now darkened foyer with one dim light burning in a corner. She had to ring the bell three times before anyone came to the desk.

'I've locked my key in my bedroom,' she told the night porter, who was still buttoning up his jacket.

'And that would be?' he asked.

'Room 307. I'm Mrs Mercer.'

'If you'll wait here, madam, I'll telephone the housekeeper.'

Satisfied that George's plan was working out well, Florence sat in the foyer smoking a cigarette and tapping her foot as if impatient. She tried not to think of what he was doing, but not for the first time wondered if a man who could so calmly plan to kill his cousin might not do the same to his wife if he ever grew fed up with her. Eyes narrowed, she considered ways of making sure she had a hold over him, and in the end concluded that her best plan would be to leave a letter in safe keeping to be handed to the police if she died suddenly – and to tell George about it.

When the housekeeper came, looking ruffled and not at all happy, however polite her words, Florence explained her problem once again then followed her languidly upstairs.

She was a little annoyed when the housekeeper insisted on coming into the room with her to check that everything was in order.

'If you can't get to your keys, we want to make sure no one has broken into your room and stolen anything, madam.'

Florence noticed the housekeeper's eyes flicker across the bed, both of whose pillows bore indentations, and then settle for a moment on the mess of towels and toiletries on the washstand. George had told Florence to clear these up when he left, but she hadn't been able to settle to anything so mundane. 'Ah, there are my keys!' she exclaimed and went to pick them up from the dressing table, brandishing them triumphantly.

'Well, that's a relief, madam.'

But as she walked slowly down the stairs, Mrs Naizley's expression was thoughtful. She always said she had seen every trick in the book during her three decades in the hotel trade and she had never seen a clearer case of someone extra using a room without paying!

Incensed, she went down to the night porter and ordered him to double check all the ways of entering the hotel. 'Every last pantry window!' she commanded. 'We've got a non-paying extra in number 307. I was sorry when *that woman* came back to stay with us, I was indeed. I'm not at all surprised that Captain Mercer is divorcing her – I'm only surprised he married her in the first place. She's as common as muck, whatever airs she gives herself. Now you go off and check everything, Stan, and I'll keep an eye on the desk for you.'

George waited in the garden of Seaview House beneath the trees. If his cousin didn't come out for one of his night walks, George would have to use his reserve plan. But somehow he felt supremely certain that Richard would take one of his regular night-time strolls now that Stenton had settled down again after the festivities.

There was a light on in one of the bedrooms upstairs, the one belonging to the boy's mother, but it went out after a few minutes. The light was still on in the library so George assumed his cousin was in there. Richard seemed to spend most of his time in that damned gloomy room. Pity the curtains were drawn and he couldn't be seen.

After about half an hour had passed George grew impatient

and crept forward to peer through a chink in the curtains, but all he could see was a bit of carpet. Feeling angry at the delays, he moved quietly back to his chosen spot. Come on, you stupid bastard! Take one of your walks.

Polly put the light off and lay down in bed, but found it impossible to sleep because she was still upset for poor Connie. After half an hour she got up again and slipped on her dressing gown then drew back the curtains very quietly so as not to disturb Billy. She often stood by the window to look down Seaview Close towards the beach at night and watch the sea glinting in the moonlight. On rough nights you could see the faint gleam of white on the top of each wave and hear them crashing on the beach. On calm nights there was a soothing tone to the regular murmur of the water.

She was leaning on the window-sill, drinking in the soft night air and thinking how lovely it would be here in full summer, when she saw something move in the shadows. Even as she watched, the dark shape of a man moved out from beneath the trees and approached the library window. Hardly daring to breathe she watched, wondering if it was a burglar. But the light was still on in the library. Surely no one would be thinking of breaking in while the owner was awake?

As the intruder drew close to the house she could see nothing because the window-sill blocked her view and if she tried to open the window further and stick her head out, she might alert him.

It seemed a very long time before the shadowy figure reappeared and then it simply moved back towards the trees. What should she do?

Polly stared down at her nightdress. Well, she could get dressed for a start. She didn't want to go downstairs dressed like this. It would look really bad if she was seen with Richard at this hour of the night like this. She tiptoed across the room, picked up her clothes and began to get dressed, keeping a careful watch through the window as she dragged the garments on anyhow. But whoever had been watching the house was either very still or had gone away.

She was going to keep watching, though! That man was up to no good.

'Come on, Richard,' George muttered, not even aware that he was speaking aloud. 'You haven't gone to bed, what are you waiting for?'

Time passed. He grew more and more impatient, feeling in his pocket for the gun and once taking it out and holding it in his hand for the sheer pleasure of it. He enjoyed the powerful feeling guns gave you, enjoyed everything about them.

Usually on these missions he could stay perfectly still for hours, but now it felt as if he'd been waiting all his life to get rid of this bloody cousin who had been held up as an example to him in his youth and had acquired all the things George had wanted for himself when he grew older. Richard had been made a Captain while George had been one of a group of men denied line officer status, told they were not suitable for commanding men but just right for special work.Oh, they'd been treated well enough, surprisingly so. But none of them had got past Lieutenant, and many of them simply had not come back from their little trips behind enemy lines.

He growled with irritation, a soft sound, barely louder than a deep breath, but enough to make him realise he was letting this get to him which could be dangerous. You had to stay in control of yourself whatever the circumstances. Muscle by muscle he forced his body to relax.

But his mind would not be still, filled with exasperation and impatience. So many nights he'd stood here and seen bloody Richard go out for a walk along the sea front. All those nights and yet when it really mattered, the stupid sod had to stay home.

He had just decided to wait a further hour, then break into the house and do the deed there when the front door opened and a figure appeared.

George straightened up, smiling. Got you, Richard Mercer! This is the last walk you'll ever take, you sanctimonious prig!

Polly heard the front door open and watched in dismay as Richard left the house, locking it carefully behind him. He didn't usually go out for a walk so late. What if the man was still watching the house? What if he chose this time to break in?

Then the dark figure reappeared and she clapped one hand across her mouth to stifle a gasp. Only the figure didn't turn towards the house. It waited at the front of the garden till Richard had moved off along the street with that long stride of his, then it began to follow him, vanishing into the shadows under the trees next door.

A quick glance showed her that Billy was sound asleep. She listened for a moment at Connie's door, hearing nothing, then crept down the stairs. She had to warn Richard.

But the front door was locked and the key missing. Richard must have taken it with him. Should she ring Constable Bulmer and tell him she was worried about Captain Mercer? No, it would take time and the man might have attacked Richard by then.

She rushed through to the kitchen and fumbled for the back door key.

Richard strode along the sea front, still feeling angry with his wife. Florence had done so much harm to Connie today. Would he and Polly be able to reassure the child and bring that happy look to her face again? Not for a while, he suspected.

When he got to the end of the promenade, he went to stand by the low wall, looking out across the sea.

Behind him a low voice said, 'That's far enough, Richard.'

Turning he saw his cousin and gasped at the sight of a gun in his hand. 'What the hell . . .'

'Keep your voice down or I'll have to silence you.'

Richard saw the gun wave about, saw the wild elation on his cousin's face and froze where he stood. He had seen that expression on too many men's faces during the war, for there were some who had enjoyed the killing. He'd always known that George was like that, too, though their paths had not crossed out there.

But the war was over now. Had his cousin run mad? Richard was about to ask why he was carrying a gun when George began to speak, his tone mockingly conversational.

'I've always hated you, you know. Right from the time we were boys. You were bigger than me in those days, but I caught up, didn't I? More than caught up. I'm not only bigger than you now, I'm a damned sight cleverer.'

'I don't understand what you want.'

'To kill you, of course. And if you want a few more minutes of life, you'll shut up until I've finished speaking. I want you to know exactly why I'm doing this, you see.'

Richard felt a calm come over him then, the sort of calm that had taken him out of trenches and across battlefields. Only the scar felt alive, burning on his cheek. He had acquired it one early-summer night just like this one, courtesy of a sniper. He'd been lucky to escape with just a graze. He was going to be even luckier to get out of this situation alive because George might have run mad but he had chosen his moment well – and his place. This isolated shelter at the end of the promenade was hidden from most of the surrounding houses, and anyway the residents would be sound asleep at this hour. There might be someone awake in the hotel, but they were probably out of earshot.

'I've already taken your wife from you. Good in bed, isn't she? Not very bright, but then I don't like brainy women. I prefer to be master in my own home. I'll marry her, of course, after you're dead, then help her spend your money. If you'd not been so greedy and persuaded old James to leave you everything, I'd not have had to kill you. But I don't know that I'm all that sorry. It's more satisfying to get hold of it all this way.'

'Actually, you and Florence won't get any of it.'

George laughed. 'Oh, no? Who's going to stop us?'

'My will. I've not left anything to her. Everything goes to Connie instead.'

For a moment George's smile faded, then it reappeared and an even wilder light seemed to gleam from his eyes. 'Oh, that's no trouble. As her mother, Flo will be appointed guardian. We'll simply take dear Connie abroad and arrange a little accident in a year or two. Nothing easier.'

There was silence for a moment then Richard said, 'I don't believe you. Even Florence wouldn't kill her own child.'

'She won't have to. I shan't even tell her, just arrange the accident. *No, don't move.* A few seconds more of life are sweet, aren't they? I've had men beg me for another few minutes. If it's any consolation, I'll make it painless for your daughter, which is more than I'm going to do for you. I reckon I'll have enough time to shoot you in the guts. I'm going to enjoy watching you writhe in pain before I put the final bullet into your brain. I wish we were somewhere further out of hearing then I could *really* enjoy myself.'

Sarge was feeling pleased with how the day had gone. The lads had thoroughly enjoyed being able to see something of what was happening and had been late getting to bed. He hadn't even tried to sleep. He had nights like this when he couldn't sleep and that was that. They were easier to cope with in the fine weather when you could go out into the garden, have a fag or two and think about life. He'd turned up a few good ideas this way, ideas for helping the lads.

For a moment, he felt the old sadness sweep over him. He missed Madge, missed her like hell. It didn't seem to get any better, either. He and his wife had been apart so much during the war, then they'd only had a short time together before that damned 'flu killed her. Not a strong woman, his Madge, but the most loving heart you could ever hope to meet. She'd approve of what he was doing here in Stenton.

He saw Captain Mercer walk past and thought nothing of it till he saw another man creep up after him. Up to no good, that one. On a sudden impulse, he went and got his service revolver. When you were dealing with men who crept up behind others, it could be useful to have a gun to threaten them with.

As he was walking towards the gate he saw another figure creeping along the promenade. What the hell was going on? He waited in the shadows and to his surprise a woman came into view, moving cautiously along the sea front. Funny bloody time of night for a walk. Only she didn't look like she was going for a walk. She was following the other fellow and kept stopping in the shadows, standing very still as if checking she hadn't been seen. What the hell was going on here? He moved silently forward to watch.

As she began to creep across the road, the moon came out from behind some clouds and he recognised her — that nice lady who looked after the Captain's daughter. What was *she* doing out at this hour? She wouldn't be up to mischief so it must be the man she was following. Why hadn't the Captain spotted him?

He shrugged. He knew why. Too lost in thought. You got like that at times. The war had left its mark on them all.

Without making a conscious decision about it, Sarge moved

stealthily to the front gate, opened it and began to follow Mrs
Kershaw.

As she drew closer to the shelter, she began to worry that the man
might spot her, but that didn't stop her. If he did threaten her,
she had a good pair of lungs and would scream her head off.
That'd wake people up and bring them to help. Only she didn't
like to scream until she was sure there was something to scream
about.

Before she crossed the road, she took off her shoes, not even
noticing when bits of gravel dug into the soft flesh of her feet.
She got to the shelter in time to hear someone on the other side
speaking in a voice full of hatred.

'. . . I reckon I'll have enough time to shoot you in the guts.
I'm going to enjoy watching you writhe in pain before I put the
final bullet into your brain. I wish we were somewhere further out
of hearing then I could *really* enjoy myself.'

'You'll never get away with it, George.'

'Oh, but I shall. I've planned it all very carefully indeed.
And sadly your time has run out now so . . .' George raised the
gun.

Richard watched his cousin's hand shake and swing about
wildly, as if he couldn't control himself properly. George had a
wild look in his eyes, as if he had run mad. When he saw that
hand twitch on the trigger, Richard dived sideways just as a
woman's voice screamed behind them.

Polly had seen Richard walk to the end of the promenade,
with the stranger moving carefully behind him. She moved quietly
along the promenade, creeping in short bursts from one patch of
darkness to another. When Richard disappeared behind the
shelter, going to stand in his favourite position at the end of the
promenade, the stranger followed.

Distracted, George jerked round and saw Polly rushing
towards Richard, heedless of her own safety.

'Two at one blow, then!' He raised the gun again.

Polly flung herself in front of Richard, who rolled sideways with her immediately. Not quickly enough. The shot hit him in the arm and he could not hold back a gasp as pain seared through it. But he kept on rolling because although he stood little chance of saving them now, he was not going to stop trying till the last breath left his body.

Another bullet just missed them. Richard was surprised by that. George had to be a crack shot to have served in the Special Corps. Only his cousin was beyond reason tonight, was acting so wildly he probably couldn't exert his usual control.

George was surprised, too. He never missed. Hatred blazing from his eyes and his face a gargoyle mask, he sprang forward, intending to finish them both off at closer quarters then wing it along the beach.

Just then another voice yelled 'Hey!' and something hit him on the side of the head. The object was soft and all it did was attract his attention, but when he swung round he saw a burly figure pounding towards him brandishing a revolver.

Three were too many to take on, especially when one of them was also armed. Cursing, George leaped over the low wall, landing lightly on the sand before running for his life. A quick glance over his shoulder showed that no one was following him but he didn't slacken off until he got to the other side of the hotel.

Damn! Damn! Damn! How had he managed to miss? It had been a simple enough shot. His whole body shaking with rage and frustration, he slipped round the side of the hotel and retrieved his jacket, wiping his face on the sleeve before heading for the small window he had unlocked earlier.

Plans formed and re-formed in his mind. He'd snatch his wallet and make his escape. Florence had her alibi – or would have if she'd done as he'd told her. If not, it was her own fault.

He'd have to get out of the country for a while. Richard knew who he was, even if the others didn't. He'd be back one day, though, He'd not rest till he killed his damned cousin.

He pushed the window but it didn't open. Hell, what next? Some fool had locked it. He wasted valuable time rattling it, then trying the ones next to it.

A quick glance around showed that the hotel and its gardens were dark. Tugging his sleeve down to cover his hand, he smashed the window with one swift blow, pulling out the shards of glass impatiently so that he could get his hand inside and unlock it.

But a light came on inside the hotel. He saw it faintly, then the brilliance grew as other lights were switched on, getting closer and closer to where he stood, casting elongated squares of brightness across the gravelled paths and smooth, manicured lawns where he'd show up very clearly.

With a curse he moved back. He wasn't caught yet. Oh, no! If he couldn't outwit a hotel porter . . .

But a man came round the side of the hotel and saw him, shouting out, 'Hey, you!'

He turned the other way, only to skid to a halt as a burly figure appeared between him and the gate. George recognised him now. That fellow from the rest home. He was the one with the gun.

When George glanced to the other side, he saw his cousin, easily recognisable in the moonlight. 'You're going with me at least,' he muttered and raised the gun. But Richard had enough sense to duck behind a statue.

Three of them! And one armed! Cursing under his breath, George edged backwards, breath rasping in his throat as he sought a way out. There had to be a way out!

More lights went on above him, illuminating the scene clearly.

Hell, he was trapped! They'd shut him up in prison for this. Visions of the cellar flickered into his mind. Well, they weren't going to lock him up again. By hell they weren't. He might have failed, but he wasn't going quietly. He was taking his bloody cousin with him. Taking huge care, he loosed off another shot at

Richard who was peering out from behind that damned statue. For a moment he thought he'd hit him, but the shadow moved and the voice he hated called. 'You missed me again. Give yourself up. You can't get away now.'

He had failed, then. For a moment the whole world seemed to stand still. Failed. The word echoed in George's ears. But he had one last resort and in that he couldn't fail. He'd cheat them of their prey at least.

'Damn you all to hell and back, Richard Mercer!' George yelled and took the only way out left to him. He raised the gun to his own mouth and pulled the trigger.

The sound of the shot seemed to echo across the lawns. The second sound, George's body hitting the ground, was so quiet that if you hadn't been listening for it, you'd have heard nothing.

Sarge, who was closest, walked forward. No mistaking a lifeless man. There was something in the way dead bodies crumpled to the ground that you never forgot, though it had been a year or two since he'd seen one. He pulled out his handkerchief and was about to cast it over the ruined head when Richard's hand stopped him.

For a moment the two men stared down, then Richard sighed and stepped backwards. 'Can we keep Mrs Kershaw out of this? Pretend she wasn't there?'

'Of course.' Sarge hesitated then asked, 'You all right, sir?'

'He hit my arm but it's not serious.'

Polly, hiding behind the gate, turned and fled in her stockinged feet when she saw George fall. She knew now that Richard would be safe which was what mattered most. He had told her to go home and lock the door because he wanted her kept out of this, but she hadn't been able to stay away, not while he was in danger.

After the noise and horror of the hotel garden, the rest of Stenton seemed abnormally quiet. How could people still be sleeping peacefully when a man had just tried to murder her and Richard, then shot himself?

She didn't let herself give in to the tears that were blurring her vision until she had crept up the stairs and got safely into her own bedroom. There she checked that Billy was still sleeping and went downstairs again. She could not go to bed until she had seen Richard back safely.

On the way down she peeped into Connie's room and saw that she was sleeping peacefully too, so closed the door quietly again.

There was only one place Polly wanted to wait. The library. Richard's room.

She got there without making a noise, switched on the light and sat down in his big armchair. Only then did the shuddering start. It turned into violent shaking that racked her from head to toe. Silent and alone, she fought against it. She wanted to weep, to abandon herself to hysterics – she nearly did. Surely you had a right to have hysterics after a night like this?

But her mother had used hysterics as a weapon to control them all and Polly had once vowed that she would never go down that path. So she let the tears flow silently and hugged herself, rocking to and fro until the shaking stopped.

His cardigan was still hanging on the back of the chair and she pulled it round her, finding it a big comfort. There was even a handkerchief in the pocket. With a sound between a laugh and a sob, she used it to mop her face.

What was happening now at the hotel? Constable Bulmer would have been called in and he'd have to phone his superiors. It'd be a while before Richard could get home again, she guessed.

She couldn't sit still so got up and wandered round the room, touching his things for comfort, breathing in the essence of the man she loved and who had said he loved her. She hugged that thought to her and it helped.

After a while, as he still didn't come, she poured herself a small whisky. She didn't like the stuff, but its warmth in her mouth and in her throat was comforting.

When she had finished it, she set the glass carefully on the desk and sat down in Richard's chair again, feeling exhausted.

As Richard and Sarge stepped backwards from the body, the third man, the hotel porter, edged forward for a look. 'My God, he's killed himself!' he said in a loud voice. 'Who is he? What's going on here?'

'Keep your voice down!' Richard ordered, but he could see that the man was nearly hysterical.

'We've sent for the police,' the porter said, sounding terrified.

'Hey!' roared Sarge suddenly. 'You lot keep back.'

The porter turned to see guests spilling from the hotel. Recalled to his duty, he drew himself up and moved forward, telling people to please move back in a loud voice.

'All wind and piss, that one!' Sarge muttered.

And to his surprise Richard found himself smiling. Alive and smiling, with Polly waiting safely for him back home. The moonlight seemed suddenly glorious. When you had just survived danger, you tended to appreciate life more than at any other time.

'Thanks for your help, Sarge,' he said quietly.

'My pleasure, sir. Hope the lady's all right.'

'I'm sure she is.' And he was. Polly was a strong woman in all the ways that counted. He admired her as well as loved her. Hell, it was so good to be alive!

Upstairs, Florence had watched in horror from her bedroom window as the drama was played out in the manicured gardens below. She couldn't at first make out what had happened. Had George killed Richard or had he failed? Whatever, it had all gone wrong. If he'd killed Richard, they would hang him. They might even hang her because the housekeeper would tell them she'd had someone in her room. What was she going to do?

When George raised the gun and shot himself, she screamed, but there were other watchers and other cries so no one came to investigate hers.

When the porter's shout of, 'My God, he's killed himself!' echoed up through the night, she whimpered.

'Get up, Georgie!' she muttered. 'You're just fooling them. Get up and run away!'

But George didn't move. He lay so still that the realisation he was truly dead crept through her. *He* was dead and *she* was alone. She'd have to face Richard, the police, prison. A vision of a noose had her backing away from the window, arms hugged tightly around herself.

Moaning, she tried to think what to do. She couldn't get out of the hotel now, with everyone awake, and by morning the police would be questioning all the guests she was sure. They'd put two and two together and arrest her. She'd seen it in the cinema. The police always caught the guilty ones in the end, then they took them away in black vans and locked them in prison.

Feverishly she began to pace the room. Footsteps sounded in the corridor outside. Voices muttered in the rooms next to hers.

Another glance through the window showed a policeman now standing by the body.

What was she going to do?

She stood very still as she realised that George had shown her what to do. If *he* had seen no other way out, how could she find one? The only thing she was certain of was that they were not going to lock her up in prison, put her on trial, then hang her by the neck until dead.

She opened the suitcase and scrabbled through it for George's service revolver. She didn't know why she'd packed it, really, when he'd left it behind in his drawer at the flat. It had just made her feel safer to have it with her, so she'd hidden it under her clothes.

She pulled it out, handling it gingerly. She knew it was loaded because he had boasted that there was no use having a gun if it wasn't ready to use. She even knew how to take off the safety catch.

The gun felt heavy and yet so smooth and comforting. She was smiling as she lifted it.

Richard was not able to make his way home until dawn had started brightening the sky to the east of the hotel. He parted company with Sarge outside the rest home, shaking hands and then clasping his other hand over Sarge's rough hand for a moment.

'Thank you. You saved my life.'

'Mrs Kershaw saved it. I wouldn't have been in time otherwise.' Then Sarge grinned. 'But I did play my part.' He pulled his hand away and gave Richard a push. 'Go home and set her mind at rest. She'll be worrying.'

So Richard walked slowly along the deserted promenade. The light was grey, without the colour and warmth it would have later, and dawn was only just bringing everything into focus.

His bandaged arm was beginning to sting. His shoulders were stiff with tension and he rolled them as he walked. It seemed incredible that two people could have died so violently when this side of the village was still wrapped in slumber. He'd never have believed Florence would have the courage to shoot herself. She must have been desperate – and she must have been involved in George's attempt on his life. Had she really hated him so much she wanted him dead? That thought saddened him. Whatever else, she had been the mother of his child.

He shuddered and quickened his pace, eager to get back to Polly, sure that she'd be waiting up for him.

The house was silent as he let himself in. It was shadowy enough inside the hall for him to see a light shining under the library door. When he opened it, he smiled at the sight of the woman curled up in his chair, sleeping peacefully. His Polly, the embodiment of all that was sane in the world. He chuckled as he saw a glass standing on the desk. When he lifted it, he could smell whisky.

As if she felt him watching her, she moved a little, then opened her eyes. The minute she saw him she was up and rushing across the room to fling herself into his arms.

He pulled her close and bent his head to kiss her, but mostly he just wanted to hold her, feel her warm soft body pressed against him. They stood like that for several minutes before he said quietly, 'It's over.'

'I know. I followed you and saw your cousin shoot himself.'

He drew her across the room to the same big leather chair, still warm from her body. Sitting down in it, he pulled her on to his knee and she nestled there as if made for him. He sighed in relief as her mere presence began to drive away the last horrors of that dreadful night.

'There's more, my little love.'

She stiffened against him. 'What?'

'Florence was at the hotel as well. She must have been helping George in this. A few minutes after he'd shot himself, she did the same thing. She used his service revolver.'

'Oh, Richard, no! Did you have to – identify her?'

'Yes. The hotel staff knew she'd had someone staying in her room. They were as kind and helpful as they could be.'

'What are we going to tell poor Connie?'

'The truth. If we try to hide it from her, she'll hear it from somewhere else. She's old enough now to face it – as much as anyone can face such a dreadful thing.'

He could see that Polly's thoughts were all on his daughter so he cleared his throat and she looked up. 'Once it's all over, this horrible mess, you and I will be free. Am I wrong in thinking you'll marry me?'

Her eyes were big and wide, then the love seemed to spill from them and without a word, she pulled his head down so that she could kiss his lips. 'Of course I'll marry you. But not till – till it's proper.'

They didn't stir from the armchair until they heard Doris moving in the kitchen. Then they smiled at one another and got up, ready to start telling their household the dreadful news.

EPILOGUE

August 1921

———◆———

The events of that terrible night took their toll of everyone at Seaview House, even Billy growing quieter in the troubled atmosphere. There had been reporters and visits from detectives who had to have every detail proven and explained several times over, it seemed, and other people just stood outside, gaping at the house and its notorious occupants.

Then there had been the further stress of the inquest and at long last the burial of Florence Mercer and George. This time the rest of the Mercer clan did not attend the funeral. Indeed, Richard insisted on going on his own until Polly had persuaded him that Connie needed to put her mother to rest, too. By convincing Connie that her father would need her support, Polly gave the girl a sense of purpose and usefulness that carried her through the ordeal.

While the funeral was taking place Polly sat at home with Billy in the back garden, watching a white butterfly visit the cabbage patch and wondering if she was doing right in staying on at Seaview House. But she knew Richard and Connie both needed her, and that it was going to be her permanent home soon, so it seemed silly to leave it now, just because people might gossip. Let them! She knew she was doing nothing wrong.

When Richard and Connie came back with strained expressions on their faces it was Billy who diverted them. He had just managed to stand up and walk properly for a few paces without supporting himself on the furniture on his own. And although it took a huge effort, the little boy was so transparently thrilled with his new achievement that it seemed to ease all their hearts.

'That lad is a ray of sunshine in this house, Polly,' Mrs Shavely had said only that morning. 'No one else can bring a smile to the master's face like he can – not even you.'

Polly looked at her anxiously. 'You know, don't you?'

Mrs Shavely smiled. 'Bless you, me and Doris could tell almost from the start that he loved you and we wished you well, too. We knew you wasn't after his money. And we knew better than anyone what he'd had to put up with from *her*. But there, we won't speak ill of the dead.'

'I do love him,' Polly said wistfully, 'but is it right for him? I mean, I'm not of his class. I don't want to . . . to let him down in front of his friends and family.'

'Eh, love, Mr Richard has never been one to bother about things like class. Since he was a little lad, he's allus spoken to everyone nice as you please. His uncle was different. Mr James's generation set great store on everyone keeping their place. But since the war, who knows what a person's place is, eh? Rich and poor died shoulder to shoulder in France, didn't they? Lived and fought together.' She patted Polly's shoulder. 'I'm that happy for him.'

Polly was moved to hug her, then Doris as well for good measure.

Now, three months later, Polly and Richard were to marry in the little church of St Paul's in Stenton. On a warm morning in late August she slipped into her wedding dress, tugged it into place then stared at herself anxiously in the mirror. The ankle-length lace dress showed the pale pink silk lining beneath it. The wrapover neckline was open to the waist with a pink silk infill and a matching silk rose at the waist. The lace hemline was scalloped and looked so pretty against her white silk stockings that she stuck out her foot and turned it this way and that to admire the effect. She had refused to wear a veil, since this was not her first wedding, but she had a wonderful new hat, made of delicate white straw with a broad brim and a wreath of silk flowers in many shades of pink around the crown.

She had been shocked rigid at the price of her dress when she and her sister found it in an elegant little shop in Blackpool, but Lizzie had nodded vigorously in approval when she'd tried it on. Even then, it was not until Polly saw Connie's reverent expression as she fingered the beautiful material that the matter was settled. Not only did she buy the dress for herself, but she bought another one in a slightly deeper pink for Connie to wear as brides-maid. Like Richard, she would do almost anything to bring that happy expression back to the face of her step-daughter, and at last they seemed to be succeeding.

Eva could not come over until the day before the wedding, because although Alice had not declined in health as quickly as the doctors had feared, she was fading and could not have much longer to live. So Lizzie had chosen a toning material for her and Eva's dresses, because of course, Polly insisted on having her two sisters as attendants.

When they were all ready in their wedding finery, Toby drove Polly, Lizzie, Eva and Connie to the church in his big car. He looked wistfully at Polly as she was helped out by Percy who was to give her away. Sighing for what was not to be, Toby went to leave his car further along the street and then join the other guests in church.

There was a small crowd of sightseers waiting outside the church and Polly clutched Percy's arm tightly as he led her through them, half expecting them to call nasty things out at her, as had happened a couple of times. 'Whore!' one woman had called her. That had hurt.

But today all she heard were good wishes and instructions that she was to make Captain Mercer happy as he deserved. She looked around her more closely and relaxed as she saw several people she knew from her walks around the village with her son.

Inside the church, Lizzie fussed over her sister's dress, then over Connie's, and Percy waited indulgently for them to signal that they were ready. He knew Lizzie was determined everything would be perfect for their little sister 'this time'. Well, anyone who knew Polly would wish her well. She was the kindest, gentlest person Percy knew, with not an ounce of malice in her.

When he gave the signal, they waited for the tune to end, then the little harmonium swelled into the Bridal March and Richard moved into position at the front of the church, turning to watch his bride walk towards him.

The mere sight of him lifted Polly's heart and her face was glowing with love as she stepped slowly down the aisle.

Behind her Connie walked confidently, ready to hold the bride's bouquet. The limp was gone completely now and as they passed one pew, the girl beamed at her friend Morag who had come down from Oban 'specially for the wedding. Beyond Morag stood the Misses Drummond in new dresses and hats, and in the next pew was Sarge, wearing his medals and with his hair plastered flat with brilliantine. Mrs Shavely and Doris were beside him, also resplendent in new finery but of a very old-fashioned style. No one was going to persuade Mrs Shavely to wear skirts short enough to show her legs like some folk did who should know better.

Sunlight slanted across the altar and lit up Polly and Richard as they made their vows. A bee had blundered into the church and buzzed drowsily in and out of the two vases of flowers at the front. Outside seagulls were calling plaintively from the beach. The flowers perfumed the air in a way not even the most expensive perfume could imitate.

You could not, Lizzie decided, as she stood behind her sister, have a nicer wedding than this. Tears filled her eyes suddenly and she signalled quickly to her Peter, sitting in the front pew with his mother and their children. He had been forewarned to have a handkerchief ready to pass to her and he did so now. 'I'm so happy,' she mouthed to him and he gave her a mocking grin as he took back the dampened handkerchief.

She turned to look at Eva and found that her other sister also had tears in her eyes, but Toby had seen that and had duly produced a handkerchief from the other side.

As the words, 'I now pronounce you man and wife!' rang out, everyone in the church smiled and there was a buzz of comments about the 'radiant bride' and the 'handsome groom'.

Afterwards they all went back to Seaview House where the assistant cook and a waitress from the Bella Vista Hotel were ready to serve a buffet meal in the little-used dining room, because Richard had insisted on Mrs Shavely and Doris joining in as 'proper guests' today, to both women's huge delight and unconvincing protests.

It seemed a long time to the newly-weds until people began to leave, many going back to the hotel where the rest of Polly's family were staying.

'Be happy!' Lizzie whispered, hugging her sister at the door. She let go, then grabbed her and hugged her all over again.

'He's a lovely man,' whispered Eva, giving her a few more hugs.

'Now if I can do anything to help you . . .' Polly said. 'You know you have only to phone.'

'Alice and I manage very well. Don't worry about us. Just be happy. You deserve it.'

'You've done well for yourself,' Percy said, with Emma beaming at his side. 'He's a fine man, Richard is.'

Johnny just gave his sister a hug and a grin.

As they watched the last guests leave, Richard put his arm round Polly and his daughter. His smile was tender as he said, 'You're really, truly "our Polly" now, you know. Isn't she, Connie darling?'

The three of them stood close for a moment then Polly said in a choked voice, 'I've never been as happy in my whole life.'

Richard suddenly began laughing. 'You and your sisters have been saying that all day, but all three of you have done nothing but weep.'

'Well, what a thing to say! Those are just happy tears,' she said indignantly.

'I don't want any sort of tears on this special day,' he said softly.

Connie watched them indulgently. She liked the way they were always going moony over one another. She waved vigorously to Morag who was watching from across the street and tugged at her father's sleeve. 'Me and Billy have to go now.'

She walked across the road pushing Billy's chair for the two of them were to stay with the Drummonds that night, both women insisting they could care for Billy perfectly well, thank you very much, and that if there was to be no honeymoon, at least there should be no worries or interruptions for Polly on this special night.

'Billy's going to be my real brother now, you know,' Connie had declared several times during the last few weeks.

As Richard and Polly turned to go back into the house, he scooped her up in his arms and carried her across the threshold. Then he locked the door and whispered, 'Just us now!'

'I can't imagine anything nicer,' she said, her voice a little breathless with nervousness nonetheless.

As they walked slowly up the stairs together, her head leaning on his shoulder, his arm around her, he said very solemnly, 'I didn't think it was possible to love anyone as much as I love you, Polly Mercer.'

She stopped to mouth her new name and tried to smile at him.

'Woman, you're not weeping again, are you?' he demanded with mock severity.

'I'm just so very happy.'

He dabbed away the tears. 'It seems to be a Kershaw trait to cry when one is happy. I don't know who's shed the most tears today, you or your sisters.'

'You'll have to get used to that.'

'I shall, shan't I? But I want no more tears tonight, Mrs Mercer. I want to take my bride to bed and show her how very much I love her.'

Shyly she walked into the bedroom, caressed the flowers on the dressing table, then even more shyly donned the new lace-trimmed nightdress that had been Lizzie's present.

By the time he had given her a long, lingering kiss, the momentary shyness had vanished completely. It had never been like this with Eddie, not this sense of joy and utter rightness. Nothing furtive about loving Richard Mercer, no hiding under the bed-covers, either. It was a celebration of their deep feelings for one another, and it felt as if the whole room was echoing with their joy and love.

She lay awake for a long time after he had fallen asleep, happier than she could ever remember in her whole life before. She hoped they would have several children. She knew they would be happy together in a way she and Eddie could never have been.